"YOU KNOW I HATE BLIND DATES,"
STACIE WHINED.

"They're just so weird. Hell, we're in Atlanta. Who can't find a date here? Half the people here get picked up just by walking down the street. There must be something wrong with him," she stated.

"There's nothing wrong with him," Tameeka said. "Honest. Tyrell and I just thought it would be a good idea for you two to meet. Then if you guys hit it off, and I know you will, we can double-date."

"I don't know . . ."

"Just look at it as an adventure. Please think about it. Okay?"

Stacie shrugged. "I might, but don't be mad at me if I say no. I'm not totally feeling a blind date."

"Why? Because he doesn't meet the requirements on your list?" Tameeka asked in a snippy tone. Her friend started keeping lists in high school and hadn't stopped since.

"Don't be getting tart with me," Stacie said curtly. "I haven't even met him so how can I know how he ranks on the list?"

Tameeka shook her head, disappointed in her friend. "You and that damn list. You know what?" she asked, and Stacie glanced at her. "That damn list ain't gonna keep you warm at night."

CRAZY LOVE

Desiree Day

POCKET BOOKS

New York   London   Toronto   Sydney

POCKET BOOKS, a division of Simon & Schuster, Inc.
1230 Avenue of the Americas, New York, NY 10020

Library of Congress Cataloging-in-Publication Data

Day, Desiree.
Crazy love / Desiree Day.
p. cm.
ISBN-13: 978-1-4165-0350-7

I. Title
PS3604.A9865C73 2005
813'.6—dc22
2005048856

First Pocket Books trade paperback edition September 2005

10 9 8 7 6 5 4 3 2 1

Manufactured in the United States of America

For information regarding special discounts for bulk purchases,
please contact Simon & Schuster Special Sales at
1-800-456-6798 or business@simonandschuster.com

In loving memory of my mother

Acknowledgments

First of all, I would like to thank my agent, Bob DiForio, who is amazing, for his guidance and his support of my work. A very big thanks to Amy Pierpont, who is an awesome editor, for her advice and suggestions on *Crazy Love*.

Thank you, Megan McKeever, for all your help and answering all my questions.

A million thanks to family and friends for your continued support.

Thank you, Mr. Lee Meadows. You gave me some much-needed exposure about six years ago and I am truly indebted to you.

Thank you, RMJ, for all your advice

And a very special thank you to you, my readers. Y'all are phenomenal!

1

What I Want in a Man

1. Must be nine inches or bigger
2. He must be six-feet-one-inch or taller
3. He must have light eyes, green or gray
4. Must have soft curly hair—none of that nappy shit
5. Gotta have Shemar Moore's cheekbones
6. Gotta be able to wear a mesh muscle shirt and look good in it
7. His ride gotta be phat
8. He must be making at least $80K (after taxes)
9. No kids—I don't need any baby momma drama
10. He'd better be a freak in bed

Stacie Long ran her index finger down the list and mentally placed a check mark after nine of the items. This was her list. The nonnegotiable items she wanted in a man. It had been revised, scrutinized and analyzed more than Bill Clinton's love life. A frown marred her pretty face, so much so that the space between her eyebrows looked like a halved prune. She was draped across a velvet couch, reviewing her list as if it was the Holy Grail. So intent on her list, she missed the hateful glares that were shot at her from the women who wanted to sit and rest their feet.

"Nine out of ten . . . not bad. Not bad at all," she said, laughing softly. Her body tingled with excitement. If she hadn't been sitting in the ladies' lounge in the Marriott Marquis in downtown Atlanta on New Year's Eve, she'd be howling with joy. Right now all she dared was a smug laugh. It was too easy . . . way too fucking easy, she thought.

Men usually sniffed after her the same way a fat man sniffed after a Big Mac, with desire, longing, greed and lust. At five-feet-nine and one hundred thirty-five pounds, she was all woman; the red sequined dress she had slithered into earlier that evening *loved* her because it hugged every inch of her body. The color of warmed honey, with high cheekbones and full lips, she had a butt that made many a man stop dead in his tracks. Depending on when you saw her, her hair was either grazing her shoulders or kissing her ears. Tonight, she had it parted in the middle and the bone-straight strands framed her artfully made-up face. Blush lingered on her high cheekbones; fire-engine red lipstick glistened on her full lips and little sparkles glittered playfully on her mascaraed eyelashes.

Two women dressed to the nines were standing a few feet away from Stacie. Their heads were so close together that they looked like Siamese twins. "You know what? You can't take *us* out anywhere, look at her," muttered the one wearing a pair of toe-pinching shoes. "It wouldn't surprise me one bit if I saw her walking out of here with a plate of food. I bet she has a roll of aluminum foil in that Wal-Mart–looking bag of hers."

"Mmm," the other one agreed. "We should tell her to get her ass up!"

"Yeah!" The lady in the toe-pinching shoes hissed to her friend. But neither moved. Instead, one reached into her purse for lipstick. The other grabbed her cell phone and shrugged lightly; who needs a fight on New Year's Eve?

Stacie snuggled deeper into the plush cushions. A satisfied gleam brightened her eyes. This was her type of party. Men, *fine* men, were everywhere for the taking, fine, *wealthy* men, that is. They were like apples on a tree, hanging around for the picking. Atlanta had a lot of them. Not only that, but only the crème de la crème attended Atlanta's Annual Sexy and Sultry New Year's Eve Bash. So far she had spotted the mayor doing her thing on the dance floor, former Ambassador Andrew Young and Denzel Washington huddled together near the buffet and a former child star working the room like a twenty-dollar-an-hour whore. Yep! This was her type of party.

It was only ten o'clock, but her evening purse was bulging with business cards. Where other ladies had to work for the numbers, men nearly threw their cards at Stacie. She'd hold on to them and sort through them tomorrow morning. Then she'd organize them by jobs—doctors, lawyers and professional athletes on top, everybody else on the bottom. But tonight, she'd gotten the one number she'd been chasing for the past six months, Crawford Leonard Wallace III. An NBA player and a multimillionaire, his family was well known and respected in Atlanta. Single, six-foot-seven, curly, sandy-colored hair and hazel eyes, he was as fine as Shemar Moore and sexier than Michael Jordan.

Stacie was so excited that she shimmered, and that's how her best friend and roommate, Tameeka Johnson, found her: stretched out on the couch and wearing a grin so wide that it looked painful. "Whassup with the grin? You look like you just found a million dollars."

"You close, girl. Very close," Stacie crowed gleefully. She didn't say anything for a couple of seconds, but then her secret started bubbling up and she whispered to Tameeka, "You are not gonna guess who I met tonight. You're not gonna guess. I know you're not," she taunted her friend. Before Tameeka got a chance to reply, Stacie blurted out her news and a collective gasp of envy went up throughout the lounge, followed by dead quiet. All ears turned to Stacie.

"Oh, is that all?" Tameeka gave Stacie a dismissive wave of her hand. "I thought you had hooked up with a *ten-incher*. That's cool, girl. So you finally snagged your baby's daddy. He's aw'ight, but I've seen *better*." Tameeka sniffed, then turned to the mirror and pretended to check her makeup. She was really watching Stacie's reaction to her reaction and trying to suppress a laugh at the same time.

Where Stacie was drop-dead gorgeous, Tameeka was borderline pretty. The color of creamy peanut butter, five-foot-five and one hundred seventy-five pounds, she was rarely treated to a head-swiveling, tongue-dropping look from a man. If she did, it was because his eyes zeroed in on her size 44D breasts.

"Meek!" Stacie wailed.

Tameeka couldn't hold in her laughter any longer. "You know I'm only playing, girl," she said. "Whassup? Have you whipped that Stacie magic on him yet?" she teased good-heartedly.

"Oh, I'll do that later," Stacie answered in a voice dripping with confidence. "Maybe *sooner* than later," she said. Then she looked around at the other ladies, who were all pretending not to be listening, and said very loudly, "He's a ten-incher or more," she boasted. "Dude got three legs. I can tell these things. Some women look at the shoe size, I look at the finger width. If he got thick fingers, then he got a thick di—*you know what*. The pants were loose, but it was in there!"

"Girl! You gotta get a piece of that. If you don't, somebody else will," Tameeka threatened.

Stacie gave a short nod. "Hey, what about you? You didn't meet anybody, did you?"

"I did too meet somebody," Tameeka answered defensively, and then suddenly laughed when she realized how juvenile she sounded. "As a matter of fact, I met a *lot* of somebodies. You're not the only one who got it going on tonight," she answered as she bowed her head and hid a nervous grin. Tonight, she'd met her soul mate.

"Oh really? Do tell," Stacie encouraged. "There are a lot of fine men out there. So which bodies did you meet?"

"I'll tell you later," she said, then changed the subject. "So whassup? Why are you sitting in the bathroom talking to me, when you got Mr. Wonderful on the other side of the door waiting to sweep you off your feet?" Tameeka asked, eager to get back to her new guy friend; she didn't want to leave him alone too long, the women were vicious. Something about New Year's Eve turns a woman into a man-stealing, I-don't-want-to-spend-the-rest-of-my-life-alone ho.

"I know, girl! Give me a minute, Meek; I need to run to the bathroom," Stacie called over her shoulder as she rushed past a group of preening women.

Inside the stall, Stacie let out a long breath and frowned. She had promised herself that she wasn't going to do it tonight. The day before she had done it twenty times, and yesterday she'd done it eighteen times and earlier today she'd done it seventeen. Her face glistened; the makeup couldn't hide the sweat that popped out over her face. Her palms became sweaty and she rubbed her hands together in an attempt to dry them; it didn't work, they only became soggier. She prayed silently to herself that the urge would pass. But it didn't. As she knew it wouldn't. Instead, the urge continued to grow. It seeped into her body like a nasty virus, and there was only one way to assuage it.

"I have to do it," she said in a tortured whisper, then snatched off her right shoe, a red strappy number, and brought it up to her nose. She inhaled deeply, and then took nine more quick sniffs as a calm came over her, blanketing her with a confidence that almost covered her shame . . . almost. The left shoe was next and the smell was even sweeter. She felt reborn. And it showed. Her face glowed; her pulse slowed and a crooked smile graced her face. Eyes sparkling, she pushed open the stall door.

"Let's show the brothas how *we* do it!" she said as she grabbed Tameeka's arm, then strutted out of the room.

2

Your Expectations Can Become Your Reality

Peachtree Street was overflowing with people, the sidewalks stuffed tighter than Janet Jackson's breasts in a bustier. Rows of vendors and amusement park rides lined the street. In the midst of it all were Tameeka and Tyrell Powell, holding each others' hand, ambling along laughing and talking as if they were old friends, not two people who had just met three hours earlier.

Tameeka was smiling so wide that her lips were hurting, but she didn't care, she was ecstatic. The whole evening felt like a dream. But it was real, the cold wind that kissed her bones proved it, and she shivered slightly and tugged at her wrap. Three hours. That's how long she'd known Tyrell. Tyrell Anthony Powell.

She smiled crookedly. She couldn't believe it when he'd sauntered past half a dozen yardstick-size women and stopped in front of her. She had almost fallen over with surprise when he had asked her to dance.

After their fifth dance together something told her that he

was a little interested. But after two hours of sticking to her like half a pound of barbecue ribs, she knew for sure he was feeling her. She shook her head, amazed that a man who looked like him wanted someone who looked like her.

A dead ringer for Gerald Levert, Tyrell was gorgeous. His full lips were totally kissable, but so were his cute ears and his ginger-colored eyes. For a man his size he was light on his feet—instead of walking he glided. She glanced down at his fingers and giggled softly; they were thick *and* wide.

Every couple of minutes Tyrell found himself sneaking peeks down at Tameeka. It was as though she had cast a spell over him, because each time he looked at her, his chest tightened and it felt as though he was breathing through a straw.

Tameeka was telling him a story about growing up with her grandmother. Her face was animated and she'd occasionally let loose a wild, raucous laugh that made him so hard that he felt like he could cut a diamond. She was the most beautiful lady he'd met in a long time, and by far the classiest. The silky fabric of her dress draped conservatively over her full breasts, then dropped down to the tip of her red sandals. Her locked hair was pulled up into a ponytail; a couple pieces had gotten free and gently caressed her cheeks. I'm the luckiest man alive, he thought, and poked his chest out.

Tyrell shook his head, amazed. Three hours ago he had asked her to dance and they'd been together since. He smiled and gave her hand a little squeeze. His smile deepened when she returned it.

They made a striking couple. At six-foot-seven and three hundred pounds, Tyrell dwarfed Tameeka's five-foot-five frame. He was big and cuddly, just the way Tameeka liked her men, and husky enough for her to snuggle in his lap if she so desired. She glanced at him and was shocked to find him eyeballing a group of ladies sashaying by.

Tameeka sucked in a breath of cold air, but it did nothing to cool her down. She exhaled slowly, then, "You like looking at people, don't you?" she lightly teased.

Tyrell chuckled. "Not really . . . why do you say that?"

Tameeka shrugged. "Your eyes seem to have a life of their own . . . at the party . . . walking down the street."

"I like being aware of my surroundings. A man gotta know what's going on," Tyrell answered as he reluctantly pulled his gaze off one of the women, whose legs ended at her chest.

"Oh, is that what it's called?" she asked, cutting her eyes at him. "So . . ." she nodded to the woman in front of them. "What are her legs telling you?" she snapped, arching an eyebrow at him.

"Come on, baby, it's not that serious. I only have eyes for you." He winked sexily, then swiped his thumb over her bottom lip before slipping his hand into hers.

"Corny!" Tameeka retorted, but her grip on his hand tightened.

The blowing wind continued to slice through Tameeka's silk dress and cut her skin as though she wasn't wearing anything at all. She silently cursed herself as she pulled her thin wrap around her shoulders. Stacie had insisted that she wear the flimsy wrap and not the wool coat that she had originally chosen.

"You cold?" Tyrell asked, and immediately felt stupid. He could see her shivering. "We can go back to the hotel if you want," he offered politely, but wished that they could keep walking forever.

"No," Tameeka lied. She was freezing, but she didn't want the night to end. She felt like Cinderella; all they needed now was a horse-drawn carriage. At that very moment, her vision came to life and she giggled as a horse and carriage trotted by.

Tyrell laughed along with her. "Care to let me know why I'm laughing?" He looked down and beamed at her for the thousandth time.

"Oh nothing," Tameeka chuckled, then decided it was too delicious to keep to herself. "Okay, I'll tell you . . . only if you promise not to laugh," she said, peeking up at him through her eyelashes.

"I promise. Cross my heart and hope to die, stick a chicken bone in my eye," he said somberly.

"Boy, you crazy," Tameeka hooted. They both shared a good laugh. Then she admitted to feeling like Cinderella.

"Wasn't Cinderella the belle of the ball?" he asked, and Tameeka nodded. "Well, you're not only the belle, but you're the queen," Tyrell said, his voice ringing with sincerity.

"That's very sweet," Tameeka said, blushing; at that moment she felt as beautiful and regal as a queen.

"One day we'll take that carriage ride; it's too damn cold—" He stopped and stared down at Tameeka. "Girl, you are freezing your ass off. You killing me with trying to be cute. Here, take my jacket." He slid his tuxedo jacket off and draped it over Tameeka's shoulders. She instantly felt warmer. She inhaled deeply, and her nose was filled with his intoxicating cologne. Thank you, God, she thought. She slid her hand back into his and smiled. His hands were big and strong, just like a man's hands should be, and it felt natural holding his hand, almost as if they'd done it before in some other life.

"You work out?" Tameeka asked. Even though he was big, he was muscular too. Muscles rippled underneath his tuxedo shirt. He sauntered jacketless through the cold as though it was a balmy summer evening instead of the middle of winter.

"Yep," Tyrell answered, before stopping and flexing his biceps. "Wanna touch?" he whispered as his gaze swept over her body, then stopped on her mouth and Tameeka automatically parted her lips.

"Umm, yeah," she answered, excited by the thought of Tyrell's kiss. Tameeka reached over and squeezed his muscle—it felt like a brick. "Wow, are you a professional body builder?"

"Naw, I'm a bus driver," Tyrell said before he draped an arm across Tameeka's shoulders and resumed their walk.

"Cool, so I got the hookup . . . free bus rides," she laughed up at him.

"I'll hook you up anytime." Tyrell gave her a lazy grin, then squeezed her shoulder. "So what's your nine-to-five?"

"Heaven on earth."

"Yes you are, baby," Tyrell drawled.

"No, I *own* Heaven on Earth, that's my brainchild. I have two employees and I sell everything related to nurturing the spirit. People come to my store when they're stressed out. Last year I grossed—"

"Hold up," Tyrell commanded. "I'm not trying to get in your bank account. Just wanted to know what you did, and I'm impressed. Not only are you a business owner, but you're sexy and smart," he said. "Hey look, a merry-go-round," Tyrell then announced, and pointed to their left. "Let's take a ride." Tameeka hung back; she could see doll-size ladies stepping daintily into the teeny seats. No way me and Tyrell will fit in those little booths, it'll be like trying to squeeze a couple of whales into a Geo Metro, she thought. "Come on," Tyrell insisted, then pulled Tameeka along.

They stood in line, and when it was their turn, she could hear snickers as she and Tyrell tried three different seats before they found one that barely accommodated them. All Tameeka wanted to do was jump off and hide. "Isn't this cozy?" Tyrell asked as he draped his arm around her shoulder.

"I guess," Tameeka answered, embarrassed, but the music snapped up her words as the ride began. The whole time she sat as stiff as a mannequin, not even Tyrell serenading her with a Luther Vandross song loosened her up. As soon as the ride ended, she pulled herself out and hopped off ahead of Tyrell. "I was feeling queasy," she said in response to Tyrell's raised eyebrow. "Let's go," she said, and gently pulled his arm until he fell into step with her.

Tameeka was enjoying their walk when, without any warning, Tyrell stopped in the middle of the sidewalk and turned to her. "So what do you think about me?" he asked.

"You're wonderful, *fine* and smart," Tameeka purred as she winked at him and his heart flipped-flopped.

"I'm feeling much love. But something's missing," he said, putting his forefinger to his forehead and wrinkling his brow as if he was trying to solve a mystery.

"You're wonderful, fine, smart and *sexy,*" Tameeka whispered seductively.

"Jackpot! Give the lady a free drink."

Tameeka giggled, then peeked up at Tyrell, expecting to see him looking down at her. Instead his gaze was locked on something else. It didn't take a detective to figure out what it was; all it took was one quick glance. She followed his stare; it was glued to the gentle swaying of a passing lady's behind. Ain't this some shit? she thought. He's doing it again!

Her eyes drifted downward to her dress and she felt like an oversize tomato. She fumed and her hand itched to slap the glassy-eyed look off his face.

"How are the *surroundings?*" Tameeka asked between clenched teeth.

Tyrell shot her a confused look, then grinned sheepishly. "It wasn't like that, baby, all I'm doing is looking."

"So now you admit to looking, before it was being 'aware of your surroundings,'" Tameeka shot at him.

"It's a little of both," Tyrell admitted. "I am a man. Besides, you should be happy that I'm checking out chicks and not dudes."

"What!" Tameeka hissed. "I should be happy that you're looking at women? What kind of messed-up logic is that?" she asked.

"Don't get it twisted," he said in a heated voice. "There are a million women out here showing their asses for everybody and their daddy to see and you don't expect a man to look?"

"I . . . I . . . I . . . ," Tameeka stuttered, shocked at Tyrell's outburst.

"Come here," he murmured as he drew her near, and Tameeka rested her cheek on his chest. "As I told you earlier, it's not that serious. Let's enjoy the rest of the evening," he said, dismissing the incident.

Why spoil the perfect evening? Tameeka thought. "Oh, look what time it is," she said, glancing down at her watch. It was one minute to midnight.

"This was nice . . . really nice. Usually I hang out with my boy J and his son Jam. We'd have our butts parked in front of the TV, watching the peach drop and sometimes we'd get adventurous and switch up and watch Dick Clark," he joked, and Tameeka laughed.

"I hear you. I had a *really* good time tonight," she said softly, and the way she said it made Tyrell think that she wasn't treated special on a regular basis.

The countdown to the New Year started and Tyrell peered down at her. "Hey lady, you know what that means, don't you?" he asked, and Tameeka shook her head no. "It means that you owe me a kiss," he said, easing up to her so that her breasts kissed his chest.

"I always pay my debts," Tameeka retorted sassily.

"Then call me Uncle Sam, because here I am to collect," Tyrell announced, then abruptly gripped her waist with his baseball-glove-size hands.

"You are so beautiful," he said, then gently caressed her face with the soft pad of his thumb. As he skimmed her lips, she caught his thumb and tenderly suckled it. She groaned softly. "I've got something else you can suck on," Tyrell drawled, and burst out laughing when Tameeka's mouth dropped open. "Not *that,* at least not yet, but *this.*" He dipped down and brushed his lips against Tameeka's and her hands whipped up his back, clutched his tuxedo shirt and pulled him closer.

Tyrell slipped his tongue into Tameeka's mouth and she grasped onto it as if it were one of her favorite lollipops. Tyrell let out a soft moan, then pushed against her and Tameeka gasped with delight when his hardness pressed into her. His hands flowed underneath the tuxedo jacket to fondle her breasts, and her body rippled in response. Suddenly heart-stopping fireworks erupted and for a moment Tameeka wasn't sure if they were from her and Tyrell or from the City of Atlanta.

Panting softly, Tyrell pulled away. "Happy New Year!"

3

What Crawford and I Gonna Do
When We Get Married

1. Honeymoon in Aruba
2. Redecorate the mansion
3. Have three beautiful hazel-eyed babies
4. Travel the world
5. Write a book on how rich people make marriage work

Stacie took a sip of wine and glanced across the dinner table at her date. Out of the corner of her eye, she could see the envious looks from the other diners. Her lips curved into a smug smile. She couldn't believe her luck. She had snagged one, and snagged a *f-i-n-e* one to boot. The only thing harder to catch than a professional athlete was a New York City cab. Unless you were a blue-eyed blonde, you rarely had a chance of catching either one.

She set down her wineglass and turned adoring eyes on her date, Crawford Leonard Wallace III. His sandy-colored hair had grown longer since New Year's Eve; instead of laying flat on his head, it had sprouted into a mass of tiny curls. Feeling her gaze, he winked at her, then went back to surreptitiously perusing the restaurant for the lucky lady who'd be his date for the weekend.

Coming up empty, Crawford took a sip of his wine and

inconspicuously studied Stacie over the rim of his glass. He knew her type. The professional-athlete-chasing, gold-digging wench. The eight-by-ten glossy of her in a bikini that she sent him and the dozen calls to his office confirmed it. Yep, he knew her type. *She's a quick fuck, a disposable commodity.*

Stacie happily bit into a scallop and held back a giggle as an image of his ten-bedroom mansion flashed before her eyes. If all goes well, I'll be living there by the end of the year. I'll put it on him so good that he'll never want me to leave. Then we can start making curly-haired green-eyed babies. She stared dreamily into space, oblivious to Crawford's whore hunt.

The evening had started off like a page ripped from a romance novel. At precisely eight o'clock, Crawford showed up at her front door, looking as suave as Morris Chestnut. His tastes in gifts were impeccable; before Stacie could say hello he had presented her with two dozen red roses and a five-pound box of Godiva chocolates.

When they stepped out into the night, she wasn't at all surprised to see a sleek Jaguar arrogantly hogging three parking spaces. She would not have expected anything less from him. They slid into the cream-colored penis with leather interior and wood trim and he swept her off to one of her favorite restaurants, C'est Bon!

"Do you ever get tired of it?" Stacie questioned, pulling herself out of her daydream.

"What's that, baby?" Crawford asked, then profiled a little for his audience. Starring in a Nike commercial paid off in more ways than one; he moved his head, angling and tilting as if posing for an invisible camera.

"All this attention," Stacie gushed. She loved it. I'm dating a professional basketball player. Na na na na!

As soon as they'd stepped into the restaurant, a hush fell over the place and every head in the restaurant had turned toward them. Occasionally a brave soul would stop over and ask for an autograph and Crawford would gladly give it. "How do you deal with it? I'd go crazy. The constant interruptions, the stares. You're in a freaking fish bowl," Stacie said.

Crawford ignored his steak and leaned back in his chair, eager to be on stage. "It all comes with being a baller," he sniffed. "It was worse when I was playing for the Lakers. Bit— oops," he chuckled, then corrected himself. "I mean *women* would be throwing it at me *all* the time. I mean nonstop. One time some chick followed me into the bathroom. She wanted my sperm." He tried to sound disgusted, but his lips curved up in a proud smile.

"Nu-uh! What did you do?" Stacie asked, enthralled; she loved hearing his stories. So far he had told her which NBA players "play for the other team," and what *really* goes on in the locker room.

"I told her to get the fu—I mean, I told her to leave me alone. Naturally, we have security for people like her. But you always get some freaks who slip through," he shrugged, then shook his head as if to say "whaddya gonna do?"

He threw her a devastating smile, then settled back in his chair and worked on his steak. I wonder if she'd do a three-way, I haven't had one of those in a couple of months, he thought. Every once in a while he'd pull his attention away from his dinner and covertly search the restaurant for his next toy. He was just about to give up his search when a life-size Barbie came sauntering toward him. The closer she got, the sharper the image became; he preferred the fuzzy version. Damn, it's ghetto Barbie, he thought when she stopped in front of him. She had a head full of fake blonde hair that touched the middle of her back and blue contacts that made her eyes look like two glass marbles. But it was her breasts that got his attention; they were the size of bowling balls.

"Yo, Crawford, can I have your autograph?" she asked with an air of familiarity that made Stacie sit straight up and glare at her. "I'm not gonna lie and say I'm your number one fan. You hear that shit all the time," she said, and rolled her eyes as though that was beneath her. "But you're a fine-ass man and I would love to have something to remember you by."

"Sure, baby," Crawford drawled, then tossed Stacie a sheepish grin and she shot him an understanding smile, but watched the situation through narrowed eyes. Crawford plucked up a paper napkin. "Who should I make this out to?" Crawford asked.

He was bent over the napkin with his pen poised to write when he heard her say, "I don't want your autograph on a piece of paper. I want it here." Without any hesitation she reached into her halter top and pulled out her right breast. Stacie sputtered wine over the table, and Crawford, who was still looking down at the napkin, glanced up and his jaw dropped down to his shoes. He thought he had seen everything.

"I can't sign that," Crawford refused, but he was mesmerized by her breast. It was huge, and it was begging him to touch it.

"Come on, it'll take two seconds," she persisted. "Just sign it, 'To Taquanna, you are my first and forever love.'"

"What!" Stacie screamed. "Lady, are you crazy? Can't you see he's on a date?"

"And your point is?" Taquanna replied airily. "All I want the man to do is to sign this." She jutted her breast out and the nipple almost grazed Crawford's lips.

"And all I want you to do is to take your stank ass away from this table and leave us the fuck alone," Stacie hissed through clenched teeth as she began to back her chair away from the table. She was two seconds away from kicking off her shoes and pulling off her earrings and jumping on Taquanna's butt. "And you need to stick that basketball-size thing that you call a breast back in your top."

Taquanna laughed uproariously, as if Stacie had just told her the funniest joke instead of insulting her. "Don't hate me because I've been doubly blessed." She eyed Stacie's chest, then said snidely, "I see that you weren't so lucky." She rolled her eyes and cocked her head at Stacie as if challenging her. People at nearby tables warily watched the action, not sure whether to run for cover or to eat and enjoy the free entertainment.

"Okay, everybody calm down," Crawford said. "I'll sign it," he said, then sighed deeply as though he was making a major sacrifice. He hid a smile as he grabbed the marker, then positioned himself so that his back was to Stacie.

Taquanna looked down at the message and she broke out into a grin. Crawford had given her a bonus, his phone number. With a wink to Crawford and Stacie, she stuffed her breast back into her top, then sauntered across the restaurant to her table.

"Why did you have to do that?" Stacie asked, pouting.

Crawford smirked. "I've got to, she's a fan. If it wasn't for her we wouldn't have anybody attending the games."

Stacie rolled her eyes, but didn't say anything else on the subject. "I like watching you play. Me and my best friend Meek watch you whenever we get a chance. We were at Phillips Arena when you scored forty points. You're my favorite player," Stacie announced. When we get married I can ditch my secretarial job. I don't think he'd want his wife to work, Stacie thought.

"I bet you say that to all the guys," Crawford teased, then glanced down at his watch, and Stacie's eyes widened slightly. She had seen one exactly like it in a magazine, and Michael Jordan was wearing it. "So Miss Long," he drawled. "Are you ready for some *dessert?*"

"Huh?" Stacie asked, blushing. Dessert?

"You know, dessert. Cakes and stuff; what were you thinking about?" he asked. He meant it exactly the way she took it. He was testing her to see where her mind was. It was precisely where he wanted it to be.

"That's what I meant too," Stacie lied, then reached for a glass of ice water and took a deep gulp.

"Sure," Crawford joked. "Let's drive downtown and see what's jumping off." He pulled out a wad of money that was as thick as his fist, peeled off some bills and threw them carelessly on the table. All the while Stacie's mouth had gone dry at the sight of all his money and an image of her spending it danced before her eyes. Sitting on the tip of her tongue and pressing against her lips was her desire to be his dessert. She needed a quiet place to think.

"I'll be right back. I need to use the ladies' room," she said, flashing him a smile. She excused herself and hurried off to the bathroom; fortunately, it was empty. "So what are you gonna do?" she asked her reflection. "Be a good girl and call it a night. Or make crazy love with your future husband?"

4

Life Is Much Better If You Take the Time to Nibble It, Instead of Gulping

Tameeka stepped into her store and the scents of lavender, peppermint and lemongrass wafted over her and immediately calmed her. The stiffness from her neck and shoulders magically evaporated. Smiling, she tentatively rolled her shoulders, then moaned out loud. Atlanta traffic always unnerved her. Anywhere else a twenty-minute drive would be just that, twenty minutes, but in Atlanta, multiply that by three and that was her daily commute.

She inhaled deeply, filling herself with the store's essence. This was her home. Her taste of heaven. Her soul fortifier. Her store. Heaven on Earth. The stress, the traffic and the momentary shoulder pain all ceased to exist as she sauntered to the middle of the floor. Her face glowed with pride. Not bad for a nappy-headed little girl from the wrong side of the tracks, she told herself. Last year, Heaven on Earth grossed over one hundred thousand dollars in sales and her financial advisor had forecasted that the next year would be even better.

A mere three years ago, a blink in time really, the three-story house was a rat-infested, urine-soaked hellhole that vagrants occasionally called home. But with financial help from the city, she transformed it into a slice of heaven. The walls looked like they were dipped in sunshine, mint-colored fabric embraced the window frames and rainbow-hued, plush throw rugs decorated the floor. Four couches and dozens of hard-backed chairs and recliners with oversize cushions were strategically placed around the room to provide readers or people who simply wanted to sit and mingle a comfortable arena to do so. Shelves and displays were chock-full of vitamins, minerals and herbs and everything else that aided in the wellness of the body, spirit and mind.

She loved the location; it was her dream spot. The Real Estate Goddess herself couldn't have picked out a better location for her. Little Five Points, Atlanta, Georgia. The size of a postage stamp, it was the part of town that, depending on whom you asked, was Atlanta's lump of coal or shiny diamond. Bars, coffee shops and brightly lit boutiques lined the streets. Each building was more outlandishly decorated than the last. No matter the time of day or year, there was always a carnival air simmering about.

The seed for Heaven on Earth was planted at Spelman, the historically black college. Thinking about the business plan she'd created there still made her laugh. She and her business professor had argued about the assignment. It was her senior year and she had taken his Life 101 class as an elective. If she hadn't needed the credits to graduate, she would've dropped the class faster than a coed looses her panties during spring break. She'd surprised herself by getting a B+ on the paper. It was forgotten until five years ago, when she was cleaning out her closet and had come across the project. It was as though she had found her lifeline; she snatched it up and never looked back, leaving behind a well-paying but stressful business analyst position at a Fortune 500 company. It didn't take long before Corporate America became a blurry nightmare.

Tameeka crossed her arms and gave herself a big hug. All her friends and family had told her that opening Heaven on Earth was a stupid idea. "Who's stupid now?" she wondered aloud to the empty room. "Stupid like a rich M.F. y'all hear me? Cha-ching!"

It was 7:00 A.M. and it would be another two hours before Bea, her assistant manager, came in and they'd open for business. Trent Lock, her part-time employee, didn't come in until after three o'clock. Tameeka sashayed across the room and pushed open the door to her office.

If the store was heaven on earth, then her office was the beach. Everything was aquamarine, sand-colored, or seafoam green. She eyed a stack of paper on her desk, then shook her head. "I'll get to that later," she muttered, then sauntered back into the store. It was time for her morning meditation.

Skipping across the room, which was something that she did only when she was alone, she dimmed the lights, put on a nature effects CD and placed six lit sandalwood-scented candles on the floor. Easing herself down on her favorite plush rug, she crossed her legs, then closed her eyes and started on the path to enlightenment. Her early morning tension was on the verge of melting away when a loud noise broke her tranquility. Opening one eye, she peeked at the ceiling; Mohammad Abdul, her upstairs tenant, had come into work early as well.

Ten years ago, Mohammad's work was too ethnic for some, but now his paintings and sculptures were hotter than bargain-priced Manolo Blahniks. On any given day, it wasn't unusual to see Shaq O'Neal or Madonna strutting up the stairs to his studio to peruse his latest masterpiece.

Tameeka pulled herself up and went through her routine. She replaced the nature effects CD with one of ocean sounds, then breezed throughout the store, turning on several strategicly placed lamps. She moved to the counter and brewed a pot of hazelnut coffee, her favorite. The aroma wafted up through the vents and invited Mohammad down.

"Hey! Hey!" he called as he slipped through the front door and made his way across the store. "How ya doing?" he asked, settling in an armchair across from her.

Tameeka grinned to herself as she poured coffee into the extra cup she had set out earlier. Their morning coffee-drinking session was a ritual that they both looked forward to. Tameeka leaned back on the couch, tucked her feet underneath her and observed Mo over the rim of her coffee mug. He was five-feet-eight, with dreadlocks that danced around his ears, full lush lips and a chest as wide as a minivan. He had a penchant for wearing khakis paired with loose-fitting shirts and today was no exception.

Her eyes danced appreciatively over his lips . . . remembering how they had felt on her skin. Years ago, really two, she and Mohammad had shared more than a pot of coffee; they had meshed their bodies together in a six-month relationship that left them both deciding that they were better friends than lovers. She thought about Tyrell and broke into a smile.

"Look at you, all lit up like a Christmas tree. Who making you glow?" Mohammad asked. He chuckled as Tameeka nearly choked on her coffee.

"What are you talking about?" she demanded, glaring at him, then averting her eyes when he gave her a knowing smile. "It's the cold air," she lied. She wanted to keep Tyrell all to herself, like a good secret.

"The cold air? You little liar. I remember a time when I made you glow. So I know that it is something *hot,*" he whispered as he slowly rounded the table until he was in front of her. Tameeka giggled and continued to sip her coffee. Mohammad was harmless and he liked to tease. "Is it something hot, Meek? I bet it was something *big* and *hot* . . . just like this," he murmured seductively as he grabbed her hand and placed it on the growing bulge in his pants. It took Tameeka a heartbeat to process the situation.

She snatched her hand away and smacked him hard across the face. She looked down at her hand with disgust; it was stinging, and she wasn't sure why. It could've been from the slap she had just given him, but she'd bet that it was from the heat rolling off his erection.

"Mohammad!" she screeched. "What the—? Why did you—? Why would you—?" she sputtered, her whole body trembling with rage.

"Oh, shit, Meek, I'm sorry, I thought you wanted me to," Mohammad apologized. "You had that glow . . ." He looked like a little boy who had broken his mother's favorite vase and Tameeka felt embarrassed for her outburst, and the anger slowly seeped out of her. She reached over and touched Mohammad's thigh.

"I'm okay," she assured him as she composed herself. "You caught me off guard. You can't be putting ladies' hands on your crotch, that thing is dangerous," she joked. "Do that to the wrong lady and you might get a little bit more than what you bargained for."

Mohammad laughed. "So you think *this* is dangerous?" he asked, jutting his lap up at Tameeka.

"Back in the day it was bad enough to make me do things that made me blush, but not anymore. You're getting old, Mo," she teased, as she relaxed against the couch.

"We're the same age," Mohammad retorted.

"Yeah, but I got a glow and you don't," Tameeka joked, throwing his words back at him.

"That's true, but I was the first one to ever make you burn," he gloated, and Tameeka's lips curled up; of all her boyfriends Mohammad had been the only one who played her body like a fine violin. She was so lost in the daydream that she didn't realize he was next to her on the couch until she felt the heat rolling off of him.

Mohammad's lips hovered over hers, and before Tameeka knew what she was doing she stuck her fingers in his hair and cupped his head, pulling his mouth to hers. She sighed against his lips, they felt so familiar, yet different than she remembered. Her lips were slightly parted when Mohammad slid his tongue into her warmth. A jolt of excitement shot through her and exploded where her legs met. Tameeka raked her fingernails up and down his back, and he shivered against her. Grabbing his waist, she pulled him to her and plunged her tongue into his mouth. He captured it and caressed it with his own.

"Mo," she groaned as she pulled him closer.

After what seemed like an eternity to Tameeka, but yet not long enough, Mohammad pulled away and looked down at her with hungry eyes.

"Just tell me when, pretty lady," he said softly, before strolling out the door, leaving Tameeka in a daze. It took her a second to catch her breath before she jumped up and rushed to the door.

Tameeka watched as he swaggered up to his studio, then turned to face her reflection in the mirror hanging beside the door. "Tameeka Jaquisha Johnson, what the fuck have you done now?"

5

How to Make Your Relationship Sparkle

1. Treat him like a king
2. Make Victoria's Secret your best friend
3. Know the phone numbers of all the restaurants that deliver
4. Make crazy love to each other like there's no tomorrow

Stacie looked around the hotel room and scrunched up her face. She was draped across the full-size bed with Crawford asleep beside her, snoring softly. This wasn't what she had envisioned when he suggested that they get together. A month, a whole month I've given this fool, and all he does is take me to hotels, Stacie fumed.

"Shit!" was the first thing that popped into her head the first time she walked into the room. It had to be one of the nastiest hotels in Atlanta. The walls were depressingly mud-colored. Two pictures of an orchard of wildflowers were slapped up on the walls in an attempt to brighten the room. They didn't. The bedspread looked as if it hadn't been changed in weeks. A quick glance told her that the rust-colored stains were not part of the pattern. The room's only redeeming quality was its view: At night, the Atlanta skyline twinkled and blinked like a Fabergé egg.

This is only temporary. Or so Crawford had reassured her when she'd asked him why he was staying at such a crummy hotel. He was quick to explain that his mansion was being reno- vated, and to blame his damn assistant for setting him up in a crap hole of a hotel.

"Yeah, I'll blame your *damn* assistant," Stacie muttered, glancing down at Crawford's sleeping form. "It's not your *damn* assistant that makes your ass see me only on Wednesdays. And it's not your *damn* assistant that keeps me from seeing your mansion. And it certainly isn't your *damn* assistant that keeps you from taking me out on a decent date," she said softly, and glared down at him. Then her face softened; he looked so cute. His eyelashes were so long that they kissed his cheeks, and his light brown hair was tousled, making it even curlier. Still . . .

It was only seven o'clock in the evening, but he was knocked out like it was the middle of the night. Stacie glowered at him. If he stuck to routine, he'd wake up, order room service, take a second nap, jump in the shower, dress, then they'd leave in sep- arate cars, each going in different directions; she on her way home and he off to one of his dozens of business meetings.

She leaned back and rested her head against the head- board, gazing out at the Atlanta skyline. "I'm so sick of this shit!" She punched the pillow, inches away from Crawford's face, and he popped up, eyes wide open and arms flailing, as if she had punched *him*. After he realized what had happened, they both laughed. He sat next to Stacie, his head resting against the headboard. The blankets had slipped down and bunched around his waist, and Stacie's eyes feasted on his chest. He once told her that he was a gym rat, pumping iron five days or sometimes more a week. And it showed. His pecs looked like Michelangelo had chiseled them.

"Yo, whassup? You hungry?" he asked sleepily as he knuck- led his eyes.

Stacie shook her head, then playfully ran a finger over his

chest, teasing a nipple. "Crawford?" When he didn't respond, she leaned over and flicked her tongue over his nipples; that got his attention. "How come I only see you on Wednesdays?" she asked.

Crawford sharply cut his eyes at her and withheld the urge to snap at her. "You know my schedule, baby, it's busier than Oprah's. Besides, I'd rather spend all my time with you," he said, nuzzling his face in her neck.

She swatted at him. "But you make me feel like a piece of ass," she admitted. "We don't go out in public and when we do see each other, we can't seem to make it out of bed. It just seems . . ." she faltered, then her voice grew stronger. "It just seems that all we do is make love—I mean, fuck," she quickly corrected herself.

"I did take you out . . . even bought you a dozen roses," Crawford objected, skirting the sex issue.

"Yeah. You took me out *once,* and you spent the evening autographing ladies' titties," Stacie pouted.

"It wasn't *ladies,* it was one, a very devoted fan," Crawford said, and turned his face to hide a smile. Taquanna had turned out to be one of the freakiest ladies he'd ever met; she'd kept him and his teammates busy for a week.

"I just don't like feeling like a piece of ass."

"Well, it's my ass," Crawford answered, then reached down and cupped Stacie's behind.

"Stop!" she protested, though her lips were turned up at the corners. "And," she continued. The way she said it made Crawford groan with frustration. Whenever a woman started her sentence with an "and," shit was sure to follow. "I'm not feeling this hotel room. When are you going to take me to your mansion?"

"Just as soon as the renovations are done," he responded smoothly. "Right now it's torn up, plaster and wood is everywhere. I don't want you tripping over anything and hurting your gorgeous body. Besides, I like having you all to myself."

"You like having me all to yourself, my ass! You're either a cheap son of a bitch or you're hiding me from someone. Which one is it?" she demanded.

Crawford simply shook his head and gave her an indulgent smile. "Neither," he answered as he gathered her in his arms. After he felt Stacie calming down, he said, "I got a little sumthin' sumthin' for you. It's in my briefcase." He jutted his chin out toward the case, signaling Stacie to get it for him.

Stacie slid off the bed, snatched up his briefcase and was back at his side in record time. Crawford pulled the briefcase onto his lap and opened it just wide enough for him to stick his hand in and pull out a long, slender jewelry box. Stacie didn't know that inside his briefcase were half a dozen identical boxes. All inscribed with the same thing: *To my reason for living*.

Stacie ripped off the wrapping, slid off the top and her eyes widened with surprise. Lying inside a nest of rose petals was a platinum tennis bracelet. To her practiced eye, it looked like he easily paid two grand for it. As soon as the shock wore off she gave a shriek of delight, then crawled on top of Crawford and rained kisses over his face. "Oh baby, this is so beautiful. Thank you so much," she gushed. "Am I really your reason for living? No, no, don't answer that, I can tell by the look in your eyes that I am." She bent down and gave him a kiss that left them both gasping for air.

"Let's order room service." He reached over, scooped up the menu and perused it, more out of habit than necessity; he already knew what he wanted to order. With his head bent, he missed Stacie rolling her eyes. She really wasn't in the mood for the greasy Buffalo wings, greasy French fries and greasy onion rings that he always ordered. But she smiled anyway, then stuck her arm out and admired her new piece of jewelry.

An hour later Crawford was fast asleep. He was satiated, above and below the belt. For the second time that evening Stacie found herself staring listlessly at Atlanta's skyline. Soon she found herself twiddling the blankets, fiddling with her hair and fumbling the remote control. "This ain't cutting it," she muttered. With a backward glance to ensure that Crawford was still asleep, Stacie pulled back the covers and slithered out of bed and reached for her shoes. A pair of sneakers. Her favorite. She brought the right one up to her nose and inhaled deeply. She moaned softly, then buried her nose deeper for a second whiff. By the time she was on the left shoe she was in heaven. Drool trickled from the corner of her mouth, her eyes closed in ecstasy.

"What the fuck are you doing?" Crawford barked. He found his voice after the shock had worn off. And when she didn't answer he repeated the question, louder this time.

Stacie's eyes snapped open. "Nuthin'," she denied, looking down at her shoes. They sat helplessly in her hands. Her high was suddenly gone. Deflated like a ten-cent balloon. She felt the wetness on her face and knew that her chin was glistening. She self-consciously swiped her hand across her mouth and chin.

Embarrassed, she pushed herself up, and on shaky legs made her way around the room. She snatched her panties off the lampshade, plucked her blouse from the dresser top and grabbed her skirt from the bed.

She dressed silently, perched on the side of the bed, occasionally throwing sidelong glances at Crawford. She glanced at him one last time and wished she hadn't; his glare was so cold that it'd cool Atlanta on an August day. She was at the hotel room door, her hand on the doorknob, when Crawford called her name.

6

If You're Ever Lucky Enough to Receive a Piece of Heaven . . . Don't Blow It

Tameeka smiled as Tyrell trotted around his truck, then stopped at the hood and made a funny face at her before coming around to the passenger side and opening up the door for her. Their whole day was like that. He'd do something silly to hear her laugh and she'd comply and laugh until her stomach hurt. Tameeka stepped out of the truck and they walked hand-in-hand to her apartment. At the door Tyrell pulled Tameeka into his arms and rested his chin on the top of her head. Tameeka sighed happily as she relaxed against his chest; she had finally found happiness.

"I had a wonderful evening tonight, lady," Tyrell said, thrilled that the day was better than he had anticipated.

"Me, too. The swimming, the beer making and dinner—you're spoiling me," she said, grinning up at him.

"Isn't that what a man supposed to do?" he asked softly as his eyes caressed her face. Then, "When are we going out again?" Tameeka and Tyrell said at the same time. They both burst out laughing. Tyrell stopped long enough to say, "Later this week is cool with me."

"I'ma have to check my schedule. Bea is supposed to have a day off and I'm going to have to fill in. After all, I am the *owner,*" she said, and Tyrell winced. This was the tenth time today that she'd mentioned she owned a store.

"I know you're the owner, hell, everybody in Georgia knows that you're owner of Heaven on Earth. You don't have to keep announcing it every five minutes," Tyrell said dryly.

"Announcing it?" Tameeka sputtered, and her happiness suddenly shriveled up. "Oh, now I see, you're a brother who's threatened by a strong black woman," Tameeka snapped.

"Hardly," Tyrell scoffed. "But, baby, give it a rest. You're the owner of a shop, it's all good." Tameeka crossed her arms over her chest and glared at him as though she wanted to kill him.

"Come here," he demanded, then opened up his arms, inviting her to step in. "Come give your teddy bear a big hug and kiss." He winked and wrapped Tameeka in a giant hug and her anger instantly disappeared. She tilted her head back and their lips met. His kisses were like lush drops of chocolate and she couldn't get enough.

"Wow!" Tameeka breathed and leaned back against her door and fanned her face. "Wow!" she repeated. "Where did you learn to kiss?" That was the best kiss of her life.

Tyrell smiled modestly, then said, "It wasn't me. It was all about you, baby."

"Wow!" Tameeka repeated, beaming.

"Hey, what's up?" Stacie waltzed up to her friend, and she couldn't help noticing her glazed eyes and smeared lipstick. She gave Tameeka a wink, then turned to Tyrell. "I'm Stacie . . . Tameeka's roommate."

"Tyrell," he stated as he inhaled Stacie. She looked hotter than Beyoncé.

"I'm sorry," Tameeka sputtered, pulling herself out of her daze. "This is *Tyrell.*"

"Well, it's very nice meeting you. I have to run." She turned to Tameeka and whispered in her ear. "He's cute. And by the way I won't be home tonight." Before Tameeka could say anything, Stacie was halfway to her car.

Tyrell stared after her. "What?" Tameeka asked, as irritation worked its way up her neck.

"I think she'll be a good match for my boy Jackson," he answered, then glanced down at his watch. "I didn't realize how late it was. I'd better get going. I'ma have to work tomorrow. They're offering overtime and a brother can definitely use the extra money, especially if I expect you to keep me around. And I don't know a woman who wants a broke-ass man," he said with a laugh.

"Oh," Tameeka said as her smile dimmed. After the magical day they had spent together, she had assumed that he would want to make the night even more special. Visions of them making love fizzled before her eyes. Just as well, she thought, and to her surprise, relief shot through her. The ten pounds she had lost last month returned along with some friends, and they had happily taken up residence in her stomach and thighs; she wasn't ready for an open house.

Still, her body throbbed for him. She wanted to feel him inside her. Lowering her gaze, she tried to think of what Stacie would do in the situation. Then it came to her, the oldest trick in the world. She lifted her head and gave Tyrell a calculating grin, then began talking in a breathy little girl voice. "Can you do me a *big* favor before you go? There's this *humongous* box in my bedroom that needs to go on the top shelf of my closet. It's *too* big for me to lift. Can you come and move it for me?" she gently pleaded, then looked up at him and batted her eyelashes.

"Er-sure-no-problem-just-show-me-where-it-is," he stuttered.

Tameeka hid a grin as she unlocked her door and led Tyrell into the apartment.

"C'mon, my bedroom is this way." She tugged at Tyrell's hand and led him down the hallway.

"There it is," Tameeka said, pointing to the box. The "humongous" box was roughly about the size of a twenty-pound box of laundry detergent. Tyrell's mouth twitched with amusement. This is definitely something she could've done herself, he thought, as he scooped the box up with one hand and effortlessly placed it on the closet shelf.

"Thank you *so* much," Tameeka gushed. "You really helped me out a lot." She had moved to the bed and Tyrell was standing in the middle of the floor, unsure of what to do. He really had to leave, but Tameeka looked good sitting on the bed. "Come, on stay a while. I'll pop some popcorn, we can watch a couple DVDs . . ." She didn't dare look him in the face lest he figure out her intentions. Instead, she plucked at some invisible lint on her comforter.

Tyrell silently appraised her bowed head and had a nagging suspicion that popcorn wasn't going to be the only thing popping tonight. "Sounds cool, baby," he said, then shrugged out of his leather jacket, tossing it on a chair, before joining her on the bed.

"Yay!" Tameeka cheered happily. "This will be like a slumber party. Maybe we can have a food fight," she teased.

"Yeah. Mashed potatoes are good. They always end up in the oddest places," he whispered, then touched her cheek softly before leaning in and kissing her. Tameeka's body melted as Tyrell nudged her back and slid on top of her.

"Mmm," Tameeka moaned as she pushed Tyrell off. "I need to take off these clothes," she explained, and gave him an apologetic look. "I'll be right back." Before Tyrell could protest she rushed into her bathroom. Slamming the door shut, she slumped against it. "Oh my God! What the hell am I doing?" she whispered to herself. "This is it, girl. He's gonna see me . . . every goddamn square inch. There's no more hiding."

On shaky legs, she walked to her full-length mirror. She averted her eyes as she unceremoniously pulled her clothes off and dumped them into the corner. It wasn't until every inch of clothing was off that she allowed herself to look. A mixture of self-loathing and embarrassment darkened her eyes as she studied her reflection.

"I look like the Pillsbury Dough Woman on steroids," she muttered as she eyed her body. Her legs looked like someone had injected tubs of tapioca pudding in them, her stomach looked like she had swallowed a ten-pound watermelon. "Oh Lord, this is what he's getting." The confidence that was so strong in her ten minutes ago dwindled down to a teeny, hard ball of self-hatred.

"Hey, what's taking so long? Do you need me to come in there?" Tyrell teased, but she heard some seriousness in his voice just the same.

"I'm coming. I'm brushing my teeth," she lied, then reached for the toothpaste. She opened it and squeezed the tube until a glob squirted into her mouth. Using her tongue, she quickly swiped it across her teeth, then spit it out and rinsed her mouth. She frantically searched the bathroom until she found her bathrobe peeking at her from a pile of clothes on the floor. She snatched it up, then sniffed it. It doesn't smell *that* bad, she thought. "I'll be damned if I walk out there naked," she grumbled as she pulled on the robe and knotted the belt tightly around her waist.

She peeked at her reflection. The robe was magenta-colored and made out of a jersey material that itched her skin. It wasn't the sexiest thing in the world, but it did stop right above the knee, hiding her stomach and thighs. She took a deep breath, turned out the bathroom light and then opened the bathroom door.

"It's about time—" He stopped in surprise; Tameeka had turned off the bedroom light before sliding into bed next to him. "Why did you do that?" he protested.

"I like making love in the dark. The darker the better," she lied. "Come on, kiss me!" she demanded as she pushed her face toward him.

"Nu-uh," Tyrell said, and Tameeka could feel him pulling away from her. "I like to see who I'm making love to. Where's the light?" he asked as he began fumbling around the nightstand.

"No!" Tameeka shrieked, and Tyrell froze.

Settling back against the pillows, Tyrell crossed his arms over his chest, then asked, "Whassup, Meek?"

"Nuthin'," she lied. "Just kiss me," she pleaded as she pressed her body against his.

"Come on, Meek, talk to me," he gently demanded.

"I . . ." She faltered, then began again. "I don't want you to see my body," she said softly.

"Why not?" Tyrell asked, clearly confused. "You *are* a lady aren't you? There isn't any funny stuff going on here, is there? No extra body parts?"

"No. I'm all woman," she said, then blew out a stream of air. "That's the problem. I'm way too much woman . . . I'm *too* big," she said, then held her breath and waited for him to laugh or, worse yet, agree.

He laughed. The blood rushed to Tameeka's face and she clutched the front of her robe closed. "Is that all you're worried about?" Tyrell asked. "Girl, puh-leeze! Give me some credit. I have some idea of what your body looks like, and trust me, I am not turned off. Besides, you aren't the first big woman I've dated." He pulled her in his arms and gently nuzzled her neck.

"Tameeka, I care about you. I am attracted to the whole package, your mind, soul *and* body. Besides, look at me, what am I gonna do with a little piece of a woman? C'mon, turn on the light. Would you do that for me?" he asked in a voice so sweet that Tameeka was tempted to say yes. Yet Tyrell sensed her hesitation.

"What if we leave the bathroom light on and close the door halfway. C'mon, now you can't beat that," he teased. Tameeka considered it, then nodded and did as he suggested.

She turned around and saw Tyrell reclining on her bed as if he had been there a thousand times. He was naked. His six-foot-seven frame seemed to take up the whole bed.

Her eyes wandered south, then stopped and she suppressed a giggle; Stacie's theory was right, thick fingers do yield a thick dick.

"Drop the robe," Tyrell whispered, his voice husky with desire. Tameeka opened her mouth to protest, but promptly closed it. They had a deal. Her hands were trembling as she undid the knot, then let the robe slip off and puddle at her feet. "Come here."

Tameeka slid into bed beside him. "You're beautiful, you know that?" he asked, tenderly stroking her cheek.

"Thank you," Tameeka whispered, then looked up into his eyes and saw her beauty reflected there.

"You are so sexy," he whispered as he gently kneaded her breasts. He bent over and began suckling her rock-hard nipples, taking one in at a time, and occasionally two. He was feasting on them as if they were oversize ice-cream cones. To her horror, he began kissing her stomach, his mouth leaving a wet trail over her excessive flesh. She tensed up. "Relax," he murmured into her stomach. "Lie back and enjoy." She nodded, but squeezed her eyes shut as his mouth moved over her.

Enjoyment only came when he slipped his hand between her legs and her inhibitions were swept away. He slid his fingers into her mound and with deliberate care began sliding in and out, his strokes causing fireworks to explode inside her.

"How ya feelin', baby?" Tyrell asked, grinning down at her. Her eyes were closed and she was panting softly.

She opened one eye and smiled weakly. *"Damn,* you got skills," was all she could get out before closing her eyes.

"Hey!" Tyrell protested. "You'd better not be falling asleep on me. I'm not done with you yet." Tameeka giggled, then looked up at him.

"Well, cutie, I haven't even *started* with you." Tameeka pulled his face toward hers and lightly ran her tongue over his lips, then breathed into his ear, "I wanna be on top."

"That's what I love. A take-charge woman," Tyrell teased as he rolled onto his back and pulled Tameeka on top of him.

"You're sexy, baby," Tameeka murmured as she gently blew on Tyrell's nipples until they were as hard as chips of chocolate. "And you're delicious," she cooed. His skin was like sugar to her lips, she couldn't get enough as she rained kisses on his chest. Inching down, she nibbled his legs, biting the inside of his thighs. She moved down to his feet, where she sucked his toes.

Tameeka reached down between his legs and cupped his sack and gently cradled it in her hand. Wrapping her hand around his penis, she stroked him and caressed his tip until Tyrell began whimpering. She smiled to herself; she had hit the spot.

"Does it feel good, baby?" she asked softly, and all Tyrell could do was moan. "I know . . . I know," she chuckled. She bent over so that her mouth hovered above his penis. Dipping her head, she slowly enveloped him in the warmth and moistness of her mouth.

"Um—Meek, I wanna be inside you," Tyrell groaned, and Tameeka pouted as she pulled her lips off him.

He reached down for his pants and pulled a condom out of his pocket. "A man's gotta be prepared," he said in response to Tameeka's surprised expression. She watched through half-closed eyes as he expertly slipped on the condom, then strad-dled her. Tyrell leaned down and grazed her lips with his. He pulled back just enough to look into her eyes, then asked if this is what she wanted, and Tameeka nodded. A smile broke over his face, and his eyes glazed over as he slid himself into her.

"You're beautiful," he said with each stroke. "You're beauti-ful!" Pretty soon he was chanting it and Tameeka moved along with his hips. When he exploded she exploded along with him.

"Oh Mohammad!" she shouted as her body shuddered.

Tyrell froze midstroke, then pulled out and glared down at her. "Who the hell is Mohammad?" he demanded.

7

List of Books That I Want to Read

1. RM Johnson, *The Harris Men*
2. Everything Zora Neale Hurston has written
3. John Grey (*Men Are from Mars, Women Are from Venus*)

*T*hrrruuump pow, thrrruuump pow, thrrruuump pow.

"What the—?" Tameeka let out a panicked yelp and turned frightened eyes onto Stacie. It sounded like Stacie's car was about to explode. Yet her friend calmly navigated the car through traffic, looking as if nothing out of the ordinary was happening. *Thrrruuump pow, thrrruuump pow, thrrruuump pow.* "What the hell's wrong with your car!" Tameeka yelled, and clutched the leather seats, her knuckles whitening. The noise roared through the car at an ear-splitting level. And every time Stacie stepped on the gas, the sound mushroomed a notch. It sounded like someone was sitting under the hood whacking the sides of the car with a hammer.

"Oh," Stacie answered, dismissing it with a wave of her hand. "That's nothing. You'll stop in a little while, won't you, Lexie? You always do," she cooed and stroked the steering wheel. "What's wrong, baby?" she whispered, then glanced down at the gas gauge. "You can't be hungry, Mommy fed you yesterday, so I know your belly is full. Come on, Lexie, please stop acting up," she begged softly. And to Tameeka's surprise, the noise stopped and Stacie shot her a triumphant look.

Lexie was Stacie's pride and joy. Her 1998 black and silver Lexus was a gift from a former boyfriend, Malcolm. During the six months they were dating, he bought her many gifts, but the Lexus was her favorite.

Tameeka watched her friend, amused by her behavior. "You're sick, you know that, don't you?" she asked while shaking her head in delight. "You need to get it fixed, instead of talking to it like it was a baby. You know what?" she asked. "Take it to the shop on Fourteenth Street, my boy Thomas will hook you up. Remember, he repaired my Escalade a couple of months ago."

"Maybe I will," Stacie said airily, lying through her teeth. She didn't tell Tameeka that the car had been making that sound for the past month. Nor did she tell her that she couldn't afford to fix it; her pile of bills was higher than Patti LaBelle's hair. Her fourteen-dollar-an-hour secretarial job, which she was holding onto by a thread—she was one late day away from getting fired—barely allowed her to keep her head above water. She definitely didn't tell Tameeka that she was scared shitless because she was driving around in a thirty-thousand-dollar car that she couldn't maintain. Over the years Tameeka had loaned her so much money that she was embarrassed to ask for any more.

Instead, she vibrantly said, "Grammy's gonna be surprised to see you." They were almost to her mother's house. Tameeka's grandmother lived across the sidewalk from Stacie's mother. "When was the last time you saw her?"

"A couple weeks ago," Tameeka replied, then sighed deeply. She absentmindedly watched the passing scenery; the houses were becoming smaller and shabbier and corner stores with names like Big Daddy's and Mom and Pop Liquor were the only stores in sight. "I can't wait to see her!" she said, brightening.

Grammy. A warm smile spread over Tameeka's face at the thought of her grandmother. For the past twenty-two years, Florrie Ann Johnson had served as her mother and father. When she was ten, her parents started paying more attention to their drugs than to her, so Florrie Ann swept in and scooped her up and brought her to live with her.

"How's Nevia doing?" Tameeka asked.

"Cool. She's been working at DeKalb Medical Center for two years now. I can't believe she found steady work. I'm so proud of her. She came a long way."

"That's for sure." Tameeka knew Nevia's story very intimately. Back in the day, Nevia was so strung-out on drugs that she had broken into her grandmother's house and tried to steal her microwave. Fortunately, her grandmother had been home and was able to prevent the theft.

They sat in comfortable silence, then, "How's everything with that man of yours? What's his name?" Stacie teased, feigning forgetfulness. "Tyrell . . . that's it. How is he?" she asked, and grinned when Tameeka began to fidget in her seat.

"Hmmm . . . he's fine," Tameeka stammered. When Stacie's brown eyes widened slightly as if she was expecting to hear more, Tameeka said, "He's a nice guy."

"Okay, listen up. You'd better tell me some dirt or I'ma stop this car right in the middle of the street and not move until you do," Stacie warned. Then her voice mellowed, "Tell a sistah something," she pleaded.

"You might be doing Lexie a favor. She's on her last wheel anyway," Tameeka joked. "It's not that I don't want to tell you. It's just . . . I don't want to jinx it, you know?"

"Yeah, I understand," Stacie answered softly, and reached over and squeezed her friend's hand. She was quiet for a heartbeat, then burst out with, "So you feelin' him? What size is he?

Is he good in bed? Where's the brother working? What kind of car does he drive? Does he own his own home?" The questions poured out of Stacie.

"Hey! What happened to all the understanding?" Tameeka laughed through mock anger. " 'K, ask me again. One question at a time, please!"

Stacie smiled smugly. The order of the questions was all jumbled in her head, so she threw out the first one that came to mind. "Is he good in bed?" Confusion colored her face when Tameeka burst out laughing. "What?"

"How did I know that that would be your first question? Miss Hot Panties," she teased. Then her voice went dreamy. "He's banging in bed! One time T put it on me so good that he made my *toes* curl."

"It's like that? Dang! So . . . is he a seven-incher?" Her eyes widened at Tameeka's smirk. "Bigger? Wow!"

"You know what? Your ass is getting too damn nosy!" she said, then playfully stuck her tongue out at Stacie before turning toward the window to hide the blush that was a sure giveaway of her true feelings for Tyrell. No man had ever treated her as well as he did; Tyrell gave her a sense of peacefulness.

"*Humph!* He must be a six-incher. Otherwise you wouldn't have the 'tude," Stacie snickered.

"Whatever!" Tameeka grinned and kept her secret to herself.

"So where's the brother setting down his briefcase?" she asked. Tameeka strained to hear the question. The *thrrruuump pow, thrrruuump pow, thrrruuump pow* sound had returned. She shook her head and glanced at her friend, amazed that the ear-splitting noise didn't bother her. She was still driving along and humming to one of the songs on the radio.

"He doesn't have a briefcase. He drives a bus . . . a city bus. He works for the City of Atlanta."

"That's *interesting,*" Stacie said. Then continued to hum along with the music.

Tameeka bristled, then asked loudly, "What's so *interesting* about that?" She had turned in her seat, cocked her head to the side and glared at her friend.

"It's just interesting, that's all," Stacie answered, then pulled her eyes away from the road to smile weakly at her friend. "Look at you. You own your own business. A *thriving* business, no less. You got a phat ride," she said. "And you're the smartest person I know. Whassup with a bus driver? How come you can't find a man at all the Chamber of Commerce meetings you go to?"

Tameeka rolled her eyes. The men she met at those meetings all wanted petite women with long, flowing hair and slamming bodies. "He's a good man," Tameeka said, and let the matter drop. "We should double-date. Me and Tyrell and you and Crawford. That'll be cool. Hanging out with an NBA player."

Stacie hadn't told Tameeka about Crawford kicking her out of his hotel room; the embarrassment and hurt was too fresh.

"Stacie?" Tameeka called softly when her grandmother's and Stacie's mother's apartment building came into view.

"I'm okay," Stacie answered, reassuring her friend.

"You're sure?"

Stacie turned a bright smile on her friend and nodded. "I am."

Tameeka eyed her skeptically. "Well . . ."

"Trust me, I am," Stacie said.

Tameeka gave Stacie's hand a comforting squeeze. Growing up, Stacie hardly talked about her father, but when she did it was with a bitterness that left Tameeka wondering what he had done to her friend. Whatever he did made Stacie fearful every time she went home. Even from the grave he's still hurting her, she thought, and shook her head.

Stacie pulled her Lexus into the parking lot and stopped in front of the prison-looking apartments. They were shaped like giant refrigerator boxes; three levels, tall and muddy brown-colored, they were configured into a giant U. In the middle of it all were broken-down picnic tables and naked trees. That's where she and Tameeka had spent summer days playing hopscotch, jump rope and kick ball. Each apartment had a patio, which was really just a piece of cement about the size of a slice of bread, barely big enough to hold a barbecue grill and chaise lounge.

Auburn Heights was just like any other project in the ghetto: women were grandmothers by the time they were thirty, a gold tooth was a fashion accessory and work was harder to come by than a thirty-year-old virgin.

Stacie was halfway out of her car when she remembered where she was. She shook her head and screwed her face up into a frown. The world ran differently in Auburn Heights. There were four classes of citizens: those who sold drugs, those who bought them, those who died either selling or using and those whose daily existence was making themselves invisible to the first three. Egos were galaxy-size; honor was thick and the rules changed on a daily basis.

Stacie surveyed a group of young men and her lips turned up in a smile when she saw a familiar face, her cousin Pimp. She asked Tameeka for money, then ran over and was pulled into a bear hug, which ended with her sticking a fifty-dollar bill in Pimp's pocket. Her car was safe. But that didn't stop her from activating the alarm. Not that that even mattered nowadays; nobody even blinked at a car's hysterical shriek. It was about as common as a baby crying.

"Call me at my mom's when you're ready to roll," Stacie said as she headed toward her mother's apartment and Tameeka walked in the opposite direction to her grandmother's place.

Stacie walked up the steps to her mother's garden-level apartment, shaking her head at the garbage strewn across the neighbor's yard. Old newspapers, crumpled soda cans and torn candy bar wrappers dotted the postage-stamp-size yard. Then she surveyed her mother's yard. It was a miniparadise. Two rose bushes framed her front door, the little bit of grass, too small to be called a lawn, was lush and green. Two little frogs sat on the top step. They croaked every time somebody came to the front door.

She pushed open her mother's front door and was struck by three things: the sour smell of cooked cabbage, the stench of baby poop and the cloying scent of floral perfume.

"Aw shit!" Stacie groaned, and resisted the urge to cover her nose. She should be used to the smells, but they only seemed to get worse with every visit. Closing the door behind her, she maneuvered her way between a green velvet sectional with over-stuffed pillows, a black lacquer coffee table and a twenty-seven-inch TV to the windows, which she raised, hoping for some fresh air.

Turning away from the window, her big toe connected with a hard object and a string of expletives escaped her lips. She reached down to stroke her injured foot and that's when she saw her niece's wooden building block. Her sister, Nevia, had never been a very good housekeeper. Twenty-six years old, Nevia had lived harder than a Snoop Doggy Dogg groupie. At one time, drugs, prostitution and shoplifting were her lifestyle. After a ninety-day stint in the Fulton County jail, she reevaluated her life and decided that she could do better. She had gone back to school sacrificing nights and weekends for a medical assistant certificate.

Stacie plucked up the block along with other toys that littered the floor and turned to her sister's bedroom door, ready to give her a piece of her mind, but got a pleasant surprise instead. Standing at the threshold was her two-year-old niece, CoCo. She had waddled up to the threshold of her bedroom door and stopped; she rarely ventured from her safety zone.

She gave a wickedly delicious laugh like only a two-year-old can, peeked over her shoulder and, knowing an opportunity when she saw one, began to make her way to her aunt. She had her bottle, or her "ba ba," as she called it, clutched to her chest as if it was a foot-long piece of chocolate.

Stacie bent down and plucked her niece up, showering her face and rounded belly with butterfly kisses. CoCo giggled joyously and grabbed hold of the attention the same way a drowning man would a life preserver. Stacie's nose didn't miss the undeniable pungent smell of baby poop clinging to her niece. She needed a diaper change.

With CoCo in her arms, Stacie strolled into her sister's room and stopped dead in her tracks. She screwed her face up in disgust. The room was a pigsty. Empty fast-food containers littered the floor, a pile of dirty diapers lay in the corner and the bed was heaped with clothes, dirty glasses and wrinkled newspapers. Nausea rose in her throat and threatened to explode through her lips. She covered her mouth as she inched into the room and rooted through the pile of junk for clean diapers and a reasonably clean towel. As soon as she found both, she raced out of the bedroom.

"Damn. Your momma's a freakin' pig," she said to CoCo, who was oblivious to the mess. She was used to it and besides, she was too young to know that anything was wrong.

Just as Stacie laid CoCo on the couch, her mother stepped into the living room. She was wiping her hands with a dishrag. "Hey, baby, I didn't hear you come in." She kissed Stacie on the cheek, then playfully poked her granddaughter in the stomach and was rewarded with a wide grin. "Hey, cutie," she clucked. She glanced over at her daughter's open door and her eyes clouded over. CoCo was momentarily forgotten as she walked to her baby daughter's door and peeked in. She shuddered, then firmly shut the door behind her. "I can't stand to look at it," she said, then sat down next to Stacie.

At forty-five, Gladys could easily pass for someone ten years her junior. She was a beautiful lady. Her skin was the color of an eggplant and just as smooth. Her hair was pulled back and coiled into a tight bun, and on the rare times when she let it down, it kissed the middle of her back. Years of power mall walking kept her in excellent shape.

"Momma! Why don't you make her clean up?" Stacie protested. Although she and her sister were close, she had no problem voicing her complaints about Nevia. Stacie placed the towel on the couch and laid CoCo on top of it. With the efficiency of someone who had diapered hundreds of babies, she had CoCo's diaper off and a clean one on her in thirty seconds flat.

Her mother shrugged. "She'll clean up when she gets a chance. She's busy at the hospital. People don't stop getting sick, you know. Besides, it's not that big of a deal. I'm just so proud of her, she's thinking about going to nursing school. Did she tell you?"

Stacie shook her head. "That's wonderful, Momma. I think she'll make a good nurse."

Her mother nodded in agreement, then asked, "Have you read any of those books yet?"

"Oh crap! Sorry, I meant to say no. I've been busy," Stacie whined, reverting to her preteen years. "I don't have the time."

Her mother looked at her and rolled her eyes before she walked out of the living room and returned with a book in her hand. "Here, read this," she said, handing it to Stacie.

Stacie read the title out loud, "Hurston, Novels and Stories."

"It's a collection of all her works," her mother said.

"I guess it helps having a mother who's a teacher," Stacie teased. "I'll read it," she promised. "Where are my other nieces?" she asked, as the apartment was surprisingly quiet without the kids.

Her sister had three babies. Designer babies, is what Stacie and Tameeka called them. CoCo, the middle baby, was black and Hispanic. Three-year-old Chloe, the oldest, was Japanese and black. Lastly there was Connie. At six months old, she looked like an angel. She was black and Italian. The fathers were picked for their good looks and not necessarily their dick or wallet size.

"She has them. She said something about taking Chloe and Connie to see their fathers. CoCo was napping when she left, so I told her to let her sleep. So what's going on at the law firm?" she asked; she loved hearing Stacie's stories about the people at her job.

"Same old, same old," Stacie answered vaguely as she played with CoCo.

"Have you been promoted yet?" she asked, and Stacie shook her head. "Well, they should, you practically run the office," she said. "How long have you been there?"

Stacie shrugged. "About eight years. But I've been having problems."

"What kind of problems?" Gladys asked, concerned.

"They've been watching me. I've been getting to work—"

At that moment Nevia strolled into the house and Stacie's mouth gaped open. While Stacie had gotten her looks from her father, Nevia had inherited their mother's eggplant coloring, sheath of long glossy hair and even after three kids, her body was still tight. She had no problem with showing it to everyone and anyone. The denim shorts she had on barely covered her rear end, her buttocks peeking out like two ripe peaches. The white halter top was nothing more than two handkerchiefs sewn together with string drawn through. It barely covered her breasts. Chloe was at her side and Connie was sleeping in the stroller.

"Damn, girl," Stacie said. "Do you have to go outside like that? Momma, look what she's wearing." Stacie turned to her mother and pointed at her sister.

Gladys simply nodded her head. She and Nevia had argued so much about her choice of clothing that she was tired of it.

"Momma's okay with what I wear," Nevia said, and pranced into the room. "You're just jealous because your old ass can't wear something like this."

"Nevia!" Gladys warned. She didn't allow cursing in her home.

"Sorry, ma'am," Nevia said, feigning remorse. "I see you're still driving that old as—" she shot a look at her mother. "I mean, that old piece of junk around."

"Excuse you," Stacie said. Her sister was unbelievable. "So what are you rolling in now? Last I heard, you and the city bus drivers were on a first-name basis."

"That's about to change," Nevia answered mysteriously. Then in a spiteful move, she lifted CoCo from Stacie's leg and set her on the floor. But CoCo toddled back over to her aunt and pulled herself up on the couch and into Stacie's lap. Despite herself, Stacie stuck her tongue out at her sister.

"What have you gotten yourself into now?" Gladys asked, warily eyeing her daughter.

"Nuthin'," Nevia lied, then began talking really fast, which instantly tipped Gladys off that she was lying. She listened anyway, nodding her head when it seemed appropriate. "Last week, I went over to CoCo's daddy's house. Carlos had some family visiting from Puerto Rico and they wanted to go car shopping, and I hung out with them. So when we got there, I started looking at the cars. Then his uncle offered to buy me a little Honda Accord, wasn't that nice? He's the nicest man I know. The car should be here tomorrow, they have to finish the paperwork and stuff," she finished, and let out a deep breath as her gaze bounced from her mother to her sister.

"Well—er—that's nice, Nevia," Gladys stuttered, stunned by the news.

Stacie shot her mother an incredulous look that said: If you're not going to ask her, I will. "Let me get this straight. Carlos's uncle, a man you just met, bought you a car, for no reason at all, other than the fact you thought it looked nice? Is that what you're telling me?"

Nevia nodded. "Yep, that's what I'm telling you," she said,

and inwardly cursed herself. She had to go ahead and blab about the car while Stacie was there. She knew that her sister would grill her like Judge Mathis. "It happens all the time. Some cultures are just more generous than others. Whenever I go over to Carlos's house, his mother always cooks for me and CoCo *and* she sends us home with a plate. Doesn't she, Momma?" She turned wide eyes on her mother, who was watching her with pinched lips.

"Hold up, a car is a lot different from dinner," Stacie snapped. "And a heck of a lot more expensive, more like fifteen thousand more. And you didn't have to do anything for it?" Stacie questioned. "He just gave you the car—free and clear?"

"No, I didn't have to do anything for it," she answered. Then, to avoid her sister's accusing eyes, Nevia bent down and peered in Connie's face; who was still peacefully sleeping in the stroller.

"You don't even have a driver's license," Stacie pointed out. "How do you plan on driving it?"

Nevia sighed and pulled herself upright and faced her sister. "Manny, that's Carlos's uncle, plans on teaching me. He said that he'll take me out for as long as it takes for me to learn to drive. Isn't that sweet?" she asked.

A sudden thought struck Stacie. "Does Carlos know who bought you the car? Or have you even told him about it?" she asked. She knew the answer as soon as Nevia began moving her lips and nothing came out. Her sister had never been good at coming up with a lie at the spur of the moment. Then Nevia suddenly found her voice.

"He's okay with it," she said. "I told you, his family is very generous and he wants to make sure that his daughter is taken care of."

Stacie knew Carlos; he'd shoot you first and ask questions later. His boys called him Fierce for both his temper and his quickness with a gun.

Nevia reached over and plucked CoCo off Stacie's leg, causing her daughter to howl. Hurt flashed across Nevia's face and she swallowed a lump of jealousy, then cut her eyes at her sister. Things always came easy to Stacie; she got the best grades in high school, men constantly flocked to her and she got the tight job at a law firm. Now she got my daughter, Nevia thought.

Nevia dropped CoCo back onto her aunt's legs. Her howls stopped and she began gurgling happily. Nevia angrily smacked her teeth, grabbed Connie and Chloe and flounced off to her bedroom, where she slammed the door, rattling several knick-knacks on the shelves hanging outside her room.

With her sister out of the room, Stacie angrily rounded on her mother. "Momma! Why didn't you say something to her? You know that man didn't just buy the car out of the goodness of his heart."

"Maybe he did," Gladys argued weakly. "There are some good people out there, Stacie," she insisted.

"Yeah, there are. But not buy-a-stranger-a-car good people," she said, and dropped her voice lower. "Come on, Momma, what do you think Nevia had to do to get that car?" she asked, as she anxiously looked at her niece.

"Stacie! What are you saying about your sister? She wouldn't do anything like that! The *old* Nevia would, but not now, not now," she said, vigorously shaking her head. "Your sister has changed," she insisted.

"I don't know, Momma . . ." Stacie said, shaking her head, hoping that her sister wasn't backsliding into the life she had left, where drugs and money ruled and bodies were disposable commodities. What the hell did Nevia have to do to get that car? Stacie wondered. The phone rang and she stretched over and brought the receiver to her ear. She blanched when she heard the familiar voice. "Nevia!" she yelled. "It's Carlos!"

8

Putting Life on Cruise Control Is the Only Way to Go

Who the hell is Mohammad?" Tyrell repeated. He had sprung out of bed.

"Nobody," Tameeka stuttered. The flush of her orgasm cooled down to a clammy veil.

"So you just call out any dude's name?"

"He's nobody," Tameeka insisted, then tugged at Tyrell's hand, pulling him toward the bed.

Tyrell snatched his hand back. "Who is he?"

Tameeka hung her head. "An old boyfriend," she admitted.

Tyrell exhaled. "So whassup?"

"Nothing. There's nothing between us."

"There must be something between you two if you're calling out his name," Tyrell fumed.

"It's nothing. Honest, baby. I don't know why I did it. I wasn't even thinking about him," she answered truthfully. "I was totally enjoying your body."

Tyrell cradled her face in his hands. "If you got something

to tell me, now is the time to do it before we get too deep in this."

"There's nothing to tell, I made a silly mistake."

"You'd better tell me if something changes. I don't like surprises."

Tameeka nodded. "I will. Now make me scream, Tyrell."

That was two days ago. Tameeka shook the memory away before glancing at Tyrell, who grinned, then winked at her.

"Hey baby, where do you want this?" Tyrell held a candle sporting a leopard design. "A whole box of them just came in." Things had been going well despite her accidentally calling out Mohammad's name.

"My wild thang candles are here," Tameeka squealed, then rushed over to Tyrell and kissed him as if he was the one who actually manufactured the candles and hand delivered them. "Put those over in the corner," she demanded. "I'm going to create a special display for them." She tilted her head to the side and studied the candles. Then she said, "Something wild and funky," she decided.

Tyrell did as she requested, then sauntered back to her side. It was two o'clock on a Tuesday afternoon and he was helping her out at Heaven on Earth.

"Open this and see what's in it!" she ordered, and shoved an oblong box in Tyrell's hands. He opened his mouth to say something, but clamped it shut; he swallowed his irritation and instead slit the box open and examined its contents. That was the third time today that Tameeka had bossed him around as though he was one of her employees. This wasn't what he had in mind when he agreed to spend the day helping her around her store.

He glanced at her out of the corner of his eye. She was across the store helping a young lady who had come barreling through the doors; she was looking for some vitamins and nothing else. She was pretty adamant about that. Now her basket was not only filled with half a dozen bottles of vitamins, but candles, a miniature water fountain and books on stress release. He shook his head in admiration: Work it, girl!

Tyrell returned his attention to the books and began unpacking them and lining them up on the bookshelf. The routine job was repetitive, down . . . up . . . stretch . . . down, and pretty soon he eased into a rhythm that suited him just fine because it allowed him to slip into daydream mode.

Several pictures flashed before his eyes. He and Tameeka exchanging wedding vows, he and Tameeka buying their first house as man and wife, then he and Tameeka bathing their firstborn, Tyrell Jr. I'm blessed. I am truly blessed, he thought to himself, then broke into a wide grin and began whistling softly.

The visions were still fresh in his mind and the music on his lips as he reached up to place a book on the shelf. Suddenly, Tameeka snatched it from his hand. He was instantly snapped back to reality. Tameeka's eyes were bright with rage. "These don't go here!" she barked. "I told you not to shelve anything before checking with me first." She began pulling down the books that had taken him more than a half hour to put up. "I'll do it myself. Maybe you should work the cash register. You should be able to handle *that.*" She was bent over, returning the books to the box, and didn't see the hurt and embarrassment on his face.

"Um—baby?"

Tameeka continued to box the books as though she hadn't heard him. So he called her again. This time she answered, "Give me a minute. I need to put these books back in the box."

"Tameeka!" Tyrell barked, and Tameeka was so startled that she dropped the stack of books she had been holding.

"What's wrong?" she asked.

"I need to talk to you."

"Oh . . . ," she said, relaxing, then went back to the books. "I'm listening."

"I—want—to—talk—to—you—in—private," Tyrell hissed.

Bea was standing a few feet away and had been keeping a concerned eye on them. Experience told her that something was going to burst. The day a woman starts treating her man like a child is the day that he's gonna start looking for a lover instead of a mother. "Young people," she clucked, then eased over to Tameeka and Tyrell.

Tameeka was holding a book and staring, dumbfounded, at Tyrell. Bea grabbed the book out of Tameeka's hand, then patted her on the shoulder. "Go on, baby, I'll take care of this." She watched as Tameeka followed Tyrell back to her office.

Inside the office, Tameeka was sitting on one end of the couch and Tyrell on the other. Tameeka crossed her arms over her chest and rolled her eyes at Tyrell. "So you wanna talk? Well, talk!"

"You need to chill, bossy lady." Tyrell said it as gently as he could.

"What?" Tameeka sputtered, then pointed to herself. "*I* need to chill?" When Tyrell nodded, she let loose. "Let me tell you something. Where the hell were you when I had to work twelve-hours days, seven days a week—by myself, mind you— because half my friends and almost all my family members thought that a black woman couldn't own a successful wellness store. Where the hell were you when I had to sleep on that cot right there." She pointed to her army-issued cot, which she'd picked up from an army surplus store. "Because I was afraid that if I got in the car and drove home, I'd fall asleep at the wheel. Where were you—"

"Hold up . . . time out." Tyrell grabbed Tameeka and pulled her into his arms. Holding her body against his, he began talking softly. "I'm not disrespecting you or taking away your accomplishments. You're my queen, I told you that when I first met you and you'll always be. But baby, you can't talk to me like that. You heard the old saying: It's easier to catch bees with honey than vinegar. Well, throw a brother some honey once in a while, that's all I'm saying."

Tameeka pulled out of his arms, then glared up at him; his mouth was twitching at the corners as if he was trying to suppress a grin. That made her even angrier. "Well, I'm not bossy. When it comes to my business, I know how things should be run. I didn't get to be the owner of a store by letting people tell me what to do!" she shouted, and soon her whole body began shaking; she was making soft hiccupping sounds and crying quietly at the same time. After some time the room was quiet. Then Tameeka looked up at Tyrell.

"You must think that I'm the most horrible person in the world, don't you? Don't lie . . . tell me the truth," she demanded, and Tyrell shook his head.

"I'm not thinking anything like that. If I was I would've told your bossy ass off in front of everybody. You've gotten a little swollen, that's all."

"And you decided to stick a pin in me?" she joked, suddenly feeling better. She grabbed Tyrell's sleeve and began wiping her face.

"Hey, do you see Kleenex stamped on my sweatshirt? Go get some tissues."

Tameeka hopped up and grabbed some tissues and wiped her face. "So how bad am I?" She had tossed the soiled paper in the garbage and was sitting comfortably in his lap.

"Well, this is you on a good day," he said, and began mimicking her. " 'Put that down, I can do it better. Don't touch that, you don't know what you're doing. Sweep the floor, at least you can't mess *that* up!' "

Tameeka's heart banged against her chest. "I don't do that," she protested, horrified at Tyrell's portrayal of her.

"Yeah, you do," Tyrell said. "And it makes me feel like shit," he admitted.

"Oh baby, no! I didn't mean to," Tameeka exclaimed as she gently stroked his face.

"I could be somewhere else on my day off. But I chose to come in and help you out. I really want to spend some time with my lady."

"Do I really sound like that?" Tameeka asked quietly.

"Yep. You sound like a drill sergeant whose jock strap is two sizes too small," Tyrell answered, breaking it down for her.

"No I don't!" she argued heatedly, then her voice suddenly softened. "Yeah, I do. Bea's told me so . . . on many an occasion." She laughed self-consciously, then continued. "She says that I treat people as though they were mindless idiots. But I don't mean to," she said, and hung her head, ashamed at her behavior.

"I hope you don't," Tyrell answered.

"It's just that I'm so stressed. I have to deal with upset customers, vendors who want their money, I have to make sure that the rent is paid on time, I—"

Tyrell placed his hand over her mouth. "Be quiet!" he instructed. "You're making excuses," Tyrell said. "And excuses are like credit cards—everybody has them. So you gotta come better than that, baby," he said before removing his hand.

Tameeka sighed. "I don't have time to think about how I talk to people."

Tyrell stood up, stretched and sauntered to the door. He had his hand on the doorknob, then he turned back to look at her. "You'd better start thinking about how you talk to people, because if you don't, you might not have anyone around to listen to you." He strolled through the door leaving Tameeka gaping; a heartbeat passed before she raced after him.

9

Why Every Woman Needs a Best Friend

1. You'll have a 24/7 confidante
2. You'll have a permanent shopping partner
3. You'll have someone to swap clothes with
4. You'll have a sounding and crying board
5. You'll have someone there to catch you when you fall

Tameeka stirred the pot of lima beans, then sat at the table across from Stacie. It was dinnertime and it was Tameeka's week to cook, which both of them were grateful for; culinarily challenged, Stacie's fanciest dish was tuna casserole, and even that was hit or miss.

"So Carlos still doesn't know about the car?" Tameeka asked.

Stacie shook her head. "Nope. I thought she was busted. Remember I told you he'd called her? All he wanted was CoCo's shoe size."

"The Lord must have been looking out for her. 'Cause as soon as Carlos finds out about that car, the shit is gonna hit the fan," Tameeka vowed.

"I know," Stacie lamented, worried for her sister. "I don't know what possessed her to do something so stupid. She's finally getting herself together. All her efforts are going to be crap when Carlos finds out. You know what they call him on the

street, don't you?" she asked, giving Tameeka a knowing look.
"How could she possibly think the shit she did won't come back
and smack her in the face? And what was she doing, screwing
around with that old man and letting him buy her a car? I don't
get it," Stacie said, then finally noticed what her friend was
cooking. "Aw crap! Are you on the bean diet again?" Stacie
asked, alarmed. Every time Tameeka went on one of her diets,
she had to suffer through it with her.

"Nu-uh, I had a taste for some lima beans, barbecue turkey
wings and corn bread," she answered, and Stacie breathed a
sigh of relief.

"Girl, you always cooking something," Stacie teased. "Even
when we were little, you were burning in your Easy-Bake Oven."

"It calms me, girl," Tameeka answered, and turned to the
refrigerator, pulling out a tray of seasoned turkey wings. "After
my store, it's the next best thing to sex."

"I don't know about all that. More relaxing than sex? You
crazy, girl. *Ain't nuthin' better than sex.*"

"You just got hot panties. Everybody ain't like you. We all
don't live and die for the dick. So how many men do you have
lined up for the week?" Tameeka asked.

"Not a lot . . . just Dennis," Stacie mumbled under her
breath.

"Dennis?" Tameeka asked, her voice incredulous. "The same
Dr. Dennis who promised to take you to Savannah, then called
to tell you that he and his wife reconciled? That Dennis?" She
shook her head.

"Yeah, *that Dennis.* They separated again, this time for good."

"Whatever," Tameeka sniffed. "Tyrell was telling me about
his boy, who, by the way, is unmarried. I think you should meet
him."

"Meek, you know I hate blind dates," Stacie whined.
"They're just so weird. Hell, we're in Atlanta, who can't find a
date here? Half the people here get picked up just by walking

down the street. There must be something wrong with him," she stated.

"There's nothing wrong with him . . . honest. Tyrell and I just thought it would be a good idea for you two to meet. Then if you guys hit it off, and I know you will, we can double-date."

"I don't know . . ."

"Just look at it as an adventure. Please think about it, okay?"

Stacie shrugged. "I might, but don't be mad at me if I say no. I'm not totally feeling a blind date."

"Why, because he doesn't meet the requirements on your list?" Tameeka asked in a snippy tone.

"Don't be getting tart with me," Stacie said curtly. "I haven't even met him, so how can I know how he ranks on the list?"

Tameeka shook her head, disappointed in her friend. "You and that damn list. You know what?" she asked, and Stacie glanced at her. "That damn list ain't gonna keep you warm at night," she said, then turned back to the stove and muttered about women not appreciating a good man when they have one.

"Like *you* don't have a list." Stacie glared at her friend.

"I don't," Tameeka replied.

"Like hell," Stacie snorted. "You review your list every time you meet somebody. Now tell me I'm wrong," she challenged.

"You're wrong," Tameeka replied in a singsong voice. "I don't have a list," she insisted.

"You crazy, girl! Whether or not you want to admit it, you—have—a—list!" Stacie said as she pounded her fist on the counter. "Check it out. What do you do every time a man step to you?" she asked, but plowed on, not giving Tameeka an opportunity to answer. "You decide, based on the standards that you have, whether or not to let him have the digits."

"That's not a list—*list,*" she said. "It's just my way of weeding out the jerks," she explained.

"Sounds like a list to me," Stacie muttered. "Okay," she said in a patient voice, "so if it isn't a list, then what is it?"

"Well, it's a *system* that I use. And this *system* does require me to note certain information that determines whether or not the man is worthy of my time," she answered slowly and deliberately.

"So when you *note* your information, how do you keep a running tab of it?"

"In my head," Tameeka answered, then tapped her temple. "It's all here."

"Ah-ha! You're keeping a list. Only it's internal. That's all I'm saying." Stacie smiled triumphantly. "There ain't nothing wrong with keeping lists, they keep things organized."

"They do," Tameeka agreed. "But why don't you admit it, your list is c-r-a-z-y. You're over thirty years old and you're still keeping a 'what I want in a man' list. That's just crazy," Tameeka said as she made her way over to the table.

Tameeka's words stung. "It might be c-r-a-z-y, as you put it, but I will be going out with my green-eyed, six-foot-two doctor. Who makes over six figures," she sang. "And he's good in bed. So something's gotta be right about *the list,*" she bragged as she pranced around the kitchen.

"Is that all you think about?"

"What else is there?" Stacie shrugged. "Other than sex," she added.

"You're serious, aren't you?" Tameeka asked, but she didn't need to. The finality of Stacie's words said it all. She suddenly felt sad for her friend. "Stace," she started gently. "There's more to life than sex and money." She began ticking items off with her fingers. "There's friends and family, good health, good spirit—"

"Blah, blah, blah," Stacie murmured. "Ain't hearing it. There's nothing wrong with money and dick. But you know what would be better?" she asked. "A dick wrapped in money." They both laughed, then lapsed into a comfortable silence.

"You know . . ." Tameeka started, as she put the pan of turkey wings in the oven.

"Do I know what?" Stacie asked when Tameeka turned around to face her.

"Don't get mad," Tameeka hedged. "Promise me you won't get mad."

Stacie shook her head. "Nope, I'm not making any blind promises. The last time I did, I ended up driving a man to Dallas," she said.

"Well, don't you . . . have you ever thought that . . . ?" Tameeka stammered, then she breathed deeply and spat out her words. "I think you and Nevia are like two peas in a pod."

"No we're not!" Stacie hotly protested.

"Yeah you are," Tameeka shot back at her. "You two have always been alike."

Stacie rolled her eyes. "How? Tell me how we're so similar," she challenged.

"Both of y'all use what's between your legs to get things from men."

"Nu-uh," Stacie objected. "I don't do that."

"You do," Tameeka firmly countered. "Do you need me to break it down for you?" she asked. Stacie smacked her teeth but nodded her head. "The car is one—"

"But that doesn't count. Malcolm gave me Lexie because my Geo Metro broke down."

"That's no excuse, you still accepted it. You could've gone out and got one on your own," Tameeka retorted. "The second is the jewelry. Both of you have enough ice to open a freaking store." Stacie didn't say anything; all she did was glare at Tameeka. "And the clothes," Tameeka continued. "I don't know who has more, you two or the Hilton sisters."

"Are you finished?" Stacie asked. "Let me clarify one thing: I'm not like my sister. Just because men like to give me things, it doesn't mean anything. I just happen to pick generous men."

"How many of those men gave you their gifts before you

slept with them?" Tameeka asked, pinning Stacie with a pointed stare.

"I don't know. I don't keep track of stuff like that," Stacie huffed, but with a sinking feeling she realized that she had slept with each one of her benefactors *before* the gifts came.

"Like I said, you and Nevia are alike."

"Do you really see me that way?" Stacie asked in a dejected tone.

"Yeah, but that's who you are," Tameeka announced in a matter-of-fact tone.

"I think you're jealous because I get all the men and you don't!" Stacie said, and Tameeka drew back as though she had been slapped.

When she talked her voice was heavy with unshed tears. "You just don't get it, do you?" Tameeka said, then sadly walked out of the kitchen.

Are Nevia and I really alike? Stacie wondered. Do I use my coochie as an ATM card? The answer flickered in front of her, but she swiped it away. "Meek! Hold up, I'm sorry, I didn't mean it," Stacie apologized and took off after Tameeka. "I'm sorry, Meek!" Stacie said, and Tameeka looked her in the eyes before slamming her bedroom door in Stacie's face.

10

Fear Sprouts from Ignorance . . .
Confidence Flows from Knowledge

When she heard the front door close, Tameeka slipped out of bed and strolled into the living room.

"A-ha!" Stacie shouted. "I knew you've been avoiding me."

Tameeka froze in her tracks. "Nu-uh," she hotly denied.

"Have too. For the past week you've been avoiding me like I was a Jehovah's Witness."

"Whatever," Tameeka said, shrugging. "I've got to get ready for work," she said, and turned toward the bathroom.

"I'm sorry, Meek. I'm really sorry for what I said," Stacie apologized, her voice ringing with sincerity. Tameeka stopped, and Stacie talked to her back. "I was being a bitch. Can't we forget about it?"

Tameeka looked over her shoulder, then said, "I don't know. You really hurt me." She quickly showered and hurried off to work, leaving behind an upset Stacie.

Tyrell happily rang up the customers' purchases and they all walked out of Heaven on Earth with smiles on their faces. Tameeka had to admit that he was a natural people person; the customers loved him. This was only his third weekend in the store and he already knew more about her regular customers' personal lives than she did. He was friendly and funny, a winning combination in any profession, but very lucrative in retail.

She noticed that he had put a customer's purchase in a bag that looked like it was too small and she started toward the register. Halfway there she stopped herself and thought that if the customer didn't complain, then she shouldn't. Turning around on her heels, she headed to her office where she had a stack of invoices two inches thick that needed to be taken care of.

Tyrell grinned as soon as he saw her walk toward her office. He had seen her hovering nearby, pretending to arrange a display, but he knew she was really keeping an eye on him.

"You must really like your job," a teasing voice said, pulling his attention back to the counter.

"Huh?" Tyrell answered and found himself face-to-face with one of the most beautiful ladies he had ever laid eyes on. She was drop-dead gorgeous. Suddenly his tongue felt too big for his mouth. "Er—I don't—um, do this full time, I'm helping out a friend," he managed to sputter out, and she giggled.

"Well, you should be doing it full time, you're good with people."

Tyrell shook his head and as his senses returned, he began scanning her purchases. "Thanks, but I enjoy my full-time job," he answered.

"So what do you do?"

"Drive a bus . . . I'm a bus driver for the City of Atlanta."

"So you still deal with people. Well, you are wonderful at it," she complimented, and smiled widely at him. "Is that any good?" she asked. Tyrell had just scanned her mango-scented massage oil and was about to drop it in the bag, but his hand stopped midair. He chuckled. He was remembering the time he had used it on Tameeka. "Ooh, it must be *good*. Listen to that laugh, it sounds downright naughty," the customer flirted.

Tyrell smiled and totaled her purchases; he waited while she wrote him a check. She passed the check to him, along with her driver's license. He glanced at her driver's license, then glanced at her. "You really aren't that old, are you? Oh, my bad. I didn't mean for it to come out like that," he apologized, but the customer simply laughed.

"I'm not *that* old. But yep, that's my age," she said proudly; she was used to people's reactions.

"Damn, you look good! I say this for all the brothas—please keep doing whatever it is you're doing."

"It's nothing but good genes and healthy living," the customer replied humbly. Then when Tyrell was expecting her to pick up her bags, she handed him her business card instead. At that very moment Tameeka stepped out of her office and stopped in her tracks. She cocked her head and watched the scene through narrowed eyes. "I'm the manager of Customer Service at Coca-Cola, call me if you want to change careers *or anything else,*" she said, and gave him a playful wink.

Tyrell slipped the card in his pants pocket and turned to watch her walk away. Even carrying two plastic bags, she managed to look sexy.

"Wow!" Trent sauntered into the store just in time to hear the customer's parting comment. "She was all over you!" He pulled off his backpack and flung it behind the counter.

"Naw, man. She was being friendly, that's all," Tyrell replied modestly.

"She was tight!"

"She was aw'ight," Tyrell said in a way that let Trent know that the subject was closed.

"I thought she was fine," Trent muttered, then headed back to Tameeka's office to clock in.

Tameeka still hadn't moved. She was so still that if the store had had mannequins she would've been mistaken for one. She's everything that I'm not: thin, sophisticated and drop-dead gorgeous, Tameeka fumed. Finally she unstuck herself and rushed over to Bea. She wanted to fling herself into Bea's arms and cry; instead she hissed through clenched teeth, "Did you see that? Did you see Tyrell flirting with that lady? He even took her business card."

"You know, Meek, jumping to conclusions isn't an exercise that you'd want to spend your day doing," Bea said wisely. "Tyrell's a good man. He wouldn't do anything to hurt you."

"Sometimes people can't help hurting people," Tameeka said, then she hissed, "especially when somebody is pushing their titties all up in their face." She glared at Tyrell; she wanted to go over and ask him what was going on.

"Don't you bother that man," Bea cautioned, reading her mind. "He didn't do nothing but take her business card. And I didn't see him offer her anything."

"Just because he didn't give her *his* phone number, doesn't mean that *he's* not going to call *her*," Tameeka bristled.

"Tameeka . . ." Bea started, but Tameeka was already on her way across the store.

"Hey, baby!" Tyrell said as he leaned over and kissed her. Tameeka tilted her head down so that his lips fell on the top of her head.

"Don't do that here," she spat, and Tyrell drew back as though she had slapped him. "It's very unprofessional."

"What's wrong?" he asked, puzzled. During the midmorning rush, she had let him kiss her. She even whispered a naughty promise in his ear that forced him to hide behind the counter for a full fifteen minutes.

"Is there a raffle going on that I don't know about?" she asked in a deliberately slow voice.

"What?"

"The business card. You're collecting business cards. Most

times when people are collecting business cards they're having a raffle. I repeat, are we having a raffle?" she asked between clenched teeth.

"I'm not collecting bus—" He smiled as he remembered. "Oh snap, *that* business card. That was nothing, baby. She was being friendly."

"Friendly, my ass!" Tameeka shrieked. "She wasn't being friendly, she was trying to pick you up, and you ate it up, every single drop if it."

"Tameeka," Tyrell soothed; he had come from behind the counter and put his hands on her shoulders but she just shrugged them off.

"So who's it going to be? Me or the one you're swapping business cards with?" Tameeka asked coldly.

11

Single Father's Guide to Dating
Tip #25

Never, ever trust a woman who wears more makeup than a
Ringling Bros. and Barnum & Bailey circus clown.

Jackson Brown stretched his long legs and settled back in
his chair at Houston's, one of his favorite places to eat. It was
the only place in Atlanta where Abercrombie, Tommy Hilfiger
and Armani collided on a daily basis. A lady sitting across from
him caught his eye; he returned her gaze with a wink that
promised he'd hook up with her before he left. He glanced
over at his son, who was glumly staring down at his plate.
"Hey, eat your food."

"I don't like hamburgers," Jameel grumbled. "I want a hot
dog," he whined.

"Come on, Jam. If you eat your hamburger, I'll buy you a
sundae on the way home," Jackson bargained, something he
never thought he'd be doing with his son.

Jameel considered the offer, then shook his head. "I want a
hot dog," he repeated.

"Jameel, hamburgers are good for you. See, look at my muscles," he said, then rolled up his Sean John shirt and flexed his biceps.

"But, Daddy, if hot dogs are so bad, how come we ate them last night?" he argued, his face scrunched up like a misshapen potato.

Jackson suppressed a smile. Jameel had him. For eight years old he was smart. "Let's get you a hot dog." He motioned toward the waitress, Amy, a twenty-year-old Asian lady whom he'd dated a couple months ago. She had done things to him that he had only seen in movies. But he had a three-date rule; after that, the women were history. Seeing that he needed her, Amy made a beeline to Jackson, going so fast across the floor that she nearly knocked over another waiter. She took his order and rushed it to the kitchen.

"Eat your French fries," Jackson said to Jameel, who was waving them around as though they were swords. His cell phone rang, stopping him from yelling at Jameel. A quick check to the screen showed that it was his boy Tyrell. "Look who finally decided to come up for air," Jackson joked. "So you finally decided to pull your nose out of her pus—" He glanced sharply at Jameel, who'd decided to make little houses with his French fries. "So you finally decided to call a brotha," he improvised, and Tyrell chuckled; whenever Jackson gave him the rated-G version, he knew Jameel was close by.

"Don't hate, man. Where are you?" Tyrell asked, but then he heard Amy's voice as she set Jameel's hot dog in front of him. "At Houston's?" he asked, laughing. "So is she going to be the first chick to break the three-date rule?"

"Naw, man . . . not even close. That's history," Jackson snickered. "But you have to give her props for trying," he said, eyeing Amy.

"Word! So how many numbers did you get today?"

"Only three," Jackson modestly replied as he kept an eye on

Jameel as he squeezed ketchup on his hot dog, then took a big bite of it.

"If you get bored, I can hook you up with my girl's best friend," Tyrell offered.

Jackson frowned. "Thanks . . . but no thanks. I don't do blind dates. Check it out, I need to run, number four just walked into the restaurant," he said. "Damn! You're fine," Jackson whispered. She was the hottest lady he had seen in a long time.

"Ooh, you said a bad word," Jameel squealed, and Jackson quickly apologized.

"How come you heard that, but you can never hear me calling you in the morning?" he asked, and Jameel giggled in response, then took another bite out of his hot dog.

A couple tables across from Jackson and Jameel, Stacie eyed Tameeka. "So we straight?"

Tameeka smiled and nodded her head. "Girl, you're a hot mess, but we're cool," she assured her, but her next words were a warning. "But you really need to stop blurting out the first thing that comes to your mind. Next time you say some shit like that to me, I'ma kick your behind."

Stacie snorted. "Yeah right, I doubt it. You think killing an ant is murder."

"Don't try me! I'll get Tyrell and both of us will sit on your skinny butt until you're as flat as a pancake," Tameeka warned.

"Okay, okay. Dang girl, you don't have to get all tough on me," Stacie said, grinning at the lady whom she considered more of a sister than a friend. "I'll watch my big mouth," she promised. "I missed you, Meek," Stacie admitted softly.

"Missed you too girl," Tameeka confessed, then, "Check him out," she said, jutting her chin toward a man that reminded her of Mario Van Peebles.

Tameeka shook her head and grinned. Stacie's taste in men changed faster than her hair weaves. "Ask and you shall receive," she replied, nodding toward Jackson. "And don't you ever say that I never give you anything. It's time to move on, girl. Crawford is old news."

Stacie nervously cleared her throat. "Meek?" she called, and Tameeka turned her eyes on her. "You remember when I told you that I broke up with Crawford because he was bad in bed? I didn't break up with him, he broke up with me . . . well, he stopped calling me."

"Oh, I'm sorry," Tameeka soothed, then patted her friend's hand. She'd suspected as much. Stacie giving up a multimillionaire was as unlikely as Donald Trump having a good hair day. "His loss," Tameeka murmured. "Do you want to talk about it?"

Stacie shrugged. "I guess I was just another groupie in his rotation. But I liked him," she admitted. "I missed our talks so much. I don't like it when we argue. The last three weeks were horrible. I tried talking to Nevia, but she didn't get half the stuff I told her."

"I know what you mean. I tried talking to Tyrell, but all he did was look at me like I was crazy. I'm glad Lexie broke down and you had to call me. You're my best friend, let's not blow it over pettiness, okay?"

Stacie agreed. "Even though Crawford and I hardly went out, we had a good time together. I guess he reminds me of Crawford," Stacie said, jutting her chin at Jackson.

"He doesn't look like Crawford," Tameeka said, surveying Jackson. Where Crawford was the color of brown-tinted milk, Jackson was glowing bronze. Instead of Crawford's wavy hair, Jackson's hair colored his scalp. The only similarity was their height; even though he was sitting down, Tameeka could tell that he was tall.

"You're right, he doesn't, but he looks like a player. Look at him." The young lady he had been admiring earlier was standing at his table, fawning over him as though he was Morris Chestnut.

"He's gorgeous! So women are always gonna be up in his face," Tameeka said matter-of-factly. "Besides, he looks too smart to get caught up," she concluded. "And look at him with his little boy. He looks like he was born to be a father."

"Oh, you can tell all that just by looking at him? Puh-leeze! Girl, you are plain crazy."

"Well. I don't think that I'm crazy, but I'm going over to say something to him. Single fathers should be given a pat on the back," she said as she shoved her chair back, then stood up.

"Oh gawd. Meek, leave the man alone. He's probably gonna think that you're trying to pick him up. Meeka! Come back here," Stacie ordered. "Tameeka!" she repeated, then scrambled out of her seat to chase after her friend.

Tameeka approached Jackson's table. "Hi, guys," she beamed.

Jameel piped up with a cheery hello, his father quickly followed and introductions were made.

Jackson smiled as he studied Tameeka. It was a friendly perusal, not at all sexually laced. It looked like she had closed her eyes, reached into her closet and pulled out the first two pieces of clothing her hands had touched. She was wearing black-and-red-checkered hip huggers and a purple-and-green-striped shirt. She wasn't his type—he preferred smaller women—but she was genuine and he liked that.

His gaze surreptitiously slipped to Stacie, and his penis twitched with excitement; she was finer up close. She was standing next to Tameeka, with her arms crossed under her breasts; boredom marred her pretty face.

"Come on, Meek, we need to leave *now,*" she insisted. "We have that appointment, remember?" It was getting late and she wanted to get home for her date. But Tameeka ignored her and kept talking. Stacie smacked her teeth, then turned on her heels to go.

Two steps later, she heard a howl so loud and pain-filled that it caused her to stop dead in her tracks. She whirled around and saw that Jameel had spilled his cola. His face had melted and tears flowed down his face. It took less than two steps for Stacie to be at Jameel's side and only two seconds for her to scoop him into her arms. Jackson's mouth went slack with amazement as Stacie comforted his son.

"Oh baby," she cooed, using a singsong tone that she used with her nieces whenever they were sad. "It's okay. It's only soda. Did you spill any on you?" She did a quick appraisal of his clothing and she didn't find a drop of soda. "Let me dry that cute little face of yours." She grabbed a tissue and dabbed at Jameel's face. It didn't take long before Stacie had him giggling. "Come on, let's go get you another drink," she said as she held out her hand and Jameel slipped his hand into hers.

Jameel peeked over at his father, and Jackson gave his nod of approval. They walked off toward the waitresses's station. He could see Jameel yammering and Stacie nodding and smiling down at him as if he was disclosing the secret of life to her.

All the while Tameeka continued talking and Jackson listened to her with half an ear. All he heard was "wonderful single father." It wasn't that he didn't appreciate the respect, but he was watching the lady with the delicious rear end talking to his son. By now he was sitting back in his chair, his legs sticking out and his arms folded across his chest. To the casual observer, it looked like he was in relax mode, but every one of his senses was heightened. He was ready to pounce like a tiger if anything happened to Jameel. If anyone had told him that men didn't possess the same fierce, protective love toward their children as women, he'd laugh in their face. He didn't relax until he saw them returning.

"Daddee, look what Mizz Stacee got me!" Jameel gushed as he held up a giant milk shake. The cup was almost bigger than him; he had to use two hands to hold it up.

"Mmm. That looks good. Are you gonna share some with your old man?" Jackson teased.

Jameel stopped pulling at the straw long enough to think about his father's request. "Maybe I will and maybe I won't," he replied, and at that Jackson threw his head back and burst out laughing. Jameel was definitely his son. He looked proudly at him. His cheeks were pulled in and it looked like he'd inhale his whole face if he sucked any harder.

Off to the side, Stacie watched the exchange with wide eyes. The love that flowed between father and son was intoxicating. She took a better look at the father.

Damn! He's got it going on, she thought. She tried hard not to stare at his sculpted lips, high cheekbones and long eyelashes. But her eyes couldn't help but take in his body. His chest was as wide as a football field and his legs were two tree trunks. A jolt of desire hit her and she didn't dare look at his fingers. It'll be over then. Gawd, the things that I could do with that man.

She glanced up at his face just in time to see his lips turn into a sly smile and her mouth went dry, images of his succulent lips tonguing her body exploded in her head. The spell was broken by the ringing of her cell phone.

Stacie quickly pulled the phone from her purse. Her face brightened as soon as she heard the voice, and she stepped away from the table.

"Hey baby," she said seductively. "I'm fine. Lexie was sick, but she's doing better now." She listened, then nodded a couple of times. She giggled and said, "I can be there in twenty minutes," then her voice deepened, "thirty, if you want me to stop and take my panties off." Stacie said some more things that probably would've made an eavesdropper blush, then clicked off her phone.

Although Jackson could only hear bits and pieces of her conversation over the din of the restaurant, he knew that she was talking to her man. Her smile, the low voice, and her body language all screamed "sex me!"

"How come your boyfriend isn't here?" Jackson asked Stacie, and Tameeka smiled to herself.

"What are you, like a census taker?" Stacie snapped, but she was secretly delighted that he seemed interested in her. Jackson laughed.

"Naw. I drive a bus," he answered as his gaze caressed her face.

"Well you should work for the government the way you ask all the women for their info," Stacie said.

"Only the beautiful ones," he drawled. "So why is your man letting you eat by yourself?" he asked as he sidled closer to her and his body heat upped her body temperature by ten degrees.

"How—" Stacie started, but her voice cracked. She cleared her throat, then asked, "How do you know I have a boyfriend?"

"Why shouldn't you? You're drop-dead gorgeous, articulate and classy. If you didn't have a boyfriend, I'd be worried," Jackson flirted as he stepped forward and Stacie immediately scooted backward.

"Well, be prepared to be worried, 'cause I don't have a boyfriend," Stacie replied sassily, yet she couldn't tear her eyes off his luscious lips.

Jackson cupped his hands over his mouth and announced, "Hey, brothas of the ATL, watch out, Miss Stacie is on the loose," he joked, then, "So do you always give brothas a hard time?" he asked lightly.

Stacie shook her head. "I give what I get," she answered, then changed the subject. "What about you? Where do you spend your nights?"

"In my bed," Jackson answered, and Stacie rolled her eyes. "By myself." Stacie raised an eyebrow. "Okay, I'm going to fess up, you caught me. Come closer so that I can whisper it to you. I don't want you-know-who to hear," he said sotto voce as he glanced down at Jameel, who was playing with his shoelaces. Stacie hesitated for only a heartbeat before leaning in. Jackson's breath stroked her ear. "Sometimes . . ." he began. "Sometimes during a thunderstorm . . . when it's dark . . . and scary . . . Jameel sleeps with me," he said, then his voice dropped to a seductive whisper. "Would you like to sleep with me instead?"

"Oh," Stacie gasped as a shot of heat hit her mound. The thought of being in the same bed as Jackson left her breathless. She turned her head and their lips were a tongue length apart. Her eyes ran hotly over his juicy mouth and the sounds of the restaurant faded away as she slowly inched toward him. Jackson reached up and cupped the back of her head, urging her closer.

"Daddy!" Jameel shrieked, then tugged on his father's pant leg and Stacie jumped a mile high. "I'm ready to go now."

Jackson shot Jameel a look that instantly quieted him.

"It's time for me to go too," Stacie blurted, flustered. She made a move to leave.

"Hold up," Jackson commanded and Stacie stopped in her steps. "So can I get the numbers?" he asked smoothly, but his mind was reeling. If Jameel hadn't interrupted him, they would've given Houston's a free show.

"Um, yeah," Stacie answered, digging around her purse for a business card, then scribbling her home number on it. By then Tameeka had eased back over to them.

"Tell the beautiful ladies good-bye," Jackson instructed his son, then he and Jameel sauntered out of the restaurant.

Later that night, after Jackson worked with Jameel on his multiplication tables, fed him, gave him his bath, and finally tucked him into bed, he felt like he had been strapped to a nonstop treadmill. It was at times like this that he wished he were married to someone who'd love Jameel as much as he did. Just then an image of Jameel and Stacie giggling together flashed in his head. "Oh, hell no! Not Miss Attitude," he muttered to himself as he trudged down the hall to his room, pulled off his boxer shorts, and slid into his bed. The sheets were cool against his naked body. He clicked on the TV and aimlessly flipped through the channels; nothing caught his attention. He glanced at the clock. *It's still early,* he thought.

He picked up his phone, then Stacie's business card and punched in her home number. "Be home, Miss Stacie," he murmured as the phone rang.

12

What I'd Rather Be Doing Instead
of Working

1. Lounging in a chaise on a cruise ship
2. Shopping in Paris or New York City. Hell, why not both?
3. Making crazy love to Shemar Moore 24/7
4. Taking a trip to Aruba to see Sinbad
5. Driving Lexie to South Beach
6. Sleeping until the afternoon sun kisses my eyelids

Thomas, Garrett and Jefferson, please hold. Thomas, Garrett and Jefferson, please hold. Thomas, Garrett and Jefferson, please hold." The words flowed out of Stacie's mouth so smoothly that they were almost lyrical. Having said them one million, one hundred sixty-eight times had something to do with it. One day when she hadn't had that much to do, she'd figured it out. She had uttered that phrase one million, one hundred sixty-eight times. Eight years, multiplied by eight hours, and she answered the phone roughly fifty times an hour.

Her nameplate read *Stacie Long—Receptionist,* but she was really *Stacie Long, Toll Collector, Gate Keeper and Information Gatherer,* all rolled into one. And she loved it. She and only she decided who got past the solid oak double doors, whose call got forwarded to the decision makers and who got the information they wanted.

She adjusted her headset, stuck a peppermint in her mouth, took a deep breath and answered the next call. Her desk resembled a small cockpit and if the truth was told, with her black, whisper-thin telephone headset, she looked like a pilot. The high-tech telephone console spanned the entire breadth of the desk.

Being a receptionist wasn't what she envisioned herself doing when, eight years ago, she had quit her assembly line job at the Ford factory; she'd wanted to wear a white collar instead of blue. She had taken the receptionist job just to pay the bills and it was supposed to be until something better came along; eight years later, nothing better had.

The phones stopped ringing long enough for Stacie to log onto her favorite bridal website. Her brow was puckered with concentration.

That's how Quinton Jones, one of the firm's hottest attorneys, found her, staring at the computer monitor as if it was a TV.

"Hey Stacie," he rumbled. Stacie jumped, then looked sheepishly at Quinton and a smile spread over her face. She'd had a crush on him from the first day he strutted into the office wearing his Armani. He was single, thirty-three, no kids and fine as hell. He reminded her of a young Denzel Washington. He was pulling in a healthy six figures to boot.

"Hey Q," she purred, smiling brightly as she flung her hair over her shoulder and looked coyly at him. "How's your day going?"

He grimaced at the nickname she had given him; it was so ghetto. "Crazy," he answered, and ran a hand through his curly hair. "I'm in court *every* day this week. One of my paralegals just quit. And my mom will be here this weekend and I haven't planned a thing for us to do."

"Oh, I'm—" She was cut off by Mr. Peppersong's voice booming through the intercom. *"Miss Long, I need to see you. Right now."* She and Quinton exchanged glances. He gave her a little smile before making a hasty retreat.

"Aw shit!" Stacie muttered. She'd been twenty minutes late for work this morning and she'd hoped no one had noticed. But of course someone had. Lexie was sick again. Wheezing and hacking, she had barely gotten Stacie to work. Stacie glanced stealthily to her left, then to her right, then did a quick twirl in her chair. The perimeter was clear. She crouched down and reached under her desk for her shoe. It was a sling back, not one of her favorites, but it had to do. She held it up to her nose and inhaled deeply. Then again, and again. After the fourth time, her heartbeat slowed down and she was as relaxed as a well-sexed woman. She swiped a hand over her nose and stood up. A moment later, both shoes were on and she was striding to Mr. Peppersong's office without a care in the world.

She hovered on the threshold of his office. He was sitting behind his desk, talking on the phone, but he looked up, caught sight of her and waved her in. As she eased her way into his office, she got the feeling that she was walking into a bear trap; she resisted the urge to examine the floor for anything that would grab her feet. Even though Andre Peppersong was on the phone, he couldn't resist the urge to smirk at her as he motioned her to the chair in front of his desk. Stacie plopped in it, and she couldn't help but notice a red folder on his desk, her name written across the front.

Stacie settled back in the chair and perused his office. This was her first time ever crossing the threshold. It was spalike. Everything was green and cream. Floor plants were scattered across the office, a cream-colored sofa took up the back wall and half a dozen miniature waterfalls covered the countertops. Stacie's eyes locked onto one particular waterfall; the cascading water was hypnotic. She was so fascinated with it that she didn't hear Andre hang up the phone.

"How are you today, Miss Long?" he asked, and fixed her with an unblinking gaze.

Stacie gritted her teeth. She didn't mind him addressing her by her last name, but the way he said "Miss" made it sound like he had just swallowed something bitter and nasty. "Fine. Thank you," she answered primly, then ran a hand over her fuchsia colored suede skirt. The same skirt that almost caused a traffic jam on Peachtree Street the last time she wore it. Any heterosexual man would've been breaking his neck to get a look. But not Andre, she wasn't his type; he preferred a joy stick, not a button.

Andre opened the red folder and pretended to study the contents. He already had the file memorized; after all, he wrote it two weeks ago. He closed the folder, crossed his hands in front of him, looked at Stacie and said, "Well, Miss Long, I assume you know why I called you here this morning." He paused a second for Stacie to comment, and when she didn't he breezed on. "This is the third time in two weeks that you've been late. What's your excuse *this* time?" He impatiently drummed his fingers on the desk as he waited for her response.

Stacie tilted her head and stared down at the oatmeal-hued rug. To Andre it looked submissive and demure, but she was really hiding the anger that flashed in her eyes. *How dare he speak to me in that tone?* she fumed. She pushed down her anger, then met his stare. "Lexie was sick. My car," she explained at seeing Andre's raised eyebrows. "Lexie is her nickname. Her full name is Lexus Long," she said all in a rush. "She wasn't acting right this morning. I guess she had a cold. So I didn't want to drive her too fast. Just in case she really broke down." She was babbling and she knew it.

"Be that as it may, Miss Long. You are familiar with the firm's policy on tardiness." This was said more as a statement of fact than a question and Stacie merely nodded. "You have one more time, Miss Long, to be late. Any more than that and we're going to have to dismiss you."

Stacie gasped. I can't lose my job. My bills, my rent, Lexie!

Andre smirked at her reaction. He loved his job. "Oh, this is for you." He slid a pamphlet to the edge of the desk and Stacie almost sucked her teeth. The asshole doesn't even have enough decency to hand it to me.

"What is it?" Stacie asked as she flipped through the brochure. It was filled with glossy photos of smiling people. Then her eyes caught the title, EAP, Employee Assistance Program. "I don't need this," she protested, dropping it on his desk as if it burned her hands. "I don't need a counselor," she said in a heated tone.

"Mr. Kimble thought that you could benefit from the program. Maybe the counselor can figure out why you can't get to work on time . . . and why you named your car Lexie," he said snidely. "I would suggest that you sign up as soon as possible."

Mr. Kimble. Stacie flushed deeply. He was one of the partners in the firm. He knows my business. Who else knows?

"That will be all. You may leave now," he said prissily, then handed her the brochure.

Stacie was halfway to the door when he called her. "A temp will be training with you this afternoon."

"For what? I didn't request anybody," she responded, panicked. She only needed a temp when she went on vacation.

Andre smiled condescendingly, then said, "I thought it would be a good idea for you to have a backup. Just in case you're out, or *something.*"

"Oh," Stacie said, relieved. "Is that all? Betty in the secretarial pool is my—"

"I think that it'll be wise to have another," Andre interjected smoothly, and a chill went up her spine.

Before she could say anything more, he picked up his

phone, punched in some numbers and swiveled his chair around, showing her his back. Stacie hurried to the ladies' room, locked the stall door and spent ten minutes with her nose in her shoe.

Misti, spelled with an "i" not a "y", show up that afternoon, oozing perkiness. With blonde hair down to her waist and skin that looked like she and the sun were on a first-name basis, she had a breathy baby-soft voice. Every time she talked, Stacie had to strain to hear.

Stacie didn't mind it when Misti followed her around like a puppy. Stacie certainly didn't mind it when Misti transferred two calls to Andre's office and they got disconnected. But she was royally pissed that by the time they left at five o'clock everybody at the firm was in love with Misti.

Stacie skulked through the parking garage to her car. She popped the trunk, pulled out her gym bag and quickly pulled out her sneakers, then hurried back into the car and locked the doors. Then she reclined her seat back, closed her eyes and brought her sneaker up to her nose.

13

If You're Going to Play with a Rattlesnake, You'd Better Be Ready to Deal with the Consequences

Have a wonderful evening. And thanks for shopping at Heaven on Earth. We appreciate your business," Tameeka gushed as she walked the last customer out, then securely locked the door behind him. "Finally," she sighed; it had been a long day.

"Come here, baby," Tyrell called from the sofa. "Let me take care of you," he said as he patted his lap. Tameeka trudged across the store and gratefully sank into his manmade cushion.

"Ah, you're my heaven on earth," she whispered and snuggled deep into Tyrell's lap, thankful that he was there. "Did you enjoy yourself today?" she asked.

"I did. You are definitely doing your thing in here. I'm so proud of you, baby," he said as he wrapped his arms around her and brushed his lips over her hair.

"Better than the last time?" she ventured, then held her breath.

"Yep . . . a *lot* better than the last time. Not once did you mistake me for your flunky or yell at me for looking at a lady. You're getting a lot better," he praised.

"Thanks," Tameeka answered. "I'm really trying. Believe it or not, our arguments bothered me too."

"I like us like this, calm, on track and in synch with each other. If we continue like this we can do big things together, baby," Tyrell said.

Tameeka warmed inside. She liked the sound of that . . . he was thinking long term. "Like what?" she asked.

Tyrell was silent for a moment, then said, "Marriage . . . babies."

Tameeka gasped with surprise; she was thinking more along the lines of living together. She pulled out of Tyrell's arms, did a quick reverse and straddled him. "Really? You really thought about that?" she asked as she snaked her arms around his neck.

He nodded. "You're a good lady, even more so when you're not trying to rule our world. You have a lot of the qualities I look for in a woman," he admitted.

"Thank you," Tameeka beamed, and suddenly a loud rumbling reverberated through the store.

"Damn!" Tyrell exclaimed. "Was that your stomach? It sounded like Amtrak ran through here," he joked, which set them both off laughing.

"I haven't eaten since this morning," she admitted.

He drew back to look her in the eyes. "Six o'clock?" he clarified. They had eaten breakfast together.

"Yep. That'd be the correct time."

"That was fourteen hours ago," Tyrell said, then tightened his grip around her. "Oh, baby, you gotta eat. Let me go get you something. What are you in the mood for? Any dietary restrictions?" he joked.

Tameeka stuck her tongue out at him. "No diets this week . . . I could go for some wings," she decided. "How does that sound?"

"Cool. I know a good place on Ponce. I'll be back in about thirty," he said as he lifted Tameeka off his lap and settled her on the couch, then stood up.

"Wait, where you going?" she asked. "There's a guy right across the street whose wings are the bomb. And he gives the neighborhood businesses a discount."

"Okay. Call the order in and I'll pick it up," Tyrell offered as he settled back on the couch.

Tameeka shook her head. "He's really funny about stuff like that. He has to see the owner in order to give the discount."

"That makes sense."

"I'll be right back," Tameeka said; now that she had made up her mind about eating, she had gotten her second wind.

"I'll walk with you," Tyrell offered.

Tameeka smiled. "That's sweet, but it's right across the street—see." She pulled him toward the window and pointed the shop out.

"Okay." He pulled out his wallet and handed her a fifty-dollar bill. "Get some fries, a couple hamburgers, some milk shakes and something for dessert. I'm starving too," he said, realizing that he hadn't eaten since lunch.

"Thanks, sweetie." Tameeka stood on her tiptoes and kissed Tyrell. "I'll be right back," she promised. As soon as the door closed, Tyrell turned to the window to watch her walk across the street. He didn't budge until she strolled into the restaurant, then he turned to the empty store. This was the first time he had been in it alone.

Tameeka hadn't totaled the receipts yet, but he knew she had to have done over three thousand dollars in business today. He gave an appreciative whistle as he glanced around the store; it was easy to see that Tameeka had done her homework before opening Heaven on Earth. She had just about every wellness potion on the market, and even after the busy sales day, everything was neat and in its place.

"What we need," he murmured to himself, "is a place for us to eat." He slowly wandered around the store until he spied a small, round table in the corner.

"Perfect." He pulled it to the middle of the store. "Now all I need is some music and some candlelight," he decided, and began making a second trip around Heaven on Earth.

He was slipping in Prince's new CD when he heard a noise.

"Yo, Meek, you still here?" Mohammad came bounding through the door wearing his usual khakis, but was shirtless. He skidded to a stop when he saw Tyrell. "Hey, what's up?" he asked, jutting his chin at Tyrell. "Where's Meek?"

"She ran out," Tyrell answered, and quickly sized Mohammad up; there was something about him he didn't like. "What do you need?" he asked.

Mohammad grinned sheepishly. "Deodorant. I ran out and Meek always gives me some," he explained with a shrug.

"Oh, go help yourself," Tyrell said, and watched through narrowed eyes as Mohammad sauntered over to the beauty section and scooped up a bottle of deodorant. A thought suddenly came to Tyrell. "Yo, man, how did you get in? All the doors were locked. Is there some kind of security breach I should be aware of?" he asked half-jokingly.

"Naw, man. I work upstairs," Mohammad answered as he made his way across the room with an extended hand. "I'm Mohammad. Meek gave me a key to the place."

Tyrell froze and he dropped Mohammad's hand. "Mohammad," he repeated, and he got a prickly sensation in the back of his ears. "And you work upstairs?" he asked.

"Yep!" Mohammad answered as he unabashedly rolled on his deodorant. "I'm one of the best artists in the Southeast. If you're looking for really unique pieces, I'm the man."

"How long have you known Tameeka?" Tyrell spat.

The smile slipped from Mohammad's face. "Hey man, we're just friends, that's all. Very good friends," he answered as he started backing away. Tyrell slowly advanced, like a lion stalking its prey. "I don't want any trouble."

"How long have you known Tameeka?" Tyrell repeated in a deadly voice.

"A couple years. I can't remember," Mohammad sputtered, silently praying that he was close to the door.

"You can't remember how long you've known the lady you've been sleeping with?" Tyrell asked, as he pressed forward. His hands were curled into fists and the closer he got to Mohammad, the higher they inched up to a fighting stance.

Tameeka stumbled through the door with three bags full of food; she got everything Tyrell wanted and then some additional goodies. She kicked the door shut, then looked up to see Mohammad crouching and Tyrell standing over him, his hands balled into fists. Her eyes widened to the size of pizzas. "Oh, shit!" she uttered as their dinner slipped from her hands.

14

Single Father's Guide to Dating
Tip #5

One-night stands are like a roller coaster: The ride is exhilarating, you'll scream the loudest you ever have in your life, but once it's over, you're nauseous as hell.

Jackson sauntered around his bedroom, wearing nothing but a towel knotted around his waist. He bent down to pick up a stray sock and the towel slipped off, revealing his body. He had an eight-pack that rippled, muscled arms that were bigger than Mike Tyson's and a butt that was chiseled to perfection.

He slipped into his pussy prowl outfit: black Prada turtleneck, black Marc Jacobs slacks and his Sean John black leather jacket.

Dressed, Jackson strolled down the hall to the living room where his grandmother, Ettie Mae, and Jameel were sitting in front of the TV.

"See ya, Jam!" Jackson shouted, and Jam absentmindedly waved at him. "See ya, Grandma."

"Be careful driving," Ettie Mae said as she did every time Jackson left the house, as though the very words shrouded him from an accident. Jackson slid behind the wheel of his SUV and headed toward downtown Atlanta to one of his favorite clubs. A glance at his watch told him that he'd make it to the club around midnight, the time when shit got popping.

Jackson let his mind wander as he drove. He smiled at his grandmother's words; she was his second mother. When he was barely eight years old, his parents were killed in a car accident and Ettie Mae had taken him and raised him.

Forty minutes later, Jackson was inside the club and sipping his favorite drink. He lazily surveyed the crowd over his glass, passing over women whose makeup was more than an inch thick. His eyes fell on one particular lady: she was sitting in a corner table along with four other ladies. Even though she was sitting down, Jackson could tell that she had legs that stopped at her chest.

He downed his drink before walking over to the table, stopping halfway to buy a single red rose. He stopped at the table and conversation ceased; five pairs of eyes locked on him and the rose he carried.

"I wish I had a rose for each of you," he said, grinning sheepishly before he handed the rose to the lady who caught his eye.

He leaned down and whispered in her ear: "Can we go somewhere private?" After a hurried conversation with her friends, she nodded and gathered up her things and followed Jackson to a cozy booth. It took Jackson ten minutes to learn that her name was Tonia, she worked as a model part time, did temporary work the other half and had been in Atlanta over a year.

"Has anyone told you that you look like Keenan Ivory Wayans?" Tonia flirted.

"Is that a good thing?"

"Very good. I think he's sexy as hell. Have you ever thought about modeling?" she asked, taking in his smooth complexion and chiseled face. The turtleneck showed off his wide, muscular chest.

Jackson softly stroked her cheek. "Naw. I'm not the model type, but I can see how you are. You're very beautiful. What's someone with your looks doing spending Saturday night at a club?"

Flattered, Tonia gazed at Jackson, entranced. "It's better than sitting at home alone."

"You need a man who'd give you a bubble bath, feed you breakfast in bed and give you nightly massages."

"Mmm . . . that sounds delicious. Can you do all that?" Tonia coyly asked.

Jackson ran his finger over Tonia's lips. "I can do all that and more for you, baby. Wanna see?" he asked as he leaned in closer so that their mouths were only inches apart.

"Yeah," Tonia breathed.

"Do you live close by?" Jackson asked, skimming his lips over Tonia's.

"About thirty minutes away," Tonia said, then rapidly blinked as though waking up from a trance. "You mean now? You want to come over now?" she asked, then shook her head. "I just met you. I don't do one-night stands," she huffed, conveniently blocking out last month's.

"Naw, baby, that's what you think this is? Well, it's not. I'm feeling you. All I want to do is give you a massage. That's it."

"Really?"

"Honest."

Tonia hesitated, then, "Okay, let me tell my girls I'm leaving. I'll meet you out front. You can follow me."

"Cool." Jackson slapped a twenty on the table and followed Tonia. He glanced down at his watch. Thirty minutes; not bad, he mused. Jackson discovered that Tonia lived closer to the club than she'd said, and they were at her house in twenty minutes.

"You're leaving already?" Tonia squinted at the clock. "It's four o'clock. Stay and we can go out to breakfast."

Jackson slipped into his pants. The scent of sex had simmered down to a funky sock smell. "Naw, baby, I can't. I can't sleep in other people's bed. I'm funny about that."

"Are we going out later this week?" Tonia asked, her voice bordering on whiney.

"Let me check my schedule and I'll get back to you," Jackson said as he tugged on his turtleneck. "Give me your number." Tonia gave it to him and he programmed it into his phone. Tonia kissed him good-bye and watched her meal ticket drive off.

Jackson got home to find his house all lit up. His heart thudded as he jumped out of his truck and raced up the stairs. Ettie Mae was standing outside Jameel's room, her lips pressed into a thin line. "What happened?"

"He's having a bad asthma attack."

"Why didn't you call me?" Jackson asked, panicked.

"I did, but you didn't answer."

Jackson pulled out his phone. "Shit! I've had it on vibrate. Did you call nine-one-one?" he asked. Ettie Mae nodded. A couple minutes later the faint sounds of sirens could be heard.

Jackson ran out to the porch and frantically waved to the ambulance. "Over here! Over here!"

15

Whenever There's a Speck of Dirt . . . There's Always the Possibility of It Turning to Mud

Tyrell had dragged his and Tameeka's argument from Heaven on Earth to his home. Their dinner lay cold on the kitchen table and Tameeka sat mannequin still on the couch. The only things moving were her eyes, which glared at him with deadly precision.

"What part of this don't you understand?" Tyrell asked in a deceptively calm voice, his temper simmering beneath his skin. "I asked you at the store, I asked you on the way here and I asked you twenty minutes ago. Now I'm gonna tell you, I want that motherfucker gone!" he roared, his temper erupting like a volcano, spewing over Tameeka and she jumped; she had never seen this side of him.

"I can't make him," she whimpered, and Tyrell cocked an eyebrow at her. "He just renewed his lease," she hastily explained.

"For how long?"

Tameeka mentally pulled up the contract, and did some quick calculating, "Five years," she answered, and swiped at the tears that were beginning to fall.

"Break it," Tyrell said coldly.

"I can't . . . I'll end up losing money," Tameeka sniffed, and Tyrell walked over to the counter, snatching up a couple of paper towels and handing them to her.

"What's more important, money or us?"

"Us, of course," Tameeka answered before she blew into the paper towel.

"Why didn't you tell me that he worked above you and had a key to your place?"

"Because I knew you were gonna react like this," Tameeka countered.

"Do you blame me?" Tyrell asked. "Can you fucking blame me? You call out some other dude's name while I'm making love to you. You tell me that it's over . . . but you don't tell me that you see him every day and he has a key to your store—something that I don't even have!"

"You can have one if you want," Tameeka offered.

"I don't want a fucking key," Tyrell hissed. "I want him *out* of your store."

"I can't just kick him out," Tameeka argued.

"Yeah you can. Let me see that contract you have with him," he said, looking around. He stopped when he realized they were at his place and not Tameeka's. She saw his confusion and smothered a giggle.

"You laughing at me?" Tyrell asked in a gruff voice.

"Yep," Tameeka answered, then stood up and hugged Tyrell. "I don't like it when we argue."

"Then get him to move," Tyrell spat out as he disentangled her arms from around his neck, then stepped away from her.

Tameeka inhaled sharply and let it out with a loud smack of her teeth. "Oh, I get it . . . you don't trust me."

"I don't trust *his ass.*"

"No, I don't believe that," Tameeka said, her eyes refilling with tears. "You think that I can't keep my legs closed."

"No, Meek, it's not like that. I *trust* you. I'm a dude, I know how we think."

Tameeka sniffled. "How do y'all think?"

"We're all vultures, waiting until the boyfriend fucks up, then we swoop in for the scoop up."

"So you think Mohammad is circling me?" Tameeka whispered as she batted her eyes at Tyrell.

"I'm not going to let him get my baby," Tyrell said, then pulled Tameeka into his arms. She smiled against his chest.

They stood together like that until Tameeka's hand slipped down and cupped Tyrell's butt, and gave it a squeeze.

A jolt of excitement ran through him. "What are you doing?" he asked.

"Whatever you want me to," Tameeka answered, then grabbed his hand and pulled him toward the couch. She gently pushed him down and immediately straddled him, then tenderly covered his face with kisses. Leaning forward, she began blowing in his ear, soft, misty breaths that made his heart beat double time.

"You're not going to make me change my mind," Tyrell argued weakly. Tameeka smiled to herself as she gently tongued his ear. "That's not going to do it," he said. With the tip of her tongue, Tameeka stroked the back of his neck. "Let's go to the bedroom," he said, and carried her to his room.

Later that night, Tameeka slid out of bed and padded to the kitchen where she microwaved some food. She took two plates back to the bedroom for her and Tyrell. She nudged him awake.

"Who knew that eating wings at two o'clock in the morning would be the bomb?" Tameeka asked around a mouthful of poultry. She hadn't eaten in what felt like years, and any sense of decorum she usually had flew out the window.

"Hey baby, you're dripping sauce," Tyrell said.

"Where?"

"Here," Tyrell said as he leaned over and licked a dab of barbecue sauce off her breast.

"Um, baby, keep doing that and I'm gonna pour the whole bottle over me," she drawled.

"Do it and I'll lick every drop off," Tyrell promised, and Tameeka shivered with anticipation. Then her cell phone rang. "Who the hell is calling you this time of the night?" he asked, glaring at her.

"Don't look at me like that," she said. "I don't know who'd be calling me this late," she said as she ran to the living room. With barbecue-sauced hands she fished her phone out of her purse. With the phone at her ear, she wandered back into the bedroom and sat down next to Tyrell.

"Well, who was it?" Tyrell asked when Tameeka clicked off the phone and resumed eating her wings.

She continued chewing until Tyrell looked like he was going to grab the plate from her. She swallowed her food, then said, "Um, Mohammad. He was checking on me. That's all," she shrugged.

"Is he afraid that I'll kick your ass?"

Tameeka hurriedly shook her head. "Nothing like that."

"Don't think I've forgotten what we talked about. I don't want you talking to him again. I don't trust his shifty ass."

"But Tyrell—"

"You my girl, aren't you?"

"Yes, but—"

"No buts, Tameeka, either you're with me one hundred per-cent or you're not. I don't want you talking to him after he returns the key to you."

Tameeka's blood boiled. "What happens if I *lose* my keys, who'll let me in? Mohammad was always my backup."

Tyrell wrapped his arms around her. "I'll be your backup, baby. Just promise me that you'll get the store keys from him and never talk to him again." He was met with silence. "Promise me, Tameeka," he demanded.

16

What I Want in a Relationship

1. Trust
2. Spontaneity
3. Communication
4. Adventure

Do you ever get tired of it?" Stacie asked, peeking over her shoulder at Tameeka. They were standing in Stacie's bedroom and Tameeka was struggling to raise the zipper on Stacie's dress. The dress was one of Stacie's favorites; it was the color of a sunflower, it stopped at the middle of her thighs and it hugged every one of her curves. Unfortunately, it took two people to get into it. "You know," she continued when Tameeka gave her a quizzical gaze. "Getting dressed up and everything."

"I ain't the one. But you . . . I don't know another lady who dresses up, makes up and G it up more than you. You're like a freaking living Barbie doll. And just about proportioned like one," Tameeka joked.

"Don't hate," Stacie teased as she pulled away from Tameeka and admired herself in her full-length mirror. Her makeup was flawless, every hair was in place, and her fifty-dollar bottle of perfume made her smell like a million bucks. She looked better than she expected in the dress. After eating out four nights a week, she was afraid that it would take a toll on her body, but it had done the opposite. At least the food dropped in all the right places, she thought, admiring her Jennifer Lopez-size butt.

Stacie turned sideways and ran her hand over her stomach, which was still as flat as the bottom of a cast-iron frying pan. "I'm getting tired of all this. Dating ain't fun anymore. I keep hoping for my Prince Charming and all I'm getting are P. Diddy wannabes. I ain't feelin' anybody."

Tameeka gave an exaggerated gasp of surprise. "You," she covered her mouth with her left hand and pointed at her friend with her right. "Giving up on finding Mr. Right? Nooo way! Hell, you've based your whole life on rustling, roping and corralling him in. So what's really up?" Tameeka sat down on the bed next to her friend.

"That's not nice," Stacie pouted. "Just my twenties," she jokingly corrected her friend. Then her voice took on a serious tone. "I don't like all the hoping." She gazed down and admired her toes. They twinkled in the soft bedroom light; the coral-toned polish still looked good after a week. "Hoping and wishing, just like a damn fool." She stood up and began pacing around her bedroom. "Is he the one? Does he feel the same way about me? Every time I go out with somebody new, I have us married with children before the night is over," she said, and she looked disgusted with herself.

"Ain't nothing wrong with dreaming. But you can't waste your dreams on every damn clown that you meet, 'cause you know that's all they are. Damn clowns. Take your time, girl."

"I do . . . well, I want to . . . it's hard. Rather, *they're hard,*" Stacie joked, then tried to suppress a giggle, but was unsuccessful and it slipped out between her lips.

"So it all comes back to the dick?" Tameeka said smugly. "It's always the dick with you, isn't it? You're gonna die with a dick in you," she teased. "You're gonna be like this when they find you." She lay down on the floor, closed her eyes and spread her legs open as wide as they could go.

"Whatevah," Stacie laughed, then tossed a pillow at Tameeka. Tameeka burst out laughing and jumped up and returned to her spot on the bed. "Meek, I don't want to grow old by myself. I don't wanna be like Momma," she said, her voice becoming quiet, "Old, single and still living in a damn apartment."

"You'll find somebody, just open your heart, head and eyes and he'll be standing right in front of you. You'll be happy with the person He sends you," Tameeka assured her.

"I hear you," Stacie replied. Then stepped on the balls of her feet and reached her hands up high to the ceiling. The full body stretch was exactly what she needed.

"Oh, girl! You're in bad shape. Come meditate with me. It'll unclog you. All those worries will seep right out," Tameeka promised, and tugged at Stacie's hand as she sank to the carpeted floor. Stacie twisted away from her friend and sauntered toward the door.

"Nu-uh, you know I don't believe in that stuff. All it does for me is make me wanna go to sleep."

"It'll help you perform better in bed," Tameeka sang as she crossed her legs, then hid a smile when Stacie stopped in her tracks. Getting Stacie to try meditation was tougher than forcing Don King to get a haircut.

"No it won't," Stacie scoffed, and Tameeka mockingly raised her eyebrow. "Okay, okay," she said laughing. "Make a space for me, 'cause I'll be joining you tomorrow. But just so you know, I don't need any help in that department." Stacie glanced down at her watch. "It's time for me to roll, girl."

"So which one is it tonight?" Tameeka asked; she couldn't keep track of Stacie's men.

"The club owner. The six-incher. I'll be home early tonight," Stacie sighed as she sashayed toward the door. Before she could make it over the threshold, her phone rang. The tune from the latest Usher song cut through the air.

"Why do you keep your ringer so loud?" Tameeka grumbled. "It's irritating."

Stacie playfully stuck her tongue out at her friend, then clicked on her phone and was immediately showered with gut-wrenching sobbing. Her heart painfully beat against her chest. "Who's this?" she asked, and when she didn't get a response, she repeated it in a worried tone of voice.

When the caller identified herself, Stacie's legs threatened to buckle, forcing her to lean against the doorjamb for support.

Tameeka pulled herself up from the floor and hurried to Stacie's side. "Who is it?" she hissed, and Stacie shook her head, waving her away. Tameeka angled her ear next to the phone, but the words were so mushy that she couldn't make out what the caller was saying.

"Slow down," Stacie encouraged lightly, although her heart felt as though it was going to burst against her chest. Her face was gray and her hands were shaking when she clicked off the phone.

"I don't believe it," she muttered, her expression dazed. "I don't fucking believe it," she repeated.

"What?" Tameeka asked. "Tell me!" she insisted when all Stacie did was stare through her.

"That was Momma. Carlos just burst into the apartment and snatched Nevia, and she doesn't know where he took her. I knew this was going to happen. I need to get over there."

"Me too, I'll go with you," Tameeka said, jumping to action. "You think he found out about the car?"

"Don't know," Stacie said as she ran through the door with Tameeka on her heels.

"We'll find out when we get there."

17

Single Father's Guide to Dating
Tip # 11

Blind dates are to single fathers as manners are to children—they just don't go together.

Jackson grinned like a schoolboy as he watched the ball fall into the hole and the lights of the machine light up. He loved playing the pinball machines at Dave & Buster's.

"Good one," Tyrell congratulated him. "How's Jam?"

Jackson pulled his attention from the game. "He's fine, man. He scared us for a minute. Now he's back to his old self."

"Has he been having a lot of attacks lately?" Tyrell asked, concerned.

Jackson shook his head. "No, this is his first one in a long time. He'd been running around all night. He usually keeps his inhaler with him, but he lost it and his second one was in my truck. Now we have one in every room in the house. But what's going on with you? Haven't heard from you in a minute. Now that you got a girlfriend," Jackson taunted, then watched with dismay when he lost the game. He nodded toward the tables; he and Tyrell sat down and ordered beers.

"I'm good. Life is good. The job is good," Tyrell answered.

"Hey, man, my girl got a friend . . . she's tight. I can hook you up."

"Why are you pushing this so hard? She must be jacked-up."

Tyrell shook his head. "Naw, man. Not even. Tameeka thinks it's a good idea for us to double-date."

"*Tameeka* thinks so? So you a punk now?"

Tyrell frowned. "Why do I have to be a punk just because I try to keep my lady happy?"

"Punk!" Jackson goaded.

"It ain't like that," Tyrell said. He took a gulp of his beer, then, "I have a situation for you."

"Whassup?"

"What would you do if your girl had given her key to another dude and it wasn't her man?"

Jackson eyed his friend. "Tameeka gave her key to a dude? That's crazy, man. You gonna let her do that to you?"

Annoyance ran up Tyrell's spine. "It wasn't her apartment, she gave him keys to her store."

"Wow! That's even worse."

"How's that?"

"That's where ole girl spends most of her time. That's where she's making the money. She's playing you, man."

Tyrell shook his head. "She said he needs it just in case she locks herself out."

"If that's the case, she should give you the extra set."

"That's what I told her. But she doesn't want to ask for the key back. She said she's scared."

Jackson blew out a stream of air. "Scared? Scared of what? You need to control that shit. Either she's with you or she isn't. Get your shit straight, man."

"I have it under control," Tyrell reassured him.

Jackson nodded, but didn't say anything.

"So are you gonna do it or not?"

"The blind date thing?" Jackson asked, and Tyrell nodded. "Well, make it worth my time. Whaddya got for me, brotha?"

18

Why Blind Dates Are a Bad Idea!

1. He might be the featured pic on www.uglypeople.com
2. He might try to do the booty dance with me since he probably hasn't had a date in years
3. He might be weird

They should be here any minute," Tameeka whispered excitedly as she nodded toward the restaurant's entrance. She wasn't sure if she was more excited about seeing Tyrell or the fact that her best friend was meeting his best friend. She crossed her fingers and silently prayed that everybody would get along tonight.

Stacie pasted on a fake smile and silently prayed that the evening would be over soon. *God, I hate blind dates, they're nothing more than an organized way for losers to meet. And I don't need any help meeting anybody.*

They were standing in front of a mirrored wall and Stacie turned to admire her reflection. "You look too good to be on a blind date," she complimented her reflection. All the men in the restaurant silently agreed; they couldn't keep their eyes off her. With her white miniskirt and pale pink silk blouse paired with a waist-length denim jacket, she captured all the men's attention. "Don't forget that I'm hooking up with Barry tonight," Stacie said to Tameeka. "So I'm going to eat, then leave."

"Yeah, yeah, yeah," Tameeka said impatiently. "Barry the doctor, I know. Just relax and enjoy the evening."

"Do you think I should call Momma and Nevia?" Stacie asked Tameeka. Ever since the hysterical call from her mother, Stacie had been calling home every day.

"I thought you called them today?" Tameeka asked as she scanned the crowd.

"I did," Stacie answered. "But I want to call them again."

"They have your number. They'll call you if something happens."

"I know. But I feel like I need to check up on them," Stacie said, worriedly. It had been another false alarm. Carlos hadn't snatched Nevia, he'd only forced her to go to a party with him.

"They'll be okay," Tameeka reassured her.

Tyrell wandered into the restaurant and at his side was a reluctant Jackson. After a full day of begging and promising to detail Jackson's car, Tyrell finally got Jackson to agree to go out with Tameeka's friend. But anybody looking at Jackson could tell that he didn't want to be there; he was seething inside, and his handsome face was locked into a mask of disinterest. But that didn't stop the women from panting at him as he walked by.

Jackson strolled next to his friend, unaware of the attention he was getting. He hated blind dates. He hated them about as much as he hated to see the Lakers win their second straight championship. Already bored, his gaze roamed idly over the crowd, looking for his date; there were a lot of ladies sitting together who smiled and looked like they wanted to eat him for dinner, but something told him that they weren't waiting for him and Tyrell.

He continued his haphazard search and was about to give up and tell Tyrell he was leaving when he zeroed in on two ladies, and his pulse began to race. He squinted. The hairstyle was different, but the face and body were the same. It's her. Calm down man. Shake it off, he told himself. He slowed his step just enough to allow himself some time to get himself together.

"That's my man!" Tameeka squealed proudly and leapt up from the table, running into Tyrell's arms. "Omigod!" Tameeka shrieked as she shifted her gaze from Tyrell and focused on his friend standing silently next to him. She tugged at Tyrell's arm. "J is Jackson? Ain't this a trip? I—we—met him at Houston's." She turned to Stacie and said, "Stace, don't you remember?"

Stacie rolled her eyes and nodded. Of course she remembered him. Knew who he was the minute he sauntered into the restaurant. Ah! The brother who doesn't know how to use a freaking phone, she told herself. At least he could've called me. She glanced down at her shoes, a pair of cotton candy pink leather sling backs from Nine West, and her nose wrinkled. She took a couple of calming breaths, then asked, "How's Jameel?"

How's Jameel? he thought. How's Jameel? The first thing out of her mouth should be an apology for not returning my call. Jackson kept his emotions in check as he smoothly answered. "Not too good. His asthma has been bothering him. Poor guy was sick all day. He was sent home early today from school. As a matter of fact . . ." He gave them an apologetic look, then pulled out his cell phone, stepping away to make the call. By the time he got back to the table the waiter was there to take their orders.

"I'll have the steak, and"—Stacie looked coyly up at the waiter—"Rudolf, can you make sure that it's medium well? The last time I was here it wasn't cooked right. It was too dry and I got a tummy ache," she said softly and grimaced prettily.

"Sure thing, Miss Stacie. I'll taste it myself if you want me to," Rudolf offered. It took her less than five minutes, but Stacie knew the waiter's name, how long he'd been working at the restaurant and his favorite color. In that time Stacie had him falling over himself trying to accommodate her.

Tameeka watched the scene with amusement; she was used to the treatment her friend got from men whenever they were out, but Jackson wasn't.

Jackson silently studied her over the top of his wineglass; she was the type of woman who used her looks to get men to do things for her. She was the type of woman who never returned a dude's call. Hell, he knew her type all too well; Atlanta was full of them, they practically grew on the trees.

Jackson set down his glass and turned to Stacie. "So you like men tripping over themselves trying to please you?"

Amused, Stacie let out a peel of laughter. "It wasn't that bad."

"Puh-leeze. I won't be surprised if the dude comes back cradling a full bottle of Cristal. And I bet my life he won't be offering us any." Stacie shook her head and rolled her eyes. But ten minutes later Rudolf proved Jackson right. Not only did he bring her an unopened bottle of champagne, but he also promised to later present her with a free dessert.

Jackson watched as Stacie oohed and aahed and thanked Rudolf so effusively for the champagne that he turned red.

Rudolf stopped by at least a dozen times to check on Stacie. Jackson turned to Stacie. "So is Your Royal Highness happy with her dinner?" he asked. There was contempt in his voice. Stacie heard it and didn't like it one bit.

"Excuse you? What's your problem?" They locked eyes with each other from across the table. "You're jealous, aren't you? You're jealous because Rudolf is paying me so much attention. Do you wish it was you? Do you want Rudolf's attention?" she asked innocently.

Tyrell spat out his wine, Tameeka's mouth gaped open in surprise and Jackson was opening and closing his mouth, too pissed to speak.

"Hell no!" he managed to utter. "I am not jealous of you or

your new friend Rudolf. I think you are the most selfish, self-centered, self-absorbed person that I have ever met. *Your royal highness.*"

Stacie continued to calmly eat, unfazed by Jackson's outburst. "If you want to call me Royal Highness, that's fine. But I gets what I want." Then to prove her point, she sliced off a piece of lobster, holding the impaled seafood up for Jackson's inspection, then stuck it in her mouth. She had originally ordered the shrimp scampi, but Rudolf upgraded her meal, at no extra charge, to lobster. "On second thought, I kinda like the name." Smiling, she turned toward her friend. "Meek, that's my new nickname, Royal Highness." Deepening her voice, she said, "From this day forward I command everyone to start calling me: Your Royal Highness."

"Oh, you are really over the edge," Jackson grumbled. "I can think of a better nickname for you," he said as he glared across the table at one of the most spoiled ladies that he had ever met. He put a finger to his head and pretended to be in deep thought. "Umm, what about spoiled brat. No, overgrown baby," he concluded, then snickered at her.

"Whatever," Stacie answered as she continued to calmly eat her dinner. "I don't see anything wrong with having standards."

"That's what you call it?" Jackson guffawed. "That's a creative way of saying that the world revolves around me and I want everybody to do as I say." Tameeka and Tyrell watched the exchange with wide smiles. They knew that there were going to be sparks between the two, but they didn't know that they were going to turn into a forest fire.

"Fuck you!" Stacie shouted. "Screw you. You ugly Yogi Bear–looking motherfucker." She had popped out of her chair and was standing over Jackson, using her forefinger as a dagger, pointing it in his face. Jackson remained in his seat and glowered up at her. Tameeka and Tyrell exchanged glances. Tyrell wasn't sure what to do. He had never seen his friend act this way before. Tameeka reached over and squeezed his hand. He wasn't sure if it was to reassure him or to put him on alert for a full-blown all-out war; either way, he was ready.

"So how's Lexie? Is she feeling better?" Jackson asked, egging her on.

Stacie was stunned into silence. He's a mind reader, she thought. She gazed at him in amazement, then her eyes widened, remembering. He wasn't psychic or as intuitive as she thought, he was just nosy. "You're an eavesdropper," she accused. "You listened to my conversation. You sicko!"

"Like I had a choice." Jackson held up an imaginary cell phone and began mimicking Stacie. " 'It'll be longer if you want me to stop and take my panties off,' " then he giggled sarcastically.

"Aren't you just the fucking king of comedy?" Stacie said heatedly. "I bet the Kings of Comedy tour could use someone with your talent. Or better yet, maybe you could go on *Ripley's Believe It or Not!* as the Amazing Wet Man." She picked up her glass of Cristal, drew back her arm and was poised to toss the liquid on Jackson when Tameeka ordered her to stop.

"Come on!" Tameeka barked and tugged at Stacie's arm. She needed to get her away from Jackson before she did something she'd later regret. She and Jackson were already scowling at each other; they looked like they were ready to pounce. When Stacie didn't move she said, "You got cocktail sauce on your chin." That stopped Stacie in her tracks. She clamped her mouth shut and followed her friend to the bathroom.

As soon as Stacie and Tameeka were out of hearing distance, Tyrell pointed to Jackson and burst out laughing. "Dawg, whassup? I'm sensing a lotta love between you two. Should I go out and rent a tux?"

"You know what, Tyrell. You are so *funny,*" Jackson said, glowering at his friend. He was still flustered. He didn't know what just happened. Or how it escalated the way it had. His eyes narrowed. It was her, he thought. She's an evil, spoiled brat! "I need to bounce up out of here," Jackson said, and slapped his napkin on the table. "I don't need to be insulted."

"Naw, man, stay," Tyrell insisted. He could barely keep a straight face. This was better than *Showtime at the Apollo*. He surveyed the table and it looked like everybody had finished eating. "It'll only be another half hour or so. We'll order dessert and coffee, then we're out. Okay?"

"Cool," Jackson muttered. "Thirty minutes, no longer. After that, I'm gone," he promised.

After dinner they all stood in front of the restaurant deciding what to do next. Stacie and Jackson pointedly ignored each other. Tyrell and Tameeka stood together. He had his arm wrapped around her waist and she rested her head on his shoulder.

"Hey y'all, it's a nice night, let's take a walk around Centennial Park," Tameeka suggested. She loved the park. A lot of people had the same idea. Even though it was late, the park was filled with lovers walking hand-in-hand.

"Cool. I need to walk this food off," Tyrell chimed in, then turned to Jackson. "Whaddya say, dawg. Wanna hang out with us?" The ladies thought Tyrell was being polite in asking Jackson, but Jackson knew that it was quite the opposite. It was their code way of telling him to beat it.

"Naw, man. You two go on. I need to get going. Jameel . . ." He let the words hang in the air, letting them fill in the blank.

"Hold up!" Stacie shrieked. "How am I supposed to get home? In case you forgot, I came with Tameeka," she said, and pointed to her friend. She placed her hand on her hip, jutted her chin out and glared at the group. The foursome was silent, and the only thing that could be heard was the flowing traffic.

Tameeka nestled her head deeper into Tyrell's shoulder and studied Stacie through her eyelashes. Jackson was on point, he had read her friend like a book; Stacie was a little self-absorbed.

But Stacie is my girl, she concluded. She lifted her head from Tyrell's shoulder and said, "You know what? We don't have to take a walk. Besides, it's too chilly . . ."

Irritation flashed across Tyrell's face and Jackson happened to glance at Stacie and saw her smug expression. My boy ain't gonna be played like this, he thought.

He gritted his teeth, gulped deeply, then said, "I'll take you home."

"I didn't come with *you*. I came with *her,*" Stacie responded, then pointed her finger at Tameeka. "And since I *came* with her, and not *you*, I want to go home with *her,* not *you*."

Tyrell and Jackson exchanged nods that were indecipherable to the ladies. Tyrell tilted his head toward Tameeka. He didn't have to see her face to know that she was fighting an internal battle; he could feel it by the rigidity of her body. "You can't let Stacie control you. I know she's your girl and all, and I don't want to come between you." He had turned around so that they faced each other, then he leaned down so that his lips tickled her ear. "But I really want to spend the rest of the night with you," he whispered.

She absorbed his words. Her head was telling her one thing and her heart another. She quietly mulled over her options. Tyrell immediately knew when she made her decision; her body had relaxed as if a weight had been lifted from her shoulders, then she molded her body against his and whispered in his ear before walking over to Stacie. Tameeka slipped her arm around Stacie's shoulders before telling her that she was going home with Tyrell and she needed to roll with Jackson.

Stacie's mouth dropped open with disbelief. It took all of Jackson's self-control not to break out laughing. Stacie crossed her arms over her chest. "Fine!" she huffed. "Just fine." She stalked after Jackson.

19

Single Father's Guide to Dating
Tip # 150

Get the hell out of Dodge as soon as a woman starts using
her breasts as torpedoes.

Jackson and Stacie made it to his SUV without cussing each
other out. He glanced over at her; he couldn't help notice that
she looked even more beautiful in the street lighting. Not that
he would let her know it. Her profile was perfect. Admit it
Jackson, she's perfect. It's too bad she's an overgrown baby
who's waiting for life to be spoon-fed to her. He shook his head
and focused on driving. All he wanted to do was drop her off.
His gaze slid to the clock, it was still early . . . early enough for a
hookup. He mentally shuffled through his phone numbers and
easily came up with five women who would take him up on his
offer. I'll give one of them a call as soon as I drop off the
princess, he mused.

Stacie was studying the sophisticated dash of his SUV and
was unaware of Jackson's surreptitious appraisal of her. At least
he has good taste when it comes to cars, she thought. His SUV
wasn't her car of choice. She thought of SUVs as road-hogging,
gas-guzzling trucks on steroids. But at least he looked nice driv-

ing it, she grudgingly admitted. She peeked at him and watched how his hands moved confidently over the steering wheel. An image of his hands caressing her naked body popped into her head. Suddenly the truck felt too small, the scent of his cologne filled her nose; she hadn't noticed it before. Dating as much as she did made her somewhat of a connoisseur of men's colognes; she sniffed discreetly and instantly identified cedarwood, sage and ginger. Her favorite scents.

She gulped deeply and shook her head, but all that did was make her lightheaded and did nothing to erase the image of Jackson stroking her body. The last thing she needed was to get involved with somebody who thought she was a spoiled brat. Against her will, her eyes lowered to his crotch. He's probably a four-incher, she concluded, then laughed so wickedly that it drew an alarmed look from Jackson.

But neither one said a word to the other. Jackson pulled up in front of Stacie's and she had her hand on the door handle and was poised to jump out as soon as the SUV stopped.

"Hey, I have a long ride home, you mind if I come up to use your bathroom?" Jackson asked.

Stacie gave him a look that said, "Hell no!"

"Look. All I need to do is use the bathroom. I don't want anything else," he reassured her, with a smile.

Stacie sucked in her breath. This was the first time he'd smiled all evening. She stared at him, hypnotized by his sexiness. She shook her head, trying to break his spell, but she was still dazed. "Come on. You can't stay long, a friend is coming through, and I don't want him to see you here," she snapped, then jumped out of the SUV.

Not bothering to look back to see if he was following, she hurried up the stairs to her apartment. Jackson stared after her, fascinated by the way her behind moved under her skirt and the gentle sway of her hips. He imagined her body moving under him. He shook his head and the picture evaporated like a wisp of smoke. Just then, Ettie Mae's words came to him: If you're going to play with a rattlesnake, you'd better be ready to deal with the consequences.

"Sho you right, Grandma, I don't wanna get bitten." He chuckled to himself, then hopped out of the car and followed her. He had to use the bathroom *bad.* He braked to a stop in front of her door and just when she was about to close it, he put his hand out and stopped it from shutting in his face. He stepped into her apartment.

"Where's your bathroom?" he asked tersely. Pretty or not, he had had just about enough of her. He was ready to take a piss and get the hell out of her life. Stacie pointed down the hall, then went into her bedroom to check her answering machine. Surely he'd called, she thought. Sauntering over to the machine, she played her messages, all the while impatiently tapping her foot through two messages from her mother, one hang up, two telemarketers trying to sell her things she didn't need, BellSouth calling about her overdue bill, an old boyfriend, then Barry.

His sexy voice filled the room and a smile as big as Alaska spread across her face. By the time the message ended, her mouth was the shape of an upside down horseshoe. He wasn't going to be able to make it; something had come up. "Crap! There goes my sex for tonight," she mumbled, then stomped into the living room and almost bumped into Jackson, who was standing in the middle of the floor looking out of place.

"Who are you talking to?"

"Nobody," she grumbled, then asked, "All set?"

"Sure," Jackson answered, and followed Stacie to the front door. Indecision flashed across his face, he wasn't sure if he was supposed to hug her or shake her hand. *Oh hell.* "Peace," he leaned in, opened his arms and was about to pull her in when he felt a hand on his chest. She was blocking him. He looked down into her smirking face. "Whatever," he snapped, then shook her hand and let himself out. "Craaazy!"

He bounced out to his SUV, glad to be away from Stacie. He stuck the key in the ignition, turned it, and nothing happened. The headlights didn't turn on, the dashboard didn't light up and the engine didn't make a peep; there wasn't a flicker of life in the SUV. "Shit!" He banged on the steering wheel, then he leaned back into his seat and laughed. "Why doesn't this surprise me? This whole evening has been a trip." Then the seriousness of the situation hit him and he sobered up. "How am I going to get out of here?"

Inside the apartment, Stacie slithered out of her skirt, toed it in the corner, then did the same with her blouse. They'd lie there until she decided she wanted to wear them again or if Tameeka came into her room and straightened up. Wearing nothing but a red thong and matching bra, she strolled over to her full-length mirror. Studying herself the same way a scientist examines a specimen, with objectivity, curiosity, and unabashed excitement, she couldn't take her eyes off her reflection. The person staring back at her looked the same, but something was different.

She tilted her head to the side. "Am I really *that* bad? Do I really think the world revolves around me? Am I a user?" Stacie tacked on the last question. Even though Jackson didn't voice it, she was sure that's what he was leading up to.

"I'm not *that* bad. He just wanna hit this. That's whassup." She flounced away from the mirror and out of the bedroom, breezed into the kitchen, grabbed a bag of chips and was lying on the couch when the doorbell rang.

She frowned and glanced at the clock. It was one o'clock in the morning. Tameeka's spending the night with Tyrell, Barry punked out on me and everybody knows that I don't like pop-ins, she mused.

Stacie cracked the door an inch and peered through. Damnit! He's worse than a bad case of gas, he just won't go away, she fumed, then snatched open the door and stared coldly at him. Jackson, who was working up an excuse to spend the night, lost every idea he had as soon as he saw her standing at the door almost butt naked.

"My—my—my—truck won't start," he stuttered. His tongue felt like it was made of mashed potatoes. But his eyes were working and they zeroed in on her breasts. She could be arrested for indecent exposure the way her bra barely covered her nipples.

"And?" Stacie prompted, but when Jackson continued to look dazed, she said, "I'ma about to chill for a minute. My favorite movie is about to come on. You can use the phone . . ." She let the sentence drop off.

Jackson pulled his eyes away from her cleavage, then met her gaze. "I don't have anybody to call. If I did, I would've," he responded as he dangled his cell phone in her face.

"Stay right there. Let me go get the phone and directory. There's a good towing service right down the street." She turned away, but Jackson called her back.

"I don't trust tow trucks, they might scratch up my truck. And there's still the problem of getting home. I'm not about to pay them the two-dollar-a-mile fee."

"Call Tyrell," Stacie said.

Exasperated, Jackson blew out a stream of air. "You know he's with Tameeka. And I'm not about to bother him. Listen, all I need is someplace to crash until tomorrow."

"Nu-uh. Like hell! I don't know you. You could be a killer or something. I don't know anything about you," she shrieked, and did what any sane, single lady would do: she tried to slam the door shut, but she wasn't fast enough. Jackson stuck his foot in and winced from the impact. But he didn't give up. Pressing his face to the door, he talked to her through the two-inch-wide gap.

"Hold up! You know me, we just spent the last four hours together." She was silent, but the door didn't budge. He tried another tactic. "I guess I can sleep in my truck, but if something happens to me . . . who'd take care of Jameel?" He pulled his foot out and made a big show of walking down the stairs. Bowing his head, and slumping his shoulders, he walked as slowly as he could. He had to fight back a smile when he heard the door open and Stacie inviting him in. "You can sleep in Meek's room. Since this is kind of her fault. You can funk up her bed."

"Funk up her bed?" Jackson shook his head. Incredulous. "The last thing I am is *funky*," he said, irritated. "But I guess you should know funky, with all that fake hair. I can smell it over here, it's getting ripe," he retorted and waved his hand in front of his nose as if waving off fetid air.

"This is one hundred percent human hair," Stacie said, near tears. "And it probably costs more than you make in one day."

Jackson saw that she was about to cry and he felt like a bully. "I'm sorry. I really am. I shouldn't have disrespected you in your own home. You know what? I'ma shower and hit the bed."

Stacie rolled her eyes and pointed to the bathroom he'd used earlier. He quickly showered, and wrapped a towel around his waist. This will have to do, he thought, as he strolled to the living room, where he found Stacie lying on the couch, watching TV. She hadn't put on any clothes yet. She reminded him of Cleopatra the way she was sprawled out on the couch.

"Aw snap, I love this movie," he exclaimed when he saw that she was watching *Soul Food*. "But damn, don't you hate her?" he asked, pointing to Vanessa Williams's character. "What the hell was her problem, she acted like she had a stick up her ass."

"*Humph*. She was only trying to make sure her man handled his business. I understand where she's coming from. Dude could've done his music thing on the side and still kept his full-time job. She didn't marry a musician, she married a professional man." She said all this while keeping her eyes on the TV. When she finally looked up at him, he took her breath away. Water still glistened on his wide chest, thick, hairy muscular legs peeked from under his towel and his arms had more ripples than a bag of Ruffles potato chips.

"Oh, yeah," Jackson mumbled, totally unaware of the effect he was having on Stacie. "What happened to marrying for love? When they said their vows before God and all their friends and family, they both promised to love and honor each other, for better or worse, in sickness and in health, till death do them part. I don't remember a part in the wedding vows that said, 'We can break up if one of us decide to change jobs.' "

Stacie crossed her arms under her breasts, which lifted them toward Jackson and he felt Big J come to life. *"Humph,"* she repeated. "No, the wedding vows don't say that. But you can't decide to quit your job because you're tired and want to live a fantasy. Hell, if we could, we all would be doing it."

"Why can't you?" Jackson challenged, and silently prayed that she couldn't see his rising excitement. But it was getting difficult to hide; the towel was forming a tent. He averted his eyes from her breasts and instead gazed into her eyes. "I tell you why no one wants to do that. It's because we're all chasing the 'American Dream.' The two-hundred-thousand-dollar house in the suburbs, the Lexus and Benz sitting in the driveway, two kids, who are, by the way, going to private school, and at least two vacations to the islands every year. That's why we can't quit our jobs and play—we're all too busy chasing the carrot. The good ole American Dream," he finished sarcastically.

"What's wrong with that?" Stacie asked, as she pulled her eyes off the TV. He had her full attention now. "What's wrong with wanting things? It's *those* things that make our lives a whole hell of a lot easier. If we didn't have *those* things, we might as well live in caves and run around naked," she finished, and sucked her teeth.

"That's not true," Jackson argued. "We all can live without the big houses, the two cars and the exotic vacations. There's nothing wrong with buying a house that's got some years on it, or driving a car that's not brand new or spending a week in Hilton Head instead of Hawaii. That's called 'living below your means,' " he finished. Then added, "If you want all the glitter and shit, it's going to cost you," he finished ominously.

"Well, I *want* the glitter and shit," Stacie said sarcastically. Then she turned her attention back to the TV, dismissing him. As far as she was concerned the conversation was over.

"Why? Why do you want all that stuff?" Jackson demanded, easing closer to Stacie until he was only inches away from her face. " 'Cause your friends have them? Or because everybody is telling you that's what you need to be successful in America?"

Jackson was so close that Stacie smelled his lingering cologne; she turned away from the TV. "No to all of the above. I don't do shit just because somebody tells me to. I deserve all that and then some. Tell me what woman doesn't," she demanded, then gave him a challenging glare.

"I don't know if you deserve it or not. I'm not the one to decide if you're worthy. I just want to know why you want all that stuff. That's all I'm asking. Why? Just tell me why you want all that stuff!" he demanded again, and to his delight Stacie was speechless. Then all hell broke loose.

"Get out!" she ordered, popping off the couch and planting herself in front of him. Her legs were spread wide, head cocked to the side, hands on her hips; she was ready to kick ass. When Jackson didn't move, she jabbed him in his chest with her finger. "I want you to leave. Right now! Call AAA or somebody to tow your truck. 'Cause I want your ass outta here!"

Jackson winced, her fingernails were like miniature daggers. He glanced down at his chest and saw two lines of crescent-shaped indentations zigzagging across his chest. This chick is whacked! She's gonna kill me!

"I'm leaving," Jackson shouted. "You got some serious issues; you need to get professional help—and stop poking me," he yelled, then swatted at her hand, which he totally missed. He connected with her forearm instead. Stacie's mouth widened with surprise as she stumbled backward and barely missed colliding with the coffee table. It only took her a second to straighten up, her yoga training paying off, and hurl herself at Jackson.

"What? You're hitting girls now?" she screamed, and the look of rage on her face caused Jackson to step back. This situation was getting out of hand. "Oh, so you're a real man, huh?" she taunted, and butted him in his chest with her breasts. "Hitting women make you feel big and strong?"

Jackson held up his hands to ward her off. "Come on now. I didn't hit you. All I did was swat at your hands and *accidentally* hit your arm. And stop poking me with *those things,*" he complained, but he was getting more excited by the minute as Stacie continued with her butting. As soon as he saw that she wasn't going to stop, he wrapped his arms around hers, pinning them to her side. They were face-to-face. He stared into her eyes and she glared back at him.

"You cool?" he asked, loosening his grip just enough so that Stacie could feel the blood returning to her fingers. "I'ma let you go, so chill. No more breast bumps. Okay?" Stacie nodded and he dropped his arms to his side, and as soon as he did that, Stacie pounced on him, hitting him with enough force that Jackson fell back on the couch and she landed on top of him. Her breasts pressed against Jackson's bare chest and he began throbbing. He knew from experience that in a couple of minutes he'd be hard enough to cut a diamond.

"Don't you ever do that shit to me again. Who the fuck do you think I am?" she screamed. "I'm not some hoochie momma that you're used to dating. I'm a *lady.*"

With that, Jackson stifled a retort: The lady who's lying on top of me with her mouth only a tongue length away. Out loud, he said, "I never said you weren't a lady," Jackson argued, "I just think you have your priorities screwed up. You should be working on improving yourself and not on trying to fix your problems with external gratification." He finished his thought, then peered up into her eyes.

She had stopped squirming now and stared down at him and he saw something in her eyes that he hadn't seen all evening. Vulnerability. *She is human,* he thought, amazed. He reached up and cupped her face, and she leaned into his hand as if she belonged there. A jolt of desire shot through her body. Jackson caressed her face, running his hand from her hairline to her jawbone; Stacie let out a contented sigh and let her body relax against him. So much so that they melded together like gold.

Jackson felt as though he had come home, and wanted to prolong the moment for as long as possible. He pulled Stacie's face to his and gently nipped at her lips. Then he softly traced the outline of her mouth with his tongue. He inched his way over to her neck where he feasted on the soft skin behind her ears, then moved down to her shoulder bone. Stacie moaned, then turned her head to take Jackson's tongue into her mouth and she sucked on it as if it were a piece of candy. Jackson eased back to her ears.

Stacie inhaled deeply and her breath came out as a soft moan. How he knew that her ears were her hot spot, she'd never know. He gently inserted his tongue in her ear and swirled it around until she thought she would burst. Jackson's hands moved leisurely down her body and encircled her waist, he stuck his finger in the waistband of her doily-size panties and peeled them off.

They kissed long and hard, giving their tongues a workout that would make any teenager jealous. Jackson slid his hand down to her breasts, which he stroked and kneaded until her nipples were hard pebbles that poked through her lacy bra. He gave an impatient groan, then did a trick that he had mastered in high school. Unhooking her bra, he whipped it off her body, then dropped it on the floor all in less than ten seconds.

Jackson tugged his towel off and threw it on the floor and it landed next to Stacie's thong. Still got it, he gloated.

But he missed the look that Stacie gave him: a swirl of adoration laced with awe. Lying underneath her was an angel. Starting at the top of his head to the tip of his toes, he was perfect. She had been with handsome men before, but he was beautiful.

His skin glowed in the soft lamplight. His wide shoulders, thick arms and wide chest took her breath away. Her eyes traveled to his southern region, and she broke into a wide grin. He's no four-incher. Lord have mercy on me, she thought. Satisfied, she closed her eyes and focused on Jackson's hands moving over her.

Giving her a wicked smile, Jackson pulled Stacie up so that her breasts dangled over his mouth like two ripe grapefruits hanging from a tree. He leaned up and began suckling. He took a hard nipple in his mouth and sucked it until it glistened like a three-carat diamond; it tasted so good that he had to try the other one. Stacie sighed.

"So you like that, huh?" Jackson asked, and all Stacie could do was nod. She had lost the power to talk. "I like it too, baby," Jackson said, and to show her, he cupped both of her breasts and lightly tongued them, making Stacie convulse with pleasure. "Do you like this?" Jackson asked in a naughty voice before he flipped her on her back.

He kissed his way down past her stomach and flitted around her pleasure point. When his tongue made contact, it was like she had been hit by electricity. She gulped deeply as her body arched toward his mouth. "I guess you do," he chuckled as Stacie's body struggled to match his tempo. "Come on, baby, enjoy," he soothed, as Stacie felt the wave of her climax, then crested and floated back down to earth. She looked at Jackson through desire-laden eyes.

"What the hell did you do?" she croaked. She had never experienced anything like it before. She had had orgasms before, but nothing like this; it felt like an earthquake had ripped through her body.

"Nothing that you didn't want me to do. Hold on, it only gets better," he bragged, then hesitated. "Umm, you have protection?"

Stacie simply nodded, slid from underneath Jackson, ran into the bedroom and returned with the foil package. Jackson ripped it open and quickly slipped the condom on, then glanced down at Stacie. She was lying on her back, legs spread wide open, staring up at him with a look of hunger.

"I'll take care of that," he promised. Stacie gave him a perplexed look, which quickly turned to desire as soon as Jackson entered her. "Am I feeding you?" Jackson taunted with each thrust. "Who's feeding you?"

"You are," Stacie panted.

"You like Big J? Tell me you like Big J!" Jackson demanded.

"I like Big J."

"You love Big J?" Jackson asked as he swiveled his hips.

"Yeah," Stacie moaned.

"Tell me!"

"I love Big J!"

Jackson increased his tempo, thrusting deeper inside her. "Who's the best?"

"God, Jackson—you," Stacie screamed; sweat was pouring off her. "Big J!"

"Is it a big piece?" Jackson asked, and punctuated each word with a deep thrust.

"It's big," Stacie moaned.

"Too big for this?" Jackson stopped his deep thrusting and simply moved his hips, taking slow short thrusts.

"No—no—no," Stacie stuttered. "It's not too big." She cupped his behind, urging him to go faster.

"Nu-uh. I want you to feel Big J. I want you to feel every inch of him." And to prove it, he slowed his movements to an agonizingly unhurried pace. "You feel Big J? You like Big J? Well, here, you can have him," Jackson announced, as he picked up his pace, and he and Stacie rode the wave and coasted together.

Afterward, Stacie and Jackson lay on her bed. He had carried her there when the couch had gotten too uncomfortable. Jackson was flat on his back with Stacie's head resting on his chest. The soulful sounds of Anthony Hamilton filled the room.

Stacie angled her head to get a better eyeful of him. "Why didn't you call me?"

"Why didn't I call you? I called you. You never called *me* back," Jackson drawled, then wrapped his arms around her and pulled her on top of him.

Stacie looked down at his face. His eyes were closed and his lips were curved up into a smile. "I never got the message."

"I called you," Jackson insisted as his hands lazily stroked her breasts.

"When . . . when did you call?" Stacie asked, then pulled herself out of Jackson's reach.

"The same day I met you at Houston's."

"You did?" Stacie asked, warming inside, and she grinned broadly. "Wow!" Then, "Hey . . . wait a minute. What happened to the message?"

Jackson shrugged. "Don't know. I guess your answering machine was broke."

"It wasn't," Stacie said, shaking her head. "Are you sure you called the right—"

Jackson pulled her toward him and covered her mouth with his, smothering her words, kissing her until her moans filled the room. When he felt he had kissed all her words away he pulled back and said, "Let's just forget about it." In a kiss-induced daze, Stacie nodded in agreement and returned her head to Jackson's chest.

Jackson felt Stacie's fingers roaming down his chest. "Ready for some more?" he asked.

"Kinda sorta. I want some more of you," Stacie murmured, and Jackson chuckled. Stacie took that as permission and her hands wandered farther down his body. Leaning over, she flicked her tongue over his nipples until they were tiny stones, then she outlined his pecs, skimming the sensitive undersides with her tongue until he moaned.

Stacie reached down and grabbed his penis and gently stroked him. "Let me feel your mouth on it, baby," Jackson moaned.

"Not yet," Stacie said, "but soon." She kissed his lips, then traced their fullness with her tongue, all the while her hand tenderly caressing him.

"Can you kiss it now?" Jackson begged, and Stacie laughed.

"Boy, you sure are impatient," she teased. "But I'll do it." She eased between his legs and left a hot trail of kisses from his mouth down to his penis. Her mouth slid over him and Jackson whimpered as he entered the softness of her mouth. She closed her eyes in ecstasy; he tasted good.

Stacie gripped Jackson's hips as she guided him in and out of her mouth, gently coaxing him to his climax. He tensed and she pulled away, his eyes popped open and he looked at her with bewilderment. "What are you doing?" he rasped. "I was so close."

"I know," Stacie answered. "You'll come . . . I promise." She bent over and took him into her mouth again. She repeated the process until Jackson was a shaking mass of nerves, exactly how she wanted him. Stacie bowed her head and took him in her mouth, then reached down and cupped his balls, and gently rolled them around in her hand. Her tongue flicked over his tip just as she applied pressure to his balls and Jackson lost it, shouting so loudly that she was afraid the neighbors would hear.

"You said you wanted to come," she said.

Stacie jumped off the bed, her bladder felt like it was going to burst. "I'll be right back, I need to use the bathroom," she said. But she was talking to herself; Jackson was fast asleep. In the bathroom, she looked around at the piles of clothing covering the floor. "I really need to clean this up," Stacie muttered, then her gaze fell on a pair of leather pumps.

She licked her lips, then swiped a hand across her nose; the desire she had suppressed earlier now returned, this time tenfold. Her nose began itching, her palms became sweaty and her heart thudded in her chest. Maybe I'll do it a little bit. Just a little bit, she promised herself. She eased off the toilet seat, took two steps, scooped up the shoe and brought it to her nose. She took a tentative whiff; it wasn't one of her favorites, but that didn't matter.

Her nose tunneled deeper into the shoe, familiarizing itself with old territory. She groaned softly as waves of pleasure washed over her. Her surroundings became secondary as her sniffs increased with such intensity that she sank down onto a pile of dirty clothes and began working the shoe like a dog with a bone.

Suddenly the bathroom door opened. "Oh, here you are, I need to use—" Jackson froze midsentence and his words dropped to the floor. Stacie looked up at him with glazed eyes; he was nothing but a blurry figure. "What are you doing?"

Stacie blinked several times to bring the world back into focus. With a startling clarity she saw Jackson's disgust, the same look Crawford had given her. She dropped her shoe and raced out of the bathroom to the kitchen, Jackson hot on her heels.

"What's going on?" he asked.

"Nothing!" Stacie yelled. "Nothing at all," she repeated, then turned to the refrigerator and pulled out a carton of orange juice and guzzled it straight from the container.

Jackson waited while she took her drink and returned the juice to the refrigerator. When she turned to walk out, he grabbed her by the shoulders, and looked in her eyes. "Would you please tell me what's going on?"

Stacie tried to shrug out of his grasp, but it was too tight. Instead she dropped her head. "Nothing's wrong," she muttered, then glared up at him. "Aren't you gonna leave me?"

Jackson gave her a puzzled look. "Why should I leave? For one, I can't, but even if I could, I wouldn't. Tell me what's going on," he pleaded as his grip loosened.

"It's nothing," Stacie said as she walked away and headed toward her bedroom. She slipped into bed and listened to Jackson as he used the bathroom. When he slid into the bed, she was silent. When he pulled her to him, she held herself rigid, and when he called to her, she pretended to be asleep.

The next morning, Jackson pulled himself out of a deep sleep, his heart rate quickening when he didn't recognize his surroundings. It took him a minute to remember where he was. Then it all came to him and a smile blossomed on his face. He vaguely remembered carrying Stacie into the bedroom. She's not that bad after all, he thought. All she needed was a pounding from Big J, a ride on the J Coaster, and a piece of J-bone. He stuck out his chest, as much as someone lying down could.

Then just as suddenly another thought poked its way in, an image of Stacie, naked, crouched on the bathroom floor sniffing a shoe. Stacie! She wasn't there. He almost called out to her, but the stillness of the apartment told him that she was long gone. A pink slip of paper on her nightstand caught his eye, and he snatched it up.

Make sure you lock up when you leave.

Thanks,

S.

"That's it?" he muttered. "She's worse than a fucking dude. Where's the 'thanks for a good time'? And the 'I would like to see you again'?" Jackson turned the paper over and stared at the blank sheet. He was tempted to leave her a note asking to see her again.

"Fuck it! Let Miss Stacie call *me*." He slapped the paper down on the nightstand, stalked into the living room and plucked his clothes up off the floor. He was dressed in three minutes flat and marched down to his SUV, which ironically started on the first try. "Ain't this something?" He tilted his head up toward the roof of his car. "You like playing with me, don't you?" he said, shaking his head in amusement. "The last twenty-four hours have been unreal." Just as he put his car into gear, Tameeka's Escalade zoomed in beside him.

"She'll know where Stacie is," he said, and jumped back out of his SUV.

20

The Seeker of an Unblemished Rose
Always Ends Up Empty-Handed

I'm *so* sorry about Friday night," Tameeka apologized for the hundredth time that morning. "If I'd known what Tyrell had planned, I would've made sure that you drove your car. He can be so sneaky sometimes," she smiled dreamily, as if being sneaky was a good thing. "I'm glad that he did . . ."

"It really wasn't that bad," Stacie insisted, averting her eyes. She turned to look out of the restaurant's window. Sitting in front of the picture window afforded them a fabulous view of the street. It was midmorning Sunday and the neighborhood was filled with people walking their dogs. Ever since they'd moved in together, Sundays had been officially appointed their brunch day. They never made it to church, but they always tried to have brunch together at their favorite restaurant. "Jackson dropped me off and I was so tired that I went right to bed," Stacie lied, as she gazed out of the window at a six-foot-tall man strolling down the street carrying a toy poodle.

"Oh!" Tameeka exclaimed feigning surprise. "I thought you had company . . . I saw an empty Magnum wrapper in the garbage . . . and since you were the only one home . . ." She suppressed a giggle as Stacie turned panicked eyes on her.

"Maybe it was Tyrell's," Stacie weakly suggested, then her voice grew stronger. "Why the hell were you going through the garbage anyway? That's so tacky. Going through the garbage," she muttered.

"No. It wasn't Tyrell's. We don't use that brand. And just for the record, I wasn't *going through the garbage,* it was sitting right on top. A blind man could've seen it."

Damnit! "Well, I don't know how it got there," Stacie said, then stuffed omelet into her mouth. Tameeka watched her through narrowed eyes. She knew her friend was lying.

"Maybe DeWayne left it there. You know, while we were at work," Tameeka nonchalantly said, and surreptitiously watched Stacie's reaction.

"DeWayne? Office Manager DeWayne? Naw," Stacie shook her head. "I can't see that happening. He'd never do something like that."

"It's just weird, funny almost, how a condom wrapper would end up in our garbage since neither one of us left it there. Do you think we should call the police?"

"Call the police?!" Stacie shrieked and several people swiveled their heads to look at their table. "Okay—okay. I did it. I mean, Jackson and I did it," she confessed, then looked at Tameeka, who was grinning. "You knew, didn't you? You knew what happened."

"I knew something was going to happen between you two. You guys had enough sparks between you to burn down Atlanta a second time. Besides, I saw him yesterday when I ran home to pick up some clothes. How was it, girl?"

"The man put something on me," Stacie answered between laughs. Then her tone turned serious. "I don't know, girl. That man got some special powers. I've never felt that way before. It was fast and everything, but not like a wham-bam-thank-you-ma'am-type fast. It was fast and furious, fast and hard, fast and—"

"I get the picture," Tameeka said. She knew Stacie's penchant for sometimes being a little too descriptive. "So whassup between you two?"

"Dunno." Stacie shrugged and looked down at her plate. It was almost clean. She'd eaten more than she'd planned to, and now she'd have to hit the gym. "He doesn't meet all the criteria on my list," she revealed.

"Your list? Your list? Stacie, honey, girl. Here's a really good man; a very good man. He's a single dad, he takes care of his son. He takes care of his grandmother. And he's gainfully employed. What more do you want?"

"Well . . ." Stacie reached into her purse and pulled out a sheet of paper. Tameeka instantly recognized the tattered sheet as "the list," and she shook her head, annoyed. "He doesn't have hazel eyes, he has a son, he doesn't make over eighty thou a year, he doesn't—"

"Hold up," Tameeka said so sharply that Stacie jumped. The last time Tameeka used that tone with her was a couple of years ago when Tameeka caught her smoking weed in her bedroom. "When has that list *ever* done you any good?" she hissed angrily. "You read and study it like it's some type of blueprint for a man. Like if you have everything on the list, you're gonna have the perfect man. Well, Miss Stacie, I'm here to tell you that you won't," she stated. She was just getting started. "There are *no* perfect men. Hell, there aren't any perfect *women*. You know why?" she roared on without waiting for a response. "Because we're all human. *Humans are not perfect.*"

"I—didn't—say—that—I—was—looking—for—a—*perfect*—man," Stacie stuttered. "All I'm looking for is . . ." She looked at her list and again started reading off her criterion.

"Stop!" Tameeka demanded. "I know what's on the list. You've had it since high school. And it ain't working, Stacie. The list thing isn't working. *This list* isn't working," she said, correcting herself. Stacie thrived on her lists.

"But I have to have standards," Stacie argued weakly.

"And there's absolutely nothing wrong with standards. And I hope that you don't think that you should just settle. But you need to be flexible. That's all I'm saying," Tameeka said.

"I am flexible," Stacie argued. "All the guys I date don't have hazel eyes and they all don't look like Shemar Moore, and—"

"See, you're not listening to me," Tameeka insisted. "You're still looking at the external. Start looking at the man's soul." She stared at Stacie, exasperated. Then her lips turned up into a slow smile as an idea came to her. "Give me the list," she instructed as she held out her hand.

"What?" Stacie asked, blinking. "Why?"

"You heard me. Give me the list."

"No!" Stacie quickly folded it up and clutched it to her chest. "No," she repeated.

"Stacie, don't make me come over and take it from you," Tameeka warned, and Stacie narrowed her eyes, daring her to do so.

"You're not having this list," Stacie said forcibly, and moved to stick it in her purse. But before she could, Tameeka rounded the table with lightning speed and snatched the paper out of Stacie's hand, then marched back to her seat. Stacie's jaw dropped in amazement as she watched Tameeka rip the list into tiny shreds until it looked like confetti. Her eyes watered. Her map of fifteen years had been destroyed.

"I'm sorry," Tameeka whispered, and reached over to pat Stacie's hand. Stacie snatched it back and glared at her friend through glassy eyes.

"You didn't have to do that. I would've given it to you . . . eventually," Stacie sniffed.

"Yeah . . . well," Tameeka answered. She felt guilty for making her friend cry. "I'm only doing it because I love you," she said, which prompted an eye roll from Stacie.

"You don't love me. You're just jealous."

Tameeka sadly shook her head. "You've sang this song already, girl, and I'm tired of the hook. I'm not jealous of you," she gently insisted.

"Why else would you destroy any chance I have at happiness?" Stacie asked, and glowered at Tameeka.

"That list?" Tameeka asked as she pointed to the pile of paper on the table. "So that list is the key to your happiness?" she asked, incredulous, and Stacie nodded.

"It is and you're just jealous because I get all the fine men."

Tameeka pushed away from the table. "You know what? This is the last time you call me jealous. Have a drink of your happiness," she said. Tameeka scooped up a handful of Stacie's shredded list and dumped it in her iced tea, then marched out of the restaurant.

21

Single Father's Guide to Dating
Tip #50

Some exes are like weeds, they pop up in the most fucked-up places.

*B*ang! *Bang! Bang!*

"What the hell," Jackson muttered groggily and let out a stream of curses under his breath. He glanced at the clock and let loose with another round of curses. They were so blue that if his grandmother were within earshot, she'd be after him with a bar of soap. It was two o'clock in the morning, and he had to be up for work in three hours. He stepped out of bed and blindly groped around for a pair of underwear and a T-shirt.

"Who is that, baby?" Ettie Mae called from her bedroom. She too had glanced at her bedroom clock and had gotten a bad feeling; no good news was ever delivered at two o'clock in the morning.

"Don't know, Grandma, I'll go see. Go on back to sleep. Whoever it is is gonna get an ass whooping. Breaking down my door in the middle of the night like they ain't got no damn sense," he muttered. He moved confidently but sluggishly through the dark house. The knocking was growing more insistent. He stood at the door, regretting his procrastination about adding a peephole.

"Who is it?" he growled, intentionally deepening his voice and making it gruffer and thicker than it normally was. The question was met with silence. He barked it out again. This time he got a response that made his heart fall down to his feet. He didn't hear his grandmother walk up, but he felt her standing behind him.

No name was needed. He knew the voice. Age had deepened it and living the life had roughened it, yet even after nine years he still recognized it. He glanced back at Jameel's room. He had a good view from the front door. Jameel lay on his back, his arms and legs spread wide as if he was getting ready to make angels in the snow.

For the first time in his life Jackson was truly terrified. A little voice told him to snatch his son up, pajamas and all, and run for their lives. His thoughts must've shown on his face because his grandmother said, "Don't make no sense to think about doing something stupid, that ain't gonna solve nothing. Open the door, baby. You knew that this was going to happen sooner or later. Yep, sometimes sooner is better than later," she whispered, then began humming a church hymn.

Jackson suddenly longed for the days when all his troubles could be solved with a plateful of chocolate chip cookies and one of his grandmother's hugs. Everything that he loved and lived for was being jeopardized by what was on the other side of the door.

Jackson deactivated the security alarm, then pulled the door open. Michelle Jacobs, his first real girlfriend and Jameel's mother, stood on the porch. She fearfully peeked at him with eyes that looked like they had seen a million lifetimes, none of them enjoyable. The thin cotton coat she was wearing didn't disguise the assault she had committed against her body. Years of hard drugs and even harder living had ravished it. Her face was a grayish color and although she was only twenty-seven, she looked like she was forty.

Jackson and Michelle stood on the threshold staring at each other. He looked at the lady who once had his heart and wondered how she ended up taking a left in life when she should've taken a right. Ettie Mae watched the scene from a distance. It'd been eight years seen she'd seen her great-grandson's mother; she didn't like her then and she definitely wasn't feeling her now.

After watching them watch each other, Ettie Mae stood between Michelle and Jackson and invited Michelle in.

"Enough of this foolishness. C'mon in. We don't need to let the neighbors know all our business," she grumbled as she steered Michelle toward the living room. Jackson tiptoed down the hall to Jameel's room. Thankfully he was still sleeping. Jackson gazed down at him and his chest tightened.

"I love you, little man," he whispered as he kissed his son's cheek, then closed the door behind him. He wished he had a lock for it.

Back in the living room, he found his grandmother and Michelle sitting on the couch. Ettie Mae was at one end and Michelle was clutching the opposite end. They were eyeing each other like two roosters getting ready to fight. Instead of sitting down, he leaned against the wall and crossed his arms over his chest. He glared at Michelle, who was now studying the room.

Jameel was well loved. Pictures of a smiling Jameel covered the walls and tabletops. There were pictures of him taking his first steps, playing football, and riding a pony on a carousel. But it was the pictures of his birthdays that her eyes returned to. Eight years' worth. Eight years of her child's life. Eight years that she'd missed.

From across the room, Jackson saw Michelle's eyes dampen. They were glistening in the lamplight, and he almost laughed at her pain. Almost . . . but one glance at his grandmother quickly dried the urge up. He wasn't raised to be ugly.

"Why'd you come back?" The question came out weaker than he wanted it to. He cleared his throat and threw in some bass. "I thought you didn't want to be a mommy."

"Back then I didn't," she said simply, shrugging her shoulders helplessly.

"So the urge hits you at two o'clock in the morning?" Jackson asked sarcastically.

"I wanted to make sure you were home. But 'the urge,' as you call it, has been with me for a while," she answered, then tried to explain. "What could a nineteen-year-old college dropout dope fiend know about taking care of a baby? All I cared about was my next high," she said, and licked her lips as if she was remembering the taste of the drugs. She caught Jackson's questioning look. "I still want it. I fantasize, hell, I crave being high. It's a daily struggle." Jackson snorted. "But I'm clean now. Been so for six months now," she finished proudly, and Jackson got a glimpse of the girl he had fallen in love with nine years ago.

Ettie Mae joined the conversation. "What happened? How did you end up this way?" she asked, concerned. Even though she didn't care for Michelle, the girl's blood was in her great-grandson.

Michelle's hands began to tremble; she hated telling the story, but the people at rehab assured her that it was good for her. She inhaled deeply, then started. "It started small. I used to get so stressed out about taking tests, so right before a test I'd take something to relax me. It worked and I loved the way it made me feel. Soon I was popping pills to relax me, pills to keep me up, and pills to make me sleep. I was taking at least ten pills a day." Jackson pounded the wall behind him and Michelle quickly reassured him. "As soon as I found out I was pregnant, I stopped cold turkey. A cigarette didn't touch these lips, and if anyone was smoking cigarettes or some weed, I got up out of that place. I would never do anything to harm my baby."

"*My* baby," Jackson quietly reminded her. She can't claim him, he said silently.

"But what happened?" Ettie Mae questioned softly.

"I started back after I had Jameel. I got stressed again, only it was worse. Between taking care of a baby and school, I was driving myself crazy."

"It's not like you didn't have help," Jackson shot at her. Between him, her mother and his grandmother, they both had more than enough help to go around.

"I see that *now,*" Michelle replied listlessly. "But I wanted to do it all by myself. I wanted to take care of the baby and go to school full time." She shrugged, then continued with her story. "And when a friend turned me on to coke, I felt like I was superwoman. The world was brighter, everything seemed possible and all my worries flew out the window. The sky was the limit. I was the shit! Oops! Excuse my language," she apologized. "Then there was the heroin . . . and the prostitution. It was hell . . . I knew that Jackson would take care of his own. That's why I left Jameel the way that I did." She finished and looked dejectedly down at her lap.

"Touching story. You can't have him," Jackson stated flatly, but his eyes flashed angrily at her.

"I don't want him. I only want to *see* him. I want to know *my* son," Michelle argued. She had expected his reaction and would've been surprised if it was anything different. So she had come prepared to fight.

"He's *my* son. I don't want him near you. You're a crackhead. Besides, you forfeited your rights when you ran away. Where were you when he got the chicken pox? Where were you when his first tooth fell out or when he took his first steps?

Where were you when he came home crying because the other kids at school teased him for not having a mother? Where were you!" he shouted, his body trembling with rage.

Michelle shrank against the couch, pressing herself back as if she was trying to make herself invisible. Then she fought against her fear. She pulled herself up and looked him in the eye. "I'm very, *very* sorry. I missed so much of my baby's life. I want him to know how sorry I am. If I could do it all over again, I would never have gotten involved in drugs and given up my baby. I messed up. My parents wouldn't have anything to do with me. All my friends are married or doing something with their lives. I wouldn't wish this life on anybody," she said quietly, then, "I only want to see him. Nothing more. Please," she begged.

"No!" Jackson barked. "All the damn sorrys in the world don't change the fact that you left your son. You abandoned your baby!"

"Fine then. I didn't want to bring this up. Not right now. But I got a lawyer, just in case you wouldn't let me see Jameel. And she said that I have just about the same right to see him as you do. Maybe even more, since I'm his mother," she added slyly.

A *lawyer?* The blood rushed from Jackson's face and dropped to his feet. "You signed a note, giving me rights to Jameel, I still have it," he said desperately. Then he cursed himself for not getting a lawyer himself and legalizing everything. But he still made a move toward the bedroom, to get the note. After all these years he still had it. It was stuck in the bottom of a shoebox that he kept shoved back in the corner of the top shelf of his closet.

Michelle's hand dipped into her coat pocket and it brushed against her lawyer's business card. Her lawyer's promise popped into her head: We'll get Jameel back to you even if we have to cut his father's balls off to get him. Confidence and power filled Michelle, a lethal combination for someone in her shoes.

"Forget about the note. I told my lawyer about it and she told me that I had nothing to worry about," she replied airily, as if she didn't have a care in the world. Michelle strutted to the front door with Jackson and Ettie Mae in tow. "I don't want to start any trouble. I only want to see my son. Please let me see my son," she begged, then searched Jackson's eyes for a shred of kindness. Seeing none, she shook her head sadly, then left just as unexpectedly as she had come.

Jackson wanted to be sure that she was really gone, so he watched as she walked down the stairs and melted into the night. Then he rushed to Jameel's room and stood over his son's bed.

She's not taking you! His hands clenched and unclenched at his sides. "She's not taking my son!" he vowed.

22

If I Were Given Three Wishes, I'd Wish That...

1. Meek and I were talking
2. I could forget my childhood
3. I could fall crazy in love with a good man—Jackson (possibility)

Tell me again why you're going shopping with me?" Nevia asked Stacie. Her sister had called her the night before, asking if she wanted to hang out with her.

"Because you're my sister," Stacie answered as she helped Nevia dress the children.

"I am that. But we haven't hung out since high school. So what's going on?"

"Nothing's going on, stop being so suspicious." Stacie grabbed two of her nieces and Nevia had the other as they trudged down to the parking lot. "Let's take your car. I wanna see how your driving is," Stacie said. "Besides, you have all the car seats in here." It took ten minutes for her and Nevia to safely buckle all three in.

"This is nice," Stacie said, settling in. The interior was clean and the leather seats glistened. "It's almost better than Lexie."

"It's even better than that old thing you call a ride," she joked, then announced, "You came at a good time. Today is payday." She reached into her purse and pulled out a handful of money. She fanned it out and waved it in front of Stacie. "It's child support day," she sang.

"Damn, girl, you get that much money?" Stacie asked, her eyes slightly widening at the wad her sister flashed.

"Yep! My babies' daddies are loaded," Nevia bragged with a gleam in her eye as she started up the car and pulled into the street.

"Do you remember Daddy?" Stacie cautiously asked.

Nevia gave her sister a sideways glance. "Kinda. I remember that he swore like he was getting paid to do it. And smelled like he bathed in liquor. Why're you asking?"

"Just wondering," Stacie said, then glanced out the window. They were on the interstate, passing through downtown Atlanta. Stacie admired the skyline. "So you don't remember the beatings?" Stacie fished.

Nevia snorted. "The I'm-gonna-beat-the-black-off-your-ass beatings? Yeah, I remember those. Hell, I still have scars on my legs from the time he beat me with an iron cord," she said.

Stacie winced. She remembered her father giving Nevia that whipping. "I'm sorry, Nev. He was a monster. If he was around today, he'd be locked up."

Nevia agreed. "I'll tell you right now. I'll never, ever do something like that to my babies," she vowed, then glanced back at her children. All lined up like little dolls, they were peacefully sleeping. "But we survived it."

"Yes we did," Stacie mumbled. "Do you think we're alike?" she nonchalantly asked.

"What?" Nevia laughed. "You're full of questions today, aren't you? If I would've known I was gonna be questioned like a suspect on *Law & Order*, I would've taken the short cut to the mall. But hell naw, we're nothing alike," Nevia protested, shaking her head. "You're stuck up, I'm not. I have kids, you don't, I live at home and you don't."

Stacie nodded her head. "Yeah . . . that's all true, but do you think we use our bodies to get what we want?"

Nevia's mouth dropped open with surprise. "Where the hell did *that* come from? I think people are just nice."

"So you got this car from a *nice* person?"

Nevia hesitated; she nervously glanced in the rearview mirror before answering. The children were still sleeping. "He was nice and I really didn't have to do anything."

"What *exactly* did you have to do?" Stacie asked.

Nevia squirmed in her seat. "Walk around naked," she admitted.

"What?" Stacie hissed. "You walked around naked?"

"It's not like I had sex with him. He just liked looking. I wouldn't let him touch me."

"Nevia? How can you do something like that?" Stacie asked; her stomach rolled with revulsion. "I thought you were trying to get your life together?"

"I am!" Nevia protested. "But I needed a car. How else was I going to get to work, get the babies to their doctor appointments *and* take them to see their daddies? If you have a better idea, please enlighten a sistah."

"But to strut around naked in front a man . . . for a car. That's just wrong," Stacie said, shaking her head. They pulled into the mall's parking lot, and Nevia inched around the lot until she found a parking spot.

Nevia sat rigid in her seat. "You don't know how hard it is to raise three kids by yourself," she said angrily. "It's so freaking hard, sometimes I just want to hop in the car and—" Nevia's hand whipped up to her mouth and she turned her terror-filled eyes on her sister.

"Nevia, what's wrong?" Stacie shrieked, afraid for her sister. She had never seen her so scared.

Nevia pointed out the window. "It's Carlos. He's here," Nevia cried, and grabbed Stacie's arm. "Tell him that this is your car," she begged. "Please!"

Stacie linked her fingers with Nevia's. They both sat frozen as Carlos stalked toward the car.

"Get out!" Carlos yelled, and Nevia vigorously shook her head. "Get the fuck out here!" he shouted, then began pounding on the window with his fist and all three children woke up screaming.

"How did he find us? Do you think he followed us?" Stacie asked. Nevia didn't answer—her eyes were locked on Carlos. "I think we'd better talk to him," Stacie decided.

"No! Let's wait. Maybe somebody will call the police."

Stacie snorted. "I doubt it. Let's go. You're gonna have to face him sooner or later." She opened the door and stepped out. "Don't do anything to her," Stacie gently pleaded to Carlos.

"Did she think I wasn't gonna find out?" he asked Stacie, but he was looking at Nevia. She had opened the car door and was easing out. Carlos rounded the car, grabbed her underneath her shoulders and shoved her up against the car. He pressed his face into hers. "Do you think I'm dumb, Nevia? Do you think I'm one of those stupid assholes you're used to dealing with?" Nevia fearfully shook her head. "You must. Because how the fuck you gonna drive around in a car that my uncle bought you? You must've known that I was gonna hear about it!"

"I didn't do anything wrong," Nevia babbled, tears streaming down her face. "He gave it to me. He knew that you wouldn't help me."

Carlos's lip turned up. "I'm tired of listening to your crap. You're a liar, Nevia. If you weren't the mother of my child, I'd kill you right now."

"Let us go," Stacie pleaded.

Carlos chuckled nastily. "Nope. This car belongs to me. So call me the repo man, because I'm about to take possession of my car." Stacie and Nevia watched dumbfounded as he slid behind the wheel. "I can leave you guys in the parking lot or I can take you home."

Stacie and Nevia scrambled into the car. The ride home was quiet. Nevia and Stacie were silent as Carlos unhooked the three car seats and placed them and the babies on the sidewalk before driving off.

"I knew this was going to happen," Stacie muttered as she pulled Connie onto her hip and grabbed CoCo's hand. Chloe latched onto her aunt's leg and solemnly followed her.

Nevia snatched up the car seats. "That asshole is gonna pay for taking my car," she vowed.

23

It's the Behavior You Hate . . .
Not the Person

Tameeka looked over at Tyrell and laughed. He was slouched down in the booth with his chin on his chest and his belt unbuckled. "Do you think we kind of overdid it? I told you to wear something with an elastic waist," Tameeka gently chastised. "But you gotta love the buffet. Ain't nothing else like it." Tameeka giggled and settled back into the pleather seats. If she had a belt buckle to loosen, she would. Life was good.

Tyrell was the first man she'd dated who didn't grimace at the amount of food she ate. Which meant she didn't have to order rabbit food every time they went out for dinner, then gorge herself when she got home. With Tyrell she got to be herself. She glanced around their table and her lips turned up into a smile. The day had been wonderful. They went to a play, strolled through downtown and now dinner. He's a good man, she thought happily.

She peeked over at him and found him peering intently at

something across the restaurant; her eyes followed his to a much smaller girl who looked like a strong wind would break her in half. She was wearing a pair of jeans that rode low on her hips and a cropped sweater that showed off her flat stomach. "Is that what you want?" Tameeka hissed, her good mood evaporating.

Tyrell sighed and turned to Tameeka. "No. I was checking out her hair. I think that style would look good on you," he answered.

"Yeah right," Tameeka sneered. "I bet you were thinking that her *ass* would probably look good on me."

"Come on now, I didn't say anything close to that. What's wrong with you?" he asked, genuinely concerned, but a familiar lump of dread was forming in the pit of his stomach.

"Nothing's wrong," she lied, then crossed her arms in front of her chest. "Why don't you admit that you find her attractive . . . there isn't anything wrong with that. She's an attractive young lady and it's only natural to look—"

"Okay, okay, she's attractive," Tyrell admitted, his gut tightening.

"I *knew* it. You want her!" Tameeka spat and narrowed her eyes to slits. Tyrell grimaced. He knew what was coming and he prepared himself for Hurricane Tameeka. "And do you know how I know that you want her? Because you can't keep your fucking eyes on me," Tameeka shrieked.

Tyrell glanced nervously around and saw people at the nearby tables looking at them and pointing. Furious, he stood up. It was the same shit every time they went out and he was tired of it. "It's time to go. Let's go," he barked when Tameeka didn't move. He buckled his belt, then tossed two twenties on the table.

"I haven't had my dessert yet. I wanted the cherry cheesecake. You know that's my favorite," Tameeka whined, feeling embarrassed over her behavior. With Tyrell glaring down at her, she suddenly felt five years old.

"We can stop by Publix. Come on," he said as he reached over and tugged at her hand.

"Don't want no grocery store dessert," Tameeka muttered. "I want *that* cheesecake," she said, and her eyes watered as she and Tyrell passed the dessert bar and went out to his truck. Their ride home was as silent as a virgin teenager's bedroom on prom night.

"I'm sorry," a contrite Tameeka said, and Tyrell grunted in response. They were inside Tameeka's apartment sitting on the couch. "I am, baby, I'm so sorry. I can't help it. A part of me knows that you care about me, but the other part—let's call her Crazy Tameeka—doesn't get it." She peeked over at him; he was watching TV. "And that's who you saw tonight."

"And the other night . . . and the other," Tyrell said. "You need to squash the attitude, Meek. You're a *big* girl. I know it, you know it, hell, anybody who looks at you knows it. But I love it. I love your curves, I love your full face, and I love how you jiggle when you walk."

"But how come every time we go out you're always looking?" Tameeka asked in a voice that was bordering on whiney.

"First of all, it's not *every time* we go out. And secondly, I'm a man, baby. A man's gonna look, that's *just* what we do. But it's nothing to get your panties all tangled up about. All I'm doing is looking. Now I don't say anything when I see your eyes wandering a little. Nu-uh, don't even try to protest," he said as Tameeka began shaking her head. "You don't do it often, but I've seen you looking. But it's all good. I know what's up."

"Just promise me that you won't do it. It makes me feel ugly," she pouted.

"Meek," Tyrell pleaded. "That's stupid. How am I supposed to stop looking at people? You might as well make me wear a blindfold whenever we go out."

"Well, Wal-Mart has some cute ones," she joked. Then she clamped her mouth shut when she saw the expression on Tyrell's face.

"I won't be wearing a blindfold," he said between clenched teeth. Then he loosened his jaw to say, "Meek, trust me. Yes, I look. But, baby, the only time you need to worry is when I start touching."

24

Why Public Transportation Sucks

1. The seats are made of some type of slippery space age plastic
2. It's way too crowded
3. There's no privacy
4. Everybody looks like they should be in jail
5. It's a rolling loony bin on wheels

Stacie trudged down the street to the bus stop, her face set in a scowl. It was 6:30 in the morning and she had to catch the bus. "Where's the bus stop?" She had driven down this street a gazillion times, but she had never noticed the bus stops. Feeling like she was on a scavenger hunt, she trudged on.

She glanced enviously at the drivers going past. They were all wearing the same "Aw shit! I gotta go to work" look. "At least y'all got a damn car," she muttered, then glanced down at her watch. "I'll have hell to pay if I'm late again." She picked up her pace. "Damn, Lexie," she grumbled. "Why couldn't you have lasted until I got a chance to go to the bank?"

It happened last night, in the middle of rush hour, on Peachtree Street. The luxury car gave out and had to be towed away like a fifteen-year-old hoopty.

Stacie limped to the bus shelter and scooted into the corner.

Although it was early morning, the shelter was packed. There was a young girl, who couldn't have been more than seventeen years old, with two kids, a toddler and a newborn. They were hers, anybody could see that they were exact replicas of their mommy; she'd spat them out like they were watermelon seeds. Her face was weary and worn, but it lit up whenever she looked at her children.

Next to her was a lady in her late twenties, hunched over the *Atlanta Business Chronicle*. Stacie eyed the woman's suit à la Target. She looked down at the Kenneth Cole suit she had gotten on sale at Nordstrom's. She smiled smugly, but quickly turned sad, almost wistful. If she hadn't spent so much money on crap, she wouldn't be in this situation now.

Stuck in a corner away from everybody else was a black man. Stacie knew he was gay. Not because he met all the clichés— impeccably dressed, neatly groomed, not a hair out of place, and his cologne smelled like something imported from London. It was the way he looked at her. His eyes flicked over her as if she was a worm that slithered out of the ground. Stacie gave him the same empty stare, then tore her eyes away to peer anxiously down the street, frowning when she didn't see the bus's headlights. Stacie was still peering down the street when a dot appeared on the horizon.

She saw the shopping cart first. It was a regular cart, but it looked like a junkyard on wheels. It was heaped high with moldy newspapers, dirty clothes, shoes and a bunch of other stuff that she didn't dare try to identify. Stacie couldn't take her eyes off the cart as it slowly eased past her, then suddenly stopped.

The cart was being pushed by Hattie, or as she was affectionately known on the streets, Mad Old Hatter. Hattie looked like she had danced with the devil on more than one occasion. Her age was unclear. Somewhere between forty or seventy would've been Stacie's guess. Wrinkles were cut into her face, crisscrossing through it like little roads. Stacie estimated that her hair hadn't seen a comb in years; it was au natural and held back by a scrap of material that looked like it was ripped from one of her rags.

Fascinated, Stacie's gaze alternated between Hattie's face and her cart; her desire for the bus momentarily forgotten. Hattie had protectively clutched against her chest a bundle the size of two footballs and wrapped in a filthy baby's blanket. Hattie held onto it as if it were gold. Every once in a while, she peered down at it and gave it a toothless smile. Stacie noticed the mass of curly black hair peeking out.

Hattie caught Stacie staring at her and chuckled to herself. Her laugh was filled with amusement and peppered with insanity. She gestured to Stacie, who hesitated for a second before leaving the shelter and stepping over to her. "This is my baby," Hattie croaked, and she sounded as if her throat was dry, like she didn't use words often enough to lubricate it.

Stacie's eyebrows shot up. "You have a baby?" she asked, amazed, and Hattie nodded. Stacie gestured toward the streets. "And you're living . . ." embarrassed, she bit back the rest of her words.

Stacie forced a smile as she slowly pulled back the blanket and exposed more of the curly black hair and a little forehead. "I bet you have a cutie," Stacie confidently said, as though she was an expert on such matters. "Look at all your hair. Didcha get your mommy's hair?" Stacie cooed, as she pulled the tattered blanket back.

Stacie's eyes widened to the size of frying pans and her mouth gaped open, but nothing came out. Her voice was stuck at the back of her throat, but it quickly loosened and she let out a blood-curdling yell. The baby's head had fallen off and Old Mad Hatter let out another maniacal laugh. Hattie's baby was nothing more than a doll's head stuck on a sawed-off broomstick. Just then the bus pulled up.

"This is why I don't like taking the bus," Stacie muttered, and on shaky legs slowly backed away, keeping her eyes on

Hattie. "Crazy lady!" Hattie had scooped up the doll's head and was busily trying to reattach it to the stick.

Stacie pushed her way through the crowd, sprinted up the stairs and onto the bus, then immediately skidded to a stop. She stopped so fast that she almost toppled over. Him!

Jackson was taking a well-earned sip of his coffee when Stacie bounded up the stairs. Her! He choked.

By now Stacie was standing in front of him, breathing heavily, and her chest was moving up and down. Jackson couldn't take his eyes off her chest and Stacie couldn't take her eyes off the way his shirt fit tightly over his chest and hugged his biceps.

"What's going on up there?" a man waiting on the sidewalk yelled, breaking their trance. "We have places to be."

"Oh, I'm sorry," Stacie apologized, flustered. Normally she would've had a funky comeback, but seeing Jackson threw her off. Damn, he looks good. Images of their lovemaking session flashed in her mind and she could feel his lips and his tongue dancing over her body. The blood rushed to her face and she bowed her head to hide the flush.

She reached down into her purse and fished around for some change. The only things she came out with were two nickels, some pennies, a lipstick sample, and a bunch of lint. She could hear groans and muttering from the people behind her. Her billfold was on the bottom of her purse. She grabbed it and pulled out a five-dollar bill. "Does anybody have change for a five?" she asked in a hopeful voice, then added ammunition with her high-wattage smile. All she received was blank stares from the women and a couple of winks from the men. "Anybody?" she squeaked.

"Come on! We've got to get to work!" a lady shouted from the back of the bus.

"Sit down!" Jackson instructed, pointing to an empty seat.

"But—"

"Sit! You're blocking the door."

Stacie slid into the seat and turned to look out the window. Hattie was still standing on the sidewalk tucking her makeshift baby into her cart. The bus pulled away from the curb and Stacie continued to look at Hattie until she became a dot. Even though she hadn't set foot in a church in years, Stacie got an overwhelming urge to talk to God.

"Heavenly Father, I know that I don't talk to you unless I need something and this time it's no different. I need your help, but it's not for me, at least not all of it. Can you please make sure that the homeless lady finds a safe place to sleep and eat. Please take care of her baby, I'm sure she has one . . . somewhere. Amen," Stacie murmured, then lifted her head. Her eyes were glassy, but her soul soared.

From his mirror, Jackson watched as Stacie closed her eyes and moved her lips in prayer. His eyes widened in surprise before he returned his attention back to the road. So the princess got a little religion in her, he mused. He glanced at her again, only to find her looking at him; their eyes locked, then he motioned to her.

"Stand right there," Jackson instructed, and pointed to a pole behind him. "So why is the princess taking the bus? I thought it was beneath you?"

Stacie jumped as though she had been caught peeking. She had angled her head so that she could study his back. Every movement he made caused his muscles to ripple. "My car broke down," she answered absentmindedly as her gaze moved down to his hands; she remembered how they felt on her body. She nervously cleared her throat. "Hey, I'm sorry about running out on you."

Jackson shrugged. "It happens."

She glanced at his reflection and their eyes momentarily locked and his lips turned into a knowing smile. A shiver of excitement shot through Stacie.

"I know," he drawled. "I want a replay too."

"I don't know what you're talking about," Stacie denied.

"Yeah you do," Jackson said, and gestured to her. Stacie brought her ear within a breath of his mouth. "Look down," he demanded, glancing at his lap. Stacie followed his gaze and her mouth went dry. His desire was evident. "You're not going to let this go to waste, are you?"

Stacie ran her tongue over her lips. "No . . . I'm not a wasteful person."

"No you're not, you took all of my energy that night and even recycled it." Jackson chuckled and Stacie flushed. "I want you," Jackson said. "Touch it," he demanded as he expertly navigated the bus through his route.

"I can't," Stacie said. "Your passengers will see."

"They're not even paying attention to us. Just look."

Stacie slowly turned around and casually looked over the passengers. Jackson was right; they were either reading something, talking, or staring out the window. "As soon as I do it somebody will look up and catch me."

"It's not like I'm gonna whip it out, I just want you to stroke it. Touch me like you did last time," he asked, then winked and her pulsed raced.

Stacie peeked over her shoulder, then leaned even closer to Jackson. She discreetly dropped her hand in his lap, then let out a low moan; he was so hot. Her hand breezed over his pants and he lifted his hips a hair for contact. Using two fingers, Stacie firmly stroked the length of his shaft until it throbbed. She gently caressed his penis and outlined the head with her fingertip.

"See how badly I want to be inside you," Jackson said, groaning softly.

"Make it bounce for me," Stacie breathed.

Stacie's stop zoomed up just as Jackson softly nipped her ear. "Oh baby, we're gonna have some fun," he promised before she rushed off the bus and into her office building.

25

Single Father's Guide to Dating
Tip # 123

Sexing in public is never an option.

Jackson and Stacie were in Just Desserts, a small café he drove past every day. He was intrigued with the oversize muffins, giant cinnamon buns and flaky croissants that the customers munched as they sauntered out the door. Something about the name and the tables and chairs on the sidewalk told him that the place was classy enough for Stacie. He was right.

They were tucked into a corner, a tiny U-shaped nook in the back of the shop. It wasn't a privacy issue, the little shop was almost empty with only four of its twelve tables filled; Jackson picked it because of its coziness. She was sitting so close to Jackson that she was almost on his lap.

Jackson gave Stacie a sidelong look out of the corner of his eyes. It'll take only a minute for me to lift her up so that she can wrap those long legs of hers around my waist, he mused.

Keeping a close eye on him, Stacie waited until Jackson finished his coffee and ordered a second cup before she felt it was safe to talk about what had been bothering her.

She took a deep breath, then said, "I don't mean to keep repeating myself, but I just have to say it. I didn't mean to run out on you that morning."

Jackson brought his coffee cup up to his mouth to hide his smile; he'd wondered how long it would be before she brought that night up again. Taking his time, he took a long sip of his coffee. "I know, you told me on the bus. But it's cool. All we did was hit it a couple of times. It wasn't a big deal," he lied. It was the best sex he'd had in his life. Ever since that night, it replayed itself over and over in his head.

"What!" Stacie yelled. "So you think all we did was 'hit it'? That's a shitty thing to say," she hissed, slumping down in her chair.

"Isn't that how you saw it?" he asked. "Or maybe I was just a piece of dick? Or maybe I was a stress reliever for you? Or maybe it was something to do until the next movie came on." Stacie didn't respond, but she sat up, crossed her arms over her chest and glared at him. "It had to be something trivial like that, otherwise you wouldn't have just walked out on me afterward," he finished.

"I admit what I did was tacky as hell. But it didn't mean that what happened between us didn't matter."

Jackson studied her over his coffee mug. "So what I'm hearing is that you liked what happened between us?" he asked, surprised. He could barely suppress the smile that had snuck onto his face.

"Since when did you become a Dr. Phil knockoff?" She laughed at her own joke, then said shyly, "I liked what happened between us. I *really* liked it," she giggled nervously. She felt bold and vulnerable at the same time. The only person she had admitted her feelings about Jackson to was Tameeka. "But it wasn't all about the dick—oops!" She clamped her hand over her mouth and her face flushed hotly. Ugh, I'm such a potty mouth! Jackson nodded for her to continue.

"Well . . . like I was saying, it's not about the . . . dick with you. It's big and everything and you can whip it on a sistah, but you have qualities that a lot of brothers lack."

Jackson smiled mischievously, then reached over and traced his finger down her jawbone. "Like knowing what makes you hot?"

"I didn't say skills, I said qualities." Stacie sighed softly as her nipples hardened, and a throbbing started between her legs.

"Oh! So you're saying that I got over-the-top skills too?" Jackson seductively asked as he leaned over and blew warm air in her ear; Stacie let out a soft moan as her eyes closed.

"Do that again," Stacie pleaded as she gripped his thigh. "Ooh, I love that," she purred as she snuggled against him. Jackson glanced down at her face and immediately got hard. Her expression was total sex.

Jackson gently probed her ear with his tongue. "So when am I gonna get that replay?"

"Whenever you—"

"Excuse me!" Stacie's eyes popped open to find their waitress wearing an amused expression; embarrassed, Stacie quickly shoved Jackson away. "There's a motel, three blocks down," the waitress announced before sauntering away.

"Isn't it funny," Stacie began in a shaky voice, "that whenever we're together we can't keep our hands off each other. My apartment . . . the bus . . . here."

"We're fire, baby," Jackson answered, giving her a quick kiss.

"I need to straighten up," she said, then made her way to the bathroom. Halfway across the room, she looked back at Jackson, who was calmly sipping his coffee. He looked in her direction, then gave her a sexy wink.

"I'm just sorry about what I did," Stacie said when she was back in the booth. Her statement was met with silence. Jackson was pouring himself a third cup of coffee. "Well . . ." She looked at him imploringly.

"What?" Jackson set his coffee down, confused. "You don't have to apologize just because we almost sexed in public."

Stacie shook her head and rolled her eyes. "Not that. I'm talking about when I ran out on you. Do you accept my apology?" she repeated.

"I accept your apology," he said, then a thought occurred to him. "You apologize, you tell me how much you admire me, but you still haven't told me why you ran."

"Huh?" Stacie asked, pretending that she didn't hear him. When she knew that he wasn't buying her deaf act, she said, "Aw hell . . . why does anybody run?" she asked, then answered her own question. "People run because they're scared. And you scared me," she admitted in a soft voice tinged with embarrassment.

"Me?" Jackson was so shocked that he pointed to his chest. "Me?" he repeated. All he remembered was the smart-ass lady who couldn't keep her mouth shut. Nowhere in the picture was she a cowering mass of nerves. "I told you then, I didn't mean to hit your arm—"

"No-no-no, that was me. I was all attracted to you and didn't know how to act. I had this fine man up in my apartment and my brain went to mush. I think I fell for you the first time I saw you . . . at Houston's. I didn't want to admit it to myself and then when you turned out to be Tyrell's best friend . . ." She laughed softly, remembering. "Then when we went out to dinner and you kept coming at me with stuff, I wanted to kill you. Then later at the apartment, after we made love, I was completely blown away. You touched my heart," she admitted. "So do you feel better now? Miss Spoiled Brat has feelings," she said, and lost her face in her mug of hot chocolate.

"I do," Jackson whispered, and Stacie snapped her head up. "Because I feel the same way," he admitted, and Stacie broke out in a smile. "So what does all this mean?" Jackson probed.

"Well, we definitely like each other," Stacie said slowly, unsure of what he was asking.

"That's apparent," Jackson said. "Do you think it would be a good idea for us to hang out and see what happens?" he asked.

"I'd like that." Stacie blushed, then looked up.

"Me too," Jackson whispered and grinned. It was on the tip of his tongue to tell her all about his baby momma drama, but not wanting to damage their newly found friendship, he decided against it.

26

The Sand on the Other Beach Isn't Whiter, It Only Has a Different Set of Shells

H ey Meek!"

Startled, Tameeka whirled around to see Mohammad standing on the other side of the register. She hadn't seen him since she had taken her key back from him.

"Damn, Mo, you shouldn't sneak up on a sistah. How the hell did you get in here?"

"I'm magic." He grinned at Tameeka's scowl. "You left the door unlocked," he explained. "You'd better keep it locked. You know Mr. Wang? Well, he was robbed a couple days ago."

"Oh, no!" Tameeka exclaimed. "How's he doing?" She liked Mr. Wang and loved browsing in his store; he had the most exquisite knickknacks.

"I heard he's okay, but he had to stay in the hospital overnight. The robber did a number on him."

"Oh boy. You're not safe anywhere."

"I don't like it that you're here by yourself in the mornings."

Now that you're not spending them with me, Tameeka wanted to say. Instead she said, "I usually have the door locked and the alarm on. I don't know why I forgot today. But anyway, Bea is coming in early." Just then, Bea walked in and pleasantries were exchanged before she went into the back to her locker.

"So how's your thing going?" Mohammad asked nonchalantly once they were alone again.

"Tyrell is not a *thing*. And it's—we are going very well," Tameeka boasted. "We have direction, we're on a path."

"That's funny, sounds like you two are Lewis and Clark."

"What do you know about Lewis and Clark? You told me you slept through history," she teased.

"I learned a lot in school, especially about keeping away from snooty women like you," he retorted.

"Snooty!" Tameeka shouted, then plucked up a bar of soap and lobbed it at him. Mohammad ducked and it dropped at Bea's feet just as she stepped onto the selling floor. Tameeka flushed deeply. "I'm sorry, Bea," she stuttered, then glared at Mohammad, who was biting back laughter.

"No problem," Bea said, then plucked the soap off the floor and tossed it to Tameeka. She dropped it in the bin, then looked down at her watch; she still had a snatch of time to meditate before the store opened.

Foregoing the mat, she sat in the middle of the floor and got into position. Mohammad quickly followed suit and settled down next to her. Tameeka closed her eyes and ignored him.

"I'm sorry if I got you in trouble," he whispered. Even though Bea was on the other side of the store, he didn't want to risk her hearing him.

"I didn't get in trouble," Tameeka bristled. But she thought: *Even though I had to promise to stop seeing you.* "Like I said earlier, we're cool."

"I made a mistake," Mohammad admitted.

"I hope you aren't talking about the crotch thing . . . that's over with. It's forgotten."

Mohammad shook his head. "Not that," he started, then said softly, "Open your eyes." Tameeka's heart fluttered, but she kept her eyes closed. "Open sesame," Mohammad coaxed, and Tameeka reluctantly lifted her lids. He reached out and cupped her face between his hands and looked deeply into her eyes. "I made a mistake with *us*."

"What do you mean?" Tameeka asked, confused. "You don't want to be my friend anymore?" she asked.

A smile danced around Mohammad's mouth. "I do . . . but I want for us to be more. I want you back in my life."

Tameeka vigorously shook her head while pushing herself off the floor. "No! We've been there, Mo. We both know that we make better friends than lovers."

"I've grown up," Mohammad answered. "I'm ready to settle down. And I want to do it with you."

"No!" Tameeka repeated, then went to the counter, where she absentmindedly arranged lip balms. "You only want me because I'm in a happy relationship."

"If it's so happy, why didn't you tell him about me?" Mohammad countered.

"I did tell him . . . I just forgot to tell him that you worked right above me. Besides, our *thing* didn't mean anything."

"Is that so?" His eyes suddenly darkened. Bea was forgotten as he leaned in and outlined her lips with his tongue. Tameeka felt a rush between her legs. Kissing Mohammad was like kissing a tornado; he'd suck you up, then leave you swirling for days. Tameeka opened her lips and Mohammad tenderly slipped his tongue in and she tentatively welcomed it. Mohammad slipped his hands up into her hair, running his fingers through it. A sigh escaped from between Tameeka's lips; Mohammad remembered that she loved to have her scalp touched. Her arms snaked around his neck as she deepened the kiss. Mohammad backed her up against the counter, and slowly and deliberately ground his hips against hers. He pulled away and looked into Tameeka's desire-drenched eyes. "So that didn't mean anything?" he demanded.

"It didn't mean anything," Tameeka squeaked.

27

I Hate My Job . . . But I Need It, Because . . .

1. I have a bazillion bills to pay
2. I'm not sure if I can do anything else
3. I can do it with my eyes closed
4. I've been a receptionist for eight freaking long years

Stacie stared out of the bus's window at the traffic. Atlanta's traffic problem was legendary, but this? In front of her were two lanes of traffic that stretched four miles long. Jackson's dispatcher had called with the bad news: an overturned tractor-trailer had dumped hundreds of gallons of gasoline on I-75, Atlanta's artery, and closed it down. Everybody and their momma was taking the surface streets to downtown Atlanta.

She glanced down at her watch and swallowed a scream. She had less than ten minutes to make it to work, and her building was nowhere in sight. Stacie fixed her gaze hopelessly on the lines of cars. The street was packed tighter than Pamela Anderson's bra.

Staring out at the parking lot of cars, Stacie could feel her job slipping further out of her grasp. Every couple of minutes the bus would inch forward a few yards, just enough to raise

Stacie's hopes, only to have them shot down when the bus was forced again to stop.

Frustrated, Stacie blew out a stream of air. Andre's threat hung heavily over her head. She *had* to keep her job. The stack of bills that were due this month flashed before her eyes and her stomach tightened nervously. "I can't lose my job," she whispered.

"I'm sorry, baby, I can't go anywhere. We're stuck like pigs in a pile of quicksand," Jackson said hopelessly. He didn't mind the traffic, he was used to it, it came with the job. But he hated what it was doing to Stacie and he wished that he could get her to work.

He glanced at her in the rearview mirror to see how she was faring. She was a far cry from the carefree lady who, thirty minutes ago, bounced on his bus giggling and talking like she owned the world; now she looked like she could crack at any minute. Her eyes darted nervously from her watch to the traffic. "It'll be okay," Jackson murmured. His words of comfort sounded inadequate even to his own ears, but he didn't know what else to say, much less do. If he could make the bus fly for her, he would.

He relaxed in his seat; it didn't look like they were going anywhere soon. Suddenly an image of Stacie with her head thrown back and her legs slung over his shoulders burned in his head. It was so realistic that he could almost taste her. He was jarred back to the present by Stacie's voice.

"No it won't," she said glumly, shaking her head as a picture of Andre handing her a pink slip flashed before her eyes. "I'ma get fired," she said dejectedly as she glanced longingly down at her sneakers. The urge to sniff was so strong that she momentarily forgot that she was going to be late for work. "Maybe I should walk," she thought out loud. She peered out of the window. The bus hadn't moved in five minutes. It would be a good fifteen-minute walk. "But if I ran—" she mulled it over, but stopped when the bus moved forward, then just as quickly stopped again. Stacie groaned out loud. "Is there a short cut we can take?" she innocently asked, and people within hearing distance laughed. Jackson bit back his amusement as he motioned Stacie closer to him.

"Baby, trust me, if I could get you out of this mess, I would," he said, gently palming her face.

"I know, sweetie." She sighed against his hand. The simple gesture made his heart thud.

"Would you call this a date?" he blurted out.

"What?" Stacie asked, pulling away from him. "That's a funny question to ask. But no, I wouldn't call my bus rides dates."

"How many dates you think we've been on?"

Stacie shrugged. "I don't know. It's not like I've been keeping track," she said, but mentally counted off five dates they'd been on since Just Desserts, just as Jackson was doing his calculating. When they were done, they grinned at each other.

"How come your girl isn't driving you?" Jackson asked, and the smile fell off Stacie's face.

She didn't answer right away; instead she looked out the window, then said, "We had a fight, well, more like an argument, and we're not talking to each other. But she did tell me that she won't drive me anywhere until I apologize," she admitted in a hurt voice. She missed their talks and the closeness they shared.

"Deep. So when are you gonna say the words?"

Stacie crossed her arms over her chest. "How do you know it's my fault?"

Jackson reached over and uncrossed her arms. "Don't hide your breasts from me," he drawled. "Baby, I'm still getting to know you, but I know the princess caused it. So be a woman and say the words."

"I will. I just want to make sure she's ready to receive it when I give it to her. I said some mean things to her."

"I believe it. You can cut a person down with that tongue of yours," Jackson said as he nosed the bus forward a couple yards.

"I'm scared . . . I don't want to get fired," Stacie moaned.

Traffic was still inching along when Jackson said, "Why are you worrying so much about getting fired? It's not like you're late every day," he joked.

Stacie smiled crookedly and shrugged, then looked worriedly out the window. Time evaporated whenever they were together. Work was the last thing on her mind when they saw each other. She never told Jackson she was in a precarious situation at work. "Well, I am kinda . . . sorta . . . on probation," she admitted.

"Oh," was all Jackson could think of to say. He didn't know how things worked in Corporate America. "Still, I don't think that they'll fire you," he reassured her.

"I don't know . . ." Stacie said doubtfully and Andre's face flashed before her. "People get thrown out on their asses every day."

"Trust me on this, okay? They won't fire you. The worst they'll do is write you up. And that paperwork will go into your file where it'll never be seen again. It'll be eaten by the big bad Corporate America Boogie Man," he joked in an effort to make her smile. She managed a weak one.

"Okay," Stacie halfheartedly agreed, then gave him a quick kiss. But Jackson's confidence and lame attempt at humor did little to alleviate her nervousness.

Thirty minutes later, Stacie jumped off the bus and ran to her office building. It had never looked so beautiful to her. She hopped off the elevator and ran down the corridor as fast as her sneakered feet could take her. She burst through the glass doors and stopped dead in her tracks. Misti was sitting at *her* desk, answering *her* phone and using *her* headset. Stacie's mouth dropped in amazement. Who gave her permission to use my phone? Nobody has the right to touch my equipment, much less sit in my chair.

Stacie couldn't take her eyes off Misti, who looked like she had been doing *her* job forever. The greeting was flawless, the transferring of a call went effortlessly and she didn't at all seem frazzled when the phone rang off the hook. A sudden movement made her shift her gaze to the left, where it landed on Andre Peppersong. He was sitting in a chair next to her desk. Stacie had the feeling that he wasn't sitting there to greet her with a big hug and kiss when she walked through the door.

He didn't smile nor did he say hi. He crooked his forefinger and said, "Come with me, *Miss* Jones." He turned on his heels and swished down the hall to his office with Stacie in tow. He pointed to a floral-printed armchair outside his office door. "Sit there," he demanded. "I'll let you know when to come in."

She heard him on the phone and five minutes later Thomas Kimble, one of the senior partners, was walking toward her. She knew immediately that she was in trouble. His usual kind face looked like it was cut from stone. He breezed past her, after acknowledging her with a short nod and a terse greeting. He stepped into Andre's office and quickly closed the door behind him. Stacie nervously played with her hair as she mentally calculated her bills and her head reeled at the amount. She needed this job, desperately. For the second time in an hour she glanced longingly down at her sneakers. Just one whiff . . . She was debating whether to slip one off and take a sniff when Andre poked his head out and motioned for her to come in. She slid into the same chair she'd sat in the last time she was in Andre's office.

Tom cleared his throat as he opened up the red file folder with Stacie's name written on it. "Stacie, Andre has given me some disturbing news. I know that he's spoken with you already. Let me first start off by saying that you've done an excellent job.

You've handled the front desk like no other. I don't know how you did it," he rambled on, and Stacie couldn't help but notice he kept referring to her in the past tense. "You're such a nice person and I enjoyed our working relationship. That's why this is so hard for me to do." He gulped, something that Stacie'd never seen him do and her chest tightened with fear; she knew what he was going to say next. "We're going to have to terminate your employment," Tom finished.

Even though she knew what he was going to say, the words didn't register at first. But as soon as they sunk in, she felt lightheaded and the blood roared in her ears. I'm fired. I've been fucking fired!

"We need somebody who's going to be on time," he hurriedly explained. "And not only that, but they must be reliable and dependable. And," he nodded to Andre, who was trying very hard to look sad, but was failing miserably, "according to Andre, you're not. You're not getting here on time, and this morning is a prime example. And he also noted that on several occasions your lunch breaks exceeded the allotted hour." He shook his head as he studied the form. Pulling his eyes away, he looked into Stacie's eyes and she didn't like what she saw: disappointment, arrogance and indifference. "Your conduct is unacceptable."

"It wasn't my fault," she argued. "There was a big traffic jam. The tractor trailer that flipped over on I-75? I'm sure you heard about it. Traffic was jammed up everywhere."

Tom continued talking as if Stacie hadn't spoken a word. "We like you, Stacie. But that front desk position is a very integral part of our business. That person is the first contact ninety percent of our clients have with the company. And if that chair is left empty or the phones are unmanned, it doesn't bode well for the firm."

"*Please*, can't I stay? I can't lose my job. I like it here! My car will be ready soon. Then I'll be driving again. Until then I can have Tameeka bring me to work. She won't mind, she's my best friend." She knew she was babbling, but she didn't know what else to do. Her face was flushed and a sheen of perspiration covered her face. Stacie was ashamed of herself for allowing them to see her this way. For allowing herself to beg.

Mr. Kimble shook his head. "If we break the policy for one, then we'd have to do it for others. After all, *we are a law firm.*"

"I've been with this company for eight years. Y'all know my work. I've always been here and on time, except for recently, when I started having car trouble," Stacie choked out. The tears were falling now and had melted her mascara and two streaks ran down either side of her face.

Tom gave Andre an uncomfortable glance. He didn't enjoy doing this to Stacie, she was the best receptionist the firm had ever had. Eight years ago he had hired her, which made it even more painful for him to do what he had to do. But if Andre reported to him that she wasn't doing her job, well, she had to be taken care of. He tuned out her pleading as he gazed out of the window at Atlanta's skyline. He was relieved when there was a knock on the door. Andre popped out of his chair and hurried to open it. Misti stood there holding a box, which she diligently passed over to Andre. Andre closed the door and placed the box next to Stacie's chair.

"Here are your things," was all he said, before slipping back into his chair. Stacie numbly glanced down at the box through swollen eyes and they widened slightly when she recognized that it was filled with her personal belongings. Her eight years with the firm were thrown inside a box. She grabbed the box and bit back a fresh round of tears as she made her way to the door. There wasn't anything left to be said. "Stop!" Andre called, and Stacie froze in place. "Contact Human Resources about retrieving your last paycheck and information on your health insurance. Now, I need to call Security to escort you out." Andre reached for the phone and that's when it hit Stacie.

"You know what, Andre? I don't need Security to escort my black ass out. I know my way. Hell, I've been walking in and out of this office for the last eight years!" she yelled, and it felt good. She swiped at her eyes, smearing her mascara even more. "And you, Mr. Kimble, firing me? Come down here with your holier-than-thou attitude. All righteous and shit. Your ass wasn't fired when you were arrested for beating up on your wife." She gave a wicked laugh at his shocked expression. "Huh, think I didn't know about that, did you? Well, half the fucking office knows. But of course, this is a *law firm,*" she snickered. Then she rounded on Andre, who had scooted into the corner. His eyes widened when Stacie turned toward him. "I don't know what the hell I did to you to make you hate me so much. But I hope you rot in hell. You're an evil, dickless man," she spat, then turned on her heels and stalked out of the office and out of the building.

28

Single Father's Guide to Dating
Tip # 1

Your first priority in life is protecting your child.

It was nine o'clock in the morning, a time when most people were just jumping into their day not knowing whether they were going to get popped by one of life's fastballs or hit a home run. Jackson was up to bat, but he didn't know whether he'd hit it out of the ballpark or get beaned.

Jackson glanced furtively around the courtroom as he clasped his hands in front of him to keep them from shaking. He wasn't having much luck.

How Michelle's threat escalated to this point so fast, he didn't know. He smiled grimly, then cut his eyes at his lawyer, Bryant Duvall. A smooth-faced young man, he looked like he had just passed the bar that morning. His Sears suit and Kmart shoes looked like he picked them up on the way to court. Occasionally he'd shuffle his papers, scribble notes, and clear his throat in an official-type way, but he didn't say much. Standing next to Jackson, he looked more like his little brother playing dress up than the person who was fighting for his lifeline.

Jackson glanced down at his suit and prayed that it made him look like a responsible black man. He'd spent three hours last night agonizing over what to wear and finally decided on a charcoal gray suit, striped tie and white shirt.

The letter ordering him to court was lying on the table in front of him like a billboard, advertising to everyone that a crackhead was out to steal Jameel.

Jackson glared at Michelle and clenched his hands into fists. It took all the restraint he had not to wrap his hands around her pencil-thin neck and choke some sense into her. Oblivious to his thoughts, Michelle was staring reverently at the judge as if he were God.

This has got to be the biggest fucking sham in the world, Jackson thought, shaking his head, then turning to get a good look at Michelle. She was aiming for the conservative look and she hit a bull's-eye. Someone had transformed her into a preacher's wife. Her hair was slicked back into a neat ponytail, and the navy blue dress she had on resembled a potato sack with two slits for arms. The only sign of makeup she wore was lip gloss. The corners of her mouth were turned up in a little smile and her face was void of any frowns or worry lines.

Jackson turned his head toward her mother. Sitting directly behind Michelle, Mrs. Jacobs's face was twisted in a pained expression as though she wanted to be somewhere else. Jackson eyeballed her, willing her to look in his direction. If there was anyone who could stop Michelle, she could. She caught his stare, then quickly dropped her head. What the fuck? Jackson's brow furrowed in puzzlement.

His gaze shifted to the attorney sitting next to Michelle and a chill settled over him. Over six feet tall and with shoulders as wide as a doorway, she looked like a defensive back for the Atlanta Falcons. Tousled blonde hair swept over her shoulders and down her back and when she talked, which was often, it whipped wildly around her face. With big, mannish hands and feet, she looked like the type of lady who'd crush a man's balls. Jackson shuddered as Michelle's attorney addressed the judge.

"Your Honor, Miss Jacobs has been clean for six months, she has a full-time job paying ten dollars an hour and she just signed up for classes at a community college." As she clicked off Michelle's accomplishments, the shaking in Jackson's hands increased and he nearly burst when the Nut Crusher announced, "And she's ready to be a mother to *her* son." She nodded, then plopped down in her seat. Jackson could've sworn that she smirked in his direction before she turned and whispered in Michelle's ear.

Bryant Duvall stood up and cleared his throat for the thousandth time. He hated Judge Lewis—he was from the old school, the very old school. He believed that, no matter what the circumstances were, the child should always go to the mother.

"Your Honor, sir," Bryant began, his tone respectful yet firm. Jackson shot him a look of amazement. He has balls. But can they survive the Nut Crusher? "Eight years ago, Miss Jacobs walked out and left her *newborn* son with Mr. Brown. For the past eight years, Mr. Brown has been single-handedly raising Jameel. Sir, he has steady employment, he's been a bus driver for the City of Atlanta for the past six years. He owns the house that he and his grandmother live in. Jameel has grown up in a loving, well-adjusted home with people who love him to death. It would be a crime to take him away from that," Bryant finished.

"Your Honor, sir," the Nut Crusher said, standing up and gnashing her teeth together. "Miss Jacobs has a two-bedroom apartment—"

Bryant interrupted smoothly, "Yes she does. And she shares it with a man to whom she isn't married."

"Yes," the Nut Crusher hissed between clenched teeth. "But

they're engaged to be married." Then, as if on cue, Michelle lifted her ring finger and waved prettily, showing off an engagement ring that looked like it came from a bubble gum machine. "Next month, as a matter of fact," she sniffed.

"So she's marrying a known drug dealer?" Bryant quipped, then calmly reached for his water glass and took a sip. Jackson shot him a look of admiration.

"Objection! That's hearsay! There's no proof that he's a drug dealer," the Nut Crusher spat.

"Cool it. I will not tolerate any outbursts in my courtroom," Judge Lewis barked. He didn't bother to look up from his pad of paper, where he was furiously scribbling notes.

Bryant attempted to hide a smirk, but failed miserably. "Your Honor, all I'm saying is that Jameel will be in an unhealthy and potentially dangerous environment. And no eight-year-old should be put in that situation." He finished and Jackson wanted to high-five him. He was sure to get full custody of Jameel now. As though a huge weight had been lifted, Jackson happily slumped in the chair.

"Not any more dangerous than where he's living now," the Nut Crusher shot back. "Mr. Brown's neighborhood has one of the highest crime rates in Fulton County. It's all right here," she said, and threw down a three-inch-thick binder on the table. Then she turned to Bryant. "You're more than welcome to review it," she snickered.

Bryant glanced down at his notes and Jackson saw the lightbulb go off in his eyes. "Your Honor, Mr. Brown coaches Jameel's football, softball *and* soccer teams. He volunteers at his son's school and he's never missed a parent-teacher conference. He's a very devoted father," he added.

"Your Honor," the Nut Crusher jumped in, "Miss Jacobs just completed a twelve-week certificate program on parenting skills," she said smugly, and Jackson snorted. He couldn't help himself. *How can a twelve-week class teach you to be a good parent? This is bullshit!* Bryant voiced Jackson's thoughts.

"A twelve-week course? Your Honor . . . come on. This man has been taking care of his son for *eight* years. Rocking him to sleep, wiping his snotty nose when he was sick and drying his tears when he was sad. And he did it *all by himself.*"

"Your Honor—"

"Enough!" Judge Lewis growled before he stepped off the bench and swept off to his chambers to make his decision.

Jackson slapped on a smile before turning around to Ettie Mae and Stacie. Two pairs of terror-filled eyes met his. They were sitting as still as statues.

"Hey, come on you two, smile," Jackson cajoled. "We're not gonna lose. Jam is going to be with us, forever." He jutted his chin in Michelle's direction. "She's not getting him." But Ettie Mae couldn't muster a smile; her heart was telling her that her grandson was going to get hurt today. When she bowed her head and began to pray, Jackson and Stacie joined in. As soon as they uttered "amen," Judge Lewis came swishing through the door and they were ordered to stand. After both parties stood, he solemnly peered at them all over the top of his horn-rimmed glasses.

"I've reviewed the paperwork, and read over the history of both parties. I've had some hard cases, and this is a tough one." He pulled his glasses off and tiredly swiped his hand over his eyes. "I believe that a child should have its mother in its life," he announced, and Jackson pitched forward and clutched the table for support just as Ettie Mae groaned mournfully. Jackson watched the judge through terrified eyes.

"And Mr. Brown"—he nodded in Jackson's direction—"you have been doing a wonderful job with your son. But Miss Jacobs has not only shown that she's interested in being a part of her son's life, she has clearly demonstrated to me that she is sincere on her part. With that being said, I announce that Miss Michelle

Jacobs will receive supervised visits with said son, Jameel Brown. The said visitations are to commence within three weeks." Judge Lewis banged his gavel, then stepped off the bench.

"Court adjourned," the bailiff intoned.

Jackson stared at the empty bench in stunned silence. Bryant stood by, looking at everything except his client. He never knew what to do in these situations; they didn't go over it in law school. Instead of offering words of comfort, he picked up his papers and stuffed them into his briefcase.

Jackson turned to his grandmother and Stacie. "Grammy, how could he do it?" he pleaded. "How can that *white* man decide to give my son to a crackhead?"

"It'll be all right, baby," Ettie Mae, soothed as she stroked her grandson's arm. Stacie wrapped her arm around his waist.

"How the fuck can a *white* man tell me what to do with my son?" his voice escalated, his anger building. Jackson caught a slight movement out of the corner of his eye. Michelle, her mother and the Nut Crusher were huddled around their table.

The Nut Crusher gave Michelle a congratulatory hug before she hurried out of the courtroom to defend another young mother, leaving Michelle and her mother lost in their own hug.

Jackson took one look at them, and his face twisted with rage. They're celebrating because I lost Jameel, he thought. That bitch is gonna get my son. Like hell! Before anybody knew what was happening Jackson pulled away from Ettie Mae and Stacie, then charged toward Michelle and her mother. Ettie Mae reached out to grab him, but she wasn't fast enough.

The bailiff charged across the room and grabbed Jackson by the neck, stopping him before he could reach Michelle. Jackson struggled against him, but froze when he glanced over at Ettie Mae and saw the horrified expression on her face. He couldn't hurt her anymore than she'd already been hurt today. Instead Jackson yelled out, he couldn't help himself.

"This is your fault. If you hadn't brought your sorry ass back here, I would still have my son!" he screamed, his face dark with anger. Michelle smiled arrogantly.

"Justice prevailed here today, Jackson. I'll be by this Saturday at ten o'clock in the morning to see my baby," she announced, then sauntered out of the courtroom with her mother on her heels.

29

It's a Bad Thing to Shoot Yourself in the Foot . . . But to Laugh While Doing It Is Sadistic

Tameeka and Mohammad were sitting inside the store enjoying their morning coffee. Tameeka was sprawled out on the couch and Mohammad was sitting on the floor at her feet. Occasionally Tameeka found herself guiltily looking over her shoulder for Tyrell to come bursting through the door.

"I heard you guys the other night," Mohammad said slyly. "I think *everybody* heard y'all. Sounded like some heavy sexing was going on up in here."

Tameeka busted out laughing, not at all embarrassed. "Were we that loud? Damn! I paid good money to have this old house soundproofed. Damnit!"

"It's not soundproofed now and it wasn't back when we were using it," he said, studying her. "I still want you, Tameeka," Mohammad whispered. His voice lingered over her, caressing her body the same way his hands, tongue and eyes used to. Suddenly Tameeka wasn't sure what was causing the blood to rush to her face, Mohammad or the coffee.

"I can't . . . I have a boyfriend . . ." Tameeka stuttered, but she inched closer to Mohammad's mouth.

He glanced down at his watch and suddenly stood up. "Hey, thanks for the coffee," he said. "I need to run. A man from CNN is stopping by. They want me to decorate some of their offices. Same time tomorrow?"

Tameeka hid her face in her coffee mug and simply nodded as he strolled out of the store. A sigh escaped when she heard the door close. The room instantly cooled by ten degrees. *What are you doing, Tameeka Jaquisha Johnson? You love Tyrell, why would you fuck it all up by sleeping with Mo?* "Because Tyrell can't stop looking at sticks," she said out loud. Last night at dinner Tyrell couldn't take his eyes off the waitress. They fought about it. They fought in the restaurant, fought on the way to her apartment and fought inside the apartment. This morning, before she left for work, she tried to kiss him, but he had offered her his cheek instead. She was still thinking about Tyrell, when twenty minutes later she heard the door open.

"I'm back," Mohammad sang out as he sauntered over to the couch. He noticed that she hadn't moved since he'd left. "Did you miss me?" he joked, but his eyes were serious.

Tameeka rolled her eyes and ignored the question. "What happened to CNN?" she sked.

"Oh, I saw the guy," Mohammad called over his shoulder. He was making himself another cup of coffee. "He did a little talking. I talked back. He showed me what he wanted. I showed him what I could do. And *kaboom*—it was over." He grabbed his coffee cup and sat down on the couch next to Tameeka. Instead of drinking his coffee he was holding it with both hands and watching the steam float up into the air. "Hey, I want to apologize." Tameeka looked at him and he hurriedly explained. "For almost overstepping again . . . earlier this morning. I shouldn't've told you that I wanted you. That was wrong. I should respect your relationship."

"Oh, that's okay. I wasn't offended or anything," Tameeka answered nonchalantly, but her heart was beating so fast that she was afraid she was going to faint. "I've been doing some thinking," she said, then took a deep breath. "I want you too," she murmured as she leaned forward, and this time her lips touched Mohammad's. They brushed against his like a gentle promise.

He pulled back and gently appraised her. "Are you sure?" Tameeka nodded. "What about your boyfriend?"

Tameeka lowered her eyes and shrugged. "I don't want to talk about him," she mumbled, then placed her hand on his crotch and felt his dick grow. "Let's do this . . . we don't have much time before customers start coming in."

"So you're giving me time restrictions now? I want to take my time and enjoy every inch of you," he drawled as he leaned forward and gently nibbled on her lips until Tameeka was softly panting for breath.

Tameeka slipped her hands under his shirt and ran her fingernails gently over his back until he shivered. "That's right, baby, I didn't forget," she murmured as she pulled his shirt over his head and tossed it on the floor. He was exactly how she remembered him. Where Tyrell was cuddly and huggable, Mohammad was hard and sinewy. "I didn't forget a thing." Leaning over, she swiped her tongue up and down his chest, over his muscled pecs, and licked his ginger-colored nipples until they were hard. A sigh of happiness escaped her mouth as she moved down to his stomach, giving his six-pack extra attention.

Pulling her up so that they were at eye level, Mohammad hungrily seized her lips as he eagerly undressed her before slipping out of his pants and boxers. Wrapping an arm around her neck, Mohammad eased Tameeka onto her back, then gazed into her eyes.

"I can stop whenever you want," Mohammad said. In response, Tameeka placed her hands on either side of his face and pulled him closer until their lips met. Her tongue slipped past his lips and gently probed his mouth until she had him groping for more.

Mohammad's hand snaked down between her legs and tenderly stroked her button. She lifted her hips toward him and began moving at a slow tempo, matching his movements until her body began convulsing and she was gasping for breath. A smile of satisfaction was on her face as she reclined on the couch and pulled Mohammad on top of her.

"Oh, Mo, put it in," she moaned as she arched her back and spread her legs.

"Whatever you want," Mohammad answered as he lovingly stroked her stomach, causing Tameeka to purr deep in her throat.

She glanced at Mohammad while he quickly put on a condom and suddenly pictures of Tyrell flashed in her head. She stared wild-eyed around her store. What the hell am I doing?

Just when she opened her mouth to tell Mohammad that she had changed her mind, he plunged into her and all images of Tyrell vanished.

"Meek, you feel so good," Mohammad grunted as he swiveled his pelvis. "You're so wet. Am I making you wet?" he asked as he looked down at her face. She looked so beautiful lying underneath him. A light sheen covered her face, giving her a sexy glow as her body undulated with his.

"You're making me very wet and hot," Tameeka groaned. "Do me like you used to, baby," she begged, wrapping her legs around his waist, pulling him deeper into her. "Make me scream."

Mohammad grinned wickedly and granted Tameeka her wish.

The smell of sex hung heavily in the air, the scents from her candles weren't strong enough to extinguish it. Tameeka dressed and picked up her coffee: it was ice cold, but she sipped it anyway as she glanced nervously around the store. I cheated on Tyrell!

"You okay?" Mohammad cut his eyes at her as he hiked up his khakis.

"I'm cool," she answered, not looking at him. She needed Stacie, she'd know how to fix things. But ever since their argument they'd been tipping around each other like two mothers-in-law living under the same roof.

"Meek," he called softly, and Tameeka looked in his direction, "This is between us. I hope you don't do something stupid like get a conscience and tell Tyrell," he said more for his own benefit than for Tameeka's. Even though he worked out at the gym, Tyrell could still break him in half if he wanted to.

Tameeka shook her head. She had a distant look in her eyes. "I wouldn't do that to him," she said, and shook her head again as if she was sealing a deal with herself. "No, I'm not going to tell him. What good would it serve?" she asked, not really expecting an answer.

"Now that we got that out of the way, what just happened?"

"You know what happened," Tameeka answered, rolling her eyes. "Weren't you there?"

"I know what happened," Mohammad said. "But did you feel it between us, Meek? I mean, really feel it? It was good! We were good! Just like we used to be. I think we should get back together."

"Because of sex?" Tameeka asked, incredulous that he would suggest something like that. "That's not a good reason to get back together."

"It's not just the sex, it's more. We vibe on so many different levels. You know I'm right," Mohammad said.

Tameeka waved him off. "You might be right, Mo. But I'm

with Tyrell—" Mohammad snorted his disbelief. "And I really love him. This was a huge mistake. We both have to be adults and not let it happen again," she finished.

Mohammad studied her through narrowed eyes. "This wasn't a mistake. And you know what?" he asked, and Tameeka simply rolled her eyes again. "We're gonna end up together," he promised with a knowing smile.

Tameeka vigorously shook her head.

"Oh, yes we are. Get used to it," Mohammad said, and kissed her quickly on the lips before he strolled out the door.

"Oh, Tyrell, I do love you, don't I?" Tameeka asked mournfully.

30

Ways for Me to Save Money

1. Move back home
2. Sell some jewelry
3. Sell some clothes
4. Sell some shoes
5. Sell Lexie??? (Last resort)

It took Stacie three weeks to get over the shock and anger of getting fired. Three weeks of sitting in front of the TV munching bag after bag of Doritos while watching daytime talk shows. Three weeks of crying jags that left her eyes looking like ripe cherries and her throat feeling like she had swallowed fire. Three weeks of analyzing how she could've handled the situation better. Three weeks of sniffing every pair of shoes in her closet. Once the anger simmered, it grew into something she would have never thought possible—relief, which mushroomed into freedom.

The freedom didn't last long. After applying for unemployment and seeing the paltry amount she'd receive, she immediately went out and registered with over a dozen temporary agencies. The assignments trickled in, in little spurts, but nothing consistent or permanent.

Stacie pushed herself off the couch and clicked off the TV

just as Judge Judy started shouting at one of the defendants. The banging of pots and pans beckoned her to the kitchen. Stacie hung onto the door and watched Tameeka. She moved around the kitchen so fast that she looked like she was walking on air.

"This is crazy," Stacie muttered as she walked into the kitchen. "We're gonna talk." Since their argument, she and Tameeka had been as cool to each other as a pastor's wife and her husband's mistress. "Hey, girl. I'm so sorry for treating you the way I did. I know you're not jealous of me. That was my ego talking."

Tameeka gave a sigh of relief. She had been waiting for Stacie's apology. The pots Tameeka held in her hands clanked to the floor. She rushed toward Stacie with outstretched arms. "And I'm sorry for tearing up your list. I know how much it meant to you." Tameeka's arms dropped to her side. "Sit down, girl, the fried chicken is almost done."

"I know. That's why I apologized," Stacie joked. No one, not even the Colonel, fried chicken better than Tameeka.

Twenty minutes later, Stacie was slowly chewing on her piece of fried chicken, savoring it like it was her last meal. She dipped her fork in the mashed potatoes and stuck a mound of them into her mouth. She groaned in ecstasy. She was going to miss Tameeka's cooking, but mostly she was going to miss their late-night talks. "I'ma have to move back home," Stacie said out of the blue, and she immediately felt bad when Tameeka's jaw dropped in amazement. Actually she had been thinking about moving back home ever since she'd gotten fired. It made much more sense economically to move back in with her mother.

"No! We've just started talking again," Tameeka protested as soon as she found her voice. If Stacie moved out, it marked the end of an era. Tameeka jumped up from the table and went to the stove, where she loaded her plate with a third helping of mashed potatoes, asparagus and two more pieces of chicken. She eyed her plate. Well, I'll start the bean diet tomorrow, she decided, then added another piece of chicken. She plopped back down in her chair, then said, "Your butt is going to stay right here until you find another job," she demanded, then tacked on, with admiration, "which I know you will. You got skills, girl."

Stacie laughed and shook her head. "I wasn't anything but a glorified switchboard operator," she said, then giggled at Tameeka's look of astonishment. "Yep, that's all I was. I admit it. No more sugarcoating it. A glorified switchboard operator," she confirmed. "Not a secretary, not an administrative assistant, but a freakin' switchboard operator. I'm okay with it." She smiled to herself, then said, "I need to go."

Tameeka eyes glistened. "I'm really gonna miss you, girl. We've been together for like, forever," she said as the tears began falling. "Oh, I don't want you to go," she said, then jumped up and hurried over to hug Stacie.

"*Humph,* I don't *really* want to go either. But it's for the best. I'm a grown-ass woman who needs to handle her business."

"Yeah, and you look like you can handle anything with that damn chicken bone dangling from your mouth. Cavewoman," Tameeka joked. Then she turned serious. "If it's just about money, you know you can stay here until you get a real job," Tameeka offered.

Stacie smiled wryly as she shook her head. "Then that would prove your point, wouldn't it?"

"What point?"

"That my sister and I are alike."

Tameeka burst out laughing. "Hey, you don't have to open your legs for me. You know I don't swing that way."

"Me either, but seriously I appreciate the offer. I truly do," Stacie said. "But no thanks. I want to be with Nevia and Mom. And I have some other things to work out," she confessed, and Tameeka's heart hurt for her friend.

Over the years Stacie had confided in her about her father,

not a lot, but enough to know that he wasn't the nicest man. "You wanna talk about it?" Tameeka asked.

"Not yet, I still need to work through some stuff on my own before I talk to anyone. And when I do, you're going to be the first to know. I promise," Stacie said.

"I'm here for you," Tameeka said, then took a bite of her chicken. It had gotten a little cool. She picked up her plate, then stuck it in the microwave. "You want me to do yours?" she asked, reaching for Stacie's plate.

"Please do." Stacie laughed.

"What about Jackson?" Tameeka asked as she placed Stacie's steaming plate in front of her. "Have you thought about moving in with him?"

Stacie shrugged. "He lives with his grandmother, whom I absolutely love. But I don't want him taking care of me. I want to bring something to the table . . . other than my good looks," she joked. "I know this might be too soon, but I think I might be falling in love with him," she admitted.

"Miss Stacie falling in love, is it a full moon?" Tameeka laughed, and to her amusement Stacie blushed. "Oh girl, you got it bad."

"I know." Stacie grinned. "I really like Jackson. He sexes me—I mean makes crazy love to me like no man has before. Meek, he listens to me, he *really* listens, and he cares about what makes me happy. I see a future with him, something that I really didn't see with the other guys I dated."

"So how does he stack up against your list?" Tameeka asked; she just couldn't resist.

"Oh hush." Stacie laughed, sticking her tongue out. "You were right . . . I was wrong," Stacie said. "I am really, really, really really gonna miss you. You were da bomb roommate— friend," she gushed, then smiled crookedly at Tameeka.

Tameeka broke out in a laugh. "I'ma miss you too. But—this will be the last on the subject. There's always a job at the store if you want it. I'm done with that subject." She sealed her lips, then pretended to zip them shut.

The room was silent as they enjoyed their food.

"So when are you leaving?" Tameeka asked, and Stacie grinned sheepishly. "Stacie?"

Stacie ducked her head, then said, "The end of the month."

"Oh no, that's too soon!" Tameeka protested.

"I know. I decided sooner is better than later. And don't you go and tell me that you need a month's notice because you can't afford the rent without me . . . that's bull. You can probably afford to buy the whole building," Stacie said. "I don't know why you don't buy a house. That'd give you and Tyrell more rooms to sex in," Stacie said, winking, then frowning when Tameeka teared up. "I was only playing."

"It's not that," Tameeka said. "I did something bad."

Stacie's eyes widened. "How bad?" she asked cautiously.

"Really, really bad. I did something that'd even shock you."

"Oh shit! Meek, tell me," Stacie begged, scared for her friend.

Tameeka breathed deeply, then spat it out. "I slept with Mo," she tearfully admitted.

"What? Your ex-fuck buddy? When? Why?"

"It happened a couple of weeks ago at the store. Neither one of us—well, I can honestly say that *I* didn't plan on it happening. I was mad at Tyrell."

Stacie rounded the table to her friend and wrapped her arms around her and gave her a tight hug. "That's not a good way to show it."

"I know . . . I'll die if Tyrell finds out. He's the best thing that ever happened to me."

Stacie pulled her chair next to Tameeka before sitting down. "If that's the case, why did you do it? Why risk messing up something so good?" Stacie asked, perplexed. "Enlighten me, girl."

"I think I like him," Tameeka whispered, bowing her head.

"Of course you like Tyrell, silly, that's why you're scared. But why did you play the booty game with Mo?"

Tameeka slowly lifted her head and looked at Stacie with anguished-filled eyes. "It's Mo, Stace. I think I like *Mo*. I think I want to be with him instead of Tyrell. What am I gonna do?" she wailed.

31

Single Father's Guide to Dating
Tip #33

Family and friends are like tight ends, use them to run
interference when necessary.

It was Saturday morning and Jackson was mowing his lawn. He
had already finished the front and now he was tackling the
back. Thanks to Jackson, he and his grandmother had the best-
looking yard on the block. A rainbow of roses, chrysanthe-
mums, and geraniums colored the front. A vegetable garden
filled with tomatoes, cucumbers, lettuce and green peppers
graced the back. The yard was Ettie Mae's pride and joy.

It was only nine o'clock in the morning, but it was already
eighty degrees and sweat poured off Jackson's shirtless body.
The soft whooshing of the lawn mower blades provided him
with the perfect backdrop for working out his problems.

Michelle was coming today and he hadn't even told Jameel
yet. *Why do I have to fuck up his life? Why can't he . . . why
can't we keep things the way they are?* Jackson balled his hand
into a fist, he wanted—no needed—something to punch.
Instead he dragged the mower to the tool shed and set it
between a sickle and hoe.

He went into the house and took a quick shower, then went into the kitchen where Ettie Mae was at the table husking corn. Wisps of corn silk swirled around her feet like a mess of garden snakes.

"You're not cooking for her, are you?" he asked, stubbornly jutting his chin out. In addition to the corn, there was chicken frying on the stove, a pot of greens simmering and he could smell candied yams in the oven.

Ettie Mae bit back a smile; he only did the thing with his chin when he was worried and didn't want her to know. But she knew, she always knew. "Naw, baby, since when did you know me to cook for a fool? This is for my men. Gotta keep you strong. Never know when the devil's gonna come at you." They were both silent and Ettie Mae focused on cleaning the corn.

"Have you spoken with him yet?" Ettie Mae asked gently.

Jackson shook his head and meandered over to the refrigerator, more to get out of Ettie Mae's line of vision than anything else, as he didn't have an appetite.

"Don't you think you should? After all, she is that boy's mother. Regardless of what you feel about her. He has a right to know," she said, wisdom ringing in every word.

Jackson knew she was right, but still . . . "Grammy," he started, reverting to his childhood name for her. "Something in my heart doesn't sit right about her. It's telling me to run and hide."

"I know, baby," she replied. "Something in my heart isn't feeling right about her either. And I've been praying for God to tell me what to do . . . I think I wore a hole in the rug." She chuckled softly, then set down a half-husked ear of corn. "She might not have always made the best decisions, but she's here and we need to deal with it. And Jam deserves the right to know his mother," she added.

"But she's a crackhead *and* a prostitute! I don't want *that* around Jameel. Besides she had her chance, but she abandoned him."

"Yep, she did that. But who did she leave him with? You. The girl ain't *that* dumb. Don't you think Jameel deserves a chance to at least know who his mother is?"

"Yes, ma'am," Jackson replied, giving the expected response, but his heart was telling him to snatch up Jameel and head west. He slowly pushed himself out of the chair; his legs were like Jell-O as he walked to the back door and called his son. "Yo! Jam, I need to talk to you."

"Okay, Daddy, I'll be right there," he called, but he didn't make a move to come into the house. Jackson glanced down at his wristwatch. Twenty-five minutes to go.

"Jameel. Bring your butt in here *now!*" he demanded. Jameel immediately dropped his toy car and raced across the yard to his father. Jackson felt bad for using that tone; it wasn't Jameel's fault. As soon as Jameel came in, Jackson drew him into his arms and gave him a big hug. He sat him down at the kitchen table.

"We're having a visitor today . . . she's a friend of mine," Jackson said, tripping over his words. "You know, friends like you and Leila," Jackson hurriedly explained. "And she's going to spend a lot of time with you," Jackson finished and smiled weakly.

Wide eyed, Jameel absorbed the information. When his eight-year-old brain sucked up as much as it could, he asked, "Can I go over her house like I go over Leila's?" He liked visiting Leila's house, her grandmother let him eat all the chocolate chip cookies he wanted.

"No, you're never, ever going to her house!" Jackson roared, and Jameel shrank back in his chair.

Ettie Mae silently watched the scene as she husked the corn. Jackson was Jameel's father and she honored that. She rarely intervened, unless it was necessary, and it wasn't necessary . . . yet.

"You two are never to leave this house by yourselves, do you hear me?" Jackson demanded. Jameel's bottom lip began quivering and Jackson felt like kicking himself. This wasn't going the way he wanted it to. "I'm sorry," Jackson soothed. He bent down and pulled his son in his arms. Good going, he thought. Scare your son right into her arms. "I just don't want anything to happen to you, Jam," he said, then tickled Jameel in his ribs until he howled with laughter.

The doorbell rang; Jackson froze. She's early.

32

Warning! Your Past Is Like a File on Your Hard Drive—It Can Be Recovered

Tameeka glanced over at Tyrell, and her lips turned up into a wide smile; she wanted to giggle, but she didn't dare embarrass him. They were in Taste of Heaven, sitting on one of the couches. The store had long since closed and they had the place to themselves. Tameeka had lit dozens of candles and a Luther Vandross CD played softly in the background. This is heavenly . . . total bliss . . . eat your heart out, skinny ladies, she crowed silently. She was stretched out on the couch with her feet in Tyrell's lap. Her eyes returned to Tyrell's profile, and this time she did giggle, she couldn't help it. Tyrell glanced up and his eyes met hers and he winked playfully at her, then went back to his activity.

Tyrell swiped the bright orange nail polish over Tameeka's toenail, then leaned back and admired his handiwork. His full lips turned up into a smile; he had to admit it, he was getting better. The first two toes looked like a two-year-old had done them, but the last three he'd just finished were the shit!

If someone would've told him that one day he'd be spending a Sunday afternoon painting a lady's toenails, he would've punched them out.

"Hey babe, you rocking this color. Whaddya think?" he asked, giving her a look that begged for her to like the job he'd done.

Tameeka glanced down and wriggled her toes. She had to agree with him, the color looked good with her skin tone. "You know, you'll never live it down if any of your boys catch you doing this. Your new name will be Tyra," she joked, then sighed. It had been another perfect day. Tyrell had cooked her breakfast and served it to her in bed. Then he came to work with her and they worked side-by-side together. He had given her a foot rub and now he was polishing her toenails. Best of all, not once did he leer at a skinny lady. I can definitely get used to this. My life is perfect. She playfully rubbed her foot against his crotch.

"Hey, behave yourself," he scolded. His brows were furrowed as he concentrated on polishing her nails. "If you keep it up, you're not gonna get your other foot done," he said, and Tameeka chuckled nastily.

Tameeka's cell phone rang, and she automatically reached out for it, but froze midair at Tyrell's warning look. "It might be my grandmother."

Tyrell shook his head. "Your grandmother rarely calls you." In all the time they'd been dating, she had only called Tameeka twice. "And if she does call, it's on your home phone. Ignore it, baby, let's just enjoy our time together."

"You're right." Tameeka grinned, then settled back on the couch. Suddenly the side door swung open. Startled, Tameeka and Tyrell looked up to see Mohammad strutting through the door. He was halfway across the store before he saw them on the couch; he skidded to a stop.

"Hey!" all three said at the same time.

Mohammad quickly took in the scene and apologized. "I

didn't know you were still here. I needed some lip balm. If that's okay with you," he said to Tameeka.

"Sure, take whatever you need," Tameeka offered, and Mohammad snatched up his balm and hurried out of the store.

"I thought you took the key from him," Tyrell asked, as he suspiciously eyed Tameeka.

"I did," Tameeka stammered, burning under his gaze. "But I guess he had a second copy that I didn't know about."

"This needs to stop; dude's treating your store like it's his personal Wal-Mart," Tyrell fumed as he pushed himself up. "He needs to give up that key."

"Wait!" A startled Tameeka pushed Tyrell back against the couch. "No! Don't do that. I'll get it from him tomorrow."

"Why are you so scared?" Tyrell asked. "Afraid I'll kick his ass?"

Tameeka gave a nervous laugh. "You know how much I hate violence. I can't even watch boxing. Let it go. I'll get it tomorrow. Okay?"

"He acts too damn comfortable in the store. I don't like it," Tyrell grumbled.

Tameeka sighed. "I'll talk to him tomorrow. I promise," she said, then leaned over and tenderly kissed him. "Are you gonna finish my nails?" she asked, wiggling her toes at him.

"You'd better handle your business tomorrow. If not, I'll do it for you. Now give me your foot." He grabbed her foot and began polishing her toenails.

"*Mmm,* baby, what will this *do* to me?" she whispered seductively, and leaned over and ran her hand over his crotch. He was focusing so hard on her nails that he didn't realize where her hand was and what it was doing. It wasn't until she slipped her hand past his elastic waistband and into his boxer shorts that he took notice. "Ah, I think it's up," she said softly, and tenderly began stroking him.

"Come on now, I'm almost done," Tyrell complained.

"You don't want me?" Tameeka asked, and poked her lips out in a pout.

"Girl, puh-leeze, I don't know how you can fix your mouth to say something like that. I want you morning, noon and night. But I wanna fix your nails. Don't you want to have pretty feet?" he asked. He was grateful for the distraction of painting her nails; otherwise he'd be cheesing at her all day. Never did he imagine that he'd find his soul mate, things like that happened only in the movies.

"I guess. But I'd rather have you," Tameeka answered sullenly, then she got an idea. She pulled her hand off Tyrell and began unbuttoning her top.

"Hey, what are you doing?" Tyrell asked. His eyes were narrowed suspiciously as he watched Tameeka open her blouse, exposing the tops of her soft breasts. She shrugged the blouse off and tossed it on the back of the couch. He felt the stirrings of a serious hard-on.

"Oh, nothing," Tameeka answered as if it was totally normal to be shirtless while her boyfriend painted her toenails. "I want to be comfortable. That's all."

"Oh, cool," Tyrell muttered, but he kept sneaking peeks up at Tameeka's chest. "So this isn't some type of ploy to get me to have sex with you?"

Tameeka shook her head. "Not at all. This is." She reached behind her back and unclasped her bra, unleashing her melon-size breasts, and Tyrell's mouth dropped open. "So is it working?" she asked unnecessarily—her hand was on his crotch and it felt like she was touching a brick.

Tyrell set the polish down and crawled on top of Tameeka. He leaned in to kiss her, but pulled away and looked down into her eyes. She was staring at him with an expectant look. "You know, if we do this, you're gonna mess up all my hard work," he said as his eyes roamed lovingly over her face.

"Nu-uh, not if we do it like this," Tameeka said, and gently nudged Tyrell off her, then took off the rest of her clothes and Tyrell did the same. Then Tameeka got into position. "See, if I do this, nothing will get mussed."

Tyrell slipped on a condom, then gripped her hips. A soft groan escaped his lips as he entered her softness.

"Tyrell," Tameeka panted as she arched her back and pressed her behind against him. "Oh baby, do it slow for me."

"You want it slow?" Tyrell asked, and Tameeka nodded. "Well, we both want things," he said. "I want you to tell Mohammad to stay the fuck out of your life."

33

Why There Should Be a Law Against Baby Momma and Daddy Drama

1. Innocent bystanders get hurt
2. Children's well-being gets lost in the anger
3. Anger causes some parents to do some stupid things

Hey, baby. How're you doing?" Stacie said into the phone. She knew that today was Michelle's visitation day.

"Okay," Jackson grumbled.

"How's Jam doing?" she prodded.

"He's okay, excited about meeting a new friend."

"So he doesn't know he's meeting his mother?"

Jackson let out a frustrated breath: Now she's questioning my decision. "Nope. I'll drop that bomb when he's ready for it. I think it'll be a little bit too much for him to handle now."

"I agree," Stacie said, surprising him. "What time do you want me over?" she asked.

"You don't have to be here," Jackson protested. "She's doing a drop-by. She'll probably be gone by the time you get here."

"That's okay . . . I just want to be with you and your family."

"That's cool," Jackson said, trying to fight the smile that threatened to spread over his face. "Well, get here when you can."

"I'll see you in a bit then," Stacie said before clicking off the phone. She sauntered into her bedroom and began thumbing through her closet. "Is it possible to fall in love so fast?" She pulled out an outfit and dressed. "I need to check on Nevia and the babies." She scooped up the phone and dialed Nevia. She picked up on the first ring. "Hey, girl, whatcha doing?"

"Nuthin'," Nevia mumbled.

"What's wrong," Stacie asked, concerned. Her sister didn't answer. Stacie took a calming breath. So she's in a shitty mood. "Did you do anything fun today?" Stacie inquired cheerfully.

"I'm gonna get my car back," Nevia grumbled.

Stacie sighed. Ever since Carlos had taken the car, all Nevia had talked about was getting it back. "Nev, let it drop. Carlos will kill you if you keep bothering him about that damn car. You can always get another one." Stacie glanced at the clock; she had five minutes to make it to the bus stop. She hurried out the door.

"I want that car. And I'm gonna get it," she said firmly. " 'Bye!"

"Nevia, wait!" Stacie yelled. All she got was a dial tone. "Oh crap," she groaned. "She's gonna get herself killed."

34

Single Father's Guide to Dating
Tip # 49

Your child's love is brighter than any star, don't do anything to dim it.

Jackson swung open the door, eyeing Michelle, the same way he would a pile of dog shit. Smirking, Michelle raised her head, squared her shoulders and strutted into the house. "I didn't realize there was going to be a welcoming committee," she said, eyeing Stacie. She remembered seeing her in court with Jackson, and she'd wondered who she was. Michelle's eyes dropped down to Stacie's ring finger; it was bare. She's not his fiancée, she concluded. Now she stood next to Jackson, looking like a wall of protection for Jameel. "Where's my son?" Michelle calmly asked.

"*My* son is in the backyard playing." As soon as the doorbell rang, Jackson had sent Jameel back outside. "I'll go get him." Jackson turned on his heel. While Jackson was gone, Stacie and Michelle studied each other like two Rottweilers in a pit. Jackson returned and then wrapped an arm around Stacie's waist. Stacie rested her head on his chest, grateful for his strength. After Nevia's call, she had called Pimp and asked him to keep an eye on her. Stacie knew Nevia would be okay: Pimp was better protection than the FBI.

Jackson's lips grazed the top of Stacie's head. Michelle saw the tenderness in Jackson's movements and her heart thudded with envy. Not because she wanted him, but because she remembered how deeply and thoroughly Jackson loved.

A few seconds later, Jameel raced into the room and stopped dead in his tracks when he saw Michelle. He wasn't sure what to do; he looked at her, then at his daddy for an answer. Seeing his confusion, Jackson leaned down and spoke softly.

"Jam, remember I told you we're having a guest today?" Jameel nodded solemnly; something about his father's voice made his tummy feel funny. "This is Miss Michelle," Jackson forced out. "Tell her hi," Jackson instructed and Jameel held out his hand for a handshake and shyly greeted her.

"Ooh, aren't you the little man," Michelle cooed.

"My daddy taught me that," he said, and smiled brightly. "He told me that whenever I meet somebody new I should shake their hand. And I do," he said proudly, then looked over at Jackson for his approval. His smile grew even broader when Jackson gave him the thumbs-up.

"Yeah, that's good," Michelle said without much enthusiasm. "So what do you like to do?"

Jameel thought hard, then he said, "You wanna swing? Me and Leila were playing, but she got tired and I was a little tired too, so I asked her if she wanted to play cowboys and she said no, she said that she didn't want to play cowboys because I cheat too much, so I told her okay and then I asked her if she wanted to color and she made a funny face and told me no, she didn't want to because I didn't have grape color and I told her that I had a bunch of other colors, but she said that she didn't want to color without grape, so I said okay, then I asked her if—"

"Okay!" Michelle shouted and Jameel clamped his mouth shut. Michelle wearily rubbed her temples.

"Jam, why don't you go wash up."

"I'll take you," Stacie offered, and she led Jameel off to the bathroom. As soon as his son was out of earshot, Jackson rounded on Michelle.

"What's wrong, Michelle? Tired of being a mommy?" he mocked. "Aw, poor baby, you were right eight years ago. You have no business raising a child."

Michelle let her hands drop to her side. "Obviously somebody thinks that I'll be good at it. Otherwise I wouldn't be here," she quipped.

"Well, the judicial system isn't always right," Jackson angrily snapped.

"When are you going to forgive me, Jackson? Huh? Don't you think I know what I did was wrong?" She moved closer to him. The top of her head barely reached his chest. "Every damn night I cried knowing that I gave away a piece of myself."

Jackson looked away.

"I'm a crackhead and a former prostitute who sold her pussy for money so that I could get high. That was wrong. I ain't trying to sugarcoat it. What I did was wrong. I know that," she said, her voice quivering; she took a deep breath to steady it, then said, "Why can't you forgive me? He did." She pointed to the ceiling.

Jackson let out a mirthless laugh. "So you found God now? And He's forgiven you? How do you know? Did He send you a sign?" Jackson taunted. "Or since you're so important, I bet He made a special trip just to tell you that He's forgiven you. That's bullshit, Michelle. You're still the same person. You haven't changed one bit," he spat at her.

"You're the one with the fucking bullshit!" Michelle screamed, her face wet with tears. Her first visit with her son wasn't going the way she had envisioned it. "Yes, I made a mistake. Why don't you give me a chance to prove that I'm sincere?" she pleaded. "Why?"

"What will it take for you to get the hell out of our lives? Do you want money? What about drugs?" He lowered his voice, then said, "I know a dude, Li'l Dog. He can hook you up, just let him know that J sent you."

"How much money are you talking? A hundred, two hundred?" Her eyes held a calculating glint that Jackson didn't miss and his heart started pounding with anticipation.

"Nu-uh, more than that. A couple thou," he said, as he calculated the balance of his savings account. He had over fifteen thousand saved up. He'd gladly give it all to her, just to get her out of their lives.

Michelle pushed down her laughter and she was almost successful until she saw Jackson's expression. It was the same one a hunter wears when his prey steps into the trap. Her laughter bubbled up and spilled out of her.

"What's so funny?" Jackson asked, looking perplexed.

"You are. You're so fucking funny. Acting like we on TV and shit." She shook her head. "So how is it supposed to work? Huh?" she asked. "Maybe something like this: You buy me off. I quietly fade out of your life, then you and Jameel live happily ever after. It ain't gonna happen! This ain't *The Young and the Restless* and you ain't no Victor. But maybe I *should* do it," she said thoughtfully. "Then when Jameel gets old enough I can show him how you tried to keep him away from his mother."

She's right. I don't want Jam blaming me for not letting him see his mother, no matter how fucked-up she is. "Whatever. Look," he said calmly. "I don't like your ass, and I don't trust your ass. But you are Jameel's mother, so—"

"You're my mommy?" Jameel asked, wonderment filling his voice. He wanted a mommy. Everybody on TV had one.

"Aw shit!" Jackson muttered.

Stacie hurried to Jackson's side. "I'm sorry," she apologized. "I shouldn't've brought him back so soon."

"It's not your fault," Jackson said.

Michelle ran over to Jameel and pulled him to her in a hug. "That's right, Jameel. I'm *your* mother and you're *my* son," she answered as she laughed between tears. She had been waiting eight years to say those words, and they felt sweet coming out of her mouth. "You're so handsome," Michelle cooed as her hands ran freely over his face. "Just like your father. And I bet you're smart in school," she said, then looked to Jackson. He was too stunned to confirm, he simply gazed at the pair.

Jameel was momentarily dazed by the news, but quickly adapted as Michelle told him about all the fun things they were going to do together.

"Can we go to the zoo? Or maybe the park. I like the park. Can we go to Six Flags? Daddy took me and Leila there last summer, but I ate too much and got sick. I puked up all over the place. I want to go to—"

"We can go wherever you want," Michelle promised. "Come on, show me your room." She grabbed her son by the hand and he led her to his bedroom.

"That's the devil," Ettie Mae muttered from the doorway. "Just as sure as I'm standing here today, that girl is evil."

Jackson sat down on the couch and dropped his head in his hands. When he lifted his head his eyes were glassy and his cheeks slick. "How do you beat the devil?" he asked in a hoarse voice.

"By living a Christ-like life. Just be patient. She'll fall and you'll be there to catch your son."

After Michelle left, Jackson pulled Jameel into his arms and squeezed him tightly. His son felt so little, so vulnerable.

"Daddy, what's wrong?" Jameel asked as he tried to squirm out of his father's arms.

"I just want you to stay with me forever," Jackson replied.

"I'm not going anywhere . . . I promise," Jameel said. "But I really like having a mommy. When am I gonna see her again?" he asked.

35

If You're Ever Lucky Enough to Receive a Piece of Heaven . . . Don't Blow It

Tameeka glanced down at Mohammad. He was sound asleep. He'd unexpectedly showed up at her door with a bottle of wine, and she'd been too surprised to turn him away. They drank his bottle of wine and raided her liquor stash, then inhaled two more bottles of wine. Tameeka told herself that she'd send him home when they were done. When he started kissing her and tugging at her clothes, then pulled her into her bedroom, she was feeling too good to tell him no.

She'd just started to drift off to sleep when her cell phone rang. "Hey, whassup?"

"Tyrell?" Tameeka squeaked.

"Yeah, it's me. You forgot what I sound like, baby?" he joked.

"Uh, no! I was doing some paperwork," she explained as she poked Mohammad in the ribs. He simply grunted and rolled over.

"Hard day?" he asked concerned.

"Long and hard," she answered as she slipped out of bed,

wrapped a sheet around her and walked into the living room. "I'm just so tired. I think I'll go to bed early tonight."

"Aw, baby. I wanted to know if you wanted to go to the movies tonight."

Tameeka gave a shaky laugh, then glanced toward her bedroom. "Oh, Tyrell, I can't. I'm worn out."

"Forget the movie then. I'll come over and give my baby a massage."

"Don't worry about me. I'll be okay."

"Too late. I'm right around the corner from your place. I'll be there in five."

"Tyrell!" she shouted into the phone, but he had already hung up. "Oh, shit!" She ran back into the bedroom. Hurrying to the bed, she shook Mohammad and he turned over on his side. "Mo! Wake up," she insisted, her voice shaky with panic. When he didn't move, she ran into the bathroom, filled a cup with water, rushed back into the bedroom and splashed it on his face. He woke up sputtering.

"What the hell did you do that for?" he demanded, knuckling his eyes. "If you wanted to wake me all—"

"You need to leave! Tyrell is on his way!" Tameeka shrieked as she ran around the bedroom, plucking up Mo's clothes and tossing them at him.

"What?" Mohammad asked, giving her a blurry look.

"My boyfriend is on his way over. Get dressed and get out!" she yelled, as she stuck her legs in a pair of jeans, then reached for a top. Underwear be damned. Mohammad had scooped up his clothes, went into the bathroom and closed the door. "What the hell are you doing in there?" Tameeka shouted, banging on the door.

"I have to use the bathroom," Mo called back.

"There's a freaking McDonald's down the street. You can stop there. Just hurry up," she pleaded as she paced in front of the bathroom door. She anxiously looked at the clock, then resumed pounding. Mohammad snatched the door open and stepped out, fully dressed. "Perfect. Now let's go." Tameeka grabbed his hand and dragged him through the apartment.

Mohammad froze, then patted his pants. "I can't leave," he announced.

"Do you want to get killed?" Tameeka asked.

"I need my car keys," Mohammad answered.

"Oh!" Tameeka shrieked as she pushed Mohammad toward the bedroom. "Go find them!" It felt like a lifetime had passed before Mohammad emerged from the bedroom dangling the keys.

"I found them."

"Okay. Now go." They hurried across the apartment to the front door. "I'll call you tomorrow," she promised, then opened the front door to Tyrell.

Neither of the trio said a word, then, "What the fuck is this?" Tyrell roared, and Tameeka winced.

"Nothing," Tameeka weakly offered.

"She's right . . . it's nothing, man. I brought her some receipts for some bills she wanted me to drop off," Mohammad drawled. "That's it."

Tyrell's gaze went from Tameeka to Mohammad. Tameeka looked like she was ready to shit bricks and Mohammad looked like he couldn't leave fast enough. "Bullshit! One of you better tell me what the fuck is really going on. Or it's gonna get really crunk up in here," he warned in a deadly voice.

"Go!" Tameeka instructed Mohammad, shoving him out the door. She knew that if she didn't get him out then, Tyrell wouldn't let him leave without any broken bones.

Mohammad shot Tameeka a concerned glance, then raced down the steps.

Tyrell silently followed Tameeka into the apartment and

slammed the door behind him. The smell of sex enveloped him. Tyrell reached out and grabbed Tameeka's arm, forcing her to face him.

"What the fuck is going on here?" Tyrell hissed.

Tameeka looked up at him, her eyes were glassy and her lips were quivering. "Nothing, baby. It's just like Mohammad said, he dropped off some receipts for me. That's all."

"Why couldn't he give them to you at the shop?"

"Because," Tameeka stuttered. "He knew that you didn't want me seeing him," she answered, then averted her eyes.

"So y'all thought that it'd be better for him to come to your house? That doesn't make sense. Come up with something better!"

"He was in the neighborhood. It wasn't like we planned this."

Tyrell's eyes narrowed. "Planned what?" he asked, leaning closer, and Tameeka whimpered. "Planned *what*, Tameeka? Answer me!" he yelled.

"It wasn't even like that," Tameeka sobbed. "Mo—" She stopped. Tyrell had glared at her as though she had called Mohammad "sweetheart." "I mean, Mohammad and I never planned for it to happen. It just happened," she said, and it sounded weak even to her ears.

"Just happened? Just happened! Oh, now you're gonna tell me that you two just tripped on one of your throw rugs and fell right on top of each other. Well, I tell you, his dick should get a fucking award for having such perfect aim." He glared at the woman he loved; the woman who had stolen his heart. "You never did tell me. How long have you two been fucking each other?"

Tameeka's face was slick with tears and her lips couldn't stop quivering. She shrugged helplessly. "I don't know . . . It's not important."

"The hell it's not important. How—long—has—this—been—going—on?" Tyrell asked, and every word hit her like a slap.

"A month or so," Tameeka squeaked.

"Did you fuck him first, then fuck me? Or maybe you fucked me first, then gave him sloppy seconds. Is that the way you did it?" Tameeka wordlessly shook her head. "Well, fuck you!" he spat. "'Bye, Tameeka."

He walked slowly to his truck. He stopped when he saw a familiar figure leaning against a car. It took him a moment to recognize him, but when he did, he charged. By the time Mohammad saw Tyrell coming toward him, it was too late. He instantly regretted his decision to hang around to see if Tameeka needed him. He jumped up and rounded the car; he had his hand on the door handle when Tyrell grabbed his collar and whirled him around.

"So you like fucking other men's women?" Tyrell hissed to Mohammad, who cowered under him like a baby. "Well, I guess pussies like pussies," Tyrell hissed before he drew his arm back.

Some of Tameeka's neighbors had opened their doors and stepped out, the less brave ones watched from their apartment windows.

"Don't do this, man. Let's talk about this. Man to man," Mohammad begged. Tyrell's fist was as big as a cannonball.

"So you're a man now? You weren't showing me any respect while you were screwing my lady," Tyrell spat.

"She told me that you guys were having problems," Mohammad whimpered, his legs shaking. "We didn't mean for anything to happen."

Tyrell chuckled nastily; he was tired of hearing that phrase. The punches came so fast that Mohammad didn't have time to brace himself. Moments later, Mohammad slid to the ground. Gasping for breath and his chest heaving, Tyrell stood over Mohammad's motionless body.

"Somebody call nine-one-one," a female voice shouted.

36

Why I'm So Blessed

1. I have a wonderful man
2. My family is awesome
3. I'm healthy

Stacie nervously stirred the pot of chili. She had gotten the recipe from Tameeka, who had promised her that it was so easy that "even a monkey could make it." Stacie brought the spoon to her mouth for a taste. "Ouch!"

"Hey, don't be burning those beautiful lips of yours," Jackson said, coming up behind her. "Let Big J kiss the boo boo away." Stacie turned around in his arms and their lips met. "Keep kissing me like that and I'm gonna have to do you right here on the kitchen floor."

"Yeah, and have your grandmother kill us? No way," Stacie said, beaming at him.

Jackson shook his head. "She likes you. She hardly let *me* use the kitchen. I can't wait to taste your food," Jackson said, peering into the pot.

Stacie gently tapped his shoulder. "Stop looking. It's a surprise." When Jackson had told her that he liked a woman who could cook, Stacie and Tameeka scoured recipes until they found an easy one. "Can you set the table for me, please?"

Jackson patted her behind. "Man, you know how to make a brother work," he teased, but went about putting the dinnerware on the table.

"This smells delicious, Stacie," Ettie Mae said, eyeing the pot of chili. "I haven't had chili in such a long time, spoon it in." Stacie eagerly began filling the bowls with the food and Jackson blessed it. Ettie Mae took a spoonful of the chili and her eyes immediately watered. She grabbed a glass of water and gulped it down.

Jackson and Jameel looked at each other. "I'm not touching that," Jameel said, pushing his bowl away.

"Oh, no!" Stacie cried, and raced to the kitchen for the recipe, returning with it in her hand. "I put in two Scotch bonnet peppers and it only called for one. I'm so sorry."

Jackson got up and wrapped his arms around her. "That's okay, baby," he said, comforting her. "Let's order a pizza." Jameel gave a shout of delight.

"It's okay, honey," Ettie Mae said, patting Stacie's back. "Nobody's perfect."

When Stacie was out of the dining room, Ettie Mae laughed. "That's a good girl you have there, but I'll need to give her some cooking lessons."

Jackson chuckled. "That's a plan." I'll need a wife who can cook, he thought. Oh crap, where did that come from?

It wasn't until after the last piece of pizza was gone and Ettie Mae and Jameel went to bed that Jackson and Stacie had some time to themselves. They were snuggled on the couch, talking.

"It's getting pretty close to that time, isn't it," Stacie quietly asked.

Jackson grimaced and nodded. "In about three weeks. I still can't believe the courts would authorize unsupervised visits to someone who hasn't seen their kid in years. I've said it before and I'll say it again, the court system is shitty."

"Amen. I don't see how a judge can make such a bad decision. You're the perfect father. And you did a banging job raising Jam," Stacie said.

"Thanks, baby." Jackson grinned. "How's the job hunting?"

"Crappy!"

"I can always help you out. All you have to do is ask," Jackson quietly offered.

Tameeka's words sounded in her head: *You're just like your sister.* She refused him. "You're so sweet, but the princess has to say no. Speaking of jobs, let me check my voicemail to see if any agency called me back."

She flashed him an apologetic smile as she fished her phone from her purse and quickly checked her messages. "Yippee! An agency called. They have an executive assistant position that might go permanent. I can't wait to see where it is," Stacie said, beaming.

37

To Know Oneself Is to Know Your Best Friend

Tameeka walked listlessly around the store. Bea had suggested that she go home, but Tameeka waved her off. A big order was due and she wanted to be there to unpack and shelve it.

"Why don't I do that," Bea offered, standing in front of the boxes when they'd finally arrived. "You go get something to eat."

"Thanks, but no thanks. I'm not hungry," Tameeka said, managing a weak smile.

Concerned, Bea scrutinized her boss. Tameeka looked like she hadn't slept in days. She had bags bigger than Oprah's bank account under her eyes. Bea couldn't help but notice that ever since Tameeka and Tyrell had broken up, she had stopped eating. "You need to eat," Bea insisted, and Tameeka sadly shook her head.

"I don't want to sound melodramatic, but I'm full on sadness," Tameeka said as she bent over the boxes to hide her swelling eyes.

Bea patted Tameeka's back. "Let me know if I can do anything," she offered, then walked off.

Tameeka opened up a box and began pulling out items. Two hours later she reached into the last box and pulled out a book. She read the title: *To Know Oneself Is to Know Your Best Friend: How to Live a Fulfilling Life.* "I don't remember ordering this," Tameeka muttered, then glanced up at the ceiling. "God, I know that I haven't been one of Your most consistent followers, but You know what's in my heart. Thank you very much for the gift."

It was seven o'clock when she finally tucked the book in her purse and headed home. As soon as she stepped into the apartment, she heard Barry White coming from Stacie's bedroom and she couldn't stop the grin that spread over her face. Barry White usually meant that Jackson had stopped by for a quickie. Sure enough, thirty minutes later a glowing Stacie bounced out of her bedroom and into the kitchen.

Tameeka was sitting at the kitchen table with a bowl of soup in front of her. Stacie spied an empty can on the counter top.

"Meek, girl. *Canned soup?*" Stacie said, arching an eyebrow.

"I'm not in the mood to cook," Tameeka muttered, then lowered her head over her bowl. Stacie sat down at the table and Tameeka shooed her away. "Go on back to Jackson. I'll be okay."

"Jackson will wait. And you're *not* okay. Ever since you and Tyrell broke up, you've been working your ass off and you've been eating like a mixed-up rabbit."

Tameeka set down her spoon. "I don't know what else to do. It's as simple as that. I'm numb, girl. I'm so hurt, I can't feel anything," Tameeka confided. "Then you're moving out, and I'll truly be alone," she said sadly.

"No you won't. We'll still see each other. Besides we still have three whole weeks together; and I plan on bothering you so much that you'd wish I'd leave."

Jackson called from the bedroom.

"I guess he's ready for round three," Stacie said with a smile, then just as suddenly she frowned. "I'm sorry, I didn't mean to say that. That was mean of me."

Tameeka managed a genuine smile, then said, "It wasn't. Go on and take care of your man."

Stacie hopped out of her seat, hugged Tameeka and raced toward the bedroom. Tameeka finished off her soup before going into the living room to meditate. She was just finishing when Stacie and Jackson emerged from Stacie's bedroom, holding hands and shimmering with sex.

"We're going to get something to eat, wanna come?" Stacie asked.

Tameeka shook her head and averted her eyes. Seeing Jackson reminded her of Tyrell. "I'm fine," she mumbled.

"We can bring you something back," Stacie offered. "Can't we?" she asked, staring up at Jackson.

"Whatevah," he snapped. His boy had told him what had gone down; he had no respect for cheaters. Stacie eyed him sharply and he glared at her, daring her to say something. Stacie rolled her eyes, but squeezed his hand. She didn't like his attitude, but she understood it.

Stacie and Jackson walked to the door. "Well, hit me on the cell if you change your mind."

As soon as the door closed, Tameeka dragged herself into the kitchen to make some herbal tea. She brought the steaming cup into the living room and settled on the couch, then picked up the book. With each turned page, tears ran down her face.

"This is me!" she cried. "I intentionally do and say things that make people mad at me. This is me to a T. I do this all the time. But how can I stop?" she wondered.

38

Single Father's Guide to Dating
Tip #60

Remember that a lady is like fire, when stoked just right, she can burn all night long.

Jackson and Stacie walked hand-in-hand along Moreland Avenue in Little Five Points. The weather was gorgeous and half of Atlanta was out enjoying the warm sun.

Jackson absentmindedly watched the people. So far they had passed a girl with bright purple fluorescent hair, a man with dreadlocks that skimmed the ground and a teenager with so many body piercings that he'd probably spring a leak if he drank too much water. Suddenly Jackson's cell phone rang. He unsnapped it off his belt and glanced at the number; it was Amy, the waitress from Houston's. He let it go to voicemail, where he'd delete it later.

"Tell your friends that you have a girlfriend," Stacie said.

Jackson laughed. "It could've been Jam," he joked.

"If it was, you would've answered it. Like I said, tell your friends that you have a lady."

"What if I don't?" Jackson asked.

"Then I'm gonna spank that ass," Stacie threatened.

"Promises, promises," Jackson teased. "Tell me again about the dead people."

Stacie groaned, then punched him lightly in the arm. "Don't remind me. I don't want to think about that place again." Her exciting new work assignment turned out to be at a mortuary. Being so close to dead people gave her the heebie-jeebies and she'd quit after only two hours.

They strolled past several fashionable boutiques, occasionally stopping to look in the windows. When they came to a shoe store, Jackson watched Stacie stare longingly at the shoes that filled the case. "I wish I could afford those," she murmured, pointing out a pair of Franco Sarto mules.

"May I ask you something?" Jackson asked. He had said it so softly and with such concern that Stacie immediately knew what he was about to ask. She stumbled slightly, but quickly righted herself. Even though it was warm, her face and hands suddenly became clammy.

"Ask me anything you want, cutie, but be prepared for the answer. My grandmother always told me, never ask for a gift that you aren't ready to unwrap. So . . . " she shrugged. "Ask away!"

"When did you, um . . . how long have you . . ." he stammered. Asking was much harder than he thought it would be. Jackson cleared his throat and started again. "What I meant was, why do you do it?"

Shame flitted across Stacie's face. "It started when I was little," Stacie whispered, and the memories came rushing back. "I don't remember how old I was. But my father used to get shit-faced drunk. It seemed like every night he was yelling and bitching about something." She smiled sadly as she remembered. "Then when he got tired of yelling, he tried to destroy everything and anything in his path. After a few times of getting my butt whooped just for being in his visual, I learned to hide. And the only safe place in the apartment was the closet. It was junky as all get out." She gave a watery laugh.

"Everything was in there. I guess it was our junk closet. Since I was small, I was able to squeeze in between bags full of clothes and roll myself up into a little ball. Then to keep him from hearing me cry, I'd stick my face in a shoe to muffle the sound. And ever since then I knew that as soon as I got to the shoes, I'd be okay," she finished, and looked down at her hands; they were shaking uncontrollably. Tears were streaming down her face and spilling down onto the front of her blouse.

Jackson pulled her into his arms and murmured softly in her ear. There was a restaurant a few feet away that had tables and chairs out front. Wrapping his arms around her, he nudged Stacie in that direction. Jackson sat down and pulled her into his lap. He grabbed a napkin off the already set table and dabbed at her eyes.

"I'm sorry." She smiled weakly, then wrapped her arms around his waist and rested her head against his chest. "I've never talked about it before. I feel a whole lot better." She pulled back and smiled up at him. Her eyes were radiant, and he leaned down and kissed her gently.

"So, um, do you do it often? Does it have a name? Do you think you'll be doing this your whole life?" As he fired his questions off, Stacie wanted to bury her face in Jackson's chest because she didn't know the answers to his questions and he was beginning to make her sound like a freak. She resisted the urge and answered the one that she knew for sure.

"I've tapered off some. I used to sniff about thirty times a day, but now I only do it around fifteen. And I don't believe it has a name and I hope that I won't be doing it all my life. Any more questions?" she asked shyly, and he shook his head. She stayed nestled in his lap and they people watched for a little while longer.

As they made their way back to his truck, Stacie got the courage to ask some questions of her own. "So what do you think? You gonna get rid of me now that you know your girlfriend is a freak?" Stacie asked teasingly, but her eyes were serious.

Jackson stopped in the middle of the sidewalk and turned toward Stacie so that they were face-to-face. "I don't plan on leaving you, baby. You're mine, freakiness included."

"Thank you," Stacie whispered as she reached up and stroked Jackson's face. Her hand was trembling, but this time for a different reason. I love him, she realized. Jackson caught her hand and lightly kissed her palm. Stacie stared hungrily at him. "You can't be doing that to a sistah, getting me all hot," she groaned. "Heaven on Earth is right down the street, maybe we can sneak into Tameeka's office."

"Bet!" Jackson agreed as he all but dragged her down the street. They fell into Heaven on Earth and immediately bumped into Bea.

"Hey! Is Meek working today?" a breathless Stacie asked.

Bea took in Stacie's flushed face and Jackson's unsuccessful attempt at hiding the bulge in his pants and smiled to herself. Young people. "She's in her office," she answered.

Jackson and Stacie exchanged a disappointed glance, but walked back to Tameeka's office anyway.

"Hey, Meek, you've got guests," Stacie called as she pushed open the office door. "Hey, girl!" she called when she didn't get a response.

"Is she here?" Jackson asked.

"Bea said she was. Maybe she's in the bathroom. We can wait for her on the couch," she said, and Jackson grinned seductively. "Nu-uh, none of that," Stacie said, but grabbed his hand as they stepped into the office. They both saw the heap on the floor at the same time; Stacie's hand flew to her mouth. "Oh, no!" she screamed, and rushed to Tameeka.

39

What I Want to Do When
I Grow Up

1. Crap! I'm not sure.

"Tameeka, are you all right?" Stacie asked.

Tameeka blinked, then quickly focused. "I'm fine. I was so worn-out that I fell asleep. Ever since Tyrell and I broke up I haven't been sleeping well. I guess it finally caught up with me," Tameeka said. Stacie and Jackson each grabbed an arm and pulled her up. "Thanks, guys. Let me go clean up," she said, yawning. She returned a few minutes later, wearing fresh clothes. "I'm sorry, I didn't mean to worry y'all. I don't know what to do since Tyrell and I aren't seeing each other anymore. But Heaven on Earth has been a lifesaver. If it wasn't for the store, I don't know what I'd do," Tameeka said, and hopelessly shrugged her shoulders.

"Oh, sweetie, I'm so sorry," Stacie murmured while rubbing Tameeka's back.

"Hey, what are you guys doing here?" Tameeka asked.

Jackson and Stacie exchanged guilty looks. "We were coming to visit you," Stacie answered, averting her eyes.

"Yeah, right. Knowing you, you were coming to use my

couch," she said, and Stacie flushed. "Ha! I was right. Well, my office is not a motel. So go on," she said, shooing them out.

"You go ahead," Stacie said to Jackson. "Meet me out front. I need to talk to my girl." Jackson nodded, then kissed Stacie on the lips before he strolled out of the office.

"How are you, girl . . . how are you for real?"

"Hurting. I hurt all over. My heart, my head . . . whoever said that you get a broken heart is wrong. It seems like every part of my body is broken."

Stacie wrapped her arms around her friend. "I'm sorry, girl."

"I'll be okay," Tameeka answered, her voice trembling. "Go on and enjoy Jackson."

Stacie looked her in her eyes. "You sure? I can stay with you."

Tameeka clutched her chest, faking a heart attack. "What? Stacie Long passing up dick to stay with me? Lordy, things have changed. I'll be fine," Tameeka said, chuckling softly.

"Okay," Stacie said. "I'll be home later tonight, just in case you want to talk."

Stacie and Jackson went back to his house to find they had it all to themselves. Ettie Mae and Jameel were at the mall.

"What's going on with Michelle?" Stacie asked, then began stroking Jackson's chest when she felt him stiffen. "Sorry, I don't mean to make you mad."

"Naw, it's not your fault. Just hearing her name pisses me the hell off. She's coming over in a couple weeks to take Jam out on an unsupervised visit," he said.

"Oh, that's right. Is there anything I can do?"

"Naw, baby, but I appreciate the fact that you got my back."

"I'm serious," Stacie continued. "I'm here for you."

"I know. Hey, let's squash this convo. We'll deal with it when it happens."

Stacie beamed. "Yes, *we* will. So what do you want to talk about?" she asked, and felt his body relax a little.

"Well, if you had a chance to be anything in the world, what would you be? And be honest," Jackson instructed as he nuzzled his mouth against her neck; he couldn't suppress the grin that spread across his face. Who would've thought that the spoiled lady who drove him crazy would turn out to be the one who broke his three-date rule and made him fall for her? Not him.

She was like a glass of champagne, bubbly, classy and definitely didn't like to be shaken, he mused. It took him only two weeks to learn this and even less time to remember it.

"I don't know," Stacie answered slowly, then smiled shyly as an image began forming behind her eyes. When she was a little girl, she had fun playing school with the neighborhood children during the summer. She loved making up the "lesson plan" and teaching the younger kids how to read. "I know what I want," she said happily as she suddenly saw her life come together and form a beautiful picture. "I think that I would like to be a teacher. Let me rephrase that . . . I *want* to be a teacher. I want to make sure that little kids get off on the right foot," she said.

"Hey, that's good. Why don't you do it? You're still young enough to keep up with the kids," he joked.

"I don't know . . ." Stacie hedged, then said, "It's not the age thing . . . I don't know the first thing about being a teacher," she admitted, suddenly feeling stupid.

Jackson wrapped his arms around her waist. "They have this new thing called the Internet. Have you heard of it?" he joked, and Stacie playfully slapped him on his hand.

"That's a good idea. I guess I feel so overwhelmed that I don't know where to start. And I'm not sure if I have what it takes," she said softly. "I never stick to anything. I get so excited about stuff, then halfway through when it's not going well . . . I just drop it. So how do I know if I'll stick to this teaching thing?" she asked, though Jackson wasn't sure if she was asking him or herself.

"At least you act on what you want. So many people sit on

the bench and watch life go by. At least you jump in and play a little, even if you're tired by halftime. You just need to learn how to stay in for the whole game."

Stacie burst out laughing. "Thank you, Coach Brown," she said, and Jackson chuckled. "I'll give it a try. What about you? What would you be?" Stacie asked.

Jackson thought for a second, then said, "A bus driver."

"A bus driver?" Stacie asked, frowning. "That's not playing fair, you're already a bus driver. You have to pick something that you *really* want to be. Think hard. And tell the truth!" she demanded.

Jackson laughed. "Baby, I *am* telling the truth. I wouldn't make this up. If I had to be anything in the world, I'd be a bus driver. It's wonderful. I get to meet a lot of people. Case in point, I met you."

"Yeah . . . but you really didn't meet me on the bus. First you met me at Houston's, then on the blind date, *then* we met on the bus," she finished.

"That's what I'm saying. If it wasn't for the bus, we wouldn't have seen each other again," he teased, then his voice turned serious. "Besides, I'm driving people to the next step in their lives."

"Really?" Stacie asked. He made being a bus driver sound so interesting.

He nodded his head. "I'm dropping people off at their jobs, doctor appointments and job interviews. When people get on the bus they're moving . . . literally. It's an awesome job," he finished, then added, "And I like working a big piece of equipment."

"Oh!" Stacie uttered as a slow grin spread over her face. "Which one?" she quipped.

"Which one you think?" Jackson drawled.

Her hand slipped down between his legs. "This one?" she asked with wide-eyed innocence. Jackson groaned as she gently stroked his crotch.

"You're not tired, baby?" he asked. Stacie shook her head no, then pulled his pants off.

Jackson smiled. "You're a hot little something."

"You want me to cool it down?" Stacie asked as she slid down to her knees in front of him and gently began nipping at the inside of his thighs.

"Aw, hell naw!" Jackson moaned as his legs widened to accommodate Stacie. Her eyes were closed as she lovingly tongued his thighs, then gently blew warm air on the wet kisses. Stacie inched her way down to the back of his knees, where she made little circles with her lips. She grinned when Jackson's legs twitched.

"You liking this, baby?" she whispered, and Jackson whimpered in response. "Well, you're gonna like this a whole hell of a lot better," she promised, then reached up and grabbed his sack and gently rolled it around in her hand.

"Stacie," Jackson uttered in a strangled voice.

"Just playing with part of your big equipment," Stacie chuckled, then wrapped her hand around his penis and tenderly caressed it. Jackson's hips mirrored her hand movements. "Feels good?" Stacie asked, and Jackson nodded. Leaning down, she gently brushed her lips against his tip, then teased it with her tongue until it began pulsing in her hand.

"Stop playing and suck it," Jackson begged. Stacie lowered her head and took him in her mouth. Jackson slowly exhaled as her lips wrapped around him. He gripped the couch cushions as her head bobbed up and down. "Ahhh, baby, are you ready for the big equipment?"

"Give it to me," Stacie said, and waited while Jackson slipped on a condom. "How do you want it?" she asked, staring hungrily at him.

"A million ways, but right now, bend over the back of the couch."

"I'd love to do it with you a trillion times," Stacie said as she got into position and her body shuddered when she looked over her shoulder and saw Jackson staring at her with lust-filled eyes. "Do me, baby," she whispered.

"A million ways," Jackson promised as he slid into Stacie and she whimpered with excitement.

"Oh, Jackson," she panted as she pressed her butt up to meet his strokes.

"Move that ass for me!" Jackson shouted. Stacie clung to the back of the couch as Jackson leisurely pumped in and out of her.

"Princess, I lo—" Jackson heard a car door slam and he froze. "Oh shit! They're back." He was so close to coming; all he needed was a couple more strokes. He increased his speed when he heard Jameel on the other side of the door. "Stacie, baby, make me come," he begged, with one eye on the door.

40

Sometimes an Occasional Detour in Life Is Just What the Doctor Ordered

Tameeka poured herself a glass of wine before heading to her bedroom, where she locked the door. She picked up a shopping bag and pulled out a leather-bound journal. She took a sip of wine, then settled on her bed. *To Know Oneself Is to Know Your Best Friend: How to Live a Fulfilling Life* said that she should get straight to the point and write like she was talking to a friend. Tameeka thought for a moment, then her pen flew over the pages as her thoughts tumbled out.

> *I messed up—really messed up. I cheated on Tyrell. I know that's incredibly bad. Horrible!!!!! I still can't believe I did it. Not once, but twice. I had spread my legs faster than a drunk college coed at a frat party. And it was with Mohammad, my ex-fuck buddy. Crazy!!!*

> *I always teased Stacie about being a dick lover. But look at me, I'm just as bad, maybe even worse, because I'm a hypocrite. At least Stacie knows what she is and embraces it.*

I don't know how I could've done what I did to Tyrell. So what, he eyeballed women like he hadn't seen one in years, and so what if he wanted me to give up my friend? I mean, that isn't reason enough to cheat, is it?

I mean, I love Tyrell, I really do. We'd go out, he made crazy love to me, he left me breathless. Was he my soul mate? . . . I don't know, but he was close to it. But the brother couldn't keep his eyes on me. No matter where we'd go, his eyes bounced around like two balls. They were glued to some lady's ass, legs or tits. Am I wrong for wanting him to admire only me?

The cheating wasn't planned, it really wasn't, it just happened. How many times has that excuse been used? Anyway, it wasn't like Mohammad and I planned for something to happen, it just did, it truly did.

The first time it happened, at Heaven on Earth, I was mad at Tyrell. We had had a fight the night before about his eyeballing. This isn't an excuse, I'm just telling you what happened. Then Mohammad came along and he made me feel beautiful, as if he would never look at anyone else. Damn! The sex was hot. The second time when he did a pop-in at my apartment, I couldn't turn him away, he looked too adorable.

Tameeka set down her pen, then wiped tears from her face.

She really needed to be accountable for her behavior. She knew that. She couldn't blame her actions on what Tyrell had done. She picked up her pen again.

I miss him so much, I hurt. I haven't felt like eating. It's not a fun way to lose weight. Not that I lost a lot, but some. I don't think that I'll ever get over him.

*I don't know why I did it. Maybe because my parents left me to
be raised by my grandmother. So maybe I have abandonment
issues. Or maybe it's what the book says—I feel I don't deserve
love, so I sabotage my chances at it. I bet that's it. That's how I
feel. If I look back at our relationship I can see where I intentionally pissed Tyrell off. Like bossing him around and not getting the keys from Mohammad.*

Tameeka set down her pen and silently reread what she had
written.

"I need to call Tyrell and ask for *his* forgiveness. Am I ready
to do that?"

41

Single Father's Guide to Dating
Tip #2

Baby momma drama is more painful than having surgery
sans anesthesia—avoid both at all costs.

Saturday morning when Jackson pried open his eyelids, they felt heavier than a set of bricks. He hadn't gotten a good night's sleep. A quick glance at his legs told him that he did a lot of tossing and turning; the blankets were snaked around his legs like restraints.

He kicked the blankets off, then swung his legs over the side of the bed; and that's when it hit him. Michelle's unsupervised visits started today. She'd have Jameel for five hours. Five unsupervised hours outside the house.

Jackson and Ettie Mae were sitting on the couch, stiff as two statues, when at five minutes to nine there was a knock on the door. Jackson huffed, then inched toward the door. When did she start trying to be on time? he thought. He was taking longer than he should have because Ettie Mae cut her eyes at him so sharp that he swore if he'd looked down, he'd see a gash across his chest. He picked his pace up a little, but not by much. Why rush to give my child over to the devil?

There came a second knock, harder and more insistent than the first. Jackson snatched open the door to see Michelle on the threshold, glaring at him.

Their eyes locked, staring at each other defiantly, neither one willing to back down. Jackson didn't mind; the longer she played this game, the less time she had with Jameel, so he held her gaze and milked it for what it was worth. She sensed his strategy and her eyes softened. She started smiling like she had just found the biggest stash of crack. Jackson opened the door wider and she breezed in.

"Is he ready?"

"He's ready. Have him back by two o'clock," Jackson demanded curtly.

"I know what time he's supposed to be back," Michelle said amiably. She wasn't looking for a fight. "I've got the paper right here," she said, patting her purse.

"Whatever," Jackson grumbled, as he clenched and unclenched his hands. For the first time in his life he had the urge to hit a female. "Two o'clock. That doesn't mean two-thirty, two forty-five or two-oh-five. But two o'clock on the dot!" he barked. He didn't notice Jameel sneaking up behind him.

"Two o'clock. I hear you," Michelle agreed. Jameel quietly watched their exchange with wide, frightened eyes. He didn't like it when his daddy was mad.

Jackson began firing questions at her "So where you taking my boy?"

"I'm taking *our* son to the zoo, then to lunch."

"*My* son!" Jackson corrected. "Who's driving?"

"Look here, nig—" She clamped her mouth shut, silently counted to ten, then started over. "I'll be driving. Haven't had any accidents yet," she proudly boasted.

"Yeah, probably haven't had your license long enough," he sneered. He held out his hand and demanded to see her license.

She refused, then quickly changed her mind. She didn't want any arguments. All she wanted to do was get her son and leave. "Hold on." She dug around in her purse and pulled out the laminated document and passed it to Jackson, who carefully inspected it. Satisfied that it didn't look counterfeit, he passed it back.

"Where's your car?"

Michelle simply nodded toward the street. Jackson opened the front door. A shiny black 1999 Honda Accord was in his driveway. He didn't ask whose car it was. All he knew was that she couldn't afford it. "You insured?" he asked.

Michelle put her hand on her hip. "It's in my glove compartment. Would you like me to go get it?" she asked sweetly.

"Naw, that's all right. Do you have a cell phone?"

She rattled off her number and Jackson fumbled around for a pen before quickly jotting it down.

"Are you done? It'll be all right . . . I'll take care of him . . . he's my son too," Michelle said. But her reassurances fell on deaf ears as Jackson watched, openmouthed, as she grabbed Jameel's hand and sauntered to the door. At the threshold, Jameel turned to his daddy, eyes wide with confusion.

"Aren't you coming, Daddy?"

Jackson felt a tightness in his chest. "Not today. It's gonna be just you and your mo—Michelle," he said quietly.

"Your *mother*," Michelle corrected him.

"I want you to come too," Jameel whined. Jackson knew from experience that a tantrum wasn't far away. He was almost tempted to let him explode, but then thought better of it. He leaned down and pulled his son to him.

"Listen, Jam . . . I can't come. You're gonna have fun with Michelle, you guys are going to the zoo, then going to eat. I bet if you're good, she'll buy you a hot dog." He looked up at Michelle and she gave him a short nod. "We'll do something tomorrow, just us men. Okay?"

"Okay," Jameel squealed, his eyes bright with excitement. He loved spending time with his daddy.

"We'll be leaving now." Michelle grabbed Jameel's hand and trotted down the steps. Jameel kept looking over his shoulder at his father. Jackson watched as Michelle buckled him in the car; he watched as she backed out the driveway; he watched until the car disappeared around the corner.

42

Why Family Is So Important

1. They keep it real
2. They keep you grounded
3. They are always there for you, no matter what

Stacie and Jackson lay together on his bed. Jackson was on his side with his arms wrapped around her waist, and Stacie's rear end was molded perfectly to his front. Lying on top of the blue-sheeted mattress, they looked like a slice of the moon floating on the ocean. The bedcovers were strewn across the floor, along with empty beer bottles. It was one o'clock, another hour before Jameel was expected home, and Jackson was wound as tight as a pair of church lady's drawers and he had been ever since his son had walked out the door four hours ago.

She wanted to give him something else to think about, so she brought up a subject that he loved to talk about.

"I need your help," she said, and when he didn't say anything, she continued. "I don't know what I'm going to do about money. I'm up to my neck in debt. Can't afford to get my car fixed, and the money I get from unemployment isn't makin' it. And I really want to pay my bills. What do you think I should do?"

"Be more damn careful with your money, that's what I think you should do," Jackson snapped.

Stacie shot up. "Excuse you? Don't be getting tart with me, Jackson," she said as she crossed her arms over her chest and rolled her eyes at him.

"That's all you talk about, your bills, no money—"

"Well," Stacie huffed. "I didn't realize it bothered you so much. I won't . . ." comprehension dawned, her face softened. "I'm sorry, baby. I'm so sorry. Here I am being selfish, talking about my problems, and you're worried about Jam. Oh crap, all I wanted to do was to give you something else to think about, instead I've made you feel worse," she said.

Jackson tugged Stacie and she fell on top of him. "It's all good, princess. I shouldn't've gone off on you. I'm sorry," he said as he nuzzled her neck.

"It'll be okay," Stacie reassured him while hugging him tightly. "I think I drank too much juice, I need to use the bathroom."

"Okay, when you get back, we can go over some ways for you to save money."

"Cool," Stacie said as she slid off the bed, slipped her feet in her shoes, then hurried off to the bathroom where she locked the door. Even before using the toilet she had her shoe off and up to her nose. Ten minutes later, Stacie had used the bathroom and was back in Jackson's room. "So are you ready to help me now?" she asked brightly.

"Yep. Come on back on the bed. I've been thinking. Since you're so good at writing lists, why don't you make a list of things that you could do to save money," he offered. Stacie snatched her purse off the floor, then fished around in it until she found a pen and a pad of paper. Jackson shot her a bemused look and she wrinkled her nose.

"I'm a sistah who's always prepared," she retorted. "I've kinda sorta already done one, but I can always add to it," she said, then bowed her head and began working on her list.

1. Stop getting manicures and pedicures
2. Do my own relaxers
3. Buy store-brand groceries

Jackson peered over her shoulder, grabbed the pen out of her hand and scratched off the first item.

"Hey! Whassup? Why did you do that?" Stacie questioned.

"I'll pay for you to get your nails done, I can't have you walking around here with crusty heels and messed-up fingernails," he joked, then he glanced over at his nightstand. "Oh shit!" he groaned.

"What?" Stacie asked alarmed.

Jackson shook his head. "Jam's inhaler. He left it. If he has a coughing fit, he might die."

43

Single Father's Guide to Dating
Tip # 3

Remember that you should always hand your problems
over to God.

He'll be okay, won't he?" Stacie nervously asked.

"He should be. But if he suddenly has an attack, I hope to
hell that Michelle has enough sense to get him to the hospital."

At two o'clock Jackson and Stacie were sitting on the front
steps, waiting for Michelle and Jameel. At one minute after,
Jackson jumped up. "She's late. I'ma call her cell phone."

Stacie tugged at Jackson's jeans. "She's only one minute late,
honey. Give her some time. You know how traffic can be."

"Nu-uh. She's one minute late. Right now she's considered a
kidnapper," Jackson huffed. And if Stacie wasn't so sure that he
was worried about Jameel, she could've sworn that she saw a
gleam of satisfaction in his eyes.

"Kidnapper! Jackson give her some time," Stacie insisted.
"Give her ten minutes and if she doesn't show, then call her."

Jackson vigorously shook his head. "Nope. I'ma call now."
He pulled out his cell phone and dialed the number that
Michelle had given him. Stacie shook her head, then quickly

grew nervous when Jackson's face tightened and his hands began shaking as he clicked off the phone.

"Jackson? What's wrong?" She asked.

"The number doesn't exist. That bitch gave me a fake number!" Stacie heard the rising panic in his voice and she tried to soothe him.

"Maybe she made a mistake. She was probably off by one digit."

"Do you plan on trying the different combinations? Besides, I don't think she messed up. She intentionally gave me a wrong number," he barked. Just then, Ettie Mae wandered to the front door.

"Where's my great-grand? Isn't he supposed to be home by now?" she asked. She looked at Stacie's face, then Jackson's, and she knew that something was wrong. Terribly wrong. She burst onto the porch. "What's wrong? What happened?" she calmly asked, but her legs were wobbly.

"I don't know where my son is," Jackson answered. "He's out there driving around with that crackhead," he said as he stalked the length of the porch, his muscled legs rippling with each step.

"We should call the police," Ettie Mae said quietly, and Jackson nodded and pulled out his cell phone. Stacie stood by on the fringes of the Browns' dilemma, trying to think of a way she could help.

44

If You Want to Play Tit for Tat,
You'd Better Have a Big Paddle

Tameeka aimlessly wandered around T.J. Maxx. Usually just the thought of going into the department store gave her an orgasm. She and Stacie had a running joke that T.J. Maxx was her personal dildo. But today she wasn't feeling the Maxx. Usually she'd have a cartful of clothes, shoes and household items. The only items in her cart today were two white-and-yellow–striped throw pillows, which she didn't need, but felt obligated to buy. Her mind was on Tyrell; she wanted to call him and invite him out to dinner.

It was early evening when Tameeka finally made her way home. As soon as she got in, she lit her favorite sandalwood-scented candles, sat cross-legged on the living room floor and meditated until her spirit was full and her head calm. Easing herself up, she felt reborn, her worries were now memories. A smile was on her face when she picked up the phone to call Tyrell. Instead of a dial tone, she heard muted voices.

"Hello?"

"Hello. Tameeka?"

"Stacie?"

"Yeah. Hey, what happened? I didn't hear your phone ring. Anyway, girl, some stuff is going on over at Jackson's. Jam's mother took him, and it looks like that skank did a disappearing act with him."

An image of the smiling boy that she met at Houston's came to her. "Jameel is gone? I don't believe it," Tameeka whispered.

"Me either," Stacie said sadly.

"How's Jackson doing? I know he must be ready to run out and kick some butt."

"He's maintaining. I know he's hurting, but he's not letting any of us see it. I'm glad that they have the Atlanta Police force looking for Jam, otherwise I think that somebody's ass would be getting kicked."

"How are *you* doing? I know how much you care for that little boy."

"I'm scared, Meek," Stacie admitted. "And I don't want Jackson to see it. The last thing he needs to be worrying about is making sure that I'm okay. Can you come over?" Stacie asked.

"Definitely—"

"Hold on, Meek. Jackson's talking to me." Tameeka heard Jackson's voice in the background. "Hey, girl, I'm sorry," Stacie said. "Jackson just told me that Tyrell is on his way over. Maybe you shouldn't come, this will be the first time you guys have seen each other since the Mohammad thing. This isn't the time to come at him with some deep shit."

"Oh, I'm coming," Tameeka said.

45

Why Kids Are Like Rainbows

1. They are all gifts from God
2. They are all unique
3. They are all vibrant beings
4. They all are worth their weight in gold

Here, baby, eat this," Ettie Mae coaxed as she placed a plate of food in front of her grandson. She'd cooked all his favorites: fried chicken, collards, black-eyed peas, corn bread and a pan of brownies for dessert. Jackson didn't say anything, instead he looked at his grandmother with lifeless eyes. "Y'all go on and get something to eat," she instructed Stacie and Tyrell. They didn't require much pushing; the smell from the food filled up the house and they all realized they were starving. Leaning over, Stacie wrapped her arms around Jackson; he felt like a block of ice, stiff and unyielding. Tyrell gave his friend's shoulder a quick squeeze before he followed Stacie to the kitchen.

Ettie Mae placed the plate of food on the coffee table, then settled next to her grandson. Jackson stirred a little. She grabbed his hand and stroked it, trying to comfort him. "They'll find him," she assured him. "They'll find your baby." Jackson slowly faced his grandmother, and what Ettie Mae saw in his eyes made her heart jump to her throat. Her grandbaby looked like he had really seen the devil; his eyes were hollow and lifeless. "Oh, Lord have mercy," Ettie Mae howled. Stacie and Tyrell hurried back into the room. "We need to pray. Right now. Hurry!" Everybody huddled together and Ettie Mae prayed for Jameel's safe return, she prayed for Jackson's happiness and she prayed the hardest of all for Michelle. She prayed that Michelle would do the right thing and bring Jameel home where he belonged.

An hour later there was a knock on the door and everybody looked at each other wearing expectant expressions. Jackson raced to the door and pulled it open only to find Tameeka on the other side.

"Shit." Jackson stalked back to the living room leaving the door open with Tameeka standing outside. Stacie shot Jackson a quizzical glance when he flopped on the couch. Ettie Mae motioned for her to go to the door. Stacie hurried off and let in a confused Tameeka.

"He thought you were Michelle. She hasn't come back yet," Stacie explained.

Tameeka nodded, then peered over Stacie's shoulder. "Is Tyrell here?"

"He's in the living room. Remember what I told you, this isn't the time or place for you to try to talk to Tyrell. You're my girl, but this is my second family and I don't want them to have any unnecessary stress right now. So behave yourself. Come on." Stacie grabbed Tameeka's hand and once they got to the living room, she gave it an encouraging squeeze before she dropped it and snuggled against Jackson.

Tameeka looked around the room. The somber mood made her think of a funeral. She rushed to hug Ettie Mae, then moved to hug Tyrell, but his narrowed eyes and the angry tilt of his head stopped her in her tracks. She backed off and dropped down into an armchair. Throughout the evening, she couldn't help darting looks in his direction. If their eyes happened to meet, he'd glare at her before breaking the connection.

At ten o'clock the doorbell rang. A uniformed police officer was on the stoop and standing behind him was a child. All Jackson could see were a pair of sneakers. Could it be?

"We found him, sir," the officer solemnly said, then he broke into a smile as though he had just awarded Jackson a million dollars. He stepped aside and Jameel skipped forward.

Ettie Mae let out a whoop of happiness, Stacie and Tyrell beamed at each other, and tears of joy ran down Jackson's face as he leaned down and scooped up his son. "How . . . where?" he stuttered.

"I take it you guys haven't been watching TV," the officer said good-naturedly. "Because if you had been, you would've seen Jameel's picture plastered on every channel. A Good Samaritan saw them eating ice cream in the mall and called the police." Then he hesitated, unsure whether he should divulge any more information. He shrugged as if to say, *"What the hell,"* then said softly, "He was in Alabama."

"Where is she? I'll kill her!" Jackson growled, and Stacie reached for his hand and held it tightly.

"She knew we were onto her, so she ran off," the officer explained.

"She left him alone?" Again?

Jameel piped in. "She told me to stay very still. She said that she was going to the bathroom and she was coming right back. I stayed very still, Daddy, just like she told me," he said, and everybody broke into relief-filled laughter.

Ettie Mae grabbed Jameel and took him into the kitchen while Jackson conferred with the officer about what he should do about Michelle.

After the officer left, Jackson put Jameel to bed, then stayed by his son's side for over an hour watching him sleep. It wasn't until he checked the locks on Jameel's bedroom windows that he tiptoed outside and joined Stacie on the front porch.

Stacie wiggled between Jackson's legs and rested her head on his chest. "Do you think those two are gonna be okay?" Stacie asked, jutting her chin toward Tameeka and Tyrell. They were standing in front of their vehicles.

She felt Jackson shrug. "They'll come to some sort of resolution," he answered, then turned his attention to Stacie. "You know . . . I want to thank you for being here today. It meant a lot to me," he drawled.

"No problem," Stacie answered quietly, then dismissed him with a flick of her hand.

"Don't minimize this. Listen." He stood up and pulled Stacie with him and they stood face-to-face. "I *really* appreciate your being here today. You don't know how much your presence meant. I don't know what I would have done if anything happened to my son," he said.

She thanked him and said, "I love Jameel too. He's the sweetest little boy I know. He takes after his daddy," she flirted, hoping to lighten the mood.

"I *am* incredibly sweet and sexy, aren't I?"

"Yes, you are," Stacie agreed as she inched her mouth closer to Jackson's until she was but a tongue lick away. "Kiss me!" she demanded.

"A lady never has to ask for a kiss," Jackson teased.

"I'm sorry, baby, but I want those sexy lips of yours on mine. Can you do it for me?" she asked, looking coyly at him.

"So where do you want them?" Jackson drawled as his tongue slowly rimmed her ear.

"That's not where I was thinking," Stacie moaned, "but it'll work."

"I'll put my lips *wherever* you want them," Jackson breathed in her ear.

Stacie shivered. "My lips would love a visit," she said, turning so that their lips met.

Jackson pulled away and hungrily looked at her. "Baby, I want to tongue you all over. Come on, let's go inside," he said, tugging her toward the door.

"Your grandmother might hear us," Stacie protested.

"We'll be quiet," Jackson promised.

"Okay," Stacie agreed as they hurried into the house.

Tameeka watched her friend, then sighed and glanced up at Tyrell. "Hey, what an evening, huh?"

"Yeah," Tyrell agreed.

"This whole Michelle thing was crazy, wasn't it?"

Tyrell nodded. "About as crazy as it gets. Have a good evening," he said, and Tameeka's face fell.

He opened his truck door and was about to get in when Tameeka called out to him. "Tyrell—"

"I need to get going. I'm tired."

"I really need to talk to you." Tameeka rushed over to him and rested her hand on his arm. "When can I see you?" she asked.

46

The Best Gift to Oneself . . . Is Oneself

Tameeka nervously fiddled with her straw. The café was crowded, and she was grateful that she had gotten a table. She expected Tyrell to walk through the door at any minute; then as if on cue, she looked up to see him fill the doorway. He stopped at the threshold as he scrutinized the crowd; and the pause gave her enough time to check him out. He's letting his hair grow back, she mused. I like it, she decided. The black stubble covering his head gave him an unkempt, sexy look.

He looked as good as ever, but his mouth was turned down in a frown and his eyes were hooded and secretive. Once she got her heart beating at a normal pace, she stood up and motioned him over.

As he lumbered across the coffee shop, Tameeka couldn't help but notice several ladies turn their heads to watch his progress. When he got to the table, Tameeka pointed her lips up for a kiss; Tyrell bypassed them and aimed for her cheek. Embarrassed, Tameeka's face flushed hotly, and she quickly swallowed her disappointment.

"I'm glad that you agreed to meet me," she started off nervously. "Oh, here, I got you these," she said, and pushed a two-pound box of chocolate-covered raisins toward him. He licked his lips when he opened it and saw his favorite candy inside. "Do you want something to eat? They have good food here."

"Just coffee," he said, then signaled the waitress. Tameeka angrily sipped her soda as Tyrell's eyes lazily roamed over the waitress's body. She didn't say anything until the waitress brought Tyrell's coffee and he had fixed it just the way he liked it, tons of sugar and a drop of cream.

She smiled brightly at him. "So how's work? I bet you have some funny stories to tell," she gently encouraged.

"Work is cool," Tyrell answered flatly. She waited for him to ask about her store . . . he didn't. The blood slowly crept up Tameeka's face.

"How's Jackson doing? I can't believe what that crackhead did to Jam," Tameeka said as she sadly shook her head.

"J is cool," he answered in the same flat tone, then gave her a look that said, "Stop bullshitting and tell me what you want!"

Tameeka cringed. He hates me so much, she thought, and her nose and ears started itching. Don't you dare cry! she told herself. The urge was getting so strong that she had to bow her head over her drink to compose herself. When she lifted her head she found Tyrell's eyes on her. They were coolly appraising her; a chill ran up her spine, he was looking at her as if she were a stranger.

Tameeka pushed down a sob, and said, "I wanted to apologize to you in person. I'm *very, very* sorry about what I did to you. The last thing I wanted to do was to hurt you." When he didn't say anything, she said softly, "I've found some things out about myself." She glanced at him and when he didn't frown, she felt brave enough to continue. "I was afraid of being abandoned," she confessed, and this time she couldn't stop the tears, they flowed down her face, like little streams.

Tyrell's heart broke at seeing her cry. "Don't," he said. He wanted to pull her into his arms, but his own pain kept him glued to his seat. Instead he picked up his coffee cup and took a long sip.

"I'm sorry," Tameeka sniffled as she dabbed at her eyes, then blew her nose. This was turning into a tear fest, something she didn't want to happen. "I guess whenever I think about people leaving me I get a little emotional."

"I didn't leave you," Tyrell said as he slammed down his coffee cup. He leaned forward so that their faces were only inches apart. "You pushed me away. You cheated on me!" he hissed, and Tameeka shrunk back in her chair.

"But weren't you listening to anything I just said? I cheated because I was scared."

"I heard everything you said. But check this out; what happens if you get scared again, or what happens if a guy does something that you don't like. How are you gonna deal with it, Meek?"

"I won't cheat," she vowed. "Let's get back together. I'll prove it to you."

"Get back together," he spat. "Are you fucking crazy? When you had me, you didn't think that I loved you so you went out and cheated on me. Now that you don't have me, you talked yourself into believing that you cheated on me because you were afraid that I would leave you. What kind of shit is that?" He gave her a hard glare.

"I . . . I . . . I . . . ," Tameeka stuttered.

"The rationale kinda leaves you speechless, doesn't it?" he barked, then his voice softened. "I loved you, girl. I loved you with everything I had. But you went and cheated on me!" His eyes became glassy and his voice thick. "You cheated on me. The man who loved you. I wanted to take care of you. I wanted to give you babies," he said harshly.

"I'm so sorry," Tameeka said over and over until it began to sound like a mantra.

"This was a waste of my time. I need to go," Tyrell said. He snatched up his candy and ambled out of the shop.

Tameeka slumped back into her chair. It was there all the time, and I didn't believe it, she thought sadly. When she looked into Tyrell's eyes, she had seen how much love he had for her, but also mixed in was the pain she had caused him.

"He doesn't want me," Tameeka murmured, before dropping a twenty-dollar bill on the table and stumbling into the street.

47

Single Father's Guide to Dating
Tip # 10

Always marry the lady whom your children love.

Jackson raced down the basketball court with Tyrell in close pursuit. Seconds later the ball was out of Jackson's hands and flying through the air. Tyrell burst out laughing when it kissed the rim and bounced off. They were at Run N' Shoot, the Atlanta gym where serious and want-to-be ballers converged.

"Still can't ball," Tyrell taunted, catching the rebound.

"I'm a little out of practice," Jackson answered, then snatched the ball from Tyrell and shot. This time the ball easily passed through the net and Tyrell grabbed it. "I just needed to warm up," Jackson said as he pulled off his shirt and flexed his muscled pecs while bouncing on the balls of his feet. "This feels good."

"Get ready, 'cause I'ma kick your ass," Tyrell threatened before shoving Jackson, then pivoting on his heel to make a basket.

"So you think you got me? Think again," Jackson huffed, grabbing the basketball and scoring. Three games later, a sweaty and tired Jackson and Tyrell casually tossed the ball around.

"The best of five," Tyrell huffed, and Jackson shook his head. "You scared? Give a brother a chance."

Jackson looked at his best friend. He looked like he was one breath away from collapsing. Jackson motioned toward the juice bar. "Let's get something to drink." Jackson strolled through the gym, nodding and greeting the ladies; he had dated almost half of them.

They got their protein shakes and sat inside a booth. "I'ma do it, man," Jackson said.

"What, go for five? Bet. I'll be ready as soon as I finish this drink."

Jackson waved his hand. "No, not that. I'ma make it official. Do the legal thing. I'm going to ask Stacie to marry me."

"What?" Tyrell exclaimed, spurting his shake over the table.

"Hey, fountain boy, watch where you're spitting," Jackson said.

"Sorry about that," Tyrell said as he wiped up the table. "Congrats, man. I didn't see this coming at all. So when did you decide to give up your player's card?"

Jackson smiled. "The moment I saw her."

"I'm happy for you . . . but she's a little high maintenance, isn't she? What is it you call her? Princess?"

Jackson chuckled. "Stacie does keep a brother on his toes. But there's a lot that you don't know. She loves kids—her nieces worship her. She's a hard worker. She's a good lady with a good heart. Ettie Mae loves her. She got some issues, but it's nothing we can't work through," he said, thinking of her shoe sniffing. "And none of my other ladies bonded with Jam like she did."

Tyrell snorted. "That's because you've never given them a chance, Mr. Three Date Rule."

"Stacie blew that rule out of the water, didn't she?"

"Damn. Another brother down," Tyrell said mournfully.

Jackson eyed his friend. Despite the jokes, he knew how much Tyrell wanted to be married. "So how are you doing?"

"Maintaining," Tyrell answered. "Just maintaining."

"You need to get back out there, man. You know women are like paper towels, they come in a bunch of sizes and colors and, best of all, they're disposable."

"And you want to get married?" he asked, then looked Jackson in the eyes. "You know, J, I would not have thought Tameeka would do something like this to me, never in my wildest dreams. She fucked me up."

"I'm sorry, man," Jackson said.

"What would you do if Stacie cheated on you?"

"She'd be seeing the back of my ass because Jackson Brown don't play that shit. Believe that!"

48

Qualities to Look for in a Good Man

1. He must love himself
2. He must be smart enough to surround himself with good people
3. He must be a leader
4. He must know how to be vulnerable
5. He must treat me like a princess

Stacie rang Jackson's doorbell. "This is our weekend!" she sang to herself. When Jackson told her that his grandmother and Jameel were spending the weekend in Macon and that he wanted her to spend the time with him, she eagerly agreed.

The door opened and Stacie waved to Tameeka, who tooted her horn two short beeps, then drove away.

Stacie was wearing a leopard-print rayon slip dress that draped over her, but still gave a hint of the body underneath. She had matched it with a pair of brown sandals that had straps that wrapped around her calves.

"You look delicious, baby," Jackson murmured, then pecked her on the cheek. "I'm not sure what to eat first . . . you or the food."

Stacie felt the same. The jeans he had on were hugging him in all the right places. His short-sleeved shirt showed off his biceps to perfection. "Let's eat the food first. I have a feeling that I'm gonna need all my energy tonight," she said, laughing. "I'm starving." She sniffed the air. "What's that? Dang, that smells good. I feel like I wanna drop my—"

"Drop what?" Jackson leered, and Stacie shook her head with a laugh.

"Nothing. Let's eat," Stacie said as she pushed past Jackson and headed to the dining room. Stacie stood on the threshold of the dining room and smiled with amazement.

His grandmother's china and silver graced the table. Two black tapered candles were in front of the two settings and in the middle of the table was a vase filled with flowers he had handpicked from Ettie Mae's garden.

"Jackson, I love it," Stacie squealed. "And I love you," she said, nestling in his arms. An hour later Stacie was satiated. She ran her finger across the plate and skimmed up the last bit of curry. Then she stuck it in her mouth and sighed. Jackson watched her with amusement. "Do you want me to leave you and the plate alone?" he joked.

"Damn, that lamb was da bomb. Where did you learn to cook?"

"In college. I used to date a girl from the islands. It's a secret family recipe."

"Then how did you get it?" Stacie tilted her head and glared at him.

"I almost married her," Jackson said quietly, and Stacie's eyes widened to the size of half-dollars.

"Oh?"

"I was young," he said, as if that in itself explained everything. Stacie nodded and waited for more information. Jackson pushed himself up from the table and began taking dishes into the kitchen. Every time he returned he was met with Stacie's glare. She hadn't said a word to him since he'd announced that he had been engaged once.

It was so quiet it was loud. After the table was cleared, he reached for Stacie's hand and they walked into the living room and settled down on the couch.

"Her name was Cleo," he began. "She was a feisty little thing. You remind me of her," he said, and Stacie snorted. The last thing she needed was to be compared to one of his exes, most of all his ex-fiancée. Jackson nervously cleared his throat. "Well, anyway, she was always so focused and passionate . . . and she took care of me. One time after a day of exams, I went into my room and found all my clothes washed and folded. And she'd cook me some amazing dishes. And the sex was—"

"Yes?" Stacie narrowed her eyes until they were just little slits and Jackson quickly backpedaled.

"The sex was aw'ight. Just aw'ight," Jackson answered.

"So what happened to this superwoman?" Stacie asked.

"We broke up. She wanted me to go to law school and I didn't want to go. I heard through the grapevine that she's a judge *and* she's married to a lawyer."

"Good for her," Stacie said. "What's for dessert?" Stacie shot him a look that said, "Don't you dare say 'me.'"

"Um—chocolate, my grand made her chocolate cake for you."

"Cool. Feed a sistah," Stacie joked, then decided that she had punished Jackson long enough. When he returned to the room carrying two plates of cake, she snuggled into his arms.

"I take it you're not mad at me anymore."

"*Humph.* I wasn't mad at you before," Stacie lied, then pushed some cake in her mouth.

"Girl, you lie like a rug. But it's all good. Like the room?"

What was usually the family gathering spot was transformed into a spa that would rival any resort. Dozens of vanilla-scented candles were scattered throughout the room. Half a dozen oversize pillows were tossed casually across the floor. Soothing sounds of the ocean pulled it all together. Dozens of lip-shaped chocolates made a trail from the couch to his bedroom.

"Love it," Stacie said, and she did. She noticed a bottle of massage oil on the table and she jutted her chin toward it. "You plan on using that on me?"

"Yes, ma'am," Jackson drawled.

"When?"

"Whenever you're ready."

She stuck the last piece of cake in her mouth, then announced, "I'm ready now." And Jackson chuckled.

"My spoiled baby," he teased as he kissed her chocolate-stained lips. *"Mmmm,* delicious." He pulled himself away from her. It wasn't time for *that* yet. "Okay, drop the clothes," he ordered. Stacie was about to protest, but logic told her that he couldn't massage her with her clothes on. She pushed down the straps of her dress and it fell to her feet into a shiny puddle. She stepped over it, then toed it out of the way.

Jackson didn't bother to hide his admiration. Stacie was sexy as hell. In the flickering lights of the candles her skin was luminous; it looked as soft as silk, almost as silky as the two-inch piece of material that covered her privates. He gulped deeply.

"Damn, baby, do you plan on getting a massage or having me bang you until you can't walk?"

"Hopefully both," Stacie giggled, then sauntered over to Jackson. He backed up; he had a plan and he wanted to stick to it.

"Take off that Band-Aid you call panties, and your shoes," he quickly added before draping a blanket over the rug. "And lay facedown on the floor."

Stacie stuck her tongue out at him. "Spoil sport." But she did as he said. While she was getting comfortable on the floor, he undressed. "May I have one of these chocolates," she called over her shoulder.

"Sure," he answered as he reached for the massage oil. He drizzled it over her back and Stacie shivered.

"Oh, so cold," she moaned, but made mewling sounds when Jackson's hands began roaming over her body. His touch was firm yet soft at the same time.

"Is there any particular spot that I should focus on?" Jackson asked.

"Yeah, my ass."

He raised his eyebrows in surprise. "Okay . . . what about your shoulders or your lower back?"

"They're fine, just do my ass," she instructed.

"Okay, Miss Bossy Lady," he joked, and did as she wished. He loved her behind so much that he couldn't resist his next move. Leaning down until his lips touched her body, he traced the curves of her backside with the tip of his tongue; Stacie moaned loudly. He kept it up until she started whimpering and begged him to stop.

He dripped a dollop of massage oil on her butt, then began slowly kneading it. His oil-slicked hands moved over her behind like a professional's and he grabbed handful after handful and squeezed until she whimpered helplessly. Jackson smiled wickedly as he gently nibbled at her flesh. His smile grew even wider as he slipped his slicked hands between her legs and spread her slippery lips and stroked her love mound.

"Omigod!" Stacie panted, lifting her behind to give him better access. "Oh, oh, oh," she chanted as she slid closer to the edge. Then, "Oh! Jackson, I love you!" When she fell over the cliff, Jackson held her shaking body. The living room was silent except for Stacie's breathing, deep and low. "I want some chocolate," she mumbled.

"You want more chocolate? Here, have this," Jackson said and began poking her with his penis.

"I love *this kind* of chocolate," Stacie drawled as she reached out and tenderly stroked him. She felt powerful as he pulsed gently in her hand. "I wanna taste the chocolate," she drawled and bent toward him, sliding him into her mouth. "Doctors recommend a daily piece of chocolate," Stacie murmured, and all Jackson could do was nod.

Jackson whimpered as Stacie's fingers caressed his behind. Jackson could feel the pressure building.

"Nu-uh, not now. I want . . . no . . . I *need* to be inside you. Otherwise, I'ma explode all over your face," he groaned.

"And?" Stacie peeked up at him wearing a devilish grin.

"My spoiled girl is a nasty girl," he teased.

"Just trying to make you feel good, baby, that's all. Um— where's the protection?"

"Right here." Jackson slid his hand between the couch cushions and came out with a handful of condoms.

"Damn! I'm impressed," Stacie joked. "Now put it on!" Jackson slipped the condom on and gently lowered himself on top of her. His tongue slipped into her mouth and tenderly probed the soft recesses of her mouth. Her tongue greeted his like an old friend. They danced a familiar dance.

"Wow!" she said, dazed by the kiss.

"Yeah, wow!" Jackson said as he slid inside Stacie; she moaned softly. "I know, baby, I know," he panted as he slowly moved in and out of her, enjoying her wetness, her hotness and her softness. "I want to stay like this forever," Jackson moaned as he picked up his speed and Stacie met him with every thrust. "Oh baby!" he shouted as he exploded and Stacie quickly followed.

"You should see my bedroom. I hooked it up for you," Jackson bragged. They were spooning on the living room floor.

"Well, we still have tonight and tomorrow."

"True dat." Jackson was quiet, then said, "Stace?"

"Yeah?"

Jackson tugged at her hand. "Sit up, I need to talk to you."

Stacie's heart thudded at his serious tone. "What's wrong?"

Jackson cleared his throat. "Do you know why you're here?"

Stacie nodded. "Yeah, you wanted to spend the weekend with me."

"Yeah, but that's not all," he said, then, "I've never met anyone like you before. You're truly one of a kind. You stuck by me with all the Michelle drama; most women would've left. Jameel and Grandma love you and I love you. When I met you at Houston's I never thought in my wildest dreams that you would be the lady who stole my heart."

Stacie's eyes teared up. "Jackson, that is so sweet."

"I meant every word," Jackson said before he reached in between the couch pillows for the second time that evening and pulled out a little velvet box. He flicked open the lid and extended it to her. "Stacie Long, will you marry me?"

49

When Life Hands You Lemons, Make Lemonade . . . Then Add a Splash of Vodka

Trent pulled off his rubber gloves, dumped them in the garbage, then set the mop and bucket inside the broom closet before sauntering up to the front of the store, where Tameeka was counting the cash receipts. Judging by the smile on her face Heaven on Earth had had a good day. "Hey, Ms. T, I'm finished. Everything is clean and sunshiny fresh," he sang jokingly.

She stopped counting the stack of twenties and glanced up at him. "Are the bathrooms clean?"

"Yes, ma'am."

"Did you refresh the potpourri and replace the candles?" Trent made the checkmark sign in the air. "Okay, smarty-pants. Have all the rugs been vacuumed?"

"It's done," Trent said smugly.

"What about the windows? You know I hate fingerprints."

"Everything is done," Trent said proudly.

"Well, is the—"

"Ms. T," Trent said, laughing, "how long have I been working for you?" Tameeka grinned to herself as she stuffed the money along with credit card slips into a deposit bag.

"About three years," she answered.

"And every night you ask me the same thing. And I always tell you the same thing. Everything is clean and the way you like it."

"I know," Tameeka said, then sighed. "It's not that I'm doubting you. You're a good worker. I just like to make sure that everything is clean. I'm a stickler for stuff like that," Tameeka sheepishly admitted.

"No problem," Trent answered, then settled down on the couch.

"Hey, what are you doing? It's time for you to go." She glanced down at her watch. It was five o'clock.

"I'm waiting for you." He didn't want to leave her alone. Just last night he saw two suspicious-looking men hanging around the store and he warned her about them then. "I want to walk you to your car," Trent answered, and Tameeka's jaw dropped. Men twice his age were not as chivalrous as Trent. They could learn a thing or two from him.

"That's so sweet. I'll be okay. I won't be long. I need to finish some paperwork, then I'll be right behind you."

"I'd rather wait," Trent said, and to prove it he reached into his book bag and pulled out a book. He flipped it open and began reading.

"Trent," Tameeka called. "You really don't have to wait. I'll be okay. You go on home!" she demanded in a firm voice.

Trent pulled his attention away from his book. "Are you sure? I don't mind waiting."

"Go on!" she insisted.

"Okay," Trent answered slowly as he returned his book to his bag and inched toward the door. "I can stay if you want," he offered, hoping that Tameeka would change her mind.

"Go on, boy," Tameeka said laughingly, and playfully shoved

him out the door, then watched as he trotted down the street to the bus stop. She locked the door securely behind her and dimmed the lights, then walked wearily to her office. It had been a long day.

She fixed herself a cup of tea, then settled down at her desk. She shuffled some papers around, sat back in her chair and stared out into space. "You fucked up, Tameeka. You really fucked up!" she chastised herself. She reached down and tugged open her desk drawer and pulled out a picture of her and Tyrell.

They had it taken at the circus. He had his arm wrapped around her waist and her head was resting on his shoulder. Later that night, Tyrell had taken her home, where he had made hair-pulling, screaming-at-the-top-of-her-lungs love to her. "We were so happy," Tameeka whispered as the tears started rolling down her cheeks. She sobbed uncontrollably until she felt like someone had wrung her dry.

"I'm not gonna make any money crying over things that I can't change." She plucked a handful of tissues out of the box and wiped her eyes and blew her nose. "I should invest in this company, given all the tissues I've been using lately." She shook her head and threw the picture back into the drawer, then turned to the stacks of paper on her desk.

Two hours later she was still bent over her paperwork. "Oh, crap. Where did the time go?" She leaned back in her chair and stretched her arms up high over her head. "Time for me to head on home."

Tameeka gathered up her purse and the deposit bag stuffed with money and hurried to the front door. She quickly activated the alarm, then stepped out the door; even though it was early fall, it was so humid it felt like she had walked into pea soup. Tameeka plucked at her top and fanned herself. Busy fussing with her top, she didn't see the pair of cold, lifeless eyes peering out of the darkness, watching her every movement.

Just one of the drawbacks of living in the South, she silently reminded herself as she hunched forward to insert the key into the lock. "Damnit," she cursed. The keys had slipped from her hands and dropped to the ground. "That's what you get for hurrying," she muttered to herself as she bent to pick them up.

Moments later she was so intent on locking the door that she didn't hear the muffled footsteps shuffling up behind her. Nor did she feel the hot breath on her neck. She righted herself, slipped the keys in her purse, then stepped back and her foot connected with something hard and unmoving.

"What the—" Her eyes widened in alarm and she suddenly needed to pee. Her grip instinctively tightened around the money. Then just as fast as her fear appeared it disappeared and her lips curved up into a smile. Silly girl. Trent came back to help me. "You're such a gentleman. I'm glad you came—" She turned around and her mouth froze into a capital O. It wasn't Trent. Instead it was a six-feet-tall, two hundred-pound monster. He was wearing a black ski mask and peering at her with cold fish eyes.

"Thanks. Nobody ever called me a gentleman before," he drawled. Then, as if he had flicked a switch, his voice turned deadly. "Give me your money," he demanded.

"What?" Tameeka asked stupidly and suddenly an overwhelming urge to laugh blanketed her, but something told her that it wouldn't be a welcomed sound. "What did you say?" she questioned, and to her own ears her voice sounded hollow and detached, as if she was watching herself in a dream.

"What part don't you understand? Give—me—your—fucking—money—*bitch!* Don't make me have to use this," he growled, and stuck something hard into her side.

She glanced stupidly down at the cash deposit bag, then comprehension dawned. "Oh—here—you—go!" Her hands were trembling so bad that she was afraid that she was going to drop it. He must've thought so too because his hand whipped out and snatched it from her. He tucked it inside his jacket, then glowered at her.

"You'd better not tell anybody about this or I'ma have to come back and kill you," he threatened.

"I won't," Tameeka stammered, between clattering teeth.

"Just in case you think I'm playing with you, here's something for you." He pulled back and slapped her hard against the face. Her head snapped back and smacked the brick wall. All she remembered before crumpling in a faint was the shining gold tooth her attacker grinned at her as she slid to the ground.

50

Why It Makes Sense to Leave
Ex-Lovers in the Past

1. They're an ex for a reason
2. They can fuck up your current situation

Stacie stepped off the city bus and promptly sank into a pile of mud. "Damnit!" she cursed, then smiled grimly. It seemed to fit in with the theme of her day: Screw Stacie Day! She glanced down at her shoes and shook her head before trudging down the street.

Three interviews and eight hours later she was still unemployed. "I'm as jobless as a three-hundred-pound stripper." The interviews were a waste of time. They either wanted greenies fresh out of college or tired, beaten-down robots. She didn't fit either mold.

A wave a panic washed over her when her stack of bills flashed before her eyes. The pile was getter higher than Mt. Everest, and it was still growing. The worst part was, there still wasn't any money to get Lexie out of the garage.

Stacie gritted her teeth and continued her trek home. "I can't believe this," she muttered. "A whole day wasted." Waist deep in her thoughts, she didn't hear her name being called.

"Yo, Stacie!" She turned to find a familiar cream-colored

Jaguar roll up beside her. Sitting behind the wheel was Crawford Leonard Wallace III. Stacie rolled her eyes and kept walking.

That was all he needed, a challenge. Leaning out of the window, he called to her. "Come on. You're not going to say hi to an old friend?" he teased, then muttered in a playful tone, "Treatin' a brother like he some kind of dog."

Stacie stopped and glared at him. The image of him throwing her out of the hotel room flashed before her eyes. "Hi and 'bye," she spat, and continued walking, this time even faster. Crawford and his Jaguar were her shadow. "Come on, Stace," he begged. "Don't be so mean."

Just then, two thirty-something ladies dragged by. One was the color and the shape of an eggplant and the other, still wearing her hairnet, was prune colored. Both of them had on white blouses and navy pants, and looked as though they had spent the last fifteen hours voicing the all-time favorite phrase: "Would you like fries with that order?"

Crawford called out to them. "Hey, excuse me!" They both stopped in their tracks and turned weary eyes toward Crawford. The Jaguar was enough to get their attention, but the lady closest to Crawford recognized him, her eyes wide, and she elbowed her friend before whispering in her ear. Crawford grinned; he loved the attention. "I'm trying to convince this beautiful young lady to go out with me, but she won't," he said, and pulled his lips down into a frown.

The eggplant-colored lady hungrily eyed the car, then shouted, "Hell, if she won't, I will. And I'ma good cook, my son just left to live with his daddy, and I can put something on you in the bedroom that'll make you hoarse," she boasted.

Crawford laughed, but he gave her a second look. She wasn't much to look at, but you never know . . . he turned his attention back to Stacie.

"Come on, the least you can do is say hi to an old friend," he teased. "I'm sorry for the way I acted the last time we were together." Stacie stopped in her tracks and Crawford smirked. "I was the biggest asshole and I'm sorry."

"You're really sorry?" she asked, and scrutinized his face for any trace of a lie.

"I'm really, really sorry," Crawford repeated. "Come on, get in the car and let me take you out to eat."

Stacie pulled away from the car and started walking. "Can't! I have a fiancé," she called over her shoulder.

"Please let me take you out to dinner to show you how sorry I am. All we'll do is talk. Then when we're finished I'll bring you right home." Stacie stopped again and this time Crawford got out of his car and raced over to her. "Come have dinner with me. I'll have you home in three hours, maybe even less. Your boyfriend won't even miss you," he said as he subtly edged her to the car.

"Okay, three hours. No more. And I get to pick the place," Stacie relented.

"Bet." Crawford grinned as he made his way to the driver's side.

All we're doing is having dinner, nothing more, Stacie told herself as she slid into Crawford's car.

51

A Clear Head Allows for a
Clear Picture

Tameeka was huddled on the couch and her hands were wrapped around her cup of tea, but it didn't stop them from trembling. She stared up at Officer Watkins with terror-filled eyes. Lucky for her, not more than five minutes after she was knocked to the ground, a man and woman leaving a boutique saw her and called the police.

"Can you remember anything about him? An accent, his cologne, what he was wearing?" Officer Watkins asked gently.

"I told you, I don't remember anything," Tameeka answered, then suddenly she remembered a flash. "He had a gold tooth," she said warily, then looked down into her cup of tea. She looked like she had run headfirst into a brick wall. The right side of her face was three times its normal size and her right eye was puffy, with red welts zigzagging through it. Her once pretty outfit was stained and ripped beyond repair. She was wearing only one sandal, on her right foot. The left one had gotten lost during the scuffle.

"Wonderful!" Officer Watkins praised as he jotted down her comments. "How tall would you say he was?"

Tameeka knew he was tall, but not as tall as Tyrell. "About six feet or so," she answered calmly, but her hands shook as she brought the cup of tea to her mouth and took a sip.

"Good," Officer Watkins murmured. "Now we're getting somewhere. What about his weight? How much do you think he weighed?"

"Dunno," Tameeka shrugged. "He was huge," she answered weakly, and shuddered at the memory. He reminded her of a grizzly bear. "He had to have been over two hundred pounds."

"What was the color of the ski mask?"

"It was dark. Black or maybe navy blue," Tameeka answered. She was getting tired. All she wanted to do was go home and forget about everything. And she told Officer Watkins that.

"I only have a couple more questions," he quickly reassured her. Experience had taught him to interrogate the victim while the incident was still fresh, otherwise their recollection would be nil. "What about his clothing," Officer Watkins pressed. "Do you remember anything?"

Tameeka shook her head. "No. Other than it was dark too. But . . ." she paused, trying to clear her fuzzy mind. "I'ma say they were black and baggy. Kinda thuggish."

"Do you think he was in a gang?" Officer Watkins asked with a tad too much enthusiasm.

Tameeka shrugged. "I don't know what a gang member looks like," she said sarcastically.

"Sorry," Watkins mumbled.

"Do you think he'll come back?" Tameeka asked in a little girl voice. Just the thought that he was still out there and might return at any time terrified her.

Officer Watkins cleared his throat, then said, "Well, it's hard to say. Some robbers do return, others move on to another target."

"Thanks. I feel a whole lot safer now," Tameeka said; then returned her gaze to her tea.

"I'm sorry," Watkins said softly, and Tameeka looked up and saw the kindness in his brown eyes. It hit her that he was an attractive man. Over six feet and a little on the thin side, he had a kind face and a pair of sexy lips. Officer Watkins continued talking, oblivious to Tameeka's scrutiny. "But there are things that you can do to ensure that this doesn't happen again."

"Like what?" she asked as she pulled her gaze away from his lips and turned them to his eyes.

"Leave at a decent hour, for one. And if you have to leave late, have an escort. Hell, with the type of money you were carrying around, you should've had two escorts," he said, and Tameeka suddenly thought about Trent's offer.

"You can take a self-defense class. The police department offers them all the time. And lastly, get some pepper spray. That'll stun anybody," he said and laughed.

"Thank you," Tameeka said gratefully.

"Anytime," Officer Watkins said. Then they both turned toward the door. Somebody was knocking hard enough to break the door down. Officer Watkins gave her a questioning look.

"Oh, that must be Tyrell," Tameeka explained, setting down her tea and hurrying to the door. She had called Stacie, but she wasn't home. She had tried Mo on both his cell and work number but he didn't answer either. Bothering her grandmother was out of the question, so the only other person to call was Tyrell. He had promised to pick her up.

Tamecka snatched open the door and threw herself into Tyrell's arms. "I'm glad you came," she murmured against his chest.

"I wouldn't be any other place," Tyrell reassured her, and gave her a bear hug, which made her dissolve in tears. She wasn't sure if the tears were because of the robbery or because she was so happy to be in Tyrell's arms again.

"Er—um—I guess I should go now," Officer Watkins said as he inched toward the door. "You have my number. Call me if you remember anything," he said, and walked off leaving Tameeka and Tyrell alone.

52

Why You Should Never Cheat on Your Fiancé, Part I

1. You might leave behind incriminating evidence
2. You might get caught
3. Your fiancé will be devastated

Stacie turned her brown eyes to Crawford. He was sitting on the edge of the bed with his back to her. His head was bowed so low that all Stacie could see were his shoulders as she glared at him. The only sound in the hotel room came from the TV. They were watching a porn movie and the actress's fake moaning filled the room. "I don't know what happened, I thought I put it on right," he offered weakly. He had put his hands over his mouth and was speaking through the slits of his fingers.

"You thought you put it on right? How hard is it to put on a fucking condom!" she yelled. "All you have to do is unroll it and *blam!* It's on!" For the second time that day, a wave of panic washed over her. The enormity of what she had done hit her like a Mike Tyson punch; hard and painful, it left her breathless. The room began swimming and she dropped her head between her knees.

Sitting with her head dangling and sucking in the stale air, all she could think of was Jackson, and how he would feel if he ever found out. The bed shifted and she watched Crawford make his way across the room and into the bathroom. He closed the door and locked it securely behind him as if he was afraid she'd come in after him.

"I don't want you, man," she muttered to herself, then chuckled mirthlessly. "I should've said that two hours ago. Then I wouldn't have some damn busta's condom stuck up my pussy!" She pulled herself up into a sitting position and as she did so, she spied her shoes lying next to the bed. They were the pumps she had spent the day trudging around downtown in.

A second later she was on the floor and they were both in her hands. She had them up to her nose as if they were an oxygen tank. She alternated shoes, first a sniff from the left one, then the right, back and forth. Stacie didn't stop even when Crawford stepped out of the bathroom. She was too far gone to notice that he was in the room and even if she did, she didn't care.

Crawford stepped over Stacie and sat back down on the bed and stared at the TV with dead eyes. His fiancée was going to kill him if he got *another* woman pregnant. She was understanding when she found out about the cheerleader. Tolerant would best describe her reaction when a second lady turned up pregnant and pinned him as the daddy. But she was going to kill him if Stacie got pregnant.

The sniffing didn't calm Stacie like it usually did. She threw down the shoes and began to cry hysterically. "You're gonna have to get it out," she forced out between sobs, and Crawford came to life.

"Me?" he asked incredulously. "Why me?"

"It's your shit! And I want it out now!" She moved to the bed and flopped down on her back and spread her legs wide open. Crawford was a red-blooded man and normally such a sight would have aroused him to no end. But this time it sickened him.

"Oh, hell naw," he protested as he began backpedaling toward the door.

"Get your ass over here and get your shit outta me!" Stacie ordered. Her face had turned red and her eyes had narrowed to teeny slits.

Crawford fearfully inched toward her as if the devil himself was beckoning him. "What am I supposed to use?" he asked stupidly, and Stacie suddenly wondered what the hell attracted her to him. Not only was he a joke, but he was dumb as hell.

"How am I supposed to know? It's not like I get a condom stuck up my twat every day. Check your briefcase. I'm sure you have something." Just then his cell phone rang and Crawford made a move to pick it up. "Don't you dare," Stacie hissed between clenched teeth. "If you pick it up, I promise you that it'll be smashed to bits. Now let's focus on getting this thing out of me."

Crawford tightened his lips and plucked his briefcase off the floor. He could feel Stacie's eyes on him as he rummaged through it. He held up an ink pen and studied it, then turned questioning eyes on her.

"Hell naw, Crawford. You are not sticking that thing in me. I could get ink poisoning."

"Well, I don't know what to do," Crawford exclaimed, and threw his hands up helplessly. Then almost immediately a smile began to spread across his face. "What about if you try to push it out?"

"Push it out? Like I'm laying an egg?"

"No. Like you're having a freakin' baby," Crawford said nastily. "Just go into the bathroom and try. And push really hard."

"I'll try it," Stacie reluctantly agreed. She crab walked across the room to the bathroom. "This'd better work," she called over her shoulder. Stacie didn't bother to shut the door. She plopped right down on the toilet seat and bore down. She kept it up for five minutes. "It's not working," she yelled to Crawford.

Which was totally unnecessary, since he was watching her efforts from the bed.

He dropped his head into his hands. I'm dead, he thought. "What are we going to do?" he asked wearily.

"The hospital," Stacie said in a flat voice.

Panic swept across Crawford's face so fast that it was comical. If Stacie hadn't been in the situation that she was in, she would've had a good laugh, but all she could manage was a bitter chuckle. "I can't go to the hospital, somebody might recognize me," Crawford protested.

"Somebody might recognize you?" Stacie asked incredulously. "This is too goddamn much. *You're* too goddamn much. You're coming to the hospital with me, so put on some fucking clothes!"

53

Don't Go Fishing Until You Can Stomach Gutting a Fish

Thanks so much for making sure I got home okay," Tameeka said gratefully, and gave Tyrell a watery smile. Tameeka nervously cleared her throat, then laid her hand on his arm. "Tyrell—"

He shrugged her hand off as if it was an annoying bug. "Hey, don't worry about it," he muttered, then flashed her a weak smile. The billionth apology was on the tip of her tongue and he sensed it.

"Okay, I need to bounce. I'm already late for work. Need to make that cheese, otherwise this big cat ain't gonna eat. And you know how much I love to eat . . ." His voice drifted off as his gaze locked with Tameeka's. Tyrell broke the spell. "Call me if you need anything." He wrapped his arms around her and hugged her tightly and Tameeka wrapped her arms around his neck and held on for dear life. After a heartbeat, he sighed inwardly and gently untangled her arms and pushed her away.

"Take care, okay. Don't forget to call me." He was halfway to the door when she shouted.

"No! What happens if he comes back to get me?" Tameeka cried pitifully, and rushed across the room and clutched Tyrell's arm.

"Oh damn, I didn't know he got your purse too," Tyrell groaned and smacked his forehead with his open hand. "That's some shit. We're gonna have to change the locks."

"He didn't get my—"

"You okay?" Tyrell asked, concern marring his face as he looked down at the top of her head. She nodded softly and when she looked up at him, her eyes were glassy with tears. She blinked and they rolled gently down her cheeks and plopped on his sleeve and into his heart.

"He didn't get my keys," she sniffed. "But he got my purse and I had a whole bunch of stuff with my address on it," she lied, then swiped her hand across her eyes. Everything was safely tucked in her desk drawer. "He could get *me,*" Tameeka sobbed.

"That's okay, baby," he soothed, and pulled her into his arms and she nestled her tear-soaked face against his chest. "Nobody's getting in here while I'm here. I'll take care of you," he vowed, her knight in shining armor.

"You will?" Tameeka murmured; she felt Tyrell nod. "I'm ready to go to bed now. I've had a *long* day," she whispered in a little girl voice and peeked up at him.

"Yes, you have," he said, comforting her. "C'mon, let's go." He tugged her arm and led her toward the bedroom.

"Do—you—think—I—should—shower—first?" she hiccupped, then gave him a look that made his heart melt and his penis hard.

"Um—er—yeah. Go on, take a shower, I'll stand guard by the front door," he joked faintly, and silently thanked God for the baggy clothes he was wearing. He began backing out of the bedroom.

"Hey! Where're you going?" Tameeka whined. "Don't leave me alone. I'm scared."

Tyrell stopped at the door and casually dropped his hands in front of his pants. "Just giving you privacy, baby."

"Oh, thank you . . . but I'll feel a hundred percent safer if you sat on the bed while I'm in the shower . . . you never know where he might show up . . . and he is pretty big," she whispered in a fearful tone.

"Okay," Tyrell huffed, then stomped over to the bed. "I'd better call in and let them know I'ma be late."

Inside the bathroom, Tameeka stood in front of the mirror, where she knew Tyrell could see her from his perch on her bed. She giggled to herself, then put on a face of nonchalance as she began undressing.

She slipped off her top, wadded it into a ball and tossed it in the trash can; she didn't want any reminders of the robbery. Her lacy black bra was next; she rolled her shoulders as she ran her finger slowly over the left strap, then slid it over her shoulder. She did the same with her right strap. Then she let her fingers play and skip over the clasp. Tameeka peeked in the mirror and saw that Tyrell had inched to the edge of the bed wearing a look of rapture as he stared at her reflection. With one flick of her fingers her breasts sprang out like two cantaloupes and she could've sworn she heard a moan of desire coming from the bedroom.

Tameeka hid a smile as she shimmied out of her pants; then toed them into the garbage. She was glad that she had worn a thong; the silky black material was nothing more than an extra-wide piece of floss. She ran her finger along the elastic waistband and gently tugged it down past her hip. Then she pulled her hands out as if she had changed her mind. She almost giggled when she heard Tyrell suck in a mouthful of air. She seductively ran her hand over her behind as her hips began gyrating and she slowly swayed back and forth while slipping her thong down past her hips, down past her thighs, letting it drift down like a feather to her feet.

Her shower was short and quick. She wrapped an oversize towel around her, then padded into the bedroom, where she found Tyrell sitting on the bed, trying hard not to look at her.

"I feel a hundred percent better. Thank you, *my strong, black king*, for protecting me," Tameeka gushed. Tyrell snorted in response and pushed himself off the bed.

" 'K, I'm out," he announced, and Tameeka's face crumbled. She scurried over to her dresser and began rearranging her bottles of perfume, lotions and fingernail polish. "See ya," Tyrell called out to Tameeka's back. Tyrell shrugged, then ambled to the bedroom door. What he didn't see was Tameeka's mouth turning into a grin when her hand rested on a bottle of lotion.

"Can you do me one little itsy-bitsy favor before you go?" she asked in a super-sweet syrupy voice. Tyrell glanced over his shoulder and what he saw made him stop in his tracks and cause his penis to pump up to three times its normal size. Her towel was gone and drops of water glittered over her naked body and it sparkled like it was encrusted in diamonds. "I can *never* reach my back . . . can you please do it?" she asked, and held the lotion out to him.

Tyrell stared at the lotion in her outstretched hand as though it was poison.

"Er—I *really* have to get to work. Maybe some other time," he fumbled as he tried to back out of the room while keeping his hands in front of his crotch.

"It'll only take a minute. If it takes more than that, you can spank me," Tameeka teased. "Not that you haven't done that before." She winked and he flinched as though she had hit him. "C'mon, puh-leeze," she begged. "It'll help me go to sleep." It was ten o'clock in the morning and she was going on twenty-seven hours without sleep.

"Just your back. Nothing more," he growled, and took the lotion out of her hand. "Turn around," he demanded. Tameeka did as he said, but then she peeked over her shoulder.

"Right *here?* You wanna rub lotion on my back right *here?* Wouldn't the bed be a lot better?"

"Here is fine," Tyrell mumbled.

"What happens if I fall? I read a story on the Internet where a lady fell right on her face when her husband was rubbing lotion on her back; he inadvertently pushed so hard that she fell flat on her face and broke her nose. I don't want that to happen to me," she said, and pulled away from him.

"You're not gonna fall!" He glared at her and Tameeka stared at him. "Fine!" Tyrell almost shouted. "We'll do it on the bed. C'mon." He flopped down on the bed and Tameeka sat down in front of him.

"Okay, I'm ready," she whispered, and her voice was like a caress over Tyrell's skin.

"Whatever," Tyrell mumbled as he squirted a dollop of lotion in his hands. As soon as he touched her skin, he knew he had made a bad decision. Her skin felt as smooth as silk. It took every ounce of his energy to focus on rubbing the lotion in.

"Oooh," Tameeka moaned. *"That feels so good.* Can you do the front?" And before Tyrell could protest, she had turned around and had her breasts in his face. "Can you lotion these too," she whispered seductively.

"Um—er—Meek, I don't think this is a good idea."

"What? Lotioning a friend's body. What's wrong with that? C'mon now, we're past all this. Are you afraid something will happen?" she asked, cocking her head to the side.

"Not at all," Tyrell shot back. His hands wavered for a heartbeat over her breasts before he dipped his hands and started lotioning them. Using small, circular movements, he worked the lotion into her breasts, inched down to her stomach, then worked his way back up to her breasts.

Gawd, his hands feel sooo good! Her nipples hardened to dime-size buds and what had started off as a trickle between her legs had grown into a river. "Oh God, T, you make me feel *sooo* good," she moaned. "Here, baby, momma want you to taste this." She cupped one of her breasts and swiped her nipple across his lips. "Go 'head, take it," she encouraged. She sucked in a stream of air when Tyrell's hot lips clamped over her nipple. Tameeka grabbed the back of his head and pressed his face into her chest, giving him a mouthful of her breasts. "Do the other one," Tameeka demanded, and Tyrell obeyed.

"I miss this," he moaned, and gently nudged Tameeka so that she was lying on the bed facing him. He stood up and pulled off his shirt and the rest of his clothing quickly followed. Naked, he stood over her in all his glory. "My black king," she murmured, and her eyes filled with tears. *He's so beautiful.* Bending to his knees, Tyrell leaned over and showered the inside of her thighs with butterfly kisses. Her feet were next. Every toe was treated to a long, lingering suckle. Tyrell retraced his kisses and buried his face in between her legs and Tameeka clamped her legs around his head and bucked her hips. They were working in perfect harmony, her hips and his mouth.

Tameeka was muttering incoherently as Tyrell's tongue worked on her. "Oh, baby, baby," Tameeka groaned as her body thrashed wildly on the bed. "I'm about to—I'm about to come!" Her body bucked wildly and then she lay on the bed, gasping for breath.

"What's wrong? I'm too much for you to handle?" he teased, then leaned over and kissed her gently on the lips. Tameeka barely managed to shake her head. "Whatever," he grinned as he reached into her nightstand and pulled out a condom and slipped it on. "Ready or not, here I come," Tyrell sang, then mounted Tameeka and slid himself into her. For the first time in a long time, she felt whole.

"Ah Tyrell, do me, baby," she groaned. With her arms

wrapped around his neck and her hips matching his stroke for stroke, she was tasting heaven on earth.

"I'm doing you, baby," Tyrell grunted. "Do you want me to do you like this?" he asked, slowing his stroke. "Or do you want me to do you like this?" He picked up the tempo and moved so fast that it left Tameeka breathless. "Or maybe you want me to do you like this?" he teased, rotating his hips in tight little circles, and Tameeka whimpered as wave after wave of pleasure washed over her.

Seeing that she had been satisfied, Tyrell let loose. "Yeah, baby, *I* like it when *I* do you like this," he groaned, and increased his speed until he found his release.

"Man!" a dazed Tyrell murmured. This wasn't supposed to happen, he thought. And it wasn't supposed to feel good. Without glancing down at her, he rolled off of Tameeka and ambled to the bathroom.

"Thank you," a droopy-eyed Tameeka moaned with a smile. She was lying on top of the blankets, curled up into a ball, when Tyrell returned to the room.

Tyrell bent down and begin plucking his clothes off the floor and quickly dressed. All the while Tameeka was lying still on the bed. "Tameeka," he called. "Tameeka!" he repeated. "We need to talk."

"Oh, okay," Tameeka mumbled, and managed to pry open her eyes. "Wasn't this fun?" she giggled sleepily. "When are we gonna do it again?"

"We're not," Tyrell muttered, and averted his eyes.

"What?" Tameeka demanded. The shock knocked the sleep out of her. "What do you mean, we're not? You come over here and fuck me! You think you can use me whenever you want?"

"Use you? Fuck you? Listen, Tameeka. *You* called me. *You* played that little game in the bathroom. *You* played the game with the lotion." He began mimicking her, 'Here, massage me, just my back. Nothing will happen.' Well, something did happen. And I'm sorry it did," Tyrell huffed.

"You wanted me just as much as I wanted you," Tameeka said in a watery voice, and her eyes began filling with tears.

"I did want you and I still do. But it's over between us. I can't trust you, Tameeka. I don't ask a lot from my lady, but trust is definitely up there."

"Can't we try again?" she pleaded. And her heart broke when Tyrell shook his head. "We can be fuck buddies, you know. Strictly sex. What do you think about that?"

Tyrell silently eyed her while contemplating her question.

54

Why You Should Never Cheat on Your Fiancé, Part II

1. You totally lose his trust if he finds out
2. You feel like shit after doing it
3. Your fiancé will be devastated
4. You'll probably never be able to look him in the face afterward

Stacie's name blared over the PA system. She glanced at Crawford; he was sleeping. Not bothering to wake him, she scurried across the waiting room to the nurses' desk. "Ms. Long, the doctor will see you now." On leaden feet, Stacie followed the nurse to the exam room. At least she was out of the emergency room; the two-hour-long wait had been nearly unbearable. "Undress from the waist down, use this to cover yourself," she said, tossing a sheet of paper at Stacie. "The doctor will be in shortly," she announced before turning on her heel and stepping out of the room.

Stacie swore she saw a smirk on the nurse's face; but she was too tired to say anything. It was two o'clock in the morning and all she wanted was to be home in her own bed and not sitting on some life-size ice slab. As soon as she tucked the paper covering under her legs, the doctor strolled into the room. He was forty-something, gaunt, and tall. His black hair was plastered to his scalp with either water or gel; Stacie didn't know which and didn't care to find out. His clothes were wrinkled and two days of new growth hid his chin.

Without introducing himself or issuing a greeting, he said, "So Ms. Long, your chart says that you have a condom stuck inside you." He said so matter-of-factly that it made Stacie wonder if her condition was a common occurrence and he extracted lodged condoms nightly.

Even if that was the case, it didn't alleviate her embarrassment. "Yep," she muttered, and fiddled with the paper sheet.

"Okay, let's take a look," he said as he set the chart down and plucked two latex gloves out of the box, then slipped them on. "Put your legs up in the stirrups," the doctor instructed.

Stacie had been to enough gynecologist appointments to know to scoot all the way to the end of the table until it felt like she was going to fall off, then stuck her legs in the stirrups. "This will be a little cold and you're going to feel a little discomfort," he said as he inserted the speculum and expanded it. It felt like hours to Stacie as he poked and prodded her, but it was really only a couple of minutes. "Yep, there's a condom in there," he needlessly confirmed.

"Thanks for verifying that," Stacie replied in a nasty tone.

"We'll get that right out of you," he tersely replied. Then with all the warmth of an uptight Catholic schoolteacher, he inserted his finger and methodically rooted around until he snagged the offending piece of rubber. It dangled on the tip of his finger. It was empty. Stacie shot up on the table.

"What the—? What happened to all the stuff that was in it?"

The doctor gave her a strange look, then said, "It emptied inside you."

"You mean," Stacie gasped, "his *stuff* is inside *me?*"

"I trust that you were using another form of birth control?"

"No," Stacie moaned, then fell back on the examining table and curled into the fetal position.

"You know you have options," the doctor said.

"What are you talking about?" Stacie mumbled.

"We have an emergency pill just for situations like yours. It's called the morning after pill, and you take it after having unprotected sex. It'll prevent pregnancy."

Stacie's eyebrows shot up, then she slowly shook her head. "No, I don't want any pill. Sometimes life's problems can't be solved with a little pill. I'll just wait and see what happens," Stacie said, jutting her chin out.

55

Life Is Your Personal Orchestra and You're Its Conductor

Tameeka picked up the picture she and Tyrell had taken at the circus and studied it, looking for any signs that could have predicted their future. A smile teased her lips as she gently placed the picture in the "Tyrell box." The box held everything that reminded her of Tyrell. She dragged it into her bedroom and pushed it into the back of her closet.

Reaching into her nightstand drawer, she pulled out her journal, then padded into the living room and stretched out on the couch to begin writing.

> *I just packed away my last Tyrell memory. I know that memories aren't really packed away because everything is still in my heart, where I can take a peek whenever I want.*

> *I guess I should've thrown all the stuff away, but that would've been like destroying a piece of me, a part of my history. All of which made me who I am today.*

But I am so proud of myself, I did it all without shedding a tear. I thought I would be blubbering like a baby, but I wasn't.

Cheating . . . Tameeka the Cheater. Crap! It still looks bad in writing. I can't believe that I did that to another human being. Especially to someone who loved me. I guess I can tell myself that at least I didn't commit murder. But in a way I did. I broke his heart and killed his trust in me.

But I guess he's surviving, because Stacie told me that he's dating someone new. I truly wish him the best. He's a wonderful guy and he deserves a woman who can love him the way he deserves to be loved.

I've learned that life is about making choices and sometimes we don't make the best decisions. But we always have to be accountable for our actions, no matter what. It has taken me a while, but I've forgiven myself. I guess that's interesting to say . . . that I've forgiven myself, because it does sound odd to me. If I were to hear someone say that, I'd ask them: "How can you possibly bestow forgiveness on yourself?" But I believe that I must purge myself and let go of the past so that I can move forward. So that's what I mean, by forgiving myself. I don't know if I'll ever really be over Tyrell, he'll always hold a piece of my heart.

I can honestly say that I'm ready to be committed in a healthy, fulfilling relationship. Now I just have to find that right person.

Tameeka closed the journal, picked up her mug of tea and wondered what the future might hold for her.

56

What's Worse Than Taking a Pregnancy Test at 3:00 A.M.?

1. Getting a rectal exam
2. Having to take a fucking pregnancy test at 3:00 A.M.
3. Finding out you're pregnant by someone who isn't your fiancé

Has it come yet?" Tameeka asked.

"No!" Stacie moaned, then fell back on her bed. For the past two weeks, she had been doing something that she had never done in her life, praying for her period. "I'm never, *ever* late."

"Have you told Jackson?"

"Have I told Jackson? Have I told Jackson?" Stacie hissed. "Are you fucking *crazy*? Not only will I lose the best man I've ever had, but I'll hurt him and Jam. And I can't do that," she said, hugging the pillow to her chest. Her eyes welled with tears.

"Stace, I don't understand how you let this happen. Where was your head?"

Stacie shook her head. Her eyes were glassy, but she refused to cry. "I don't know. Guess that I didn't want to think about my problems. I was worried about all this shit! Finding a job. Lexie.

Having to move in with my moms. And when he offered me dinner . . ." She shrugged.

"Well, it looks like you brought home a little something extra in the doggie bag," Tameeka said half-jokingly.

"Stop being an asshole," Stacie said.

"Hey, don't be jumping on me. I told you that the dick was going to get you in trouble one day," Tameeka said.

"Well, we've both been fucked, because it got you in trouble too. So there," she said. "Meek! What am I gonna do?" she wailed. "What happens if I *am* pregnant? And it's *Crawford's* baby? Jackson ain't gonna want me then. And he's the best thing that's ever happened to me."

"So . . . you're saying that you'd keep it?" Tameeka asked incredulously.

Stacie looked at her friend as if she had just told her that she was an alien. "Yeah. What else would I do? I wouldn't want to kill my baby just because of my foolishness."

"Oh! The good thing is that at least you'll have the green–eyed, curly-haired baby that you've been fiending for all this time. But the bad thing is that you'd better get down on your hands and knees and pray hard that you're not pregnant. Because if you are, and you're gonna keep it, you're on your own, 'cause Jackson will kick you to the curb."

"Believe me, I've been praying so much that I've worn two little holes on the side of my bed." They were both silent, then in a little girl voice, Stacie said, "I really don't know what to do if I'm pregnant. I don't have a job, I don't have a car and I'm gonna be living with my moms. You were right. I'm just like Nevia."

"No you're not . . . you're human. A stressed-out sistah. I'm sorry I even said that," Tameeka said. "But have you at least taken a pregnancy test?" she asked in a quiet voice.

"No."

"Well . . ."

"Come with me?" Stacie squeaked.

"You know I will," Tameeka said, then, "I hope you don't think I was too hard on you . . . you know with what I said earlier . . . about the dick getting you in trouble?"

"I didn't appreciate your attitude. If that's what you mean," Stacie answered as she slipped into a pair of sneakers.

"I was mad at you. You saw what I went through with Tyrell because of my cheating. Now you're doing the same thing to Jackson. And I don't want to see you or Jackson hurt like I do."

"Trust me, girl, after what happened with Crawford, no one but Jackson Brown has the combination to open these legs."

Tameeka gave a nod of approval. "Good! Now let's go down to Wal-Mart and pick up that pregnancy test."

57

Good Friendships Are Like Elastic Waistbands, the Looser They Get, the More Comfortable They Are

his is our last night together," Tameeka replied sadly. She and Stacie were sitting on their balcony with four bottles of wine between them. They were already mostly through the second bottle. It was nine o'clock at night and Jackson was coming first thing in the morning to help Stacie move into her mother's apartment.

"I know," Stacie murmured. Then said, "Damn, girl, we've been living together for ten years, longer than most marriages," she joked, and Tameeka simply nodded. "And now I'm getting married," she said, eyeing her one-carat, princess-cut ring. "I truly can't believe it. I owe it all to you, girl."

"To me?"

"Yeah, you're the one who made me give up my list. Otherwise I'd still be using that as a blueprint for a man."

"You would've figured it out eventually," Tameeka modestly replied, then gulped down her wine. It was her fourth glass.

Stacie cut her eyes at Tameeka. "I am so relieved that the

pregnancy test came up negative. That was the first time in my life I was happy to have cramps. You can't imagine how scared I was."

"You got lucky. So you're not gonna tell Jackson?"

"Hell no! I don't believe in all that confession stuff. It's not good for the soul, all it does is cause a lot of problems."

"Ain't that the truth," Tameeka answered, and poured another glass of wine. "So when's the wedding again?"

"June twenty-fifth, just three months away. I can't wait. And you're gonna be my maid of honor," Stacie sang. "And when you get married—"

Tameeka gazed up at the moon. It was crescent shaped, it could've been either a smile or frown, depending on your point of view. "Stop it, don't bite your tongue. I'm okay," she reassured her friend. "And I will get married. Thanks to all my journaling I think that I've gotten to the root of my problems. I feel whole."

"I'm so happy for you!" Stacie exclaimed. "We've finally grown up!"

"I know," Tameeka said. "And I have the perfect thing to celebrate with. I'll be right back." Tameeka sauntered off and returned minutes later holding a large pizza box.

"Hey, where did that come from?" Stacie asked.

"I picked it up on the way home from work. Then I hid it in the oven," she giggled. Tameeka opened up the top and pulled out an oversize slice of pizza loaded with pepperoni, sausage, olives, green peppers, anchovies, onions, and cheese. She immediately took a big bite.

"Hey, what happened to your diet?" Stacie asked as she took a smaller slice and began nibbling on it.

"Oh, the radish and tuna diet? Had to give it up. I was eating so much tuna that cats were beginning to think that I was a big ole fish and tried to have me for lunch."

"Silly," Stacie laughed. "I'm really gonna miss you," she said softly.

"I'ma miss you more," Tameeka joked, then her voice grew serious. "You're my girl. We have our ups and downs, but we always get past it. You've been there every time I needed you. You provided me with a shoulder to cry on, case in point," she said, and rested her hand on Stacie's shoulder. It was still damp from her tears. "You've lent me an ear when I needed one and you've given me a place to call home. You've given me so much," Tameeka said, and she could feel the tears welling again. No more, she willed. "My offer is still open. You can always stay here."

"I would love to. You don't know how much I would. But moving in with Momma and Nevia will force me to do something. It'll be too easy for me to sit around and not do something if I stayed here," she said.

"How's Nevia doing?"

"I'm happy to say that my little sister is back on track. She was like a fiend for that car."

"So she never got it back from Carlos?"

"Nope. He kicked his uncle's butt, sold the car and blew the money in Vegas."

"Nu-uh!"

"Yep. That's just how Carlos rolls."

They grew silent then, both enjoying the food, the wine and each other's company.

"I have a toast," Tameeka announced, and raised her glass. "To a long-lasting friendship with my girl, to happiness, to success and to the dick," she finished, and they both burst out laughing.

58

Single Father's Guide to Dating
Tip # 100

Never leave home without condoms, breath mints and deodorant.

Jackson dropped the last box on the floor. "Damn! What's in the box? A hundred pairs of shoes? At least we're done moving."

Stacie sat on the bed and looked up at Jackson; misery was etched in her face.

"What's wrong baby?" he asked, sitting down beside her on the bed and wrapping his arms around her.

Stacie rested her head on his shoulder and inhaled deeply; she loved his scent. "I feel like I'm going backward," she wailed, relieved that it was out in the open.

Jackson hugged her tighter and glanced down at the top of her head. "Have you ever seen a sling shot?" he asked. "It starts at the same place, then it's pulled back and when it's let go, it soars to crazy heights and distances. That's you. Even though you're going back a couple steps, that's giving you strength to soar and achieve wonderful things."

Stacie looked at him in awe. "You are *so* smart. Thank you," she said, and kissed him softly. They sat in each other's arms for a while, listening to each other's heartbeat and just enjoying each other. Pretty soon Jackson's hands were roaming over her body.

"Excuse me, sir, but we can't be doing this under my momma's roof," she said saucily, but she pressed herself closer to him. "She'll put me out."

"I doubt it," he said, thinking of Nevia and her three designer babies. "Besides, we're not doing anything wrong," Jackson whispered, then slid his hand under her shirt and cupped a breast.

"What happens if she opens the door?" Stacie said between moans.

"We'll just tell her that we're playing doctor," Jackson murmured as he pulled Stacie's shirt over her head and tossed it into the corner.

"You make too much noise," Stacie said half-convincingly. She had her eyes closed and her hand was on Jackson's head, urging him to her breasts.

"Look who's talking," Jackson murmured around a mouthful of breast. He pulled away long enough to slip his hands into her shorts.

"Oh Jackson!" Stacie sighed. It was somewhere in the middle of a groan and a protest. "We can't do anything." Her hips bucked toward him as his fingers eased into her panties. The last thing she needed was for her mother to walk in and find her and Jackson christening the bedroom.

"What?" Jackson feigned innocence, then winked as he pulled off her shorts and panties and tossed them in the corner along with her top. Stacie stretched out on the bed and Jackson gazed hungrily down at her. The sunlight streaming into the room showered her body, giving her an exotic golden glow. Jackson shook his head in wonder; he didn't understand it, but she got more beautiful every time he saw her. He leaned down and kissed her eyes, her nose, then her lips, his kisses soft like

wisps of air. Their eyes met and Stacie sighed happily and settled back on the bed, her mother forgotten. Jackson kissed a
trail from her breasts to her belly button.

"You're beautiful, you know that?" he asked. "I'm so glad
you're in my life," he murmured as he moved downward and
placed his face between her legs. Stacie's hips bucked and she
began moaning.

"Here, use this," Jackson said and handed her a pillow to
cover her face. "Make as much noise as you want." He grinned,
then resumed his position. He eased his tongue into the soft
folds of her mound and swiped it over her love knob. She
moaned so loud that he was afraid that maybe the pillow
wouldn't be enough. He smiled devilishly as he slid two fingers
into her, then nibbled at her clit as he slid his fingers in and
out. Stacie's hips moved fast to keep up with his fingers, and
they were bucking when she had her powerful orgasm.

"Gawd," she said dreamily as she gasped for breath. "That
was amazing." She peeked at the door. "Hurry up," she urged,
as Jackson slipped off his clothes.

Jackson slipped on a condom and stood poised over her.
"Fast or slow?" he teased.

"What do you think?"

"We'll go fast," Jackson decided for her. He bent down and
covered her mouth with his, smothering her groans. "You feel
so good," he groaned out of the corner of his mouth. "Why do
you feel so good?" he teased, and all Stacie could do was shake
her head; he left her speechless.

"I love you," Stacie groaned as waves of pleasure washed
over her body.

"I love you too," Jackson shouted as waves of pleasure covered him.

Suddenly there was a knock on the bedroom door and
Jackson and Stacie froze. "Is everything all right in there?" Her
mother asked, concerned.

Stacie stuck her face in Jackson's chest to smother a giggle. "We're fine, Ma. A box fell on Jackson's toe, but he's okay now," Stacie yelled.

"How you doing, Jackson?" Gladys called from the other side of the door.

"Fine, Momma Gladys," he assured her.

"You need some ice? I can get you some ice. I'll be right back," she said.

"No!" Stacie and Jackson yelled simultaneously. Stacie hopped up from the bed and opened the door a crack and assured her mother that Jackson was fine and that he didn't need any ice. Stacie switched back over to the bed and plopped down on top of Jackson. "Man, that was close," she said as she laid her head on Jackson's chest.

"I know. Can you imagine her expression if she had opened up the door . . . ?"

"Crazy. C'mon." She leapt off the bed and stood in front of Jackson with her hands on her hips. "Help me unpack. I'll do my lingerie."

"And I'll do you," Jackson said, grinning as he reached for her again.

59

Let Love Find You,
Don't Go Chasing It

It was late and Tameeka had already sent Trent and Bea home. Sade was playing softly on the CD player, and she hummed along as she strolled around the store, putting stray items back in their homes. Tameeka didn't hear the door stealthily being pulled open, nor did she see the man watching her as she moved around the store. He crossed the floor and stood behind her but by the time she sensed his presence it was too late, he was on her. Mohammad grabbed her up in a bear hug and Tameeka struggled in his arms and let out an ear-splitting scream. Mohammad tightened his grip.

"Calm down, it's only me . . . Mohammad," he breathed in her ear. His arms relaxed around her and she turned around with fearful eyes.

"Mohammad?" Tameeka squeaked, trembling as she tried to squash the flashback of her mugging. "What the hell are you doing, scaring me like that?" she admonished in a shaky voice as she glared at him. He didn't look as bad as he had the last time she'd seen him, when he was being put into an ambulance. The only reminder of that night was his broken nose that had healed slightly crooked.

"Didn't mean to, baby, just wanted to hug you. It always turned me on to see you cleaning up your piece of heaven," he joked, then noticed her shaking. "Are you okay?" Mohammad asked while rubbing her arms.

"I'm fine. You scared the shit out of me though," she answered, then told him about the robbery. She left out the part of her and Tyrell's lovemaking.

"Fuck! He was probably the same man who robbed Mr. Wang. Baby, I'm sorry I wasn't here," he soothed as he pulled her into his arms and Tameeka rested against his body. "Are you okay?" Mohammad asked, tilting her face up and searching her eyes. Tameeka nodded. "So why are you here by yourself tonight? Where's your boyfriend?"

Tameeka ignored the question about Tyrell, and answered the first question instead. "I'm safe. I had an alarm system installed and I changed the locks . . . Hey, how did you get in?" she asked, her eyes wide.

Mohammad shrugged. "I walked in, the door was unlocked."

"Oh crap! I am getting so forgetful. Man, am I glad it was you," she said, giving him a weak smile. "Let me go lock it." She turned to go, but Mohammad caught her arm. She looked up at him, her brow raised.

"I locked it," he murmured, looking at her like he wanted to devour her.

A shiver of excitement shot through her. "So where have you been?" she asked.

"Traveling across the country. I had a lot of art shows, did some festivals. Even taught some classes. But it's always good to be back home," he said, eyeing her, then his hand whipped out and pulled her against him. "You didn't answer my question. Where's your boyfriend?" Mohammad asked.

"Don't have one," Tameeka muttered into his chest. "We broke up . . . the night he caught us."

"Good," he drawled.

Tameeka sucked her teeth. "Mo, why would you say something so mean?" she asked, then inhaled deeply when she saw the desire burning in his eyes.

"This is why," he said, hungrily covering her mouth with his, catching Tameeka off guard. She momentarily froze, then her body thawed under Mohammad's heat. She wrapped her arms around his neck as she plunged her tongue deeper into his mouth. Mohammad moaned against her lips.

Tameeka tenderly caressed his face as he rained kisses over her eyelids, forehead and lips. They sank to the floor, snatching off the other's clothes along the way.

"I missed you," Mohammad breathed, as his mouth moved over Tameeka's breasts, sucking on her engorged nipples as though they were lollipops. Tameeka writhed underneath him as her hands roamed freely over his body. She gasped with desire when Mohammad tongued his way down to her mound.

"Oh, Mo," she exhaled, and her hips shot up to catch his mouth as it zeroed in on her button. He gently sucked it and nibbled on it as though it was a delicacy until she felt the sweet stirrings of her climax. Then it built into an explosion that left her trembling from head to toe.

"You're shaking, baby," Mohammad said as he nipped at her shoulder.

Tameeka grinned up at him. "These are good shakes," she reassured him as she caught her breath. "I saw fireworks," she gushed.

"Good, wanna see more?" he asked, then before she could respond, he quickly mounted her and slid into her hotness.

"Mohammad," Tameeka groaned, arching her body toward him. Her orgasm came at a dizzying speed, leaving her gasping for air. "We didn't use anything . . . I might get pregnant," Tameeka whispered.

"Would that be a bad thing?" Mohammad asked, smiling at her. "I want us back together. Not just as fuck buddies, or cut buddies but as a real couple. I guess seeing you with Tyrell made me realize how much I love you," he admitted, then cupped her face in his hands and asked, "Tameeka, would you be my wife?"

60

Why It's Important to Face Your Fears

1. They can hold you captive
2. They can prevent you from living your life

Stacie pulled her eyes away from the latest issue of *Essence* magazine and nervously glanced down the hall. She couldn't see it, but it was there; the door, or more accurately, the door to *the closet.* The same closet where she had spent half her childhood hiding from her drunken father and sniffing shoes. She frowned a little, then settled back on the couch.

The place was unusually quiet. In the short time she had moved back home, she had become accustomed to family noise. The cry of a baby, women squabbling followed by gentle laughter and the soft scratches of footsteps, but now it was just Stacie, alone, in the apartment. Stacie unfolded her legs, then planted them firmly on the floor and peered fearfully down the hall.

She tossed the magazine to the side, and wearing a look of resolve, she pushed herself off the couch and marched toward the closet.

"Today I'm going to do this," she muttered as she tried to ignore her clammy hands and the roaring in her ears. This was her twentieth trip to the closet, well, actually the closet door. Ever since she had moved back home, she had been making a daily trek in that direction, but she had never gotten the nerve to open the closet door.

Stacie stopped in the same place she had stopped the last nineteen times. The door hadn't changed. It still had a hole in it from when Nevia had gotten mad at her and tried to hit her with her Easy-Bake Oven. If Stacie weren't so petrified, she would've chuckled at the memory.

She peered over her shoulder, half hoping that someone would come barreling down the corridor or at the very least call her. But all she saw was an empty hallway with carpeting the color of dirty eggs. There was no one to call her back as she gulped deeply, pulled the closet door open and flicked on the light.

She hung back, preferring to stand on the threshold. Her mouth was dry and she swallowed several times to wet it. She slowly counted and on ten, she placed one foot in front of the other and crossed the threshold.

Her eyes widened with surprise; what she remembered as a humongous haven was really only a ten-foot-long, three-foot wide closet. Back then it was huge to me, she mused. And it had been cleaned up. The trunk had long since been thrown away, as well as all the shoes. Now the closet was filled with baby clothes, baby toys and baby games.

She scooted to her favorite place, the back of the closet, eased down and pressed her back against the wall. The sniffling started first, then the trickling and lastly the sobbing. She felt nine years old again and she automatically pulled her shoe off and brought it to her nose. Taking deep breaths, she calmed herself.

Occasionally she was the target of her father's rages. He was a vicious man; sometimes he had said things that had gouged out pieces of her heart and made her cry for days.

Her father's voice roared in her ear. "You're nothing!" it hissed. "You're just like your mother, pretty but dumb as fuck," it scoffed. "You're a piece of shit!" The words had spewed from his mouth and had drenched her with their nastiness, leaving her coated with a slime that she just now had the courage to wipe off.

"Stop it!" Stacie stood up and shouted into the darkness. "Stop talking to me like that. I'm a good person!" Her words were all wet but strong as the tears ran down her face. "You're nothing but a big bully! I love you, Daddy, but you shouldn't talk to me like that! I'm smart, I'm pretty, I'm loving, I'm God-fearing and I love myself. Don't you *ever* talk to me like that again! I deserve better. You bastard!"

She could hear her father snickering and could imagine him sneering at her. "Don't laugh at me. It's your fault that we grew up in the projects. If you hadn't drunk up your pay-check, we could've had a nice house. So there!" She stuck her tongue out. "So when you said I wasn't shit, you weren't shit, otherwise you would've been a real daddy to me. You know what, Daddy?" She peered into the darkness and smiled lop-sidedly. "I got a man who adores me and calls me pretty every day. And I love it!"

Emotionally exhausted, Stacie fell against the closet wall. She felt good. She felt reborn. She felt invincible.

She regretted that she could not have said her peace to her father; but his lifestyle had caught up with him. He'd been living in a shelter and was penniless when he died of cirrhosis five years earlier.

"Good-bye, Daddy," she whispered. On shaky legs, she pushed herself out of the closet, leaving her shoe behind.

61

What I Got in a Man!

1. A man who'd battle an army of millions for my safety
2. A man who cares about what makes me laugh and cry
3. A man who knows that foreplay begins at sunrise
4. A man who looks in the mirror and sees love
5. A man who looks at his close circle of friends and family and sees love
6. A man who knows that his potential is unlimited

Hey, slow your roll, Rudolph the Red-Nosed Reindeer. I'm taking care of her needs. If she needs anything, she lets *me* know. So go on." Jackson shooed Rudolf off. He scurried away, but not before pinning Jackson with a hard glare. Stacie chuckled, feeling a little sorry for the waiter. She knew that the only reason Jackson insisted on returning to the restaurant was to show Rudolph that he had gotten the girl.

"So are you excited about starting school Monday?"

"I am. I'm gonna be a teacher," she giggled happily. "It's so interesting how one door slams shut and another opens," she said philosophically. "Thank you." She leaned over and kissed Jackson on the cheek, then settled back in her chair and fixed him with a stare.

"Whassup, baby?"

"If it wasn't for you, I wouldn't have thought about going to school to teach. I'd probably end up at another law firm doing the same old shit. Working for another Andre, answering the same old phones and saying the same old shit."

"Who would've thunk it. A bus driver with brains," he joked, reaching for a roll and slathering it with butter. There was a comfortable silence as Jackson chewed his bread. His life was better than ever. In three months he'd have a new wife, Jameel was safe and sound, but most importantly, after Michelle's foiled kidnapping attempt, she was given probation on the condition that she relinquish all parental rights to Jameel.

"Thanks for Lexie," she said softly, cutting into the silence, and he grunted. Seeing how miserable she was without her *baby,* he had given her the money to have her fixed. He had also given her enough money to keep her financially afloat until she landed a job, which she had, three weeks ago, as an executive assistant to the CEO of a major property development company. Stacie smiled, then asked, "Isn't it funny?"

"What's that, baby?"

She looked down at her engagement ring, then said, "That you and I ended up together and Tyrell and Tameeka broke up. It should've been the other way around. Don't you think?" She wrinkled her nose and glanced up at him, then rushed on to explain when she saw that he had raised his eyebrows so high that they almost touched his hairline. "I love you . . . I really do," she quickly assured him. "But, dang, we had so much stuff going on. You couldn't stand me. I couldn't stand your arrogant ass . . . and still can't sometimes. But look at us—we're together. *Happily together.* And we're getting married."

Stacie grinned as she gazed over at her fiancé; ever since he had come into her life, things had gotten better. Her list for the perfect man had long been scraped, she had stopped her shoe sniffing, but most importantly, through him she had found herself.

"That is funny," Jackson said, then focused on his food.

"Meek was the one who gave me advice on you—on us. She was my man expert. Not that she isn't now, but you know . . ." Stacie let her sentence drift off and she looked imploringly at Jackson.

Jackson sighed and put down his fork. "It's very simple. Tameeka and Tyrell would still be together if she hadn't cheated on him. She deserved what she got."

"But she didn't mean it. She was all screwy in the head. But she's okay now, she and Mohammad are burning up the sheets."

"*All screwy in the head?* Well, that just excuses it all. She didn't mean to cheat on her boyfriend, but since she was *all screwy in the head* it made it all right," Jackson mocked, then picked up his spoon and began shoveling soup into his mouth. As far as he was concerned the conversation was over.

"Well," Stacie muttered. "She was going through things that made her screwy in the head."

"Yeah, whatever. Mohammad had better be careful, because dude will be her next victim." Jackson looked her dead in the eye, then said, "You'd better not cheat on me."

An image of her, Crawford and the stuck condom popped into her head. "I . . . um . . . er," Stacie stuttered, then averted her eyes.

Jackson set his spoon down and turned to his fiancée; concern was in his eyes. "Whassup, Princess?"

"Nothing," she lied, bowing her head and fussing with her napkin.

"You sure?" Jackson reached out and grabbed the tip of her chin, forcing her to face him.

"Yeah, I'm cool. It's like you don't trust me or something," she said, laughing nervously.

"I trust you! Now tell me that you'll never cheat on me," Jackson demanded softly, his eyes glinting dangerously in the soft restaurant lighting.

"I will never, ever cheat on you," she solemnly pledged. I will never, ever cheat on him again, Stacie vowed to herself.

They locked eyes and Jackson searched hers looking for any speck of a lie, and not seeing anything, he grinned. "I know you won't." He bent down and kissed her. "Who's Big J?" he murmured against her lips.

"You are, baby," Stacie breathed.

CPSIA information can be obtained at www.ICGtesting.com
Printed in the USA
LVOW11s1521031214

416961LV00002B/361/P